IMPACT

Kelda Laing Poynot

ISBN-13: 9781793136008

DEDICATION

To my beloved, who constantly supports and encourages my dreams.

I love you.

ACKNOWLEDGMENTS

Thank you, Lord, for giving me the ability to communicate with words.

Sarah, thank you for reading every word I've written.

Your prayers and encouragement are priceless.

My small group girls: Abbey, Aubrey, Emily, Maddy, and Rachel.

Thank you for your youthful enthusiasm

and for believing I could do this.

Special thanks to: Becca, Carla, Kelly, Ethan, and Matthew

Cover art by Chelsea Guidry Poynot

PREFACE

We'd been traveling all day, and I was ready to be home. It had been hard driving in the foul weather. A late-season hurricane in the gulf was casting its angry force out in bands, hundreds of miles out from the eye. I knew it was time to be home and hunker down until the dreaded storm made landfall a few hundred miles west. We were under minimal threat, but a few days of family time and a pot of gumbo were always welcomed.

I scanned for a radio station to give me an update on the weather. That song, I knew that song. I smiled. It had been decades since I'd heard it. Bobby Darin's voice crooned, *Once upon a time, I met a girl with moonlight in her eyes...put her hand in mine and said she loved me so... but that was once upon a time very long ago...*

The rain fell in bands of heavy showers, and a break allowed just enough sunlight to cascade through the clouds. The most magnificent rainbow shown in the sky as I drove: red, orange, yellow, green, blue, indigo, and violet. Each color crisp and defined. The colors were bright above me; they almost looked tangible.

"Look, honey! Isn't it beautiful?" I exclaimed.

An 18-wheeler came up on my left and vibrated the car as it passed, spraying water across the windshield. The driver was going too fast on the wet road. The large silver truck entered the colors and reflected the light into my

3

eyes. The glare took me by surprise as the colors filtered through my windshield. I lifted my hand to shield my eyes from the glare.

Suddenly, the truck veered back and forth across the lanes, trying to regain control. The back end tilted off its axels with too much force to regain its balance. The truck swerved and its brake lights flashed. Reflexively, I gripped the steering wheel and slammed on the brakes. I instantly regretted that decision, as my car went careening into the back end of the 18-wheeler. I jerked the wheel to one side to avoid the truck, but there was nothing I could do to avoid the impending crash.

The 18-wheeler teetered and fell onto its side, skidding along the asphalt, sending wet spray and mist up from the road. The metal grated loudly, brakes squealed, and the cab quickly followed the trailer onto its side. Tires lost traction. Our bodies braced for the impact that was sure to follow. Instead, our car hit the wheels of the 18-wheeler and, like bumper cars, sent us spinning off the road and into the trees.

Funny the thoughts you remember when your brain fights to remain conscious: the rainbow and the colors, driving along the interstate in the pouring rain, a passing 18-wheeler, and the distant memory of Noah and a flood and a promise, the distraction of the colors in the sky, the vibrancy of the colors, and then a kiss and the warmth of the winter sun. He'd kissed me at the alter on a winter's day, surrounded by flowers.

I coughed. The sound was wet and red spewed forth from my mouth onto the steering wheel. I could taste the heavy, metallic flavor of blood. I blinked.

4

IMPACT

Then came the light. A flash of light. The brightest light I'd ever seen. It threw

me back into the rainbow and the force shattered me into tiny fragments of light.

Nothing made sense. Scraping metal, shouts, sirens, and flashing lights.

Opening my eyes periodically only confused me, so I closed them again.

Fractured body. Fractured light. Blinding light. Total Darkness.

I felt tiny, huddled in a large black space. It was cold and void of feeling. I

was small but gradually assumed the space I'd been thrust into.

CHAPTER 1

"Beth, Beth can you hear me?" I think I shook my head. "Beth, it's Darren. Can you hear me? Whenever you're ready, wake up; I'm here." The decidedly male voice spoke low and even into my ear.

There was a touch on my hand. Smooth fingertips and the soft pad of a thumb stroking over my knuckles. Soft lips and a gentle kiss on my forehead. A whisper in the dark, "Beth please wake up." Another whisper, "Beth, can you hear me?" I could smell the hint of peppermint when he spoke. It was pleasing, and I preferred the traces of mint over the nauseating waves of antiseptic and other sharp odors that often assailed me in his absence.

I wished beyond anything that this Beth would wake up so that I could sleep. The voice was constantly waking me up. For the most part, I was in a dark place, barren of light. It was cool and comfortable and there was no pain. When I tried to respond to the voice, my head ached. To avoid the pain, I faded back into the peace and stillness that surrounded me. When the voice wasn't speaking, I heard other sounds: beeps and clicks, the whooshing of air flowing through tubes, and the crinkle of the mattress under the rough, cotton sheets.

"Beth, it's Darren." Yes, he said it so confidently; it had to be his name. "How are you feeling?" he whispered intently. His voice was familiar. My foggy brain acknowledged him, and my ears were attuned to his voice.

"Darren," I tried to say aloud, but the oxygen mask on my face and the tubing were in the way. It sounded like a garbled mess.

At some point, I blinked at the unfamiliar face smiling at me. His hair was a blur of dark brown and his brown eyes were encircled in black frames. My vision was unclear, but I could tell this man was happy to see me. He smiled, encouragingly. My brow furled. It was painful to focus for any length of time.

"Hi, there, Beth. It's good to see your eyes. Can you hear me?" He smiled tentatively, expecting a reply.

Beth? I didn't know that name. I shook my head and tried to acknowledge his words through the haze of my mind. That same interaction happened several times. Each time I opened my eyes, I saw his face and felt his hands on mine. I sensed his presence each time my brain tried to fight the fog. The faint traces of peppermint lingered in the air between us.

My head ached and I felt like I'd been hit by a truck. Darren came and stayed with me and called me Beth. Time passed in waves and days and nights were disconnected. I found myself looking forward to him being there, feeling the mattress depress at my hip when he sat near me, the warmth of his hand on mine. But, I didn't *know* him. I didn't know myself.

Once the nurses weaned me from the strong sedation and pain medication no longer dripped constantly into my IV, my thoughts began to connect and my brain could reason. In a day or two, I woke fully. The nurses propped me up and I began to process my surroundings.

"Where am I?" I asked, groggily.

"You're in the ICU at General. You were in a car accident. You had trauma to your brain and were kept sedated until we could assess your brain function. You're slowly coming around," the nurse said kindly.

I was confused and frightened and looked forward to the regular injections that made me sleep for hours and momentarily forget. I didn't mind Darren's presence, but my brain was too foggy for coherent conversation.

The evaluating neurologist, Dr. Saunders, made his usual rounds. Finally, I was able to formulate my questions. "Why don't I know my name? I can't remember how I ended up here, and I don't recognize anyone." Fear laced every word, and I was on the verge of tears as I confessed this. "Please tell me that I'm going to remember something."

He didn't do much to comfort me. Instead, he looked down at my chart. "Your name is Beth A. Rust. You were born in 1991. Darren Fitzgerald is your next of kin. He's eager to see you through this. He knows more of your history and can help you piece it together." His eyes were genuinely persuading. "Beth, it's only been a couple of days since you were weaned from the sedation. It was necessary for you to be put under, but now that your brain inflammation has been reduced, you should gradually regain some memory."

Later that morning, they moved me from ICU into my own room. The walls were covered in textured, taupe wallpaper. The coordinating curtains were pale with mint green and mauve stripes. Prints of pink cabbage roses were framed and hung on the wall over the sofa and next to the television, directly across from my bed. The curtains were pulled back, and the sunshine coming through the windows did wonders for my attitude. The aids settled me in the large bed, but said very little to me. Soon, a large, older, African-American nurse entered my room, smiling broadly and pushing a machine on casters.

"Here, honey," she said placing the thermometer in my mouth and wrapping the blood pressure cuff around my arm. "I'm Sadie. I'll be your nurse for the next three days. If you need anything, don't hesitate to ask. Just press this button. I know you must be really confused right now, but I'm sure you'll be at a hundred percent soon enough." She removed the beeping thermometer and the blood pressure cuff and documented her findings.

She then went to the dry-erase board across the room from my bed and wrote her name and a time and some other information. "You have surely been through it, honey. You don't worry, now; you leave that to the doctors. They have a higher paygrade. You just rest and let your noggin heal. It's been through a great trauma." Her eyes were kind and her large, dark hand covered mine. She spoke casually to me, and I was drawn into the sound of her voice. The ICU nurses had taken good care of me, but none of them made any effort to draw me from my silence. Maybe they thought I'd lost my ability to speak along with my memory.

"Sadie, may I have a mirror?" I asked. "I want to see what I look like."

"Are you serious?" she asked perturbed, placing her hands on her broad hips. "We are so stupid, sometimes. We don't think to give a woman a mirror. Of course, you need to see yourself." She pulled out a mirror from the side-table drawer.

I took the mirror from her and looked at my reflection. My eyes went directly to the large bandage above my left eyebrow. The bandage was about three inches long and the skin around it was a mixture of colors from the bruising. My left cheek and eyelid were both scratched with tiny lacerations. I was thinking it looked like glass slivers. My hand instinctively went to touch it.

"Sweet girl, don't go messing with that. I'll let you have a proper look when we change the dressing in the morning," Sadie promised. I nodded obediently.

I stretched my arm out and moved the small mirror to see more of my reflection. My hair was cut short and spiked out in several different directions. The color itself was nothing natural. Chemical enhancements had layered it in a variety of browns with bleached tips. It was dramatic to say the least. My eyes were light brown with severely tweezed brows and tiny lashes. My teeth were straight and my lips were a soft pink color. I was definitely Caucasian, and underneath the pale skin, I showed freckles across the bridge of my nose.

Before leaving ICU, I'd taken a quick inventory of my hands. My nails were clipped short, neat and clean, without any traces of polish. My feet didn't seem to be too large in proportion to the length of my legs, and my toenails looked professionally pedicured. My wrists bore the faint vertical scars of a horrendous accident or self-infliction. I would happily give up any memory of what desperation may have caused self-harm.

Before I was really settled, some flowers and balloons and a plant were delivered to my room. I didn't recognize any of the names on the cards. At lunchtime, Darren came in to see me; he'd apparently spoken with the neurologist.

"I know you don't know me yet, but we *will* figure this out." The determination in his voice wasn't frightening. He was confident and sure of himself; I couldn't deny his resolve. Darren promised to take me home as soon as the doctors released me. My mind was blank.

When he came in, he handed me a cup. I took a sip and made a face. The coffee was surprisingly sweet. "What's wrong?" Darren asked, noticing my reaction. "Four sugars. Three creams."

"It's so sweet," I complained and covered my mouth, offering the cup back to him.

He took a sip of it. "It tastes exactly like you drink it." He handed it back to me and I took another sip. This time it didn't surprise me and tasted better. I settled back with the cup in my hands and savored the sweet aroma. I think I preferred the smell over the flavor.

"There for a second, I thought you'd wrecked your taste buds." He laughed at his own joke and set his steaming cup of coffee on the rolling table at the side of my bed.

"Darren," I asked tentatively, "don't you have to be at work or something?" He was there every time I woke up. He never seemed to leave.

"Now that you've been moved into your own room, Mrs. Moore gave me off until the end of the week and then next week is Thanksgiving break. Just four weeks after that until we're off for Christmas. I also called Dr.

Montgomery. I hope you don't mind," he said sheepishly. "I thought she should know why you weren't in class. You don't have anything due since you'd already turned in your paper. She's excusing you from the defense, so you don't have to worry about the final."

Class? Paper? Final? Mrs. Moore? Dr. Montgomery? I had no connection to his rambling, but I felt instantly relieved that I didn't have to defend anything. "Darren, I'm sorry, I have no idea what you're talking about." I wasn't frightened, but I was suspicious of the familiarity. My mind searched again frantically to find a trace of this man with the kind eyes and friendly smile. Nothing. He took my hand to comfort me. My body relaxed instantly at his touch. I may not have recognized him, but my body never flinched or doubted him.

"I brought some photos. You can look at them when you've finished your lunch. What are they serving you today?" He looked over my plate hesitantly. "Anything good?"

"It tastes fine, but I don't have much appetite. My head aches a bit and I'm definitely not burning a bunch of calories lying here in this bed. My nurse, Sadie, says she'll get me moving around tomorrow and PT should send a tech to evaluate me this afternoon."

"So, now that we don't have deadlines and rigid visiting hours, where would you like to begin?" Darren asked.

I was glad he'd asked. I had a million questions. "Are we related?"

"No, but I've known you since college. We met our freshman year. We were both education majors. Our paths crossed quite a bit and before the end our first semester, we'd become best friends." He smiled at the memory.

"I know my name is Beth A. Rust. Not Elizabeth? Do you know what the A stands for?"

"Your parents were apparently big KISS fans. They named you after a rock ballad, so it's just Beth. The *A* doesn't stand for anything. Your birth certificate just says *A*." He shrugged.

"Are you my *boyfriend*?" I asked hesitantly, not wanting to offend him.

He looked down and a little breathy chuckle escaped. "No, but we are roommates."

"I live with you?"

"We share a townhouse and we work together. You teach kindergarten. These cards are from your students." He produced a stack of cards from his backpack. I smiled, tentatively. I looked through the stack of brightly colored cards and drawings and handed them back to him. I felt guilty that I didn't know my students.

"Do I have any family?"

"You're an only child. Your parents died when you were seven from a drug overdose. You were there when it happened. Social Services placed you with your grandmother. You called her Gram. You lived with her until you left for college. You grew up less than an hour from here. She died our sophomore year. I should have brought you a picture of her."

"Where are you from?" I asked.

"My father is retired military. We moved a lot. They live near my sister's family, now, in Illinois. I see them every Christmas and Fourth of July. You're welcome to come with me, if you're up to it." He sounded hopeful.

"Do I usually go?"

He shrugged and nodded. "Yeah, but you prefer Chicago in the summer. You aren't particularly fond of the cold. You and my sister get along pretty well, but her husband can be a real ass sometimes. He can't help it; he's a tax attorney. Mom and Dad expect you every year, but you didn't go last year."

"Why not?"

He hesitated. "You suddenly decided not to celebrate Christmas with my family."

"Do I like Christmas?" I asked.

"You do amazing things each year with the children in your classroom. You've discovered about fifty different ways to decorate and spend weeks each summer prepping for your next class's Christmas, but you don't celebrate much outside of their anticipation and excitement, except for the few days we spend with my family."

We talked a bit more, but Darren didn't think it was a good idea to cover everything all at once. He found the remote and we watched the early evening news. He offered to get me a cheeseburger or something more appetizing for supper.

"I'm fine. The food is good. What do you plan to eat?" I asked.

"I was going to get a sandwich downstairs."

When he returned, he was carrying a pillow, his backpack, and a bag of food. "Are you sleeping here?" I asked.

"If that's okay with you."

I shrugged. "I'm really fine here. The nurses are great and I don't need watching."

"I'd feel better if I stayed. Mind if we give it a try tonight?"

I sighed, resigned. "Sure, why not?" I didn't have the energy to refuse him. He obviously wanted to stay.

Before Sadie ended her shift, she came in to check on me. "You doing alright, honey? Need anything before I go?"

"Do you mind walking me to the bathroom one more time?"

"No trouble, come on." Sadie helped me maneuver the IV pole and kept me mostly modest in my hospital gown. She waited outside the bathroom door until I finished. I could stand and walk pretty well, but my body ached from the bruises and I suspected the pain meds were making me loopy.

I heard Sadie talking low to Darren. "Is this young lady your girlfriend?" she asked, pointedly.

"No, we're roommates. We've known each other for a long time."

"She looks scared half out of her wits, like she just fell out the sky, but she's not afraid of you."

"She's got no reason to be. I'm here to look after her," Darren sounded protective, almost defensive.

"I've taken a liking to her. But those scars. You know anything about that?"

"Yes, ma'am, I do." Darren's voice lowered to a whisper.

I flushed the toilet and stood to wash my hands. I walked the few steps to the sink and looked in the large mirror. My reflection was the same and still unfamiliar.

Sadie cracked the door open when she heard the water running in the sink. She helped me back into the bed and fluffed my pillows and straightened my bedding. I was tucked in tightly like a burrito.

"Thank you, Sadie."

"You get some rest tonight. I'll see you in the morning," Sadie said eyeing Darren as she left.

"I don't think she knows what to make of me," Darren laughed. "She's intimidating as hell. I wouldn't cross her, if I were you."

"I don't plan to."

Food service brought me my dinner and we ate.

"Want to watch some TV?" Darren asked.

"No, focusing strains my eyes and I don't think I'm processing everything well. It gets muddled."

"I brought a book. Would you like me to read to you?"

"No," I said politely. I had more pressing thoughts and questions. "I'd like to know about my scars."

Darren's face changed instantly. "Beth, I don't want to talk about that right now. Please, can you ask me something else, anything else." The look in his eyes was pained and he suddenly looked vulnerable and sad. I didn't want to hurt him so I dropped the subject.

"I'm just going to rest, then. Do you mind dimming the lights over my bed?"

He stood and, after a couple of attempts, managed to turn off or lower all the lights. He smiled in the dim light and patted my hand gently. His tender touch comforted me. "I'm sorry, Beth, I know it's confusing. We can talk about it tomorrow if you want." I nodded and he kissed the top of my head.

Even in the dim light, my head throbbed. The night nurse injected something into my IV and the pain instantly subsided. I closed my eyes and drifted into sleep.

CHAPTER 2

At some point in the night, I awoke screaming and panting like I'd been running. "No!" I screamed. "No!" I knew consciously that I was having a nightmare, but it was the vivid variety. The kind where you think and reason and all of your senses are engaged. I was trapped, pinned against something heavy. I couldn't breathe. I was gasping for breath. My hand was on someone's chest. There was someone next to me, but I couldn't see who it was. Vibrant colors swirled through my mind, then a flash of blinding light, followed by total darkness.

I heard sirens approaching from far away and men's voices commanding loudly over me. The weight wasn't pinning me down anymore. I could breathe, but I couldn't find the person next to me. My hand searched and groped in vain. The pain, excruciating pain. Blood flowed everywhere! I gagged at its smell and taste. My eyes stung as the blood clouded my vision; I couldn't see anything.

Darren was at my side, sitting on the bed. His hands were on my shoulders. "Beth, wake up. You're having a bad dream."

I wiped my eyes to remove the blood, but there was nothing there. The blood had only been in my dream. When I opened my eyes, Darren was right there. His glasses were off and his brown eyes were concerned. Instinctively, I leaned into him and allowed him to take me into his arms. "You're okay. You're safe. I'm here. Take a deep breath," he said stroking my back and easing me into him. "Shhh, you're going to be fine."

The night nurse ran into the room sounding frantic. "You okay?" she asked.

I didn't answer. "She's just had a nightmare. She's fine," Darren answered

for me like I had them all the time, but he didn't release me. "She'll be fine in

few minutes. I'll call you if she needs anything."

When I stopped panting, Darren released me and looked into my eyes. "I'm

a complete mess," I confessed.

"Here," he said handing me a glass of water. I drank dutifully.

"Do I have those often?" I asked.

"Not anymore, but there was a time when you did. What was this one

about?"

"I think it was the crash. Was there anyone else in the car with me? Were

you in the car with me?"

"No, you were alone. You were driving back from a teacher training in

Natchitoches. Why?'

"I felt like there was someone else. I could feel them, but I couldn't see

them." I wiped tears from my cheeks. "It was so real."

He took me back into his arms and stroked my back. His hands were strong,

yet gentle. The warmth of his chest comforted me. He then eased me onto the

pillows and tucked me in again like Sadie had done. He stood and looked at me

warily. "Would you like me to lie down next to you until you fall back asleep?"

My mind was reeling and my body was shaken; I didn't really know what I

wanted, but his hands on me comforted me and his voice in my ear settled me.

"Have you done that before?" He gave a little side nod and lifted his chin in a way that told me to scoot over and make room for him. I rolled over onto my good side and he eased in beside me. He wrapped his strong arm over me and pulled me into him gently. I was instantly settled.

"Thank you, Darren," I whispered.

"Shhh. Close your eyes. I won't move until you're asleep."

I closed my eyes. Darren breathed steadily behind me. He smelled clean, and with him at my side, barely any remnants of the nightmare lingered.

***

Sadie entered my room the next morning, just as sunlight was making its way into the room. "Good morning, sleepyhead."

I rolled over gently and opened my eyes. Darren was already dressed and reading on his tablet. He placed it in his backpack and smiled at me and then at Sadie. "I'm going to get a cup of coffee. Either of you want anything?"

I shook my head and looked up at Sadie. Her eyes were curious as she watched Darren leave. "You sleep fine last night?" I shrugged. "The night nurse said you had a nightmare. Later, she came in to find you and *roommate* sleeping together in the bed. That goes against hospital policy, but she said you were both settled and you didn't cry out anymore in the night. You make a habit of that?"

"I have no idea, but as soon as he was next to me, I was asleep, until now. I don't remember him getting up."

Sadie put the thermometer in my mouth and the blood pressure cuff on my arm. She turned my hand over and placed her hand on the scar on my wrist.

20

"Honey, I used to work in a psych ward. These are old, real old. Whatever haunted you then isn't a part of you now. I don't see a lick of crazy in your eyes." She smiled reassuringly.

What a thing to say. I appreciated her boldness, but I didn't know what to make of it. "Thank you? I don't feel crazy, except for not remembering, and I don't feel the least bit suicidal."

"Good. I don't have time to deal with that today. I have two more intakes and two discharges on this floor before lunch. Let's change that dressing and take a good looksee." She opened a drawer and pulled out the necessary supplies and handed me the mirror from yesterday. Her latex gloves snapped over her large hands. She gently removed the tape and bandage as I watched in the mirror. The laceration was a couple inches long and I could see a great many stitches. The bruising was extensive and the skin looked puffy and tender.

"I'll have a pretty big scar, huh?"

"Yep, you will. Maybe you can change your hairstyle and let your bangs grow out. We'll send you home with ointments and some special scar tape. It can do wonders over time."

"Sadie," I began. She looked down into my eyes. "How do you know I'm not crazy?" I asked.

She smiled as she worked. "Some call it a sixth sense, but I just call it intuition. You're not right, but you aren't mentally ill. I worked with psych patients off and on for nearly thirty years. I worked with women and adolescents mostly. Abuse and neglect are hard things on any mind."

"What made you stop?"

"I'm not as young as I used to be. Psych floors are physical places. They require more than what I could do anymore. I'm older than I look, honey, and much wiser than I'd care to admit. I miss it, though. There's something powerful in a healing mind. I guess that's why I've taken such an interest in you."

"You're funny, Sadie. You're the only one who's been able to make me smile or laugh even a little."

"That fella, you know him at all?" My smile faded instantly. Sadie stopped and lowered her hands. She looked into my eyes. "I'm sorry. I didn't mean to upset you."

"I'm not upset, just confused. He looks at me and touches me with such familiarity. He knows me better than I do. I can't bring myself to not allow his touch and comfort. It's the only thing I know right now. I don't know how to explain it."

"Hmmm," Sadie considered as she resumed her work on my forehead. "That is interesting. Funny how our bodies have their own memories even when our minds don't recollect. Scents, sounds, touch, all of our senses mark us in some way. I've always had a theory that we were connected in a variety of ways. Our brains may be the command center, but the Good Lord has a great sense of humor, and I figure he'd have wired us so that no matter what, we'd have experiences beyond our reckoning. There, you're as good as new." She smiled and took the mirror from me.

"I'll send the aide in after lunch to help you get a shower and wash your hair. Let's get you up and into the bathroom. Where's your toothbrush?"

When Darren returned to the room, he brought in another bag. "I brought you some clothes. I thought you might be more comfortable in your own PJs."

"That's very thoughtful. Sadie says I can get clean after lunch. I'm really sick of this hospital gown."

PT arrived after breakfast and told Darren he could walk with me to the end of the hall after my bath. Once I could make it to the elevator and back, I'd be ready to try stairs with the tech and then they'd assess me for any discharge exercises. My morning was filled with doctors making their rounds; the neurologist, Dr. Saunders, introduced me to the psychiatrist who I would be seeing once I was released. I liked them all, but none of them could tell me when I'd begin remembering.

After lunch, the aid came in and helped me into the shower. I sat on the bench seat that lowered from the wall. She adjusted the water setting and helped me maneuver the hand-held sprayer. Getting cleaned up and washing my hair improved my attitude more than the sun. Hot water might not return any memory, but I loved how the heat and steam relaxed me.

She helped me put on the pajamas that Darren had brought me. They were soft and well-worn, in the best way, like maybe they were my favorite ones and he knew they'd make me feel most comfortable. He also brought me a light fleece hoodie that felt like a cloud.

When I came out of the bathroom, Darren smiled. "That's better."

I was able to make it to the elevator on our first walk. I also convinced Darren to let me take the stairs. It was easy and I never missed a step, but I was tired once we returned to my room. Darren waited outside the bathroom and then helped me into the bed.

"I'm going to head to the house and take a shower and get a change of clothes. Do you want anything? I'll be back after supper, and I plan to stay the night again."

"I can't think of anything I need." I shrugged. For some reason I found that really funny. "I have absolutely no idea what's at home that I might actually be missing." I said between giggles.

Darren smiled, appreciating my sense of humor. "I'll see you after supper. Rest, okay?" I nodded obediently.

CHAPTER 3

My head ached again and I was exhausted. A nurse came in and injected meds into my IV; the familiar fog fell over me again. Sadie came in before shift's end. I'd fallen asleep after Darren left. She checked my vitals and asked where my friend had gone.

"He went home to take a shower and eat supper. He'll be back tonight," I said.

"You're lucky to have a friend like that. He doesn't take you for granted. The ICU nurses said he refused to leave you. They said his relief was palpable when you finally opened your eyes. They were all relived for him. I can see it as plain as the nose on his face. Girl, if I didn't know better, I'd say he loves you more than anything in this world."

Darren returned, stirring the stale hospital air. He brought with him the clean scent of soap and aftershave. He also brought me a chocolate milkshake and it tasted amazing. I sipped and relished the cold, creamy goodness. The long, afternoon nap left me well-rested and fully awake. It might have been the chocolate shake, too. Regardless, I was in a talkative mood, and, for the first time, my head didn't hurt.

"Do we have any pets?" I asked.

"No."

"What's my favorite color?"

"It depends."

"On what?"

"The weather, the day of the week, the cycle of the moon, whatever's clean," he chuckled.

"What's my favorite food?"

"That's easy. Chili cheese fries and chocolate shakes."

"Favorite movie?"

"It depends, again. Depends on genre. You love sci-fi and fantasy with intricate battle scenes, but you're a sucker for anything by Austen or Dickens."

"Am I a romantic?"

"No, you like the way they speak."

"Am I athletic? Do I like sports?" During my shower, I noticed that my body was lean and curvy in the right place.

"You're not athletic. You run occasionally, but mostly you just use the equipment at the gym near our complex. Your job with the kids is pretty physical, so you don't sit much at work. You swim more than anything else. As far as sports, you are extremely tolerant during basketball season. You don't ever complain when I'm watching a game. I think you are secretly a basketball fan, but won't commit to a team."

"What was I like when we first met?"

That was the perfect question. He talked for nearly an hour, smiling and remembering in complete detail our time together. He was a vivid storyteller and I was drawn into his narrative. He told me how we had ended up having most of our classes together our freshman year. He laughed telling me how some guy kept asking me out.

"This loser was relentless. He wouldn't take no for an answer. You and I had only spoken a couple of times, but I could tell this guy made you very uncomfortable. Hell, he made me feel uncomfortable and he wasn't asking me out. Then one day, you came into class and sat in the desk in front of me. It couldn't have been better if we'd rehearsed it. You took my hand and looked longingly into my eyes. 'Daddy says we can't see each other anymore,' you said breathlessly like it was the saddest thing you'd ever uttered. 'I'm sorry, but I can't go against his wishes. I'd hate for anything to happen to you. I couldn't go through that again.'"

"It took all I had not to laugh, but when you looked down at our hands, and stroked your thumb over my knuckles, I had the craziest thought. I squeezed your hand. 'Is he going to make you marry that other guy?' I asked under my breath. You shrugged so convincingly. 'I don't think he will, but the elders at my church said I need to consider my future. He's already got two wives, I don't know why he needs a third. My daddy only has two. Besides, he's married to my sister. I can't see that working out well for any of us.'

"You really threw me a curveball with that one. The guy was watching us and taking in every word. His eyes were bugging out of his head. He had no idea what he was witnessing. 'I'm so sorry; I shouldn't have let you believe I could do otherwise.' Your lip trembled and I thought for sure you were going to cry. That guy never spoke to you again, and from that day forward, you and I did most everything together."

"What made you go to school in the south?" I could tell from his accent, he didn't speak like most everyone I'd come in contact with so far.

"My dad was stationed in north Louisiana. It was only three hours away from my parents, and I based my choice on their special education program and who paid me the most in scholarships. I knew I didn't want to go into debt to attend college. I was even able to save my college fund for graduate school. He and my mom went to Germany for three years before he retired. We spent two Christmases there. It was absolutely beautiful. Do you remember when we…" his voice trailed off. "Sorry, I shouldn't have led with that."

"It's okay, Darren. I'm getting used to it. It's strange, but I'm not even really trying right now." There was an awkward silence. "How long have we lived together?" I asked changing the subject.

"Well if you count school breaks, summer vacations, and all the times we stayed in each other's dorms, I'd say we've lived under the same roof since we were eighteen, so almost ten years? We got our first jobs together. You've been taking some graduate classes at night. You're a wonder at the early childhood development center. You're additionally PreK and kindergarten certified. I thought for sure you'd go back to middle school, but it was too much for you. You're better with the little ones." I was silent again, but not in the awkward way. "Are you ready to go to sleep, now?" Darren asked.

I nodded and pulled back the covers. I walked to the bathroom and was able to do everything to ready myself for bed on my own. I washed my face and brushed my teeth. I didn't even have to fight the IV pole as I got myself back into bed.

Darren had changed into plaid lounge pants and a dark green hoodie while I was in the bathroom. He tucked me in and adjusted the lights. He kissed the top of my head as he'd done before. It seemed to be his habit. "Goodnight. Sleep well."

I lay there, but couldn't fall asleep. My head was swimming with all that he'd told me tonight. "Darren," I said, breaking the silence. "Are you asleep?" I could still see a faint light and thought perhaps he was reading on his tablet.

"No, just reading. What do you need?"

"Will you tell me, now?"

He sighed exasperated. "Yes, but I still don't want to." There was a long silence before he closed his tablet and rolled over to face me. I adjusted the bed so that I could see his face. He sat up and pinched the brim of his nose like he had a headache. He fished for his glasses and came to my bed and gestured for me to move my legs over. He sat on the foot of the bed facing me.

He looked into my eyes and pursed his lips like he was bothered by the entire topic. "Last week wasn't the first time I've been relieved to see you open your eyes." He blinked hard and looked away like he was reliving a nightmare. "You struggled with depression after Gram died. More than once, you attempted to take your own life. Obviously, those scars are a constant reminder of a very dark time."

He took my hand and ran his thumb over the scar on my left wrist. "The first time you tried to overdose, but thankfully the medication you'd found in your grandmother's medicine cabinet wasn't as effective as you'd hoped. We'd gone to her house at the beginning of summer break to clean it out to sell it. She'd only been dead a couple of months. You found a box in the attic that forced you completely over the edge. It contained the police report and the recommendation for foster care. Why your grandmother held onto that is beyond me. It should have been burned." Distaste and disdain laced every word.

"After a lot of therapy, you remembered finding your parents dead. They overdosed in the night while you slept. You woke up in the morning and poured yourself a bowl of cereal and went to dress for school. You were only seven and you were already getting yourself ready for school. You walked into your parents' room and found them dead. You had the sense, even at seven, to call 911, but the rest you'd blocked out.

"The doctor called me out into the hall after they pumped your stomach and said that he was concerned about the long-term effects on the baby. You could have mopped me up off the floor. I didn't know. You *obviously* didn't know. He was talking to me like I was the father. I just stood there trying my best to process it all. I was relieved that you were going to be okay, but I couldn't figure out how you'd gotten yourself pregnant. We were together all the time. I sure as hell knew it wasn't *mine*." His voice was sharp.

"When I entered the hospital room and saw you lying there, pale and weak, I was livid, but then when you opened your eyes, the anger completely left me. I hated being the one to tell you about the baby. I hated being the one who found you catatonic on the floor of your bedroom. I hated even more that you told me you planned to have an abortion. I thought those were the hardest days of my existence, but I was wrong."

"If it wasn't yours, why were you upset that I wanted to terminate the pregnancy?" I asked.

He looked at me incredulously. "Because you knew taking another life was wrong, and I knew you wouldn't be the same if you went through with it. I was right. God! I didn't want to drive or pick you up from that damn clinic, but you begged me, and I knew you had no one else. I tried to convince you to give it up for adoption. I promised you we'd raise the child together if you decided to keep it, but you were determined to go through with the abortion. I couldn't understand why."

"Did you know the father?"

"No, and neither did you. Apparently, there was more than one possibility. You never told me. I think you were afraid I'd do something stupid. I'm not particularly violent, but I could feel the rage just under the surface. You were protecting me, I'm sure."

"What happened next?"

"The worst was yet to come. I sat up with you all night while you cramped and bled and cried. You had a reaction to the pain medication and you started talking out of you head like you were possessed by demons. A week after the abortion, we were back in the ER, but this time you'd decided that pills weren't going to fix you. I found you on the floor of the kitchen in the middle of the night. Here we were trying to ready Gram's house and you made the biggest mess all over her kitchen floor. Do you have any idea how to get blood out of grout?" I shook my head. "Neither did I. I bound your wrists with dishtowels and threw you into my car. I drove like a crazy person to the hospital, praying the entire time I wasn't too late." The grief as he spoke was too much to bear. His words had weight and pressed in on me, forcing tears to stream down my face. "*Those* were the hardest days of my existence."

I looked down at the scars on my wrists and covered them self-consciously, not understanding how someone could even imagine taking her own life. This body was beautiful and fit and healthy. I had a good life and an amazing friend. Darren's hand squeezed mine.

"I'm sorry, Darren. I'm sorry I asked and put you through it all again."

"You need to know, but you don't remember, do you?" I shook my head. "Good, I'll happily allow that memory to never return. You're *good* now. You've been good for a long time. You dealt with your childhood and your grief and learned to live with the guilt and consequences of your choices. It was hard work, but you did it! You are such an amazing woman and I'm so proud of the changes you've made in your life. You've come a long way, and although those scars are a daily reminder of a dark time, they're also a reminder of how far you've come." He smiled encouragingly and leaned over to kiss the inside of my wrist. I placed my hand on the top of his head and stroked down his hair. He

didn't flinch; he just sighed.

"I'm ready to go to bed, now," I said, exhausted from the story.

"Me, too." He stood and kissed my head again and returned to his guest

bed. "Goodnight, Beth."

CHAPTER 4

The hospital couldn't keep me any longer. Other than the stitches and amnesia, they couldn't find any medical reason. The doctors assured me that I'd regain more memories once I returned to my home and familiar surroundings. They were confident that in time I'd be myself again. I was sore and the bruising was evident across my face and arms where the airbag had deployed. The stitches across my forehead pulled at my hairline. Sadie said if I was careful, I could wash my hair again in a couple of days. I just needed to make sure to keep the stiches dry.

Sadie began the discharge process. Darren assured her that he'd see to everything. He was so confident that no one doubted him, even me. I didn't know what else to do, so I allowed this mostly-stranger to bring me a change of clothes. He left the room when the nurse's aide helped me dress, but it probably wasn't necessary. I had a feeling he'd seen this body naked before; he was entirely too familiar with me.

Sadie came into the room one last time. "Beth, I don't make a habit of this, but you look like you may need a friend, someone to talk to. Here's my number. You call me, you hear?" She said handing me a Post-it note.

"Thank you, Sadie, I really appreciate it." I smiled, but tears stung my eyes and I blinked them back. My apprehension was mirrored in her eyes.

She looked down at Darren who was sitting on the sofa. "This is for you," she said pulling out another Post-it from her pocket. "You take care of our girl.

She's a special one." He nodded obediently to this commanding woman. No one in their right mind would have intentionally disappointed her. I had a feeling she wasn't accustomed to being refused.

Just then the aide returned with the wheelchair. Sadie hugged me and eyed us both like she wanted to ask a question, but just shook her head and stepped out of the way. While the aide helped me into the wheelchair, Darren packed my toothbrush and the cards from my students into a bag. He followed the aide down to the lobby as she wheeled me to the main doors.

The hospital valet had already been notified to bring Darren's car to the front entrance. I waited patiently for him to move forward when his car approached. I had no idea what he drove. The valet pulled in a dark blue, four-door Toyota. It wasn't new, but it was clean and smelled like its owner and traces of peppermint.

Darren drove us about twenty minutes through a town that was mostly familiar to me. That gave me hope, until he pulled into a small community of townhomes and parked. He told me to stay put and then ran around to open my door. He helped me steady myself before he grabbed the bags from the backseat. He walked me to the door of the second townhome from the left. I faced a dark red door with a black 2B in the center. I chuckled to myself thinking of Hamlet's monologue. Random.

Darren unlocked the door and helped me step over the threshold. "Welcome home," he said smiling. The downstairs was an open floor plan. The living room and the kitchen and dining area could all be seen from the front door. It was spacious. The lighting was good through the large windows and neutral colors flowed throughout the space.

I walked into the living room and looked around. There were photos in frames, artfully placed on narrow shelves. Most of them were of Darren and me in various locations. I picked up the one of a younger me with an elderly woman. She was wearing a Christmas vest and large, green and red Christmas light earrings. The two of us were smiling and our eyes were bright. I couldn't help but pause and smile at that one.

"That's your Gram. She was a trip! That was taken the last Christmas before she died." Although I didn't recognize this woman, I hoped that I would. I wanted to know her. Nothing was familiar, though. "There's a half-bath here," he said pointing to a door under the staircase. I placed the picture back onto the shelf carefully and looked up the stairs. "Your room is the one on the left. Let me put a casserole in the oven before I help you get settled."

I couldn't disguise my surprise when I entered my bedroom. "Don't be upset. I cleaned up a little before I went to the hospital last night. I didn't want you to trip over anything." I looked around tentatively.

"I take it that I'm not usually tidy."

"You're incredibly organized when you need to be and there's nothing out of place in your classroom, but at home, in your room, no, you're *not usually tidy*." He eyed me and stepped back. "You okay?"

I shrugged. "I'm just disappointed. I was hoping there'd be something, but nothing." I couldn't hide the despondency in my tone.

He nodded. "Me, too. I can tell," he said looking me in the eyes. His gaze was penetrating like he could see all the way to my soul. "Look, I'm going to change clothes and send a couple of texts. I'll let you get comfortable."

He left the door open when he left the room. I sat down on the bed and looked around the room, taking it all in. The bedding was garish and unwelcoming, almost offensive. This was not a room for an adult woman. I still had concert posters on the walls, for goodness sake. I opened the top drawer to the dresser and peaked in. There were underwear and socks neatly folded, and it looked like a box of condoms had been emptied into the drawer.

I opened the closet and stroked the fabric of the clothes hanging there. I pulled out the first jacket that my hands touched. I put it on and slipped my hands into the pockets. I pulled out another condom. *What the heck?* Out of curiosity, I opened the bag from the hospital that lay on the bed. On top was a cell phone. It was dead. I reached down into my purse to search for a charger and instead pulled out three more condoms. This was ridiculous! I had a serious problem. I dug further and finally found the charger. I plugged in the phone and swiped my finger across the screen. The page was filled with texts.

After dinner, Darren cleared the dishes from the table and put them in the sink to soak. We had eaten in virtual silence. "That was really good. Do you always cook like that?"

He laughed. "Not usually. We typically eat sandwiches or takeout or cereal at night. Some teachers from school brought meals for the freezer. They thought it would be a good way for you to regain your strength. Honestly, I don't think they trust that I'm capable of feeding you. They really do underestimate me sometimes."

"I think it's kind. Having food in the freezer makes it easier for the caregiver. So, how do I spend my free time?" I asked.

"Your days are pretty full and you study at the library a couple evenings a week. You like to listen to audiobooks. I'm in class two nights a week most semesters, so I don't usually see you until around ten. On weekends, we go Cajun dancing with friends sometimes or listen to bands downtown. You love Mexican food and margaritas, and you're a sucker for movie marathons."

"What are you studying?"

"Special education and administration. I plan to submit my dissertation proposal next fall."

"*Dr. Darren Fitzgerald, PhD*. Impressive."

"Thank you, I think so, too." He smiled.

CHAPTER 5

I was feeling down, frustrated that my memories weren't coming back in the right way. Nothing fit. Other than Darren's accounts, I still had no idea who I was. I'd spent the better part of the morning with the therapist from the hospital. She assured me that brain injuries took time to heal, and that once the swelling was completely gone, I should regain more memory.

Darren was determined to help me along in the process of regaining familiarity with my past. Music played low over the speakers. He was reading on his tablet while I looked over a photo album for the hundredth time. I shut it more forcefully than was necessary. He stood and faced me. "Here," he said, smiling and putting out his hand.

"What?" I didn't understand what he wanted me to do.

"Dance with me."

I shook my head, disappointed. "I don't dance."

"That body you're in has danced with me for as long as I've known you. I'm sure it remembers even if your brain doesn't." He offered his hand more directly. "Let's give it a try. What can it hurt?"

I took his hand and stood begrudgingly. He stood several inches taller than me. He put my hand on his shoulder and then put his hand around my waist. He took my other hand in his and swayed side-to-side with the beat of the music. "Close your eyes," he instructed.

"That can't help. I need to watch my feet. I don't want to step on you."

He shook his head. "Just do it, please," he said with a hint of impatience.

I closed my eyes and listened to the music. I allowed Darren to sway me back and forth. "Do I like this song?"

"Not particularly, but I do. You surprised me with tickets to his concert for my birthday last summer. I think it's quite possibly the most thoughtful thing you've ever given me." He moved slightly, causing me to go rigid, and I opened my eyes. "Relax. Just allow me to lead you. It's not hard. Try again."

I closed my eyes and the song changed. It was slow and the melody was easier. "I like this one."

"Yes, you do." There was a smile in his voice.

Before a minute had passed, I was keeping pace with the beat of the song and Darren's leading. I couldn't help but smile. It was strangely familiar. When he pulled me closer, I could tell we'd turned, and I hadn't fought the change. My breath caught as the song ended on the sweetest note. Darren pulled me closer and held me securely in his arms. My head rested on his chest and I could feel the smooth muscles of his shoulder. He breathed against the side of my head and his lips whispered into my hair. "See, you do remember." He sounded so relieved that his little test had worked.

My heartbeat increased at our closeness. It happened every time he touched me and being this close and feeling his hands on me was a pleasant sensation. "And you're sure we aren't *together*?" I asked almost in a pant.

"Positive."

"How can you hold me like this and not feel…" I couldn't finish.

"Oh, I feel it. I've just been refused for so long that I know not to hope or act on it." He released me and put a respectful distance between us. "It gets easier with time. I decided a long time ago that if I pressed you, you'd run. I like having you around too much to change that."

***

We spent a quiet Thanksgiving, eating a store-bought turkey dinner. "Wouldn't you rather be eating with friends or family?" I asked, but Darren insisted that I stay home for a few more days as per the doctors' recommendations. He was resigned not to leave me except for brief stints to the gym or to run to the grocery store.

All day Saturday, Darren watched me like a hawk. "What? Why do you keep looking at me like that?"

"It's Saturday afternoon."

"So?"

"You don't miss confession and mass for anything."

"I don't?"

"Would you like me to drive you?"

"I guess so. I didn't know I was Catholic. Are you?"

He shook his head. "No, I'm not particularly affiliated with any one congregation. I was raised in a Christian home and grew up attending church with my family. I believe in God and was baptized when I was twelve, but I don't attend regularly."

"Do you mind going with me?" I asked.

"Not at all."

As soon as we entered the church, I was overcome with the strangest feeling. This place was familiar. I smiled and Darren saw the change in me right away. "I've been here before. I know that altar. I recognize those windows. Someone I know got married here. There were flowers everywhere." I dipped my hand in the holy water and made the sign of the cross over myself and genuflected. Darren lowered his head in a bow toward the altar before we sat in the carved, wooden pew.

The priest and altar boy entered the sanctuary and I was instantly drawn into the order of worship. I surely must be Catholic because I knew what to do. This body knew when to kneel and when to stand. I remembered the prayers and the words and the way of things. Darren sat next to me, watching me the entire time. He walked behind me when I went up to receive communion. Taking the host and drinking the wine wasn't incredibly spiritual, nor did it miraculously give me any memories. It was more like a settling in my soul. Darren crossed his arms over his chest and received a blessing from the priest. He didn't receive communion.

After mass, he asked if I'd like to go out to eat. We went to a local Mexican place. It was delicious. I absolutely loved Mexican food. I was still taking medicine at night to help with the inflammation and headaches, so neither of us ordered alcohol.

That night, I tossed and turned in my bed for an hour. I couldn't settle. Something was terribly off and I couldn't put my finger on it. I finally stood and walked across to Darren's room.

"What's wrong?" I heard his voice in the dark as soon as I opened his door.

My throat was tight. "I can't sleep," I confessed. Along with the words, from out of nowhere, tears began to fall. I sniffed and swallowed, trying to regain some control.

"Come here," he said, but I hesitated at the door. "Beth, are you okay?" I sniffed again and wiped the tears that were streaming down my cheeks.

"I don't know why I'm crying. I'm sorry I woke you. I'll go downstairs so you can go back to sleep."

"Beth," his voice was so compelling that my feet refused to retreat. He stood from the bed and walked toward me wearing boxers and a t-shirt. He put his hands on my shoulders and looked into my eyes. The light from the hall was dim, but I could see his eyes through my tears. "Hang on," he said and turned back into his room. He put on a pair of lounge pants from the foot of his bed and grabbed his pillow.

He led me back to my bed and let me get settled before he once again lay down next to me. He lay on his side and placed his arm over me protectively. He was lean but solid and I could feel his heartbeat and his breaths as he inhaled slowly, willing me to relax. I closed my eyes and was asleep in about two seconds.

Sunday morning, I woke to the smell of bacon. My mouth was already salivating when I opened my eyes. I jumped out of bed and nearly ran down the stairs. "Breakfast!" I exclaimed. Darren smiled, pleased that once again, he knew exactly what I liked. I went to the fridge and poured myself a huge glass of milk. "Want one?" I asked.

"Sure."

The easy morning was enjoyable. The newspaper came and I felt like a little kid reading the funnies in my PJs. "You have to go back to work tomorrow," I said.

"Yep, but I'm glad I've had this week with you. Are you going to follow-up with the sheriff's department tomorrow? You also need to call your insurance company. You can't drive until the neurologist clears you, but you can at least be thinking about what kind of car you want."

"Darren, I have a problem. I can't remember the password on my laptop and I have about fifty texts from people I don't know. I hate to be rude, but I just want to clear them."

"Bring them down, I'll get you in." I brought him all of my devices. He patiently entered in the same password. "It's *thisisBS91*, capital B, capital S."

"Really? How cynical," I said.

"It's not cynical at all," he defended. "You can call out BS faster than anyone I know. It keeps your priorities straight. You have two classifications: Bonus and BS. I'm happy to be in the Bonus category."

"What resides in the BS category?"

"Anything or anyone that hurts you or anything from your past that
threatens to harm your future. It's not a complicated process. You just call it BS
when necessary."

That wasn't as bad as I initially thought. "I like that. How assertive of me.
Do I say it out loud?"

"Sometimes, but thankfully not in faculty meetings or with your students.
The parents didn't understand when their kids came home saying *BS*. It didn't
go over well. You finally started teaching them *bologna* and *hogswallop*.
You've broadened their vocabulary, if nothing else."

***

I was pretty sad to see Darren leave for work on Monday morning. The
house was painfully quiet. I cleaned the kitchen and started a load of laundry. I
took a bath and carefully washed my hair. By ten o'clock, I'd called the
insurance company and gave them what information I could. I also found out
that I drove a red Honda Accord and that I should receive a payoff check within
ten business days. I explained that I was unable to drive and that a rental wasn't
necessary.

Before noon, I called and left a message with the sheriff's department.
After lunch, an officer called me. Lt. Miller's voice was deep and authoritative.
"I need you to come in and sign some paperwork. When would you be able to
do that, ma'am?"

"I haven't been released to drive and my roommate is at work until four. I
guess I could take a cab or something."

"Honestly, the sooner the better. Between you getting released from the hospital and my being out last week, my report's been delayed long enough. If you could be here within the hour, I'd appreciate it. Are you at home now?

"Yes, why?"

"Do you have Uber on your phone? It's pretty reliable on that side of Lafayette."

"Hang on," I said and thought through his request. Sure enough, I had an Uber app on my phone. "Okay, what's your address?" I asked.

A little over an hour later, I sat at the sheriff's department waiting on Lt. Miller. The receptionist called my name and I entered a large room filled with desks. She led me to the lieutenant. He was a stocky, dark-skinned man with short hair and a thick neck. He had an authoritative demeanor and his muscles flexed under his uniform.

"Ms. Rust, thank you for coming down. I have a few forms for you to sign. It won't take long." Neatly stacked files and papers were arranged on his desk. "I have to say, you look a considerable dose better than when we pulled you from your vehicle." All of his features softened when he smiled.

"You were there?" I asked.

"Yes, ma'am. I was the first officer on the scene."

My stomach ached when he mentioned the accident. He pulled a folder from the stack and opened it. He read over the report and turned the folder towards me. "I spoke with your friend while you were in the hospital. I know you have no memory of the crash and are having a hard time piecing it together, but I still need you to read over my report and sign it."

"Was it my fault?" I asked hesitantly.

He shook his head. "No, the best we can figure from the witnesses is that an 18-wheeler was involved and that the two vehicles skidded at high speeds on a wet road, during bands of hurricane rain, and both drivers lost control of their vehicles. Traffic was backed up for hours."

"Do you have photos? I'd like to have some memory of it."

"Are you sure you want to see that? They're pretty graphic." He looked concerned.

I nodded as confidently as I could, and he allowed me to flip through the photos in the file. I didn't recognize the red Honda at all, but the other vehicle I knew. I knew it well. It was a white, four-door, Volvo. The interior was tan leather with silver and faux wood trim. The seats were heated and cooled and there was a small scratch in the dash. I knew that scratch. My fingers lingered over the photos. I was terribly confused. "The other car, were there any survivors?" He shook his head. "How many people?" I asked.

"Two. A man and a woman."

"They were married."

"How did you know that?"

I shrugged. I had no idea why I'd said that aloud. "I just guessed. Married couples drive Volvos, right? Was the woman driving?"

"Yes. They probably died within seconds of one another. They didn't have a chance." He shook his head, saddened at the memory.

"May I have their names?" I asked.

He opened a file on his desk. "The victims were a forty-nine-year-old Caucasian woman, Katherine Hebert, and her husband, Victor, fifty-three."

"Katherine and Victor," I repeated, distractedly as I flipped back to the report and read it thoroughly. I batted back tears, again, and I was deeply saddened at the destruction and loss from the photos. My heart ached for this couple and their deaths. I took the pen Lt. Miller offered me and signed my name. "Is there anything else?" I asked.

He shook his head. "Do you have a ride home?"

"No, I have to Uber back, but I left my phone," I said frustrated at myself for forgetting it.

"Do you want a ride? I'm off the clock in ten minutes, and my mama doesn't live too far from your address. I can drop you off on my way."

"I don't know. I don't want to be a bother. Do I have to ride in the back like a criminal?"

"No, ma'am." He laughed in his deep voice. I liked his smile. "Let me go file this and I'll be right back."

CHAPTER 6

"How long have you been with the sheriff's department?" I asked making conversation on the ride back to the townhouse.

"Five years. I was in the Marine Corps for ten before I decided to come home for good. Besides, I missed my mama's cooking." He laughed, his deep voice resonating.

Darren's car was parked outside when we arrived. He walked outside looking frantic when he saw me getting out of the patrol car. "Are you okay? Where have you been? I've been texting you for an hour! Is everything alright, officer?" he asked Lt. Miller, and then they recognized each other.

"I'm fine. I had to sign a report. Lt. Miller was kind enough to drive me home," I interjected.

"There's no trouble. I was headed to my mama's. It's on the way."

"Thank you. Darren Fitzgerald," he said and put out his hand to shake the officer's. "I didn't recognize you. You were the officer at the hospital, right?"

"Marcus Miller, pleasure to meet you again."

"Is everything finalized, then? Is there anything else to be done?" Darren asked.

"Nope, it's all wrapped up."

"Thank you, Lieutenant," I said and returned his smile.

"I hope to see you, again, under better circumstances. Take care," he said and gave a little nod like a salute.

Darren eyed me once we were inside. "Where's your phone?" His voice was sharp; his eyes were sharper.

"Upstairs. I plugged it in and forgot it when the Uber arrived. I'm sorry. I didn't mean to worry you. Why are you looking at me like that?"

"Did Marcus ask you out?"

"No, what gave you that idea?" I asked, surprised at his question.

"Never mind," Darren said.

"Darren, I don't understand. I'm sorry I didn't have my phone, and I'm even sorrier that I made you worry, but I can tell there's something else."

He hesitated and stammered. He walked to the kitchen and put another casserole in the oven. He laid his glasses down on the counter beside him and rubbed the bridge of his nose as he'd done just before he'd had to tell me the awful story about my scars.

I sat down on the sofa and waited. I braced myself because I could tell it was bad, and I shook internally. I looked up at him and could see that he was still struggling. I took a deep breath, guessing, "Does this have anything to do with the number of condoms I've found in everything I own?" They were everywhere: every drawer, every jacket pocket, my purse. "What the heck, Darren? Am I some kind of pervert?"

When Darren didn't answer me, I suddenly felt dirty and violated. The truth was painful. I felt it. I knew instinctively that this body had been used a lot and not in a good way. "Does that make me a whore or a slut?" I asked lowering my gaze into my lap. I couldn't look him in the eye. My stomach hurt and I thought I might throw up.

"Whore implies money or property was exchanged. I prefer the word promiscuous," he said numbly. I looked up into his face again, curious to know more. "I've begged you not to, but you insist on sleeping with every guy you go out with. Wait, let me clarify." His voice rose and I could tell he was having to work to control his temper. "You're determined to have *sex* with every guy you go out with. I've made a habit of supplying you with condoms and not asking questions." Disappointment crossed his face. He hated every word he spoke aloud.

"But I've never slept with *you*," I guessed.

"Oh, as you already know, you *sleep* with me all the time, but you've never, ever let me even imagine having sex with you." His candor tore at my heart.

"Why not?" I asked cautiously, curious to know more.

He considered me for a few moments, deciding on what to reveal. I wondered if he forgot sometimes that I'd lost my memory. "I honestly have no idea. I kissed you once, romantically, and you asked me to never do that again. You told me I'd seen all your ugly, and you were afraid that would taint our future. I didn't have any way to convince you otherwise." His words were a little sad and held a hint of regret.

"Is that why I go to confession every Saturday?"

Darren shrugged and almost looked thankful for the shift in topic. "I don't know; maybe." He chuckled humorously, "I suspected once that you had a thing for your priest, but that was just my own insecurity."

I looked at Darren and examined him more closely. For the first time, I really looked at him. He was handsome and kind. He was smart and had a good sense of humor. He had a scholarly look about him like he was already a college professor. I wondered why he hadn't been snatched up already.

"Do you date?" I asked.

"Sure, I've dated a few women, but I didn't love them, so, I don't pursue relationships that I can't keep platonic. Most of the women we know either assume I'm gay, or you and I are really together." He shook his head. "By the way, I'm not gay. I'm deeply in love with a woman and in a committed relationship, even if the commitment is one-sided."

I understood. He loved me. Well, he obviously loved Beth and had for a long time. Sadie and the other nurses had noticed it immediately. He was taking care of me, not just because he was my friend, but because he loved me.

"I think you're a masochist. Maybe you should tag along to my next appointment. You may have some things to figure out with my therapist." The sarcasm ran deep.

"Believe me, Beth, I've never received *any* sexual pleasure from our relationship." His tone was hard, resigned to the truth.

"That's disappointing. I'm sorry. I truly am, but if it's the least bit reassuring, I don't have any attraction toward Marcus. I also don't have any desires toward anyone else." Darren furled his brow, not understanding. "I don't feel any urges to go looking for it, okay?" I said defensively, unsure of why I needed to say that out loud. I lowered my gaze and blushed all over.

He chucked in relief and shook his head. "I've never seen you blush before, not like that, not about sex." I could feel his stare.

"When did I lose my virginity?" I asked looking up at him.

His face looked pained again, no, it was definitely anger I saw, but I didn't think the anger was directed towards me. "I suspect that you were abused more than once before you went to live with your Gram. I don't think your parents protected you from much. As far as when you chose to become sexually active, I don't have any details. I know it was in high school and you were probably sixteen or seventeen. You never had a boyfriend. Gram was delighted to meet me because you'd never brought a boy home before. She told me once that I was the best thing that ever happened to you. I disagree; I'm just the thing that's stuck around the longest."

I didn't know how to respond. It was obvious he'd been rejected and denied, and I could do nothing to reassure him. Darren looked around the kitchen and then sighed. "I'm going to take a shower. I'll be down to eat."

I remained on the sofa, numbed by the knowledge of what a selfish, disgusting, unlovable person I was. At dinner, I sat across from Darren and we ate in silence. I concentrated unnecessarily on my plate and the food. I couldn't look at him. I felt shame and guilt and every sort of vile thing I could think of. How could he live with me? How could I live with myself?

The shame affected my senses. The clink of our silverware on the plates was annoying. I could hear every time Darren swallowed. The few bites of food that I was able put in my mouth turned into flavorless grit on my tongue. I was chewing dirt. I rose from the table suddenly and vomited in the sink. Darren was at my side immediately. He held my shoulders until the dry heaves subsided, then he dampened a paper towel and offered it to me. I wiped my mouth and turned into him, sobbing uncontrollably. He walked me to the sofa and sat next to me. He let me cry for a long time. He didn't try to shhh me or tell me to stop. He just held me and rocked me back and forth soothingly.

When I was all cried out, I sat back and looked him in the eye. "This is BS! It's all BS! I'm not going to be that person *ever* again." I was surprised at the resolve in my voice. His eyes mirrored my determination and I could tell he believed me. "I'd like to be alone, Darren. I'm going to take a bath and go to bed." He nodded and I could feel his gaze follow me up the stairs.

I lay in the bed for a long time. I couldn't fall asleep. I scrolled through the photos on my phone. I studied the faces of the children in the photos. I smiled with them and could see the pride in each of their innocent eyes. I assumed the people in the photos were my friends. There were so many selfies with Darren but no other guys. I considered getting up and finding Darren, but that was cruel. I didn't want to abuse his friendship like that anymore.

I lay there, taking inventory of my body. I closed my eyes and started at the top of my head. I thought it would be the most neutral place, but the only thing I could feel was Darren's kiss that sent warmth all the way down to my chest each time he kissed me in the hospital. I could feel his hands on my face, my shoulders, my back. I remembered the way he held me when we danced. Ed Sheeran's lyrics played in the back of my mind like a movie soundtrack.

So, open your eyes and see, the way our horizons meet

The intensity of his eyes penetrated mine.

And all the lights will lead, into the night with me

His arms holding me, protecting me from myself.

And I know these scars will bleed,

but both of our hearts believe

His tender voice saying my name, comforting me.

All these stars will guide us home

Our bodies lying together as we slept. I imagined him there with me. I imagined his slow breaths at the back of my head. I felt the security of his arm around me and the warmth of his chest on my back. Before two more breaths, I was asleep.

CHAPTER 7

Darren was already gone when I woke up. There was a note on the counter.

B,

You were sleeping soundly. I didn't want to wake you.

Have a good day. If you leave, please take your phone.

I'll call you at lunch and check on you.

D

I had no appointments and I had nothing to do. I ate a bowl of cereal and folded a load of towels. I made my bed and found an empty shoebox and cleaned out all of the condoms I could find from the clothing and bags and drawers. I took an inventory of my bedroom and my closet. There were only a few articles of clothing that I would call professional. I found a couple of blouses and a skirt that were reasonably adult-looking. I apparently preferred t-shirts and denim.

My shoes looked comfortable and practical with only three pair of heels. I supposed teaching little kids in heels was an absurd concept. There were several pairs of sneakers. I really liked the pair of cowboy boots in the back of the closet. They were well-worn and fit my feet perfectly.

Once the hangers were arranged and weeded through, I moved to the shelves at the back of the small, walk-in closet. I refolded a blanket and found an old quilt behind it. I pulled it off the shelf and held it close to my face. I could smell faint traces of something familiar. I went to the bed and removed the ugly comforter and replaced it with the quilt. I liked it much better. I decided

not to keep the comforter which made more room for a stack of sweaters.

Cleaning out the condoms from my dresser, I found a jewelry box and a

small, wooden box that contained a variety of photos and birthday cards. The

photos were of me as a child. I had an overbite and a slight gap between my

teeth. My hair was long and straight. A couple of school photos showed me with

bangs. There were two photos of an infant and a couple. The woman wasn't

more than a girl. She looked so young, but I was definitely related to her. I had

her eyes. The other one was clearer and I presumed the young man was my

father. He was smiling at my mom. He had the same small gap between his

front teeth. I stacked the photos neatly and placed them carefully back into the

box.

I opened the cards and read each one of them. They were all from Gram.

She had a peculiar sense of humor. They made me laugh. I really wished I knew

her. Before I could begin reading through them more carefully, I heard my

phone ring. I jumped. It wasn't a sound I'd heard but a couple of times. It was

Darren, his smiling face appeared on my screen. I swiped it open and said,

"Hello?"

"How's your day so far?"

"Good," I said. I wasn't sure if I should mention last night or just leave it

be, but Darren cleared the air easily.

"I'm really sorry about last night. Are you alright?"

"Darren, I'm okay. None of this is easy. I need to just take it as it comes."

There was a brief silence as he accepted my words. "What are you doing?" he asked.

"I'm cleaning out my closet." Dead silence. "Are you still there?"

"Yes, I'm here. You're cleaning?" he asked.

"Well, sort of. I don't know what I have to wear. I've only worn real clothes like three times. I guess I'm taking inventory more than I'm cleaning."

He laughed at that. "That's a good idea. Found anything interesting?"

"I really like my boots. I also like that hoodie you brought me in the hospital. I have two of them. Bonus!" He laughed again.

"Hey, you want to go out for dinner tonight? I don't have class and I thought you might want to get out."

"That's nice, but I don't think I'm up for it. May I take a raincheck?"

"Sure. I'll be home by four."

"Hey, do we have stuff to make spaghetti? I'm really hungry for spaghetti."

"I'll pick it up on my way home."

"Okay, thanks. Bye."

"Bye."

I'd heard the buzzer from the dryer go off a couple of times. I went downstairs and made myself a sandwich and wiped down the counter. Darren was extremely neat. I didn't feel particularly slobbish, but I would make an effort to be useful and not make messes I wasn't able to clean up. I folded the clothes from the dryer, stacked the folded towels, and went back upstairs. I placed Darren's towels in his bathroom on the shelf above his toilet. His bathroom smelled like him: his shampoo and aftershave, his deodorant, and even his toothpaste.

I put my towels away and looked around my room. The most inviting thing about it was the quilt. I lay down and traced my fingers along the stitches and felt the different textures of the fabrics. My head ached some and I felt tired, so I closed my eyes and brought one side of the quilt over me. It was the perfect weight. I breathed in and out a few times and fell asleep almost instantly.

When I woke, I heard Darren's shower running. I sat up and checked my phone; I'd been asleep for a few hours. I went downstairs and found where Darren had unpacked the groceries onto the counter. I pulled an apron from the drawer, opened the package of ground meat, and started browning it. I found the pasta pot and filled it with water, adding a dash of salt and a bit of olive oil. I unwrapped the garlic cloves and mushrooms. I held the knife and cloves of garlic and wondered where the cutting board might be. I hadn't heard Darren come downstairs and jumped when I saw him. He was giving me a really funny look.

"What?" I asked.

"You're cooking," he said.

"I'm sorry, did you want to cook?" I asked. "I thought I'd get things started."

"No, go ahead," he mused. It was easy again with Darren; the tension from the evening before had completely dissolved.

"I don't normally cook, do I?"

"You could say that. You make French toast and pancakes and can roast marshmallows perfectly over the BBQ pit."

"Stop it! You're teasing. I know how to make spaghetti. Everyone knows how to make spaghetti."

Come to find out, I did know how to make spaghetti and it tasted good, and I was pretty proud of myself. Darren and I cleared the dishes and put the leftovers in the fridge. The kitchen was clean and I joined him on the sofa.

"How was your day?" I asked. I was interested in how he'd spent his day.

"It was good. I have a new kid this year. He's all over the place. He's challenged me in ways I can't explain."

"What's his name?"

"Tommy. He's fourteen. I had to call his mom today. The cafeteria ladies refuse to serve him anymore. He's incredibly picky and even more eloquent with his words. He'll be brown-bagging it until the end of the year."

"Poor kid. You should take him some spaghetti tomorrow."

"Maybe I will. What did you do this afternoon?" he asked.

"After we talked, I ate lunch, folded some laundry, and took a nap. I found a box with old photos and birthday cards from Gram. They made me laugh. She had a great sense of humor, didn't she?"

"Yep."

"I found a quilt, too."

He looked surprised. "I didn't know you still had that. Where'd you find it?" he asked.

"Behind a blanket in my closet."

"Where is it now?"

"On my bed. I think I'm going to get rid of the comforter."

"That's a good idea." He nodded encouragingly, like it was a good thing.

"Why didn't you have class today?" I asked.

"My professor is out of town. He assigned some readings and discussion questions for next week. I should probably work on those tonight. They'll most likely be on the final. He's spiteful like that."

CHAPTER 8

Since I only went to therapy once a week and hadn't yet been released to drive or go back to work, my days were solitary. I was allowed to walk, so I took a lot of walks. I tried to read, but it gave me headaches, TV, too. Audiobooks were tolerable, but music was the only thing that didn't provoke the throbbing. I cooked dinner on nights when Darren didn't have class and I slept a lot.

Darren drove me to mass on Saturdays, but I didn't feel the need to go to confession. If nothing else, amnesia was a great form of absolution. I figured I'd already confessed the stuff I'd learned about myself, and with so little contact with other humans, I wasn't particularly sinful. Maybe monks had the answer. Living apart from the world, gave me fewer opportunities to screw things up.

The faculty Christmas party was in two days. I didn't know why I needed to go, but Darren insisted. He said it wasn't healthy for me to be isolated and at home all day, alone. He explained that it would be held at our head mistress's house. Her husband was a cardiologist and they had a home large enough to host everyone. I pilfered through my closet to find something both festive and professional. The only dress I thought was the least bit appropriate for such an occasion, hung at the back of the closet with the tags still on it.

I looked in the mirror and continued to be disappointed with my hair. The stitches were to be removed the following morning, and I assured Darren I could Uber to the clinic by myself. I decided that I'd do something about my hair after that appointment. That would give me a couple of hours to get ready for the party.

Before I left for the clinic, I grabbed a photo from the ones on the shelf and slipped it into my purse. The stylist that took me into the back of the walk-in salon looked at the photo considering. "Is this your natural color?" I nodded. "I like it. It will soften your skin tone considerably. You should be out of here in a couple of hours."

"Is there any way you could tone down these spikes?" I asked. "I know it's already so short, but I don't know what to do with this hairstyle."

The stylist ran her fingers through my hair and nodded approvingly. "I think I can trim and shape it a little. I'd like to color it before we cut it though and neutralize the bleached tips. It might have a softer look with just the color change."

"May I get a pedicure, too?" The shoes I'd chosen were open-toed, and I didn't want the nasty chipping to be obvious.

"Sure, I'll seat you with a nail tech while your color sets."

I left the salon feeling more confident about my appearance than any other day preceding. I was not only pleased with the color, but the trim softened the shape of my face. I smiled approvingly. Darren wasn't home from school when I arrived, so I decided to get a bath and shave my legs before getting dressed for the party. I wrapped my head in a towel before taking a long, hot bath. The hot bath eased my anxiety about attending this party.

I went downstairs in my bathrobe with my head still wrapped in a towel to get a snack. Darren came in from school and found me in the kitchen. "Is there any more of that?" he asked looking at my reheated leftovers.

"No, this is the last. Want to split it?" I asked.

"Sure," he said grabbing a fork from the drawer. "How was your day?"

"It was good. I got the stitches out." I gestured to my forehead. He nodded chewing a bite of food. "Then I went and got a haircut and my toes done on my way home."

"You cut it?" he asked disconcerted.

"Just a trim," I assured him. "It was growing out all wonky on one side." I didn't mention the coloring because I wasn't sure how he'd feel about me making such a drastic change. I figured it would be best to just show him the finished product.

***

I stood looking at myself in the full-length mirror. I liked the change to my hair. The coloring had softened my features, and I didn't look so angular and dramatic. I put on a little bit of makeup and then pulled the dress over my head. It was a rich grey, long-sleeved, knit dress. It was opened on the shoulders and the hemline went just past my knees. It was flattering and feminine.

I dug around in the dresser and found the small jewelry box. There were a few pair of earrings and several necklaces. I chose a long, old-fashioned locket and a pair of pearl earrings. I only found one more condom to add to my collection in the shoebox under the bed. So far, I'd found thirty-seven. This one made thirty-eight. I took another look in the mirror and turned to see my backside. I liked the overall transformation. I adjusted the sleeves to cover the scars on my wrists.

"Darren, I'm going to wait downstairs," I called toward his bedroom.

"I'm already here," I heard him call back. I hadn't heard him go downstairs.

I descended the stairs tentatively. I was suddenly unsure about my choices and doubted whether or not I should go back upstairs, find my hoodie and leggings, and just stay home after all. When I rounded off the stairs, I saw Darren looking down at his phone. He was wearing khakis and a navy blazer. His hair was still damp from the shower and the hint of dark brown waves brushed the edge of his collar. When he looked up from the screen, his eyes bugged out a little and his mouth gaped.

"Too much?" I asked, self-consciously.

He was obviously surprised, but then he smiled approvingly. "No, perfect. You look really pretty."

His words washed over me like a wave and I smiled at his satisfied expression. "Thank you. You clean up pretty good, yourself."

He acknowledged the compliment and cocked his head to one side. "Your hair. I haven't seen it that color in a long time. Do you like it?" I nodded and took the locket into my hands, giving me something to hold onto. "Do you have any inclination that I gave you that necklace?"

I looked down at the locket in my hands and shook my head. "Sorry, no. I just thought it went well with the dress."

He reached and took it gently from my hands. He opened it and showed me the small photos inside. On the left was Gram, and on the right, was himself. "It's so you're never alone. We're always with you." He smiled remembering something. "I'm glad you agreed to come tonight. We're going to have a good time." He kissed my cheek, grabbed his keys from the table behind me, and we left for the party.

***

"Darren, I don't know how I'm going to fake knowing any of these people. How long do we need to stay?" I was feeling nervous and a little nauseated.

"They know that you've not regained your memory, yet. They also know that you're most likely not going to recognize them. I asked them to introduce themselves and to just let you have a night out. For the most part, I think they'll be understanding."

Mrs. Moore answered the door and welcomed us into the party. She was a tall, middle-aged woman and looked like I had imagined a headmistress of a school. Her smile was warm and welcoming. "Beth, Darren, it's good to see you. Won't you come in?" Her voice was maternal and sincere. "Beth, I'm Christina Moore, your headmistress. We've missed you." She smiled and took my hand and looked into my eyes. "You look beautiful. I love what you've done with your hair. Everyone's gathering around the bar; make yourselves at home," she directed.

"Thank you," I said. "Everything is lovely." Her home was decorated for the holidays: trees, lights, garland, and mistletoe. The entryway led into the dining and living areas. There were already about twenty people there, mingling and holding glasses of wine and other drinks. On one side off the dining room was a bar with a server and on the other, a long buffet table covered with food.

"Red or white?" Darren asked.

"Red, please." He nodded and stepped away.

A young brunette approached me and looked into my eyes, expecting a response. "Hi," I said, trying to be friendly.

"Hi, Beth, I'm Molly, Molly Kennedy? I'm your kindergarten co-teacher. I'm really glad to see you. We were so worried about you."

"Hi, Molly. Thank you. Other than the memory thing, I've recovered well." I smiled. "So, how are the kids doing? Who's taking my place while I'm out?" I asked making conversation.

"The kids are good. Mrs. Moore hired two substitutes and we already had a student teacher, so we're handling it well. Some of the moms have been rotating, too, volunteering to help me out. It's taken a small army to replace you." She laughed nervously.

"I'm glad to hear it's going well. I hope to be back soon," I said sincerely.

"Are you hungry?" she asked, motioning toward the buffet table. Just then, Darren joined us and handed me my glass of wine. "Hello, Darren." Molly's face changed and her eyes fluttered self-consciously. She was admiring him in a way to which he was completely oblivious.

Darren and Molly took it upon themselves to introduce, or reintroduce, me to everyone there. I met my colleagues and their spouses and significant others.

We played a few games and there were prizes awarded to the best teams. Molly, Darren, and I won movie passes. I had to admit that I had a good time. I thanked some of the ladies who had prepared food for me. Their concern was evident.

It was nearly midnight when we left the party. I couldn't believe we'd stayed so long. "Goodnight, Beth. Goodnight, Darren," Molly's voice rang out toward us as we got into the car.

"She likes you," I said.

"Molly? Did she tell you that?"

"No, but it's pretty evident in the way she looks at you."

"I'm a lot older than her. I don't think we have that much in common. It's just a crush. She'll get over it."

"Darren, when was your last date?"

He cut his eyes briefly in my direction. "Let's just say it's been a while."

CHAPTER 9

Christmas break arrived, and Darren convinced me to go to Illinois with him. He had delayed purchasing an airline ticket in advance because he wasn't sure what I may need, so we ended up driving the fifteen-plus hours to his parents' home near Chicago.

"Do you and I exchange gifts?" I asked.

"Yes, last year, you gave me a goat," he smirked, trying to hold his amusement.

"You're lying. That's a lame present. Really, what did I give you?"

"Honestly, you gave me a goat, but it was wrapped in potholders."

"That's ridiculous."

"No, really, you donated a goat to a family in Haiti in my name. You wrapped the picture of the beast in a potholder you'd made as an example for your students."

That wasn't as bad as I thought. "What did you give me?"

His smile broadened and a flash of something shown in his eyes. "The dress you wore to the Christmas party."

"Thank you. You have really good taste."

"I think so, but I wasn't sure you liked it. That's the first time I've seen you wear it."

"It still had the tags on it," I said sheepishly.

A few days before we planned to leave for Chicago, Darren lifted my suitcase down from the top of my closet. He reminded me to pack in layers: thermals, sweaters, hats, and gloves. He said his mom and dad kept plenty of heavy coats on hand if we needed them, along with our ski gear.

"I can't believe I'm going to arrive at someone's home for Christmas empty-handed."

"You aren't empty-handed. I've shipped gifts for everyone. Thanks to Amazon, they are already wrapped and ready. My family is just happy to know you're coming. They will love having you. It's not about the presents; it's about spending time with my parents. They've been worried about you, and it will comfort them to see you."

We headed out of town early in the morning. We were on the road before six. Darren drove ten hours the first day. We stopped in a little town in northern Missouri and checked into a hotel. We walked a block to a local pizza place for an early dinner. The crowd was light but the staff was friendly and the food was delicious. There was a dancing pig on the jukebox. I was glad we arrived when we did; before we left the restaurant, the place was packed.

"What do I need to know about your family before we arrive? What can I expect?"

"We'll arrive and my mother will hug us to death. My father will hug us, too, but he'll hug you more. You and I will stay upstairs in the guestrooms. We'll share an adjoining bath. My sister, Allison, and her husband, Lance, will come for dinner. They'll bring their son, Michael. He's nine. I'm his self-declared favorite uncle, and I spend as much time with him as possible. We play video games every day, and I'll take him to a winter sports park a couple of times. He enjoys cross-country skiing. You and I will take him shopping for his Christmas present. His parents will protest and put up a fuss that I'm too indulgent. That's their fault; they're the ones who asked me to be his godfather. I save all year so that for his birthday in July and Christmas, I can do just about anything I want to make those days special."

"What price range are we talking about?" I asked.

"It depends. I've promised to buy him a dirt bike when he's twelve. Don't worry, I have his parents' permission. This year he wants an Xbox, but I've included a flat screen for their basement and rechargeable batteries for the remotes. That part will be a total surprise."

"Does your family open gifts Christmas Eve or Christmas Day?"

"Christmas morning. We'll go over to my sister's house early and watch Michael open his presents. We'll have a huge breakfast and hopefully there will be Legos to assemble and games to play. We'll set up Michael's gaming system in the basement and spend the entire day there. Christmas Eve we'll go to church with my parents. Michael will sing with the children's choir, and we'll all have chili or soup of something like that for dinner. Like I said, it's about being together as a family. I know you can't do any of the athletic stuff, but you'll have a good time." Darren made it sound good. He assured me that it would be relaxed and fun.

We arrived at his parents' house in the early afternoon. Sure enough, his mother, Mary, squealed and hugged us and hugged us some more. She kissed our cheeks and made over us like we were the prodigals returned. Their house smelled like fresh baked cookies and cinnamon and hints of peppermint like Darren's car. His father, Tom, was an older version of his son. He had the kindest eyes. He hesitated at first when he saw me and then grabbed me like a doll and hugged me. It wasn't awkward or weird. It was like hugging an older version of Darren. It was familiar and safe. I instantly liked it there.

Darren helped me carry my suitcase upstairs. He showed me my room and the bathroom and where everything was kept. I freshened up and went downstairs. Mary was in the kitchen with Tom.

"It's good to see you, Beth. We were so worried about you. DJ texted us every day. He was a mess. Any improvements on the memory at all?" Mary asked, sincerely.

"No, ma'am. I have a few hints here and there. Dreams. Nightmares, mostly, but I recognized my church the first time Darren took me to mass. I'm really thankful for everything he's done for me. Your son is pretty amazing." His parents eyed one another and smiled proudly. "You already knew that, though," I said shyly.

"Beth, I can't imagine what you've been through. I can't imagine what you're going through, now. We're here for you. You can count on us," Tom said as he hugged me again. This time he didn't let me go and kept his arm around me protectively. Darren came downstairs. "DJ, how was the drive?" Tom asked.

"Good. We stayed in Charleston last night. We ate at that pizza place with the dancing pig on the jukebox."

His dad laughed. "That's the same place Alli beat you at pinball."

"The one and only time she beat me at pinball!" They laughed together; their voices resonating. "Need any help, Mom?" he asked kissing her cheek.

"No, everything's in the oven. Alli and Lance are bringing the salad. Pot roast is easy. You could bring in some more firewood before it gets dark. Dad's boots are next to the backdoor."

"Tom, why don't you take Beth on a tour of the house. She's probably curious."

Tom did as he was instructed and led me on a tour. The dining room was spacious and formal and led into an office. There were two desks and everything was neatly organized. "Our bedroom is through that door. We took in a formal living room and added on a sunroom to make a downstairs master when we bought the place. We knew in time we wouldn't be able to make those stairs every day."

Tom then led me into a family room with a couple of sofas and lounge chairs and a fireplace. A real Christmas tree stood in the corner. It was decorated with a hodge-podge of ornaments. Some were obviously homemade and probably from when Darren and Allison were children. I gradually moved around the room; there were photos everywhere. I was in many of the photos with this family.

"When was this taken?" I asked looking at a photo of me in a large field with mountains in the background. I was standing with Mary and we were making silly faces at the camera.

"That's from a summer vacation in Germany. It was your second time there. You'd come the Christmas before. We skied those very mountains behind you the next Christmas you two visited."

"It's beautiful," I commented. Then there was a photo of me holding a baby. "Is that Michael?" I asked.

"Good job. That is. He was a tiny little fart. Now he's my favorite medium fart," Tom laughed.

"What do you and Mary do these days?" I asked.

"Mary still works part-time at the hospital. She's a nurse. She and Allison work together. Alli's a nurse practitioner in the ER. I putter around here and take care of Michael after school. Lance is a tax attorney and works long hours at different times of the year. I volunteer a couple days a week through our church, and I manage the shooting range on the weekends and during the summer."

Tom spoke to me like he'd known me my entire life and like a new acquaintance at the same time. "Thank you, Tom," I began but I could feel the tears welling in my eyes. I didn't want to cry, but I was suddenly overcome with emotion. He had known me for a long time and his affection for me was as evident as Darren's.

"What for?" He turned and looked at me. He read my expression. "Awe, sweetheart, come here." He enveloped me and rubbed my back.

In this stranger's embrace, the tears fell freely. "I'm sorry. I was nervous about coming. I asked Darren about a hundred questions. I feel so silly. Ya'll are awesome."

Tom laughed and held me tighter. "You're going to be just fine, sweetheart, give it time." And for some strange reason, I believed him.

"You okay, Beth?" I heard Darren say. He must have come in with the logs.

"She's fine, son. She just needed a hug," Tom said without letting me go. I couldn't see either of their faces, but I was sure they were sharing a glance or concern was mirrored in their faces. I felt Tom give a nod, possibly answering Darren's unspoken question, and then he kissed me on the head just like Darren. He hugged me closer and then stood back taking a good look at my face. "I'll leave you with DJ."

I nodded and smiled wiping the tears from my face before turning to face Darren. "Sorry," I said.

"Why do you apologize every time you cry or need encouraging?"

"I don't know. I feel helpless and wish I could do something productive." I crossed my arms over my chest and exhaled, allowing the emotions to pass. I smiled realizing something. "*DJ*, huh?" I asked. He nodded once with a grin.

"Did *I* call you DJ?" He nodded again. I pulled in my bottom lip considering. "When did I stop calling you DJ?"

"You always called me Darren at work and in any professional capacity. You were careful not to call me DJ in front of anyone; you reserved that at home and with my family."

"Would you prefer I call you DJ?"

He considered for several seconds before he answered. "I don't think I have a preference."

"Is there more? That took you long enough to answer."

"I've always been DJ to you. It's familiar and it's right somehow, but for the past month you've called me Darren and somehow that feels right, too. Please don't overthink it. Call me whatever feels right in the moment." He smiled and I believed him. "I have another load of wood to bring in. Want to come outside with me?"

"It's freezing!" I complained.

"Yes, but it's sunny and beautiful. Let me show you around outside before it gets dark."

I put on Mary's boots that were next to the backdoor. I put on a parka and some gloves. We went into the backyard. The snow was piled high along the path that led to the outdoor shed. Darren pointed out Mary's garden and a trail that led from the back of their yard through the neighborhood. I could see his breath as he spoke.

Allison and Lance arrived with Michael for supper. The house was warm and the love from this family even warmer. Allison hugged me like Mary had. Lance smiled and shook my hand, but I could tell he was uncomfortable. Michael was the least inhibited of them all. He looked me in the eye and introduced himself. "I'm Michael. I'm nine-and-a-half and I've known you my whole life." He gave me a quick nine-year-old-boy hug and then tugged me into the dining room. He told me where I should sit and explained everything to me in detail. I liked him instantly. He would surely be my favorite medium fart, too.

We joined hands around the table and Tom blessed the food. He gave thanks for the family and for our safe arrival and asked God to help me heal. This felt all kinds of right.

After supper, we cleared the table and everyone helped put the food away and straighten the kitchen. They worked like a well-oiled machine. Michael asked me to help him wipe off the table and the counter. In less than fifteen minutes the kitchen was clean and the dishwasher was running. I followed Michael into the family room and he carefully lifted the cover from the small table.

"Do you like puzzles?" he asked hopeful.

"Sure," I said.

He took out some folding chairs from a narrow cabinet and I sat next to him, helping him assemble the large face of a mountain lion.

"Come on, Michael, we need to go," Allison said after we'd been working on the puzzle for about an hour.

"Awe, can I stay, please?" Michael whined.

"Maybe tomorrow. I'm sure Beth and your Uncle DJ are tired from their trip."

"I'll drop him off on my way to the office in the morning," Lance said, and we all hugged goodnight.

Tom and Mary asked if we needed anything. Darren assured them that we were fine before they went to bed. Darren and I sat in the living room. "I'm so comfortable here with your family. I know you didn't grow up here, but it feels like you did. Was every home you lived in like this?"

"Mostly. We liked some places better than others. We liked some climates and some schools better, but overall, our home was consistent. Mom made sure of that, even when Dad was called away. You learn to rely on one another."

I yawned big. "I think I'm ready to call it a night. Do you mind if I take a shower?"

"Go ahead. I'll be up when I hear you get out."

I was sitting on the edge of my bed putting lotion on my hands when I heard a light tap on the door. I looked up to see Darren standing in the doorway.

"Goodnight," I said and smiled.

"I plan to sleep in here with you, tonight."

"Why? I haven't needed you for weeks."

"Because I don't want you to have a nightmare and wake alone in a strange bed, in a strange house. Mom and Dad don't need to be awakened like that."

"But we're in your parents' house. I don't want them to be offended," I whispered. "I'd be mortified."

"Don't worry. They know. I don't keep things like that from them."

"Do they know *everything* about me?" I asked self-consciously.

He shook his head. "No, I've never told anyone. That's yours to tell, not mine. They know you took Gram's death really hard. They know you had some demons to wrestle, but they've never judged you for that. They've claimed you for a long time. I think you feel that, even if you don't remember. It wouldn't be the first time they've seen us sleep together."

The next morning, Darren was already dressed and downstairs. He was at the kitchen table with Michael.

"Good morning, Beth," Michael said.

"Good morning, Michael."

"Want some cereal?" he asked through a bite he'd not quite swallowed.

"Sure," I said looking at Darren. He stood and got me a bowl and I sat down next to Michael. "So, what are we doing today?" I asked.

"We are going to the mall. Tomorrow we are going to the sports park. Then it's Christmas Eve and Christmas Day, and then we'll go back to the sports park. Oh, and Uncle DJ says we can see a movie and maybe to go the children's museum in the city. Want to come?" Michael asked. His enthusiasm was contagious. I wanted to do everything he mentioned.

"I can't do the sports park, but maybe I can come watch," I suggested. Michael seemed pleased by that and I returned his smile.

After the mall, we went back to Tom and Mary's. Tom was home, then, and we all ate lunch together; Mary would be home after her shift. Tom started dinner while the three of us worked on Michael's puzzle.

That afternoon, Allison came by to pick up Michael. He asked if he could stay the night. Darren looked to me for confirmation. I shrugged. I didn't have an opinion and I didn't think I had any authority to dictate whether or not someone else's child spent the night at their grandparents' house.

"He can stay," Darren said. "We don't have any plans tonight."

Michael's eyes were unnecessarily pleading; he knew he'd gotten his way. "Alright, I'll bring him a change of clothes and his ski gear for tomorrow," Allison said. Michael high-fived both of us like he'd won a championship round.

After supper, we built forts in the family room with blankets from the hall closet. We stacked up several cushions and used flashlights. Michael told us a few ghost stories. We watched *A Charlie Brown Christmas* and toasted marshmallows over the logs in the fireplace. Michael asked if we could sleep under the fort in sleeping bags. Michael dozed off with a full belly of marshmallows, and after a mug of hot cocoa, I was having a hard time keeping my own eyes opened. The fire crackled low as the last of the logs burned themselves out. I blinked lazily, staring at the lights on the Christmas tree.

"We can go upstairs, if you'd be more comfortable. He's out," Darren said, looking over at Michael.

IMPACT

I looked down at Michael in his sleeping bag in front of my sofa. He was sleeping peacefully. There was something innocent and sweet about a child sleeping, especially one sleeping under the glow of a Christmas tree. "No, I'm cozy here by the fire. This sofa is so comfortable. Can we get one?"

Darren laughed in a whisper. "I think it's circa 1990." He was lying on the sofa adjacent to mine.

"Is yours this comfortable?"

"I think so."

CHAPTER 10

The next morning, I awoke to the smell of fresh coffee and pancakes. Mary was in the kitchen making us breakfast. I loved her as soon as I met her, but this sealed the deal.

"Good morning," she said in a whisper. "Are Michael and DJ awake, yet?"

"I think Darren's upstairs. Michael's still asleep on the floor."

"Do you mind giving him a nudge? He needs a good breakfast before he hits the trails."

I returned to the living room and knelt down to gently shake the sleeping child awake. "Michael, Michael, wake up," I said. When I lifted my hand from his shoulder, I had the strangest sense of de ja vu. I'd done that very thing before. I closed my eyes and tried desperately to recapture that memory, that feeling, but it was gone.

When I opened my eyes, Michael was looking at me. "Are you okay, Beth?" he asked in a husky, morning voice.

"I think so."

"You looked worried. Is everything okay? Where's Uncle DJ?"

"He's upstairs. Everything's fine. Your grandmother's making pancakes."

The smile on his face reflected the same feeling I'd had when awakened with that same knowledge. He was on his feet instantly, stretching and yawning. He looked like he'd slept on his head.

We layered and put on ski clothes. I was content to sit in the stands and watch as they made their way through some of the trails. I was also content to sit in the warmth of the concession stand and found a cozy lodge with a fireplace. I looked around and took in the beauty of the snow and the season. There were Christmas decorations hung everywhere throughout the park. I'm sure it was beautiful at night with the lights strung across the trails and around the buildings.

That evening, Allison refused to allow Michael to sleep over. He needed to get a good night's sleep before his Christmas Eve performance. Apparently, he had a solo and needed to be in top form.

I told Darren that he didn't need to sleep with me. He nodded and went to his own room. By two a.m., I was regretting that decision. I woke in a panic. I hadn't needed Darren in the night for weeks, but this dream was horrific. I was putting a small child to bed. He couldn't have been more than two or three. He was feverish and I didn't know how to help him. He was burning up. I tried to wake him, as I'd done Michael in the morning, and that's when I realized that this child was unresponsive. I shook him and cried out to him. I shook him and shook him, but still, he didn't respond.

I threw off the covers, panting, and went to the bathroom. I patted my face with cool water and tried to bring myself back to the present. I couldn't do it. I went back to the bed and tried to go back to sleep. I couldn't do that, either. I sighed, exasperated with myself. Finally, I rose from the bed and walked into Darren's room. He was sleeping soundly, probably exhausted from the exertion of the sports park and trying to keep up with a nine-year-old. That's also probably why he didn't argue when I told him I could sleep alone.

I eased into his bed silently, desperately not wanting to wake him. Without touching him, I settled myself into the pillow and formed my body around his shape. I breathed in a few times, settling into his presence, and was lulled into a peaceful sleep.

Before I opened my eyes, I could feel him staring at me. I think I could hear him blinking. He wasn't sure what to make of my being in his bed. I suppose I didn't either. I assumed this was out of character for me.

"I couldn't sleep," I said without opening my eyes.

"Are you okay?"

I opened my eyes and his eyes were piercing me through. His gaze was so much more intense when he wasn't wearing his glasses. I could see his dark lashes as he blinked and the different shades of brown in his eyes.

"I had a bad dream. I couldn't go back to sleep. Is this okay? I didn't know what else to do."

"It's fine. It's not your *usual*, but it's fine." He smiled a sleepy grin.

"Thank you," I said and sighed.

"Come here," he said as he pulled me into him. He held me close and kissed my forehead. He was so warm. I exhaled. I was instantly relaxed and calmed. I closed my eyes and wrapped my arms around him, returning the embrace. I nuzzled my face into his chest and inhaled all of him. God, he smelled good, clean and masculine.

Darren moved his hand down my back and pulled me closer to him. There was a tug at the bottom of my stomach. My heartbeat increased and my breath caught. I went rigid, so did Darren.

I moved my hands to his chest and braced myself, feeling self-conscious and ashamed for the feelings that covered our embrace. "No, Beth, stay. Just relax. Take a deep breath." He inhaled and exhaled slowly. "It's okay." I breathed with him a few times and relaxed back into his embrace. I was about to apologize when Darren interrupted me. "Don't say it. Don't you dare say you're sorry." I nodded into his chest and allowed my arms to embrace him once again.

I think we both fell back asleep. I know I did. Again, like yesterday, I was awakened to the smell of coffee and something mouth-watering. "I think I love your mother; she cooks breakfast," I said lazily rolling over to get out of bed. I really needed to pee.

Darren chuckled. "I'll bet that's Dad. I smell bacon. Mom doesn't cook bacon."

"Okay, so I may love your dad, too." He laughed again.

I went downstairs in my PJs and socks unable to resist the lure from the kitchen. Sure enough, Tom was plating up a pound of bacon. "Good morning. Hungry?"

I nodded eagerly. "That's the best smell in the world." I gave Tom a side hug since his hands were full.

"How do you want your eggs?" he asked.

"I'm not picky. Whatever is easiest."

"Do you want some toast?" He gestured towards the toaster and an open loaf that was lying on the counter. I walked over and pressed a couple of slices down.

I poured myself a cup of coffee and asked Tom if he'd like one, too. We sat together at the kitchen table and ate breakfast. Mary was working an early shift for Christmas Eve. She would also cover a late shift on Christmas Day so that some of the younger women could have time with their children and families.

Darren came downstairs already dressed. He went to the stove and cooked a couple of eggs for himself. He poured a cup of coffee and joined us. I looked at the two of them together. Their eyes and eyebrows, the shape of their chin and their ears, they definitely had the same ears. How funny.

"What?" Darren asked. He could tell I was watching him.

"It's like having two of you," I said.

Tom looked at his son and shook his head. "Poor dude. His mom is much prettier."

CHAPTER 11

Mary came home from the hospital and began preparing a chili for after the Christmas Eve service. I stayed with her in the kitchen, chopping onions and peppers.

"We'll come back here afterwards. Nothing formal. We'll eat dinner and maybe watch a holiday movie together. Does that sound good to you?" Mary asked.

"Yes, it sounds wonderful." I said.

"Is there anything we can do to make things easier for you?" she asked.

"Everything's fine. I don't have any expectations. I don't have any memory of past Christmases. To some degree, not having a memory helps for there to be little disappointment." I laughed. "I'm not sure how I should feel about things, though. I'm not sure how excited I should be. I want there to be some sense of anticipation like it's a magical time, but honestly, I'm good with whatever."

"That part hasn't changed about you," she said patting my hand. She looked into my eyes reading me. "How are things between you and DJ?" Her question was kind, but direct.

I couldn't escape her eyes and my stomach did that tightening thing again. My cheeks flushed, and I swallowed. "I'm not sure. What do you mean?" I asked.

She cocked her head in the same way Darren did when he was trying to figure out something. "I know I'm prying. It's probably none of my business, but there's something different between the two of you."

"*Everything's* different between the two of us," I remarked wryly.

She nodded her agreement. "Understood."

"Mary, he's amazing. He's honest, even when he knows the truth might hurt me. He's kind. He obviously loves me. Why weren't we ever *together*?" I asked. "Did I ever tell you why?" I was curious, sure, but my voice was pleading. I really wanted to know.

Mary considered for a moment before she answered. "Once, a couple of years ago, you, Allison, and I were here together. The men had all gone fishing or some such. Allison decided we needed a girls' night and brought over a huge bottle of tequila. After several rounds of margaritas, you told me you wished things were different between you and DJ. You told me you wished you could take it all back. You didn't say what you wished to take back, but that you wished you could just start over again and do things better, do things right. Allison had fallen asleep by this point and you looked sad. So, we sat together and drank your misery away. You never mentioned it again and I never asked."

"What does DJ say?" I asked using their nickname. It felt natural to refer to him like that with his mother.

"Hmmm," she speculated. "He hasn't said anything for years. When he first met you, he talked non-stop about you. He smiled every time he spoke your name, and still does, for the most part. He'd only dated a couple of girls in high school, but we moved half-way through his freshman year and then got transferred half-way through his junior year. That doesn't really allow for you to develop any sort of meaningful high school romances. So, when he came home during your first year in college, I knew he had it bad. I thought for sure you'd be my daughter-in-law before you two graduated." She smiled remembering.

I felt a little sad at that possible reality. "I hurt him; I know that. I can't remember it, but I know it. I can tell. He still loves me, doesn't he? Can you see it, too?"

Mary nodded knowingly. "Mothers know their sons."

"What should I do? I don't know how I'm supposed to feel, but I feel like I'm supposed to be with him all the time. Is it because he's the only thing I know now?"

Mary shrugged. "Beth, I know it's complicated. You aren't the same, but you're still *you*. You're still the sweet, beautiful young woman we met when you were what, eighteen or nineteen? Your laugh and your smile, the way you look at DJ, none of that has changed. Your feelings for one another, well, I guess only time will tell. You'll figure it out. You two always do."

"Did you and Tom object when we moved in together?" I asked.

"Why would we object?"

"Wouldn't you want him to pursue a relationship with someone that was more promising or with someone that would make him happy?"

"Other than a few times, I've never doubted his happiness with you, and that was only because he couldn't fix whatever was wrong at the time. I asked him once what his intentions were, but I never objected his choosing to share a home with you. I also never doubted his resolve. He wants to share his life with you, Beth, and he's willing to do whatever it takes to make that happen."

"I don't think this is a very healthy relationship, Mary. It's all one-sided. What do I do to reciprocate? He does everything."

"What are you talking about?" Mary asked incredulously.

"Since I left the hospital, he's seen to everything. He's responsible. He's smart and he's kind. I don't see where I contribute much at all to this relationship."

Mary laughed. "Oh, my goodness!" she exclaimed. "You have lost your mind! Beth, you're his best friend. You make him laugh and you encourage him. You're the reason he works with gifted kids. You sit up with him when he's studying. You proof every paper he turns in. You make sure he eats and has clean laundry. You two are a pretty great team. Do I wish he were married and had kids? Sure, if that's what he wanted, but he's never had to defend his choices to us, none of them. Do you understand that?" I nodded, but I wasn't sure if I completely understood. "He's a grown man and we're proud of the choices he's made, even the ones regarding you. I want to make that perfectly clear. You may have awakened into this life unsure of who you are, but be confident that this relationship has never been one-sided." Mary spoke with the same conviction and love as her son.

"Thank you. I don't want to hurt him."

IMPACT

"No need to worry about that. You have other things to focus on for the time being."

That evening, we set out for the Christmas Eve service. Tom and Mary attended a non-denominational church. Darren had asked me if I wanted to go to an afternoon mass, but I declined.

The sanctuary was packed. The music began and we were instructed to stand and sing along with the band. The music was lively and wonderful! I stood between Darren and his dad. They were singing and their combined voices resonated deep in my chest. I had heard Darren sing a few times in mass, but he didn't sing out like he was tonight. The pastor welcomed us and gave a brief sermon on the true meaning of Christmas and our hope and salvation coming into the world. I took it all to heart. I didn't feel like I needed to be saved, but I was definitely searching for something more and meaningful. I needed hope. Since the crash, I felt lost. I needed direction and I desperately needed answers.

After the sermon, the children entered the sanctuary and made their way onto the stage. There were probably about thirty kids. Michael and two other children were set apart near microphones. He smiled and waved to his family when he found us. He didn't look nervous at all.

The music began and they all sang together. The little girl to Michael's left sang her solo first. The second soloist sang his part with the other children singing back-up. Before the last song began, Michael stepped forward. The lights dimmed and Michael was in the spotlight. He looked intently at the music director waiting for his cue; she gave a little nod. The pianist gave him one note and he closed his eyes and took a deep breath. He began singing *O Holy Night* acapella. I blinked, unbelieving. Goosebumps covered my arms and I'm sure my mouth gaped. The entire sanctuary was held in rapt silence. When he finished the song, he smiled proudly and gave a little bow. The children were escorted from the stage to the applause from proud parents, grandparents, aunts and uncles.

The pastor spoke again and wished everyone a Merry Christmas. He then prayed and we lit candles and sang *Silent Night*. The service couldn't have been more beautiful or more meaningful for me. I was surrounded by love and acceptance. I was a part of a wonderful family and I wanted desperately to remain there.

After supper, we watched *It's a Wonderful Life* and Mary and I cried at the end. No one seemed surprised at this.

"We'll head over to Lance and Alli's by seven. Michael will be calling us before 6:45. You might want to set your alarms," Tom instructed. Tom and Mary headed to bed, and Darren and I sat watching the fire.

The lights from the Christmas tree were bright in the corner of the room. Darren brought me a mug of hot tea and sat next to me. "So, how's it going?" Darren asked nonchalantly.

"It's going well. Tonight was amazing. How can that voice come from such a little kid?" I asked.

Darren chuckled. "He came that way. He's been singing since before he could speak. Alli and Lance are both musical. Lance is all uptight and reserved, now, but he played guitar and bass in a band in high school. He even has tattoos." I laughed at the thought. Lance did not look like a man with tattoos. "Alli and I learned to play the piano and sang growing up. She stuck with it longer. She's way more accomplished than I ever hope to be."

"Do you ever play?" I asked.

"Not the piano. It's not as portable. I play guitar at school with the kids sometimes. I keep one in my classroom. *Music has charms to soothe a savage beast.*" He laughed.

"I'd like to hear you play sometime," I said.

"I can arrange that," he said, smiling.

"I liked singing with your family tonight. I've liked everything about your family," I clarified.

"They're your family, too, you know?" I smiled between sips of tea.

"That's sweet. Thank you."

"Want to go outside with me?" Darren asked.

"Why?"

"I don't know. I feel sort of cooped up and want some fresh air. Come on, I promise you can come in when you're ready, and I'll build up the fire when we get in."

I begrudgingly agreed. We walked outside on the trail that meandered through the neighborhood. The night was clear and the half-moon reflected off the snow, illuminating the night. Mary's boots crunched along the path. I hung back and picked up a handful of snow and formed it into a ball. I looked at Darren and wordlessly challenged him.

"Are you sure you want to go there? Think carefully. It won't end well," he said gravely.

I think I raised my eyebrow; I was sure I wanted to. I couldn't resist. I stepped back a few paces and lobbed the snowball right at his head. It hit his stocking cap and exploded into a million flakes.

He smiled menacingly and gathered a handful of snow. He took his time, forming it perfectly. I stepped back again and formed another ball. We lobbed them at each other at nearly the same time. His hit directly into my shoulder and sprayed across my jacket.

I reached to get more snow. He was reloading as well. He was faster this time. The snowball hit me right in the chest and sprayed up across my face. My snowball hit him in the leg. "Oh, that was lame," he laughed.

I formed another ball and threw it and then ducked, making his ball miss me completely. I laughed and ran to get another ball formed before he could get me. He lobbed two more at me in rapid succession. I managed to turn in time for them to hit my back. I rounded and lobbed one. He ducked, but it hit him right in the face. I bent over laughing.

He walked towards me, looming large and threatening. He had a handful of snow. He put his cold, snowy glove over my face. I pushed him off and he was laughing. I stepped wrong and slipped. He caught me, but it was too late; I was already in the snow. I gasped as I fell.

"Are you okay? Did you hit your head?" he asked, his voice full of concern. The laughter between us faded instantly.

"I'm fine." I said. "I expected it to be colder, but it's not." I lay back in the snow and moved my arms and legs. He stood and offered me a hand to get out of the snow. I looked back satisfied at the snow angel I'd made.

It was late when we arrived back at the house. My clothes were wet and I was covered in snow. I stripped down to my thermals in the mudroom. My nose was running from the cold. I ran into the living room and wrapped a blanket around myself. I sat as close to the embers in the fireplace as I could manage and let the warmth thaw out my toes.

Darren joined me wearing his thermals, too. He looked down at me and smiled. He put another log on the fire and stoked it. "Tea or cocoa?"

"Tea, please."

He returned from the kitchen a few minutes later and handed me a steaming mug. I just wanted to hold it in my hands and breathe in the steam. He pushed one of the sofas closer to the fireplace and sat down behind me. I could feel him staring at the back of my head.

"What?" I asked, not turning to face him.

"Merry Christmas," he said.

"Is it midnight, already?" I asked as I turned to face him. I stood and joined him on the sofa. I took a few sips of tea and let the warmth penetrate my body. We sat in silence watching the fire. It was fascinating.

"I have a confession to make," I began. Darren turned to face me, looking expectant. "I didn't get you a Christmas present. I didn't know what I could do that would possibly compete with last year's goat, so I didn't do anything. I hope you weren't expecting anything great."

He shook his head. "I told you that this time was about family and spending time together. It's not about presents. It never has been for me. I indulge Michael because he's a kid and he wants stuff, but more importantly he wants me to spend time with him. He doesn't just *want* stuff. Your agreeing to come here with me is the best gift you could have given me." His eyes were sincere and he took my hand to reassure me.

I placed my mug on the table next to his and leaned back so that I could see his face. The reflection of the fire shone in the lenses of his glasses. It looked like a small fire was burning in each of his eyes. The look on his face was pleasant and he almost smiled. Without hesitation, I leaned in and kissed him. It was the easiest thing in the world to do. His mouth was soft but received my kiss reluctantly. Within a few seconds, he collected his thoughts and placed his hands on my shoulders keeping me in place. He sat up, pushing himself away from me. His face was pained.

"I'm sorry," I said, realizing that I'd probably just sent him reeling. He shook his head and closed his eyes. He took in a deep breath. "DJ, I'm so sorry. I don't know what came over me."

"Shhh," he said, calming us both. He allowed his hands to slide down to my elbows and then he took me into his usual embrace. "Why did you call me DJ?" he asked, but I couldn't tell what his tone implied.

I shrugged against him. "It's who you are here, especially when you smile at me. I won't do it if it bothers you?"

"No, it's good," he said shaking his head. There was a long pause before either one of us spoke again. "Beth, why did you kiss me?"

I shrugged again and sat back to look into his eyes. "Why does anyone want to kiss someone else? I'm attracted to you. You're kind and handsome. You obviously love me and deserve to be loved in return. It's confusing, but this body loves you, and every time you touch me, it makes me want more. I'm conflicted and unsure about nearly everything I do on a daily basis, but I'm not conflicted about the way I feel about you." He smirked, understanding, but my explanation brought genuine delight to his eyes. "I know kissing may complicate matters. You're trying desperately to help me figure things out; I should have better self-control." I placed my hand on his chest, apologetically. He took my hand and held it there over his heart.

"I never thought I'd ever say these words aloud while looking into your eyes, but I'm not sure this is a good idea."

My stomach did that stupid tightening thing again and I blushed all over. Hopefully he couldn't see it in the dark. I nodded and lowered my gaze. I felt like a child being reprimanded. I didn't have the guts to look at him. Tears welled in my eyes and I tried desperately to blink them away. With my face tilted, gravity pulled them down and onto the sofa between us. I sniffed reflexively.

Darren tilted my chin upward and wiped the tears from my cheeks. He held my head between his hands and forced me to look into his eyes. His brown eyes were piercing. He leaned over and kissed my forehead. "Damn it, Beth. I'm sorry; this is so unfair!" he whispered. I could feel the tension in his hands.

We sat there for a few minutes with his lips lingering on my forehead. I managed not to cry again. I would be satisfied being there with him and leaving well-enough alone. He released me.

"It's late. We need to go to bed."

"But not together," I guessed.

He shook his head. "Not tonight." He stood aside and let me go ahead of him up the stairs.

"Goodnight, Beth," he whispered before I entered my room.

"Goodnight," I said but I couldn't look him in the eye.

CHAPTER 12

I surprisingly slept well for what remained of the night. The next morning, I could hear Darren's alarm beeping from the other room. I grabbed a change of clothes and went to the bathroom to start the water in the shower. As I was toweling off, I shut the door to my side of the bathroom so that Darren could get a shower, too. I heard the water running seconds later. I brushed my teeth and combed my hair. I went back into my bedroom and found a box on my bed.

I looked around to see if anyone else was in the room. I sat on the edge of the bed examining the colorful box. There was a card on top.

To: Beth

From: Darren

Merry Christmas!

"Am I supposed to open this, now?" I called into the next room.

"Yes," came Darren's voice. He was standing in the doorway, waiting. "Go ahead. It's not a big deal."

I wasn't sure how we would be this morning after I'd gone and kissed him last night. He surely hadn't made it awkward; it was me. He smiled encouraging me to open his gift. I untied the ribbon and lifted the lid to the box. Inside was a small instant camera with a photo album and a journal.

"I thought you'd like an opportunity to make some new memories, ones you can be sure of."

"That's an awesome idea. Thank you. That's very thoughtful." I smiled. "And the journal?"

"I know you have glimpses of things. I thought it might be good to have some idea of what's happening and if there are any connections to the present. You used to journal a lot. I thought it might help."

"You're the best." I smiled, again, but when I looked into his eyes, my smile waivered. He had the strangest look on his face. I sat there, feeling self-conscious and vulnerable. "What?" I asked, knowing he wanted to clear the elephant from the room and address my impulsive kiss.

He stepped into the room and lowered his voice. "I'm sorry if I hurt your feelings last night. That wasn't my intention and I don't want it to put a damper on today." I shook my head, disregarding his need to apologize; it was all my fault. "No, Beth, hear me out. I will never deny the way I feel about you, and I hope you know that I'd like nothing more than for you to kiss me, but I don't want to take advantage of you in your current condition. I don't think that's fair, do you? When you know yourself better, we'll see how you feel about kissing me then. Deal?"

I swallowed hard before I spoke. I didn't want my voice to break. "Deal. No more kissing, then," I replied with my best effort at a genuine smile. "Where do we stand on hugs and sleeping together when I have a bad dream?"

He shook his head. "Come here," he said and met me half way. He took me in his arms and hugged me. He kissed the top of my head. "I will never stop hugging you, ever."

Tom's phone rang at 6:35. We were already in Mary's car. "We're on our way, Michael. Yes, everyone is together. No, we didn't forget Beth; she's right here. Did Santa come already? I don't care if you don't believe in Santa anymore, I do. I want to know if he brought me anything. I have been extremely good this year. I hope he remembers that I like the soft peppermints and not those hard ones." Tom laughed at something Michael said. "Sit tight. We are seven minutes away. I promise." He laughed again.

Michael was waiting eagerly for us to arrive. He threw the door open wearing a Santa hat, fleece pants and a hoodie. His eyes were wide and expectant. Lance and Allison's home was less homey and more modernly decorated than Tom and Mary's. Beautiful art hung on the neutral colored walls. Their tree looked like something from a magazine layout. There were a few photos of Michael and a couple of the three of them together. The furniture was sparse and I couldn't see a speck of dust anywhere.

Michael led us to the kitchen. Allison was wearing a Christmas apron and a reindeer headband. Lance was looking quite festive in a red sweatshirt that said, *Bah Humbug*. The smell of fresh baked cinnamon rolls wafted out of the oven. The aromas of coffee and bacon and a frittata welcomed us, too. My mouth watered and my stomach growled. I think breakfast was quite possibly my favorite meal with these people.

During breakfast, I showed Michael my camera. He knew how everything worked. We took a couple of selfies and he took one of himself with Darren and me. After we ate, Michael eagerly ushered us into the living room. He reached into the pile of presents under the tree and passed them along to everyone. He opened a few and then looked expectantly at the back of the tree. He reached through and found his present from his favorite uncle. I think DJ was possibly his only uncle.

He was so excited to open it; he leapt up and down and hugged the box. Finally, he could play it. I took a couple more pictures with my new camera. When all of the presents were unwrapped, Tom cleared his throat. "Your mom and I wanted to do something a little different this year. Michael will be hitting double digits this summer and we wanted to make that extra special. So," he paused for dramatic effect, "we've decided instead of our usual vacation to the lake for the Fourth of July, we'll be taking an Alaskan cruise."

Gasps and cheers. Michael jumped up and hugged his grandfather. "That's the coolest thing, ever!"

"Well, working on your social studies project got me thinking; Alaska would be a great place to visit," Tom said.

Caught up in the excitement, I commented, "Alaska is beautiful in the summer. The whale watching will be a highlight for sure. There's also this amazing excursion you can take with the train. You won't be disappointed."

Darren stopped and looked at me. "What are you talking about?"

"The train. You know, the gold miner train," I said excitedly.

"I've never been there, Beth." Everyone was looking at me. They could sense a change in Darren's voice. He was eyeing me carefully.

"I've never been there before either, have I?" I whispered.

He shook his head. "Not that I know of."

I felt so defeated. Finally, I thought I was having a real memory, something to interject, and it was all off. I smiled and covered my blunder with a shrug. Michael diverted his attention back to his game and his need for his uncle and dad to get a move-on. We all gathered up the wrapping paper and the trash and then the men went down to the basement.

Allison and Mary asked if I'd like to join them for another cup of coffee. "Do you have tea?" I asked.

"Sure," Allison replied. "You okay, Beth?"

I shook my head. "I don't know. I thought for sure I'd been to Alaska as soon as Tom mentioned the trip. For a moment I felt like I'd been there, but now it's faded. Perhaps I watched a documentary once or something. Who knows." I rolled my eyes.

"How did you sleep last night?" Allison asked.

Mary placed the mug of tea in front of me and joined me and Allison. "Darren and I were up late last night. I'm sure I'm just a little tired." I told them not to worry.

"Would you like to go lie down in the guestroom?" Allison offered.

"Thank you. I think that's a good idea. My head is starting to ache some."

"Where's your medication?" Mary asked.

"In my purse. I can get it."

Allison showed me to the downstairs guestroom. I lay down on the big bed and she handed me a blanket. "I'll lower the shades. Get some rest. We'll check on you again before lunch."

The medicine I took for the headaches made me relaxed and combined with the lack of sleep the night before, I was able to sleep for a few hours. I heard a light tap on the door, but the smell of lunch had already awakened me.

"Beth," I heard Darren's voice as he opened the door a little.

"I'm awake," I said.

"How's your head? Mom said you've been in bed all morning."

"Better. Did you guys get everything set up?"

"Yes. Michael is showing Dad how to play some racing game. He's killing us. Lunch is nearly ready. Are you hungry?"

"Yes," I said sitting up and stretching. "Darren, can you come here, please?" He walked toward the bed and sat on the edge next to me. "Thank you." I began. "I can see the concern in your eyes. I'm not who you know me to be. I'm a stranger to us both. I know this must be incredibly hard for you, and I appreciate your patience. I just wanted you to know that."

He acknowledged my words with a nod. He didn't hug me or even try to comfort me. The truth that I was a stranger to him couldn't be denied. I couldn't read his expression in the dim light, but my body craved his touch more than my stomach craved the aromas coming from the kitchen. I placed my hand on his arm and let it slide down to his hand. My eyes were unnecessarily focused on his thumb. He just sat there in complete silence. Did he feel the intensity in my touch? Could he deny the attraction I felt for him?

"Uncle DJ, Beth, lunch is ready," Michael announced as he entered the room. "Beth, will you come see downstairs after lunch?"

"Sure," I said, distracted by Michael, but still focused on our hands.

Darren squeezed my hand gently and then released it. He stood to allow me to get out of the bed. He folded the blanket and placed it neatly over a chair. He didn't even look at me. My heart was crushed at the thought.

Michael lingered to lead us to lunch. On our way to the dining room, we passed another room. Inside was a baby grand piano and a variety of instruments hanging on the walls. I hesitated. "That's where I practice my piano," Michael said.

"Will you play for me later?" I asked.

He rolled his eyes. "I'm not very good, but Mom makes me. She says it helps with math. I'm already good at math. Dad lets me play his bass, though. Can I play that instead?"

"Sure."

After lunch, I joined Michael in the basement. It wasn't what I imagined a basement to be. It was cozy. There were area rugs and a foosball table, an old sofa, and a recliner. The laundry room was also down there. Now, there was a TV monitor and a gaming system. Michael was so proud to show me.

The concrete walls had been covered and painted a neutral taupe color. Photos covered these walls along with every ribbon of achievement, every token, or award the members of the family had ever received. This area reflected more of their personality than the rest of the house.

I watched Michael play his game for nearly an hour. He offered to let me play several times, but I declined. I was content to sit in the recliner and watch him. He pushed the controller away in frustration after he'd failed to beat an opponent for the third time.

"I think we need a break. Do you have any cookies around here?" I asked.

We went upstairs and found Tom napping on the sofa. Football was on the TV. Allison and Mary were in the kitchen talking. Darren and Lance were nowhere to be seen. Michael found the cookies and a tray of snacks on the counter. He brought me one. "Where are Dad and Uncle DJ?"

"It's halftime. They went for a walk." Michael nodded like that was normal.

Michael sat in his grandma's lap. She tickled him and hugged and kissed him. He was still young enough that it was okay for his grandma to make on over him. I was sure those days were few and she knew it, too.

Michael finished a couple more cookies and then asked if I'd like to see the music room. I followed him in there. He sat at the piano and plunked out a tune that sounded more like a warm-up scale. I watched his hands closely. I was drawn to the piano and sat down on the bench next to him. He played *Jingle Bells* and *Jolly Old St. Nicholas* without any music.

He jumped down from the piano bench and reached for the bass guitar on the wall. He reached his arms long to bring it down carefully. He plugged it into the small amplifier and listened carefully to check it's tuning. He plucked a few notes and then played the same songs he'd played on the piano. He was grinning even through a couple of fumbles of his untrained fingers.

His dad and Darren joined us; the music's call was stronger than the football game. Lance looked proudly at his son. It was the most emotion I'd seen from the man since I met him. He reached for another guitar and handed a third to Darren. There was knowing in their eyes. The three of them played bits and pieces of familiar tunes. They sang along to some of the choruses.

I remained at the piano bench, my hands drawn to the keys. I closed my eyes and felt my hands gliding delicately over them. My fingers formed chords and I gently depressed the keys in beat to the music they played. A few seconds later, I was playing along. I could hear the simple chords in my mind and my fingers knew what to do. The song ended and I opened my eyes. Darren had a look of complete disbelief on his face. I took my hands from the keys and lowered them into my lap. When I looked back at his face his gaze gradually turned to joy. He was grinning from ear-to-ear.

"You remember," he began hopeful, but I shook my head.

"My hands do, but my mind doesn't." He frowned, disappointment covering him. I felt exhausted again. He could tell. He handed Lance the guitar and put his hand on my shoulder comfortingly.

"Want to go back to Mom and Dad's?" I nodded. "Michael, play her another song; I'll be right back."

Tom and Mary decided to stay. Lance and Allison would bring them back later. Darren pulled into their driveway but didn't turn off the engine. He hadn't spoken to me once we were in the car. He sat staring, holding the steering wheel. He took a deep breath but didn't say anything. I got the feeling he didn't want to be alone with me.

"I can stay by myself. Go back and spend the rest of the evening with your family. I don't want to be a bother. I'm just going to lie down. I might journal a bit."

He nodded. "The mudroom door's unlocked. Keep your phone handy. I'll text you when we're on our way home."

"Thanks for the ride." I tried to catch his eye, but he didn't look at me. "Darren, I wish I had more answers. It's like I'm holding your best friend hostage and I can't find the key to let her out."

He turned and looked at me then. "Please keep looking; I miss her a lot." His eyes were pleading. I nodded and stepped out of the car. He waited until he saw me go into the side of the house. I heard him drive away. I shut the door to the mudroom and hung my jacket on the hook. I held onto it tightly for several seconds, needing something tangible to ground me. The weight and confusion of the day tumbled down on top of me, and I burst into tears.

I went into the kitchen and started the kettle. I made a mug of tea and sat on the comfy sofa. I wrapped myself in the same blanket from last night. I just sat there in the quiet, trying to figure out how I could play the piano and how I knew about Alaska and how I had no memory of my life before the crash. Thankfully, sleep offered me a much-needed reprieve.

When I awoke, Darren was coming in the mudroom door. "Beth! Where's your damn phone?" he asked frustrated.

I was startled by his intrusion. "Upstairs," I stammered. I sat up and blinked the sleep from my eyes.

"I've been texting you."

"I fell asleep."

"Obviously," he said flatly. "I don't like it when I can't get to you." His protective tone returned.

"Where are your mom and dad?"

"In the car. They're going to drive around looking at Christmas lights before Mom starts her shift. I thought you might enjoy that. Want to come?" he asked, returning to his natural tone.

"Yeah. I'll be out in a couple of minutes."

I rode in the backseat with Darren. The lights throughout the neighborhoods were beautiful. Churches, businesses, and homes were all illuminated in festive colors. Mary played Christmas music on the radio. I hummed along and watched the lights as Tom drove slowly around town. We didn't talk much. We just oohed and aaahed appropriately. Tom and Mary commented on a few of the homes that belonged to their acquaintants. It was a peaceful way to end my first Christmas.

CHAPTER 13

Although I had slept a good portion of the day, I still felt physically and emotionally drained. I took more medicine in hopes that it would prevent a headache and help me sleep. It may have helped with the former, but not the latter.

I lay in the bed staring at the ceiling. I heard every time the heater clicked on and when the house creaked. I could even hear Darren's light snore from the other room. I wanted to go and lie down with him, but after the stupid, impulsive kiss I was leery. Today, too, had been awkward. There were too many thoughts to turn off my brain.

I turned on the lamp and found the journal Darren had given me. I scrounged for a pen in my purse and opened the first page. In Darren's neat hand read: *Merry Christmas. I pray this leads you back to yourself. Love, DJ*

I began writing. Just lists of memories, flickers really, nothing tangible. Then, I divided the next page into three columns. I headed them: *Old Beth*, *New Beth,* and *Just Beth.* Surprisingly, I was able to list several items in each column. Old Beth was a slut, but I opted to use Darren's word, *promiscuous*. New Beth wasn't. For what all I remembered, I was a virgin. Old Beth couldn't cook. New Beth could. I listed music, Darren, and Mexican food in the third column.

The sun was barely showing itself by the time I finished my journaling. I knew Darren and Michael had plans to return to the sports park that morning. I would give them a day to themselves. I wrote Darren a note and placed it on the counter on his side of the bathroom.

Didn't get much sleep last night. I'm staying in. Have a fun day with Michael.

Beth

I woke about four hours later. The house was quiet. I ate a bowl of cereal and then loaded the dishwasher and washed a load of laundry. I fell back asleep on the sofa until the dryer buzzed. I took the load upstairs and placed the pile on the bed to fold. I picked up an inoffensive shirt from the pile and looked at it. I was suddenly overcome by gut-wrenching grief. Deep sadness washed over me. I tried to find the source of the grief, but I couldn't connect it to anything tangible. Tears burst through and ran down my cheeks. My chest tightened. I could hardly catch my breath between the sobs. I was losing it. I was absolutely losing my mind.

I lay down on the bed, clutching the shirt, but it had no power to ground me. Finally, I connected to the grief. I was falling into a memory. The crash. The pain. The light. Shallow breaths like my lung was collapsed. I was choking, gagging on my own blood. My body was shaking, convulsing. I couldn't control any part of myself.

Hands were around me, strong, careful hands. Darren's voice, "Beth, can you hear me?" I could hear him, but I wasn't able to respond. He was lifting me from the bed. "Michael, call your mom. Tell her we're bringing Beth in and grab a blanket."

I felt horrified at the thought of getting into a vehicle. The memory of the crash was still too real. I clung to Darren for dear life. "It's okay, I'm taking you to the hospital. I want them to check you out. Please, let go." I could see his face now, I think I was coming around. His hands forced my hands from around his neck. His eyes were full of concern. He buckled me in. Smaller hands tucked a blanket around me. I closed my eyes and woke again when the car stopped.

The cold air shocked me when the door opened. "Beth, it's Alli. Beth, can you hear me?" I managed a nod.

"How long ago did you find her?" Allison asked.

"Not ten minutes before Michael called you. She wouldn't respond; she wouldn't wake up." I could hear panic underlying the words.

Arms were lifting me onto a gurney. I could feel myself being wheeled away; I could see bright lights through my closed lids. The familiar sounds of the hospital roused me into fuller consciousness. I could see Alli now. She was working diligently with a nurse. They checked my vitals. She shined a light into my eyes.

"Her pupils are slightly dilated. Heartbeat stable. Blood pressure 89/50."

I opened my eyes to see Darren and Michael at the foot of the gurney. Michael was holding the blanket and Darren's arm was around Michael's shoulder. They looked pale and sickly in the hospital light.

"Darren," I whispered weakly. I couldn't hide the panic in my eyes. He walked toward me as soon as the other nurse moved from the side of my bed. He held my hand and stroked the side of my face.

"You're okay. You're safe," he whispered.

A doctor came in then and introduced himself. "I'm Dr. Abernathy," he said in a deep, midwestern voice. He asked a few questions while he shined the light in my eyes and checked my head for any exterior trauma.

Darren reported that he'd found me on the bed, unresponsive. "I was folding clothes," I said weakly.

"She was in a car accident just before Thanksgiving. She was diagnosed with retrograde amnesia. She's been working with a therapist and a neurologist at home. We're here visiting for Christmas." Darren's voice was professional and disconnected to the emotion on his face.

"Any history of seizures?" the doctor asked.

"No," Darren said.

"What medication is she currently taking?"

"Sumatriptan for the headaches." I was so thankful Darren was there. I couldn't have answered any of those questions in my current state.

"Any possibility of pregnancy?"

"No," Darren said flatly.

"Birth control?" the doctor asked.

"Depo injection. She's due in January." No wonder I hadn't had a period.

"I'm ordering an EKG and a CT scan. I'll order routine bloodwork. Do you have her doctor's information? I'd like to confer with him."

"Her neurologist is Dr. Saunders. I have his number."

While Darren retrieved the information from his phone, Michael approached my bedside. "How are you feeling?" he asked timidly.

"A little better," I whispered.

"You were just lying there," he said.

"I'm sorry. I didn't mean to frighten you. Thank you for helping your Uncle DJ. My brain isn't working right. It's not all put back together, yet." I could feel tears pooling in my eyes.

"I know. Mom says brains take time to heal. I hope yours gets better soon."

"Me too." I tried to smile to comfort Michael, but I failed miserably.

Mary came down to the ER as soon as she was able to leave her post. Tom came, too, and took Michael home. Allison helped me into a dressing gown and then she hooked me up to the EKG. I was then taken to radiology. Darren waited with his mom.

Dr. Abernathy returned. "I've spoken with your doctor. I'm admitting you for observation and an EEG."

I shook my head at Darren. I didn't want to stay. "I won't leave you," he said, but that did little to comfort me. I was a complete nuisance.

Once I was in my room, they hooked me up to a bunch of electrodes. I had to lie there, still and quiet for over an hour while the machine registered my brain functions. Darren went downstairs to find something to eat and a cup of coffee. When the test was completed, he was allowed to return to me.

Mary brought dinner to us. She also brought me some PJs and a change of clothes for Darren; he was still wearing ski gear. She helped me change and go to the bathroom. The hospital accommodations weren't as comfortable as the ones at home, so Darren had the joy of sleeping in a makeshift recliner rather than a too-small sofa.

We didn't talk much. He helped me to and from the bathroom. He made sure I drank plenty of water and was comfortable. I wondered at how many nights he'd spent with me in hospital rooms over the years. This must continually suck for him.

Early the next morning, Dr. Abernathy returned. "It looks like you've had a mild seizure. It's very common after the sort of brain trauma you've experienced. With Dr. Saunders' approval, I'm prescribing a low dose of an anti-seizure medication. I want you to follow up with your doctor as soon as you return home. I'm sending him all your results. He's expecting a call from you before the first of the year. Keep that appointment."

He keyed something into a tablet. "In the meantime, I want you to rest. You may walk a bit, enough to get fresh air, but nothing to exert yourself. I also want you to avoid television, computer, and phone screens, and straining your eyes for long periods of time reading. You should probably avoid caffeine, too. It can sometimes aggravate your recovery. Are you driving or flying home?" the doctor asked.

"Driving," I said.

"Good. Flying can be an issue. Wear sunglasses, even if it's not sunny. The bright lights at night can aggravate you, too. Just think about whether an activity has the potential to stimulate you in a different way than the day before. Take things gradually. The excitement of Christmas can stimulate even the healthiest

brain, so yours is particularly susceptible."

I nodded and thanked Dr. Abernathy. I was released and Darren took me

back to Tom and Mary's. They made me comfortable downstairs on the sofa.

Honestly, no one trusted me to be alone upstairs. I wasn't afraid of having

another seizure, but I felt safer with them near me.

Tom and Mary went to bed as was their routine. Darren dimmed the lights

and sat on the other sofa reading on his tablet. I felt as though there was a chasm

forming between us. He'd barely spoken to me. The medications they'd given

me at the hospital combined with the prescription dulled my senses, but did

nothing to dull my emotions.

"Do you need anything?" he asked as he stood and walked toward the

kitchen.

"Some more water would be nice," was what I said, but my body screamed

for him to touch me: hold my hand, hug me, kiss the top of my head, anything.

Before he returned, I felt the familiar moisture escape my eyes and stream down

my cheeks. I put my face down on my knees to dry the tears and to hide my

expression.

His warm hand rested on the base of my neck. I took in a deep, settling

breathe and placed my hand over his. I held it there firmly. I didn't want to let

him go. A small sob escaped, muffled in the blanket over my knees. He put the

cup down and eased around to face me on the sofa. He didn't try to remove his

hand. He pulled me into his side and wrapped his arms around me.

For the first time in two days, I could breathe. Being near him made me able to inhale deeply and hold the contents of my lungs. In his arms I was stronger; in his arms I was whole. I could think and reason, and he extracted the fear straight from my heart. His scent, his heartbeat, his breaths, they all grounded me in that very moment. His embrace alone gave me hope and security. It was exactly what I needed. I wasted no more tears.

He kissed my head and rubbed my arm soothingly. He let me cling to him and nuzzle myself into his side. He didn't resist my closeness. Maybe he needed it as much as I did. I breathed slowly, keeping pace with his breaths.

"Let's go to bed. You must be exhausted," he suggested. I nodded and trudged up the stairs. I didn't want to be rejected, but I was afraid to sleep alone. I turned to face him at the top of the stairs.

"Darren," I began, but before I could ask, he interrupted me.

"I'm not letting you out of my sight without constant supervision." I smiled, relieved, and then he kissed my forehead. "Let's get ready for bed."

We assumed our usual positions, but before I could fall asleep, I rolled over and lay my head against his chest. He eased onto his back and wrapped his arms around me possessively. He leaned his cheek onto the top of my head and sighed. It was nice, lying there in his arms.

When I awoke, Darren was already showered and dressed. He petted my head and looked into my eyes, studying me. "How did you sleep?" he asked smiling.

"Really well." I returned his smile. "Thank you for staying with me last night. Thank you, too, for not staying frustrated with me. I can't explain why, but I need you. You make everything better." I took his hand and opened his palm against my face.

"Good. I'm sorry, too. It's frustrating, but I'm not going to take it out on you. I know you can't help it. I told you before that we're going to figure this out. That wasn't a lie, but I need to explain. When I see glimpses of *you* in your smile and your laugh or like at the piano, I get so excited, but then when you say things or do things that you've never done before, you scare the crap out of me. I don't know what to do with it." His eyes were pleading.

"I'm so sorry, DJ," I said before I could correct myself.

"Like that. I hear it and know you mean it, but it's different and I can't put my finger on it. When you kissed me," he sighed breathlessly, "you have no idea how horrifying that was. You're a stranger inside the most familiar thing I know, and I'm having a hard time wrapping my mind around that."

"I don't want to take your kindness for granted. We both need to be patient." I said, kissing the palm of his hand. "Do you think, in time, you can accept and get used to the changes?"

"I can get used to *this*," he said, looking down at his hand.

CHAPTER 14

"Please don't cancel your plans with Michael. You already said your mom
was home today and willing to keep an eye on me. I promise I won't lift a
finger. I'll take a bath and then sit on the sofa until you return. Your mom is
more than capable of babysitting me."

Darren considered it. He was torn between going to the children's museum
with his dad and Michael and staying home with me. "Please, go. I don't want
to spoil your fun. One day, Michael will be big and think you're lame, and not
want to spend time with you and his grandpa. Go!"

Michael watched Darren and Tom each kiss the top of my head and pat my
shoulder as they passed me toward the mudroom. Michael hugged me and then
stepped back considering. I imagined a little DJ gazing back at me. He stood tall
and kissed my head, too. It was sweet.

Mary waited upstairs with me while I bathed and dressed. She made my
bed and offered to make me a sandwich. When I emerged from the bathroom,
my pile of clothes was also folded and laid carefully in my suitcase.

I sat at the kitchen counter, watching Mary make my sandwich. "How's
DJ?" I asked. Mary hesitated with the knife as she spread the mustard across the
bread. She took in a deep breath and resumed her work.

"He's worried. He's confused." She arranged the contents of the sandwich
carefully between the slices of bread. She cut it diagonally into triangles and
slid the sandwich towards me.

"Thank you," I said looking her in the eyes. "Is there more?"

She watched me, considering. "Have you talked to him directly?"

"He's guarded and I want to gain some perspective."

She pursed her lips, almost frowning. "Beth, I don't know what's going on between you two, but it's different." She shook her head. "It's even more different than it was two days ago," she clarified. "Would you like to talk about it?" she asked. I nodded, understanding her meaning, and took a bite of sandwich. I was a little hungry, but I was actually avoiding her question. "Beth," Mary said with a hint of reproof. I looked up into her eyes. She had a strong motherly expression like she could ferret out the answer to her question by just staring into my eyes. I took another bite of sandwich and then a sip of water. "Beth, are you sleeping with DJ?"

I gulped, thankful not to have choked on my last bite. "Yes, ma'am, he said you'd seen us sleep together before."

She was surprised by my response. "What are you talking about?" she asked and then connected the dots. "Oh, no, I'm asking if you and my son are having sex."

I blinked at her candidness. "Oh, God, no!" I said in a rush, shaking my head to punctuate my innocence. I blushed all over. "I would never do that, I mean, in your home. I mean, I think I'd like to, but no, I'm not. No, ma'am," I stammered.

She narrowed her eyes, examining me. "Hmmm," she pondered.

I needed to come clean. I needed for her to understand. "It's my fault. Christmas Day and all of that was because I kissed him Christmas Eve."

Her expression softened and her eyes understood. She nodded with a smirk. It was the same look DJ gave me when he was amused with me. "Of course, I understand." She patted my hand affectionately.

"Well, that makes one of us," I said taking another bite of sandwich.

"I'm sorry if I made you uncomfortable. I thought it might be best to clear the air. He seemed better this morning, but he's acting weird, too."

"I'm acting weird?"

"Uh huh, you are. I should be more specific, though; you're acting guilty, like you're up to something. I'm relieved to know you haven't muddied the waters. You're both adults; I'm sure it's crossed both your minds plenty of times, but do you honestly think that's a good idea in your current mental state?"

I shook my head. "No, ma'am; neither does your son. I'm not allowed to kiss him anymore, either." She nodded approvingly, like maybe we could be trusted after all. I took another bite of my sandwich and pinched off the crust. "Are you always this direct?"

"When I need to be. When it matters." She sighed. "Beth, please forgive me. I know it's not really any of my business, what you do privately, but I care too much about the two of you. I don't want to see either one of you damaged. I'm just being protective."

"Thank you, Mary."

She walked around the counter and hugged me. I leaned into her and she wrapped her arms completely around me. I wasn't a mom and I couldn't remember a mom, but I knew this was a mom hug, and I knew it was good and comforting and right. I knew she loved me and was concerned for my well-being. I also sensed her protection and desire, and possible power, to fix whatever was the matter with me with a hug.

I sat quietly for the remainder of the day. I dozed for a little while on the sofa while Mary folded laundry. I sat at the counter again and watched her chop vegetables and make soup for dinner. We talked and laughed, the tension from earlier passed. I asked her how she and Tom met. She told me about their mutual friends and how they met while she was still a nursing student. She said they married a week after her graduation and moved to the other side of the country. Their honeymoon was the three days it took to drive to his new post.

"We didn't know anyone but each other. Talk about a way to start a marriage, living with a practical stranger. I loved him, sure, but I didn't know anything about him, really. I think I was pregnant with Alli less than twenty-four hours into our marriage. How crazy was that? We moved into an apartment on base and began sharing our life. Nothing like hitting the ground running. It's been the most amazing adventure with that man."

She talked about Alli and DJ as children. She told me about some of our vacations. She told me about how they were in Germany for our graduations and regretted that no one was there to cheer us on. It was like she was filling in the gaps, tiny potholes, in my memory.

The guys came in later and we had dinner. Michael had worn them out. Mary and Tom went to bed and Darren and I sat on the sofa together. "Are you tired?" he asked. I shook my head.

He took my hand and held it. I couldn't help but smile. "Your mom asked me earlier if you and I were sleeping together, then she corrected herself and asked if we were having sex." He turned and looked at me, surprised and cautious.

"Why would she do that?"

"I asked how you were doing, how you were handling everything. I think it gave her an opening, and because she said we were acting *weird*, but then she clarified that we were acting guilty."

"What did you tell her?"

"Well, after I stammered and blushed all over, I think she knew I was telling her the truth. I told her I was sleeping with you, but that I wasn't allowed to kiss you or anything else. She seemed relieved that we weren't *muddying the waters*, as she put it."

Darren laughed. "I can see how Mom would put it that way. I'll talk with her tomorrow. Did it bother you?"

"No, but I wasn't prepared for her boldness. She doesn't mince words."

"No, she doesn't. You always know where you stand with her. Dad's a bit harder to read. He can mask his emotions."

"He's taught you well."

"Do you think so?"

I nodded. "Sometimes, yes."

"I made your appointment with Dr. Saunders, today," he said completely changing the subject. "He'll see you on the second. I don't have to go back to work until the third. I'd like to accompany you. I want to hear what he has to say."

"That's fine."

"Beth, are you ready to go home?" We hadn't planned to leave until the first.

"I don't want you to cut your visit short. Don't you have more plans with Michael?"

"I told him we'd go to a movie before I left. We can do that tomorrow afternoon. Dad can be home with you for a few hours if that's okay." I nodded. He stared into my eyes, looking for something, but wasn't satisfied. "I'm ready to get you home. I think this trip may have been too soon, too much new, too much stimulation. You were doing great at home; familiar is better. Besides, they're forecasting a front moving through; I'd like to get ahead of it."

Tom and Mary agreed with Darren's decision to leave a couple of days early. Michael was disappointed, but he understood the best he could. "We'll all be together again for the cruise," he reasoned and seemed pacified for the time being.

CHAPTER 15

I felt absolutely ridiculous in Tom's sunglasses. They were huge and dark on my face. He had a pair from when they'd last dilated his eyes. No one let me lift a finger to load the car. Well, actually, Mary let me carry a bottle of water and a bag of pretzels. She made sandwiches and snacks for the road, too, but she'd packed them neatly in brown paper bags inside a larger insulated tote. Mary also gave me a throw and a pillow for the ride home. She thought of everything.

"Our numbers are in your phone," Tom said. "You call us if you need anything."

They hugged and kissed us and waved enthusiastically as we pulled out of the driveway early in the morning. We'd drive another ten hours or so. Darren said it would depend on how tired I was and how much rest I could get while he drove.

We made it to Little Rock just after dark. I had managed to sleep on and off during the ride, but I still felt exhausted. We'd snacked all day, so neither of us were particularly hungry when we arrived at the hotel. We took turns showering. I lay down on the bed and watched Darren reading on his tablet. I found my headphones and played some music from my phone. I hadn't listened to anything the entire time away. I wish I had thought to do that. It helped me feel settled.

I imagined my hands on the keys of the piano. I could feel my fingers forming the chords. I felt them adjust to the rhythm in my ears. "DJ," I said aloud, insistently, probably louder than necessary, with my ears muffled from the headphones.

"What?" He sat up concerned. I'd definitely startled him.

I pushed up to rest on my elbow and pulled out the headphones. "Did I play by ear?" He looked confused. "The piano, did I play it by ear?"

"Yes, mostly, why? Someone taught you the basics, but the rest you did on your own."

I smiled. "I think I'm figuring something out. My senses."

"What about them?"

"That's where my memories are. Smell, touch, hearing, taste, everything that I *know* right now has come from my senses. Do you know what I'm talking about? Except for my vision, my vision deceives me. I don't *see* anything familiar, but the rest of them are working overtime to help me." I could see the relief in Darren's eyes. He smiled.

"Why don't we have any instruments at the house?" I asked.

"We haven't had much time to play between work and school. You have a keyboard and a guitar in the downstairs closet."

"Why didn't you mention the music?"

"Like I said, we haven't had much time to play for a few years. It hasn't been a part of our lives for a while." He looked saddened by this fact.

"Was that my choice or yours?"

"Yours."

"Do you miss it?"

"Sometimes."

"Do you care to expound on that?" I was growing impatient with his one-word answers.

He gave a smug look. "Yes." He hesitated on purpose and then smiled, knowing he was annoying me. I waited patiently, confident he'd give in. "I taught you some chords in college. You were a natural. You could just *feel* the music. Gram's friend taught you some chords on an old upright when you first went to live with her. I heard you play that old thing every time we visited her. It was so beat-up and out of tune. It's a wonder you didn't become tone deaf. You'd play anywhere there was a piano." He was smiling telling the story, chuckling at just the right times. "That's part of the reason I got so excited Christmas Day. I missed that part of you, even before the accident. Watching you there at the piano, it was like you were back, but not the you from a month ago. Does that make sense?"

I nodded. "What happened between us?"

"What do you mean?"

"I feel like there's something you're not telling me, like maybe we had a falling out." My voice went up like a question. "There's a definite before and after feel to the stories you tell. It's noticeable."

"*Before* and *after* would be a good way to describe it. There have been a couple of befores and a couple of afters. Before you attempted suicide, before the abortion, before I kissed you, and before the accident. I always think the befores are the good times, but I'm wrong. The afters are always harder, but better in time."

"Except the last after," I guessed.

He nodded. "You're awfully intuitive. It happened a little over two years ago. I decided I was ready to marry you. I had everything planned. I did everything in my power to woo you to the dark side. You were coming around. You smiled all the time; you were so happy. I knew it would take a good while to convince you, but I was patient, determined."

"What made you decide then?" I asked.

"We'd just moved into the townhouse; I was feeling all settled and domesticated after living in different apartments since college. I'd finished my masters and was accepted into the doctoral program, and we were both content in our teaching positions. We'd established our careers and it just felt right. We'd both turned twenty-five and I thought it was time to start a family."

"Did I know of your intentions?"

"Mostly, yes." He smiled. "There was a change in our relationship and you liked the security. You even stopped going out. I was days away from asking Mom to send me my grandmother's ring. You said before that I masked my emotions, well before then, I had no reason to. You knew everything. You knew when I was happy or angry or frustrated. I never concealed anything from you."

"What did I do to change that?"

The pained stare returned. He thought for a few moments. "It had rained for days. School was cancelled due to area flooding. We'd watched movies all day. We worked through our queue and ended up watching old Disney movies, reliving our childhood favorites. I was curious to know if you wanted children. It seemed like an innocent enough question. You looked at me like I expected you to divulge state secrets."

'Are they yours?' you asked.

'I'd prefer they be ours,' I clarified.

'Made the old-fashioned way?'

'Yes.'

'You'd do that with me?'

'As often as you'd allow it.'

"You just stared at me. You gave no reply like you were letting my words settle. You didn't run screaming, so I thought maybe you were considering it. Could it be that horrible to imagine me making love with you?" he asked rhetorically.

My stomach did that tightening thing again. *No*, I thought. It wouldn't be horrible at all. I imagined it more than I cared to admit. I wanted to kiss him and feel him close to me constantly.

"I refused you, didn't I?"

He smiled, but not in a happy way. "As only you could. I knew instantly that I'd rushed you. I couldn't wait, though. I want to blame it on the endless rain and being alone together for three days; we couldn't leave the house. That last night, we were just hanging out. You'd beaten me at cards and Trivial Pursuit that day. We were listening to music and folding paper airplanes. We were a little stir-crazy. You flopped down on the sofa next to me. You laughed at something so I started tickling you. You screamed and tried to get away. I caught you and held you close; we were just messing around.

"You stopped resisting and looked at me, smiling. I sat you up on the sofa and knelt down in front of you. I wasn't even nervous. I took your hand in mine and asked you to marry me. At first you smiled, but then you looked like you might cry.

'Stop messing around, DJ. That's not funny,' you said.

'I'm not messing around,' I said. 'I want you to be my wife.'

"You must have been in shock. You smiled and shook your head disbelievingly. I took advantage of your momentary distraction and kissed you. I'd never kissed you before, ever, except like I always do. I was elated when you allowed me to kiss you for several moments. It was better than I could have ever imagined.

"When I was satisfied that your answer was *yes*, I eased you back, thinking that this was the happiest day of my life. You didn't even blink when you asked me to never do that again." He paused, knowing that I knew some of this story already. "I was delusional. I'd misread everything; I felt like an idiot. That was the beginning of the end. I knew that I didn't have an ice cube's chance in hell after that.

"These past two years, you've gradually distanced yourself. You felt guilty for rejecting me and for thinking you couldn't make me happy. We delved into our careers with gusto. You decided to begin your masters. We work together; we live together. We go out sometimes and we share a few friends. Other than that, we're just roommates. You altered your appearance and seemed to reject anything that I found attractive. I felt sick when you cut off all your hair. You said it was easier than wearing a ponytail every day, but I took it personally."

"Is that why I didn't go to your mom and dad's last Christmas?"

He hesitated and looked at me. "Yes. I'm sure, that's the real reason. Are you okay?" he asked. "I shouldn't be telling you all of this. It's got to be upsetting."

"I'm fine; I want to know. I'm not afraid and I don't feel the least bit overstimulated. Honestly, I need to know."

He read the sincerity in my eyes and continued, "We'd been arguing for weeks before your accident. You were doing it on purpose. You were trying your best to push me away for good. The last conversation we had was the worst argument yet. You asked me to move out and said you wouldn't celebrate Christmas with me ever again. I didn't understand; I didn't want to hear any of it. You told me I needed to get on with my life and find someone who would love me the way I deserved and give me what I wanted. You said you couldn't do that so I needed to stop being hopeful." He slowly blinked back the pain. "So, now you know."

I watched him as he removed his glasses and laid them on the bedside table. He rubbed the bridge of his nose and leaned back into the pillows. I reached across the bed and took his hand. He looked down at it surprised, but then squeezed my hand gently in his. I rolled over and scooted into his side. He let me be near him and comfort him, what little I could.

"Beth," he began. His voice cracked like he might be holding back tears. I pulled in even closer. "Do you see why I'm hesitant? I'm selfishly taking advantage of your memory loss. That's at least two memories I'm thankful you can't recall. My greatest fear, other than losing you, is that you'll wake up and remember everything and hate me, again."

I steadied my breaths as tears rolled out of my eyes and onto his side. I didn't want to remember that, either. There was no way I could comfort that pain with words. I'd have to show him over time that I didn't feel that way at all.

I took his hand and pressed my palm against his. I didn't hold his hand, I just let our fingertips align. It was intimate and I could feel his heartbeat in my hand. He gently wrapped his hand around mine and brought it to his chest. I didn't dare move for fear that I'd attack him and kiss him again, and in his vulnerable state, he wouldn't be able to resist me.

I closed my eyes and steadied myself against his breaths. His heartbeat gradually slowed. We fell asleep that way, close and breathing together. I woke at some point in the night. I must have been crying in my sleep. My face was wet and I sniffed. Sadness surrounded me, again, but I couldn't find any hint of a dream. I eased out of Darren's embrace and went to the bathroom. I remembered to take my medicine and drank a glass of water. The clock on the desk read 3:45. I pulled back the covers and eased into the bed beside Darren.

He sensed the change and rolled over toward me. "You okay?" he asked in a groggy voice.

"Yeah, bathroom, and I forgot to take my medicine. Goodnight, again."

He smiled sleepily and drew me closer into him. He kissed my forehead and allowed his lips to linger there. His breathing eased back into sleep and his light, familiar snore returned. I nuzzled closer into his chest and wrapped my arm around him. I think I was asleep in another five breaths.

CHAPTER 16

Darren let me sleep late. He was dressed and packed when I rolled over and opened my eyes. He sat in the chair reading, and the light was bright around the heavy curtains. "What time is it?"

"Almost eight."

"Why didn't you wake me?"

"You were sleeping really well and you're supposed to be resting." There was a smile in his voice.

"I'm hungry."

"Of course, you are. Get dressed. I'll get us some food from downstairs and we can eat before we leave. There are a lot of windows in the lobby. You don't want to eat in those ridiculous glasses, do you?"

"Are you embarrassed to be seen with my stylish frames?"

He laughed. "They're lovely. You should wear them with everything."

He returned with a plate full of food and some orange juice. We were on the road before nine and made it home well before dinnertime.

"There's nothing to eat here," Darren announced after checking the fridge and the pantry. He poured what remained of the container of milk down the drain, making an unpleasant face from the odor. "I need to go to the store. Will you be okay here by yourself?"

"Do you have to go now? Aren't you tired of being in the car? How about we order a pizza or something easy and do it first thing tomorrow?"

He nodded, considering. "That's a good idea. It's New Year's Eve. Want to do something tonight?"

"Gosh! There're so many options: sleep, rest, take a walk, rest some more, unpack. I can't decide what's more thrilling. Have we been invited to any wild parties? Maybe we should call all of my closest friends, whose names and faces I don't remember, and invite them over," I said sarcastically.

"I meant like play a game or listen to music or let me read to you, but a walk might do us both some good," he said not returning my tone.

"I'm sorry. That was uncalled for. You were being thoughtful. A walk, in pleasant temperatures, sounds nice. Let's call for a pizza early and then walk after it gets dark."

"Agreed."

New Year's Eve wasn't all that exciting. We ordered a pizza and ate while Darren read the trivia cards aloud and I moved the pieces around the board. He was winning most of the game. I managed not to lose too badly.

After dinner, we took a walk around our complex. The mild weather in comparison to the cold of Chicago was welcomed. I was definitely a southern girl. It was good to be home. I went upstairs and took a shower. The familiar scent of fabric softener on the towels welcomed me. I put on my PJs. I was comfortable. I found the thought of sleeping in my own bed, under my quilt, right somehow. Darren was playing music on the stereo downstairs.

"Do you want to stay up and ring in the new year or do you want to go to bed?"

"What do you like to do?"

"It depends. We're usually at my parents' house. We watch the ball drop in Time's Square and then we go to bed an hour earlier than the rest of our time zone. It's so boring. Sometimes, Alli and Lance go out and we've joined them in years past."

"Do you make resolutions?"

"Yes." He looked a little embarrassed.

"How successful are you at keeping them?"

"Very."

"Really?"

"Yes. See that jar on the counter?" I looked over at an inoffensive jar nestled between the toaster and the coffee maker. "Each year we write our resolution on a slip of paper and put in fifty bucks. The one who achieves their resolution before the end of the year gets their fifty bucks back. If you don't, then the other person gets your fifty."

"I don't have fifty bucks."

"You can write a check to cash."

"You seem very confident."

"I am. It builds character and I don't like losing. I think it's made me honor my word better. If I write it down, it's more likely to happen."

"Do I keep my resolutions?"

"Absolutely! You don't like losing, either."

We sat on the sofa and listened to music. Darren read some and sometime around nine, I sat up and looked at the closet door. "Will you help me get out my keyboard?"

"Sure, if that's what you want."

I was sure. I wanted something to do that didn't involve reading or watching a screen. Darren walked to the downstairs closet. It was bursting with jackets and a vacuum cleaner and instruments. He pulled the keyboard out. It was safely stored in a case with a foldable stand. I unzipped the case and found the power plug.

"Where does it go?" I asked.

"You kept it over there near the window, but I don't have a preference."

"How about there?" I gestured toward a corner of the living room so it would be out of the way and wouldn't be in direct sunlight, either.

Darren lifted the keyboard onto the stand and crawled on the floor to access the outlet behind the bookshelf. I pulled a chair across the room and sat in front of the keyboard. He adjusted the height for me.

I played a note or two and lowered the volume. I looked over the computerized options and hoped I wouldn't need to do anything too technical. I closed my eyes and placed my hands over the keys. I began playing an ascending scale, feeling how the keys responded to my touch. My heart was happy there. The joy flowed through my hands and onto the keyboard. I formed the chords and combined them into simple tunes, humming under my breath as I played.

I opened my eyes and Darren looked both relieved and proud. I couldn't help but smile up at him. "Do you want to play, too?" I asked. "Get the guitar and play with me."

There was a look of disbelief in his eyes, but it didn't take him two seconds to decide. He removed the guitar from its case and began tuning it. After a few plucks on the strings, he hit a key on the keyboard to get the right tone. Satisfied, he strummed a few chords. He played some of the choruses he'd played with Lance and Michael on Christmas Day. Our first attempts were crude and we laughed together at our miserable attempts. It was easy, though, and the most fun we'd had together since the crash.

It was nearly eleven and I couldn't wave off the exhaustion creeping over me. "I don't think I'm going to make it to midnight. I'm ready to go to bed." I didn't know how it would be, returning to our townhouse. I'd slept most nights with Darren while we were away, but I wasn't sure how it would be once we returned.

"Where do you plan to sleep tonight?" I asked.

Darren considered. "In my own bed," he said flatly. I nodded, but I didn't like his answer. He could tell that disappointed me. "I'm here if you need me, but I don't think you need me every night, do you?"

I shrugged. I took his hand and held it for a few seconds. Was it need or was it want? Either way I wouldn't argue. "Goodnight. Happy New Year. I hope it's a good one." I kissed him on the cheek and released his hand before I turned and walked toward the staircase.

"Goodnight," he whispered after me.

CHAPTER 17

We scrambled eggs for breakfast and made a list for the grocery store. We were nearly out of everything. It was the first time I'd been to the grocery store since the accident. I hoped to find a more flattering pair of sunglasses. The only ones I'd found in my room were more fashion than function.

We were making our way through the aisles when I heard a deep, familiar voice. "Beth." I turned.

"Lt. Miller." I couldn't help but return his friendly smile.

"Marcus, please." He was standing tall in his uniform holding a loaf of bread and a carton of eggs. "Happy New Year! It's good to see you," he said smiling. He balanced the bread on the eggs in his left hand and reached over to take my hand. He then turned to Darren and shook his hand, too. "How are you doing?" I'm sure he was curious about the huge, dark glasses covering my eyes. He examined Darren suspiciously and then his friendly smile returned. As a police officer, he was probably trained to assume I was covering abuse with such huge frames. He knew Darren posed no threat.

"I have to wear these, now. Light might trigger a seizure."

"Sorry to hear that. How was your Christmas?"

"Good. We were at Darren's parents' in Chicago. It's nice to be back where it's warm. How's your mom?"

He smiled proudly that I remembered. "We've both been working plenty since before Christmas. I'm bringing home breakfast. Hey, y'all have plans for later today?" I looked to Darren. He shook his head. "My mama will have a ham

on all day and we have people coming over this evening. We'll have cabbage

and black-eyed-peas, too. Can't start the new year without health, wealth, and

happiness."

"I don't know," I said hesitantly.

"Come on, it'll be fun and you won't get a better meal anywhere." He was

so convincing. I smiled at his broad, dark face and then looked to Darren for

approval. He nodded.

Marcus gave us his mom's address and we resumed our shopping. Standing

in the check-out, I realized that I never paid for anything. "Darren, do I need to

give you some money?"

He chuckled as he removed the debit card. "No, Beth, this all comes out of

the household account. We have money directly deposited into a joint account

to cover the electricity, cable, wi-fi, insurance, groceries, and whatever else we

need to pay together. You have your own checking and savings, too. I guess I

should have explained all of that."

On the ride home I asked, "What about the mortgage, or do we rent?"

"We don't have a mortgage. You own the townhouse, outright. You bought

it with some of the money from your Gram's inheritance. She had a life

insurance policy and then you also had the sale of her home and the cars. You

invested a good bit of it, so you're fine financially. We got some good advice

after Gram passed. You were smart and listened and did what her lawyer

recommended. He sent us to the right people."

I felt relieved that I wasn't completely dependent on Darren. "You also have enough accumulated sick leave that you haven't lost any pay for the month you've been out."

"Funny, I haven't even thought about work or anything. I guess I should be trying to figure out what I'm supposed to do with myself once I'm cleared to return to work."

"Let's not worry about that until after you've seen the doctor tomorrow. I'm sure he'll help you make a plan."

That afternoon, we drove less than two miles to Marcus's mom's house. The aromas wafting out of the house were mouthwatering. Marcus greeted us on the front porch. He was standing outside with a couple of other men. He welcomed us and introduced us to his brothers and then took us inside to meet his mom. I didn't have to be introduced. "Sadie!" I exclaimed.

She turned from the stove and opened her arms wide. "Oh, child! I'm so glad you came." She hugged me like she'd done before I left the hospital. "When Marcus told me he'd invited you, I could hardly wait to see you." She put her hands on her hips and looked me over carefully.

"How did you know it was me?" I asked.

"A while back, Marcus told me he took a girl named Beth home. He also told me she'd lost her memory after an accident. That's a pretty big coincidence, don't you think?" She laughed. "I told him I may know you and sure enough, I do. How are you doing?"

"Overall pretty good, but I've had a few rough days."

"Your scar looks good. I like what you've done with your hair, too. How are you, *roommate*?" she asked looking over at Darren. She smiled, making light of her comment.

"I'm fine, thank you," he said.

"How's our girl? You looking after her?" I should have noticed the resemblance between Sadie and Marcus instantly. She could have been in law enforcement, too. She had that way of looking at a person like she could read guilt or innocence with just one glance.

"Yes, ma'am, the best I can."

"Good! Let's eat!" She called into the other room and we were made welcome by her sons' families and a neighbor or two. The younger boys removed their baseball caps and everyone bowed their heads. One of the gentlemen there, blessed the food and the hands that had prepared it. He asked for favor for the new year and blessings for everyone who was gathered there.

We lined up and began filling our plates. Sadie bustled in and sat with Darren and me in the living room. She asked about Christmas. She asked about Chicago and commented that she wasn't a fan of the cold. Her home was welcoming. She told me about all of her children and their children. She said that she and her late husband had raised five. The three sons lived locally, but one daughter lived in New Orleans and the other in Texas.

I told her about the seizure and that I had an appointment with the neurologist the next morning. "How are your headaches?" she asked.

"I haven't had one since the seizure, but then again, I haven't done anything to cause one. This is the most activity I've had since Christmas."

"Good, keep it that way."

Apparently, everyone in Sadie's family could bake. There were a variety of desserts to choose from. I wished I would have known that before I filled-up on the real food. I would have saved way more room for dessert.

A couple of hours later, Darren suggested we head home. Sadie and Marcus agreed with him. I'm sure I looked as tired as I felt, but honestly, it was the food. I could have passed out on the sofa. It was a good feeling. I thanked them and said goodbye to their family.

"Do you still have my number?" Sadie asked.

"Yes," I said.

"Don't hesitate to call me if you need anything." I nodded and thanked her and assured her that I would.

The next morning's appointment was delayed. Apparently, Dr. Saunders had an emergency at the hospital. We waited for a long time in his reception area. I listened to music a bit on my headphones and Darren read on his tablet. I wondered if our relationship was always this quiet or if it was just the most recent version.

"I'm bored," I confessed. "What are you reading?"

"Case studies of gifted students with anxiety and other social conditions."

"Is it interesting?" It didn't sound very interesting to me.

"Actually, yes."

"What else do you like to read?"

"Murder mysteries, some sci-fi, and teen fiction to stay current with my students. I kind of like knowing what they're reading. It gives us a neutral point of reference. They keep me on my toes, for sure."

"Tell me about your students."

"I have a mostly self-contained gifted classroom. They are mainstreamed into PE and most electives with regular ed teachers, but their core subjects are all covered in my classroom. I have five students this year. They are each unique and amazing and challenging. Let's just say it's a daily mental workout. I don't really *teach* anything. I provide an environment where it's safe and neutral and stimulating. I'm a facilitator of their education, not their teacher. In fact, they just call me Darren. It's easier."

"Why don't they have to call you Mr. Fitzgerald?"

He laughed. "Well, I started out working with little kids. Many of them couldn't pronounce my name without spitting. Mr. Darren or Mr. F. sounds weird to me, so I just let them call me by my first name. Besides, I think genuine respect and authority don't come in a title; they come from consistency and relationship. They need to trust me and I have to earn it."

We were finally called in to meet with the doctor. He examined me and looked over my file. "Any other episodes?" he asked.

"No."

"Have you been able to recall anything from before the accident?"

"Very little. Glimpses, here and there. I'm learning a great deal about my former self." I cut my eyes to Darren. He looked away and diverted his eyes toward a large poster of the brain.

"Take your time. How are you sleeping?"

"Fairly well."

"Dreams?"

"Nightmares." He nodded and made a note. He reviewed all of the reports from Dr. Abernathy, but gave me nothing new in his findings.

"When will I be released?"

"The seizure complicated things. I can't release you to drive for at least three months, and with the memory loss and your current position, I can't release you to return to work, either. I'm not going to even consider you returning this school year."

"What the hell am I supposed to do with myself?" I asked, surprised at my sudden impatience. I didn't mean to dump it all on the doctor; he just happened to be the one standing there. He and Darren looked at me, both surprised at my outburst.

"Ms. Rust, I know this must be frustrating."

"Oh, do you? You know how frustrating this is? You can't give me any answers. I'm tired of *resting* and I'm bored out of my mind because there's nothing to keep me occupied. I can't remember my friends or what the hell I do on a daily basis."

"Beth," Darren said soothingly as he stood and walked toward me.

I put my hands up in surrender. "I'm sorry. I know I have to accept things as they are right now. It's just hard, okay?"

Dr. Saunders didn't know what to do any more than I did. He had scans of my brain and he still couldn't help me. I was determined to figure this out, myself. I felt angry, but it was misdirected. I took a deep breath and exhaled slowly. "So, doctor, what am I allowed to do? And I'm just warning you, if you say *rest*, I may choke you."

He chuckled a little. I think he was used to dealing with crazy people in his line of work. "Fair enough. You have permission to do one new task a week as long as it's low-impact and minimal risk to your head. Gradually introduce printed material and screens. No more than ten minutes at a time. Any signs of stress or headaches and we agree you take a day off." I nodded. "I want to see you again in six weeks. We'll rescan then, if necessary, and adjust your medication, then, too."

He then turned to Darren. "Please don't let her lift anything over twenty pounds until her next appointment. She has permission to resume normal household and sexual activity." Darren nodded obediently and kept his expression blank. I rolled my eyes. I was pretty sure he wasn't going to let me do that, either. "So, I'll see you in six weeks. Please contact my office if you have any significant changes or episodes."

"Thank you," I said.

CHAPTER 18

Darren had to return to work the next day. He was torn about leaving me, but I assured him that I would spend the day unpacking and taking a few walks. The evening before, he helped me log onto the bank website so that I could gain some insight into my bank accounts. He also left me with numbers to contact our insurance rep from school to find out what I needed to do to activate my short-term disability policy.

There were forms to fill out and paperwork to get signed. It was a small task, really, but I suddenly felt overwhelmed at the thought of being limited. I really didn't like being told I wasn't allowed to do things. I'd have to make a point of asking Darren in which journal column I should list that personality trait.

After lunch, I took a nap and then began unpacking and started a load of laundry. I realized around 3:00 that I should probably be thinking about something for supper. I went downstairs and decided to make hamburgers.

I was playing the keyboard when Darren came in from school. He was sweaty and wearing workout clothes. "How was your day, *Dear*?" I asked in a patronizing tone.

He laughed. "It was wonderful, *Darling*. How was yours?" He kissed the top of my head as he passed me.

"Fraught with peril and endless adventures."

"Excellent. Mine, too. Did yours have minions trying to take over the world?"

"No," I feigned disappointment. "I'll have to find some of those tomorrow."

"I'm going to take a shower. I'll be down in a few."

During supper, Darren said he was considering taking a break from classes this semester.

"No, not on my account," I argued.

"But that's two really long days that you'll be alone, not to mention the nights and weekends studying and writing papers. I don't feel right leaving you like that all the time."

"I'll figure it out. Please don't delay your plans. Don't you have a couple of weeks before classes begin again?"

"Yes, but that's not very long."

"It's okay, really," I said encouragingly. He nodded, believing me.

We watched a few minutes of a movie, but I could tell Darren was tired from his first day back. "You don't have to stay up with me. You can go to bed."

"I'm fine. I want to be here with you."

I cuddled into his side and he put his arm around me. It wasn't gushy or the least bit romantic. The physical closeness we shared was never like that. I suspected it could easily go there, but it wasn't like we had to be cautious or anything.

The next morning, I decided to clean my room and bathroom. I rotated some laundry which had become my routine. I finished unpacking and tried to put my suitcase back on the shelf, but it was a little too high and something was in the way. I stepped back to see a box against the wall on the top shelf. I had to stand on my tiptoes to reach it. I pushed it over and it came down hard onto the floor behind me. The contents scattered everywhere upon impact. It contained envelopes and notes and several notebooks. I sat down on the floor and began picking up the items. The notes were actually letters, and they were all signed, *DJ.*

I picked up the letters and put them in order by the date and began reading. They were mostly from times when Darren and I were separated. He was in Germany with his parents. He was working at a camp for special needs kids. He was asking me whether we should drive or fly to Chicago for his sister's wedding. Why didn't he just email me? They all included silly drawings and sketches in the margins: happy, smiling faces, little dogs, and stick-figures with top hats. I stacked them neatly and placed them back inside the box.

I opened the notebooks thinking they were from college or important classes that I'd need to review the information. I was wrong. They were journals. Thankfully, they too were dated. I put them in order and opened the first one and began reading. It was my seventeen-year-old self, describing in vivid detail the trials and tribulations of high school. There were guys mentioned and about half way through the first notebook, I was reading, in explicit detail, what I believed was probably my first sexual encounter.

IMPACT

The details were clinical without any feeling or emotion. I wasn't sure my younger self even liked the guy. There didn't seem to be any guilt or remorse or longing in the words. It was like a scientific observation or a medical examiner's report, like the author was describing an experiment. I couldn't believe how emotionally distanced she was from the details.

I heard the dryer buzz, so I took the notebooks downstairs with me. I folded the towels and made myself a sandwich for lunch. I sat on the sofa and read the second notebook as I ate. I was about to graduate from high school and had decided to go into education. I was complaining how Gram didn't understand why I decided to move into the dorm on the main campus and not attend the satellite campus close to our house. I wanted to experience college fully and was willing to work part-time to cover my room and board. There were a few more encounters with boys, but they were mere mentions of people I'd met, where we went, and a clinical description of our intercourse. By the end of the second notebook, I found the first mention of DJ. From then on, he was mentioned in every entry.

Met a guy named DJ today in my algebra class. He's so cute and really made me laugh. I wonder if he'll ask me out. He's not like other guys I've met on campus. Come to find out, he's also in my English lit class.

Our time together was fun and sweet and I could tell how much my younger self loved this boy. I laughed at her entries. I smiled and felt how settled she was and how she dreamed and how she desired a good life. She went home on weekends and attended mass nearly every Saturday with her grandmother. It was sweet. It was endearing.

I got up twice to pee and make myself something to drink. Sexual encounters were listed by first name, location, and a number ranking. I couldn't figure out what that meant. There was rarely a name repeated. The entries that included DJ were completely separate from the sexual encounters. My younger self lived a double life. No wonder, DJ didn't know how I'd gotten pregnant.

By the fifth notebook, I was a mess. Emotionally, that is. Physically, my heart hurt and my lungs felt like I was being suffocated. I was crying; no, I was sobbing. I finally grabbed the roll of tissue from the half bath because I'd emptied the box in the living room. Gram was dead and I didn't know how I was going to make it through finals. I'd gotten the call from a neighbor that had found her dead. She was in her garden.

I wasn't even twenty years old, and I was having to plan a funeral and write papers and figure out what the hell I was going to do with myself. DJ was there through everything. He drove me to the funeral home. He waited while I met with the attorney about Gram's will and her wishes to be cremated. The neighbors' daughter wanted to buy the house so she could be closer to her parents.

Cleaning Gram's house. Found a box in the attic today. I just want to go to sleep and wake up in a world where none of this crap exists.

Two days later.

I'm pregnant. They pumped my stomach and then told me I'm pregnant. I can hardly write the words, much less speak them aloud. Congratulations, Beth, you're a fucking slut! He doesn't think I'll go through with it, but he won't stop me, either.

In a perfect world, I'm good.

In a perfect world, I don't mess around.

In a perfect world, Jesus loves me and doesn't look disappointed every time I look up at him hanging on the cross.

In a perfect world, this baby is DJs and I'm allowed to keep it.

In a perfect world, I tell him every day how much I love him and what he means to me.

I surely don't deserve him, now.

The last few pages of that notebook were empty. I threw away all of the tissues I'd accumulated around me on the sofa and put what little remained of the roll back on the roller. I had one more journal to read.

I was exhausted. I shouldn't have been reading like this. No telling what kind of episode today would trigger. I couldn't stop, though. I was too far into them now. I went upstairs and put the first five notebooks in the box on top of DJ's letters. I carried the last one to the bed and wrapped myself in the security of the quilt. I hesitated because I knew part of what was coming in this story and I didn't want to face any of it.

It was the middle of the summer. The first entry was July fourth.

Perhaps Independence Day is a symbolic enough day to begin. My therapist recommends that I begin journaling again. She's good and she knows her shit, but I don't want to write anymore. I've committed an unforgivable sin and I can't even ask God to forgive me. I'm too ashamed. I haven't been to mass in over a month. I can't bring myself to confession.

DJ returns from his parents' house tomorrow. He's called me nearly every day, but we don't say much. He asks how I am and if I'm keeping my appointments. He asks if I like my new apartment and if I can pick him up from the airport. He asks if I'm eating.

It's the same questions the counselors ask me each time I go to an individual or group session, except they don't ask for a ride from the airport. Some of those people have really big problems. I guess it helps me realize how stupid I am and how I really don't have it all that bad.

I'm working again and I have an A in my only class this session.

This notebook showed the work and growth of my younger self. I really appreciated her determination and her increased self-respect. She didn't document any more sexual encounters and the only other living person she mentioned was DJ. She wrote letters to her parents and to Gram. She wrote letters to God. She wrote a letter to her unborn child. I was crying so hard through that one that I could hardly read the words. My body felt empty and ached to have something inside me. The loss was so deep. I think I would have carried a litter of puppies if it meant I'd be free from the vacancy of my womb.

The final entry was a letter to myself. I didn't think I had any more tears, but I was wrong. I had a wellspring of them in reserve. The letter was beautiful and elegant and self-affirming. I should probably have it framed and read it every day. The final entry read:

No matter what, I'm keeping the quilt.

The therapist surely did know her *shit* and guided me through a really, really dark time. Although I had no memory of anything written in these journals, I had a physical and emotional connection. I felt all the pain and the guilt and felt overwhelming joy throughout the recovery process. Sadie had been right. There was something powerful in a healing mind.

My shirt was wet from tears. There was snot wiped all along the cuffs and the collar and even on the hem. I was disgusting, covered in goo. Just then, I heard Darren coming in the front door. I threw the notebook in the box with the rest and shoved it in the corner.

"Beth?" I heard him call. I jumped up and ran to the bathroom. I probably looked terrible.

"I'm upstairs. Give me a minute. I'll be down."

My eyes were red and bloodshot. My nose was puffy from being wiped a hundred times. I splashed some cool water on my face and patted it dry. I brushed my teeth and put on some lip gloss. I threw my T-shirt in the hamper and found something else to wear.

Darren came upstairs, sweaty again. He popped his head into my bedroom just as I was coming out of my bathroom. Panic crossed his face. I must have looked horrible. "Are you okay?"

"I've been crying."

"How long have you been crying?" Darren asked. He stepped into my room to take a better look at me.

"Since lunch?"

"What happened? Are you okay, now?"

"Surprisingly, yes. I found a box in the closet with letters from you and a half-dozen notebooks, journals really. I spent the entire afternoon reading them. I'm a mess." I sniffed and wiped my nose again.

"You've been reading all afternoon?" I nodded. "Beth, that can't be good."

I acknowledged his concern. "I know, but I couldn't help myself once I got started." I took a deep breath. I wasn't feeling sad or emotional anymore. "I think it was really good to get a different perspective on the things you've already told me." I couldn't read the expression on his face. "I'm okay, really. I know I must look horrible and I'm sure I'll pay for this later, but I'm okay." I took a few steps toward him and took his hand and looked into his eyes. "Thank you, DJ." I'd had his initials in my head all day. "Thank you for continuing to be my best friend."

He smiled. He hesitated like he wanted to hug me but remembered he was all sweaty. "It's okay. I don't mind." He smiled and hugged me close. It was the best feeling in the world. I took a deep breath and regretted it. I stepped back and looked at him. "Sorry, but you really don't smell good." He chuckled self-consciously and stepped away from me. "Hey, since you're here, do you mind putting away my suitcase? I can't reach." He turned toward the closet and easily placed the suitcase up on the top shelf. "Here, this, too," I said, handing him the box of journals and letters.

"I didn't know you'd kept all those. I figured they were buried somewhere or burned," he said, looking at the contents.

"Apparently, I thought they were important. I'm glad they were here." He smiled to himself. When he did that he was completely DJ. I couldn't help but be familiar and close to him after the intimacy of my younger self and this boy, this man, who now stood before me. It made him completely mine.

"Have you ever read them? The journals?"

He shook his head. "No, not mine to read."

"You have incredible self-control."

He chuckled, again. "Not really, I'm honestly more frightened of what I might find out."

"Well, you might find out that I've never hated you. I'm not capable. I'm so sorry."

He couldn't step away from me in the small space of the closet. He just stood there looking at me, unsure of what to make of me. His eyes looked away from the intensity of our closeness. "I need to take a shower. If I stay here any longer, I'm going to stink up all your clothes."

I stepped away so he could pass. "I didn't cook dinner. Are you okay with a sandwich?"

"No," he called back from his bedroom. "I think we need to get you out of this house. You've been cooped up again all day, and I'm not going to leave you like this. You need some fresh air. Get dressed; we're going out."

CHAPTER 19

The evening was pleasant for January. I wore jeans and a hoodie and my boots, and we ate in an enclosed patio at a Mexican restaurant. I really wanted a margarita, but knew better. DJ told me about his day and how he was planning a field trip for his students. He told me about Molly asking about me and whether or not I'd like to invite her over for dinner.

"I don't know," I said honestly. "I guess so. Has she ever done that before?"

"A couple of times. You two went to several movies, and I'm pretty sure you all had dinner with your student teachers a few times. She's only been working with you since last year. She's a sweet girl. She might make a good friend."

"I can see why you might want to share some of the friendship responsibilities," I said, making light of the comment, but it struck a nerve.

"That's not what I'm trying to do."

I laughed. "I know. I was just making a joke."

After I'd plowed through a couple of bowls of chips and a plate full of enchiladas and chili rellenos, I was stuffed and satisfied and desperately in need of my bed. "Thank you, DJ. That was exactly what I needed."

He took my hand as we stood from the table and led me back to the car. He let it go only after he opened the door for me. Before I got into the car, I looked at him and smiled, happy as all of the feelings from the journals returned.

"What?" he asked.

"Gram was right. You are the best." I hugged him. When our bodies were aligned in the parking lot next to his car, my stomach did that tightening thing. My initial response was to release him, but the comfort and security of his arms was greater. Just like in his bed in Chicago, he held me tightly. I forced my body to be still and absorb all of the physical closeness I was afforded. I took in a deep breath and nuzzled closer. He didn't push me away. The moment was intimate. He leaned his cheek against the side of my face and breathed with me.

A few moments later, I released him. I sat in the car and allowed him to shut the door for me. He didn't say much on the way home. He kept both hands on the steering wheel and only removed one of them for a moment to adjust the volume on the radio. In the confines of his small car, I knew he could feel it, too. I wondered if his stomach also did that stupid tightening thing. It was really annoying, sometimes, but I had to admit that I liked the overall feeling when I didn't fight it. It made me warm all over.

"I have a therapy appointment tomorrow," I said, breaking the silence as we entered the house.

"What time?"

"Ten thirty."

"Do you need a ride?"

"No, I just wanted you to know that I'd be out tomorrow."

"Thank you." He was focused on the pile of mail on the entry-way table.

"DJ?" He looked up, still holding a couple of envelopes in his hand and smiled. I didn't care what he said at Christmas, he preferred it when I called him that. "Will you please sleep with me tonight? I'm exhausted from today and after all that reading, I'm sure tonight of any may be a time when I need you." He considered for a few seconds and then nodded.

He read on his tablet for over an hour before he was ready to go to bed. I lay on the sofa with my feet near him. My eyes were tired and I think I may have dozed off a couple of times. He stood and stretched and then turned off the downstairs lights. He checked the locks on the doors and made a quick scan of the kitchen as was his routine. Thankfully, I'd cleaned up after myself today and there was nothing for him to do.

I stood and walked upstairs. I washed my face and brushed my teeth and got ready for bed. He joined me with his pillow. I smiled sheepishly, feeling a little bit guilty for asking him to sleep with me when I hadn't had any sort of episode. I didn't even feel addled or stirred at that moment, but I selfishly wanted him close tonight.

We got into bed and he scooted over toward the center as I rolled into his chest, breathing in his scent. I think I may have sighed aloud. He chuckled once deep in his throat. "Why do you do that?"

"What?"

"Sniff me."

"I'm not sniffing you," I said lazily. "That sounds like something a drug dog would do. I'm just taking in your scent. It's really quite wonderful." He muttered something under his breath, but I didn't catch what he said because I was already falling asleep.

I woke screaming and sobbing, clutching for dear life. "Shhh," he whispered and held me close. He stroked my head and down my back. "I'm here. You're okay. You're safe. It was just a dream. It's not real." His voice rose a little, unable to conceal his concern.

I was panting like I'd been running. "I couldn't stop it!" I gasped. "I couldn't get out of the way! It was coming so fast!"

"Let it out. Just breathe. It's over. It can't hurt you, anymore." I felt like he'd said those words in my ears before. They were strangely familiar.

I pushed myself away from him, gently, placing my hands on his tightened abs. I opened my eyes and looked at him. This was not a dream; he was real. DJ's brown eyes were full of worry in the shadows of the dark room. His hands stroked my back and shoulder, comfortingly. I took in another deep breath and settled myself.

Slowly, I sat up and walked to the bathroom. I turned on the nightlight next to the sink and splashed water on my face. DJ was standing behind me, then. His hands on my shoulders, reassuringly. I looked at him in the reflection. I wasn't sure how focused I was without his glasses, but I could see him clearly.

"The crash," I began. He nodded. "There's always so much blood." He sighed. I gagged reflexively and moved quickly away from him. In less than a second, I was leaning over the toilet and vomiting. He placed a dampened washcloth over the back of my neck and allowed the dry heaves to subside before he helped me back to my feet. I brushed my teeth and got back into bed.

"Do you want to talk about it?" he asked, holding me close to him.

I shrugged. I really didn't know what to say or even how to explain the feelings I had surrounding the images. "I can't breathe. I'm choking and gasping. I'm clutching to someone or something next to me, but I can't ever see it clearly. The pain is excruciating and I'm unable to move my legs. Everything is so heavy and I'm pinned in, unable to move. This time there was another impact and the brightest light and then sudden darkness."

He kissed my head and the warmth radiated down to my chest as it usually did. He whispered soothing words over me, again. I believed every one of them. "Do you think you can sleep again?" he asked.

"I don't know. What time is it?"

"Nearly six. I need to get up in a half-hour, anyway. Want some breakfast?"

"Bacon?" I asked. Although I'd just thrown up, bacon sounded really good at that moment.

"Sure. Get up. Let's make breakfast. I'll feel better leaving you fully awake and fed."

Breakfast was beyond delicious. Eggs, bacon, and I found some frozen hash browns in the back of the freezer. We sat and ate together before DJ went upstairs to shower. When DJ came back downstairs, I was loading the breakfast dishes into the dishwasher. He placed his hand on my shoulder and kissed my forehead. I wiped the water from my hand and I took his hand from my shoulder. I held it for a few seconds, looking into his eyes. I wanted to reassure him that I was better now.

"I'm okay, DJ. I'll talk about it with the therapist today. Maybe she can help me process the memory."

"No reading. Remember what Dr. Saunders said. You take a day off." I nodded obediently.

The Uber driver was a chatty fellow. He asked friendly questions. I wasn't annoyed in the least. It was nice to have some contact with another person in the middle of the day. He dropped me off in front of the therapist's office. Since the first time we'd spoken in the hospital, I felt like we'd made a decent connection.

"Hello, Beth, please come in," she said as she called me into her office.

"Hello," I replied with a smile. She was engaging and friendly and her office was cozy and welcoming. I guessed those were all requirements for being a good therapist. You'd have to figure out the best way to get your patients to let their guard down and be honest.

"Please take a seat. How were your holidays?" I sat in a large, leather chair and she sat in the matching one across from me.

"Pretty good."

"How was your trip?"

"Good. I loved DJ's family."

"DJ?" she clarified.

"Darren, my roommate? Apparently, that's what I used to call him. It feels right, somehow. After spending Christmas with his family and hearing them say it constantly, and then yesterday, I found a box of letters and journals from high school and college. He's in nearly every entry. I just have his nickname in my ears and it feels right in my mouth, you know?" She nodded and made a little note in my chart. "Did Dr. Saunders' office tell you about the seizure I had over Christmas?"

She nodded, but didn't comment about it. "Have you been able to access any memories since our last session?"

"I have bits and pieces. Nothing that I'd really say is an actual memory. Everything that I find familiar or that I'm able to do is through my senses."

She looked at me curiously. "Like what, exactly?"

"Like the foods I crave, textures and human touch, scents, and I can play piano by ear."

"Really? That's very interesting.

"Music has been the one thing that hasn't aggravated me since the accident."

"How are you sleeping?"

"Pretty well, but I've had several nightmares. They are increasingly more vivid."

"Would you tell me about them?"

"That's one of the many reasons I'm here," I said wryly.

"Excellent, let's begin."

I explained the dreams in the most vivid detail I could. I told her about vomiting after this morning's dream. I told her how I had glimpses and pieces of memories, but that nothing I *see* held meaning for me. "Could my body hold the memories that my mind isn't able to recall?" I asked.

She shrugged. "Our neuropathways are incredibly intricate. We have trillions of neural connections. Our brain is the storehouse of our memories, but our bodies and senses combine to create those connections. We don't have one without the other. We need the input just as much as we need a place to collect and process. So, to answer your question, I think your body remembers in ways that are not fully understood. Gymnasts and musicians practice routinely to train and create muscle memory so that they aren't cognitive of their body's ability to perform a particular task."

She articulated my thoughts. I smiled. "You say it way better than I was able to, but I feel like my senses are working really hard to help me."

"Can you discern what might agitate you? Can you tell a change is coming?"

I shook my head. "Not exactly. Screens for sure and lights. I read for hours yesterday and I thought for sure that if I was going to have a hard night, it would be after that. My eyes were really tired and I'd cried a lot. We went to bed early and it was just before daylight when I woke from the nightmare. I was so thankful that DJ had agreed to sleep with me. I don't know that I felt a change, but maybe I knew it was there."

"Would you tell me more about your relationship with DJ?"

I sat for a few seconds, thinking. I wasn't sure where to begin. "Like what, exactly?"

"You live together, and before your accident, you worked together. You've known him for a long time, but you don't *know* him as you once did."

"I can't explain that either. He's been my best friend for a long time. Right now, he's my only friend. I'm beginning to consider making new friends and expanding my circle, but that's slow going. I've thought about texting his mom and dad and keeping that connection. I don't leave the house much and I'm not allowed to do things that might provoke another seizure. He's pretty much my whole world at this very moment."

"What sort of feelings do you have towards him?"

I tried not to allow the pained expression to show. "I'm grateful and thankful for sure. He's amazing and loves me unconditionally. He's proven that countless times over the years."

"Are you developing feelings for him?"

"Is it that obvious?" I smiled and looked away. I think I may have blushed, but tears filled my eyes and I was suddenly sad. I blinked hard, trying to keep the tears inside.

"What are you feeling right now?" she asked, patiently.

"Sadness and regret."

"What do you regret?"

"I'm not sure, but I feel it. I know I hurt him and rejected him and many other hateful things, but he's remained steady. Reading my past self's version of him, drew me closer to him mentally, but my body's known him since I awoke in this life and desires his closeness and his touch. I love him but I have no way to express that."

"Does he know you have feelings for him?"

"Yes," I said wryly and rolled my eyes.

"And that wasn't received as you'd hoped."

I shook my head. "You're an excellent guesser. I'm not allowed to kiss him again until I get my memory back." My words bit at the end.

"But he sleeps with you?"

"He sleeps. I sleep. It's really quite wonderful, but no, we don't, nor have we ever had sex."

"And you'd like to?"

"Yeah, pretty much all the time." The sarcasm came easily.

She sat considering. "Do you think you're fixating on DJ because he's currently the only significant person in your life?"

I shrugged and then shook my head. I'd considered that, but no, I was pretty sure it was more than that. "No, I'm sure, I'm in love with him for real."

She made another little note in my folder and pursed her lips. "I'd like to see you again next week and continue weekly for the next several weeks. If you're agreeable, I'd like to experiment with age regression therapy."

"Hypnosis?" I asked skeptically.

She inclined her head, acknowledging my concern. "It can be extremely helpful in cases where memories are struggling to return to the surface. Please consider it. Now, for your homework," she said with a professional tone. "I'd like you to spend a little time each day journaling. I don't care what, but I want you to get your thoughts down on paper, even flickers of a memory. I also want you to document any dreams or nightmares. The third thing is that I want you to make an effort to speak to another person, other than DJ, every day. It can just be a brief, hello or an in-depth conversation, but either way, I want you talking and intentionally expanding your little circle of friends."

CHAPTER 20

"Fancy meeting you here," the same driver I had earlier said as I entered his car.

"Does this happen often?" I asked smiling back at his friendly face.

"No, but I'd call it a happy coincidence." We chatted all the way back to my house. It was lively and entertaining. Although I relied on strangers driving me often, I rarely spoke to them. This driver's friendly banter made me realize how much I missed contact with other people. My therapist was right, I needed to work toward extending myself and reach out to others. I thanked him as I got out of the car and made the decision to call Mary and Tom.

I sat outside on the back patio to get some fresh air, wearing my ridiculous glasses in the bright winter sun. Not knowing either one of their schedules, I decided to call Tom first. "Tom? Hi, it's Beth. Is this a good time?"

There was a brief pause. "Beth, of course, I'm glad you called. How are you?" I could hear the smile in his voice.

"I'm good. I have therapy homework and I was hoping you and Mary might help keep me accountable."

"Sure, what can we do?"

"My therapist says I have to talk to another human being, other than DJ, every day for a week. I was hoping that you and Mary could be two of those people." Tom laughed his familiar laugh.

"I imagine we can manage that. Mary'll be home in an hour. Do you want me to ask her to call you?"

"That would be great. How are you?" I asked.

"Can't complain. It snowed pretty hard here just after you two left. It was beautiful; wish you'd been here to see it."

"How's Michael?"

"He's great. He didn't want to go back to school this week, but what kid does? How are you doing, sweetheart, really?"

My breath caught like it had in the living room that first day with him. I was simply overcome by his goodness and genuine concern. I couldn't stop the tears that pooled in my eyes. I sniffed. He'd surely know I was crying.

"I'm okay," I finally said once I'd gotten control of my voice.

"How are you spending your days?" he asked.

"I'm here at the house a lot and I'll be seeing the therapist weekly, for a while. I've taken a few walks, too. We went to dinner last night. It was really good."

"Have you been playing your keyboard?"

"Yes." I smiled. Of course, DJ would share that information with his parents.

"Good, keep it up."

I took a short walk around the complex before Mary called me a little over an hour later. She would be delighted to call me every day or more if needed.

"Would you like us to alternate or would you prefer it to be more organic?" she asked.

"I have no idea. I have a couple of other people that I may call, too. Don't feel like it's all your responsibility."

After talking with his parents, I went inside and ate some lunch and marinated a couple of chicken breasts for dinner. I went to the sofa and lay down; I was suddenly very tired from the morning. When DJ came home, I was already awake. I'd begun chopping vegetables for a salad and I'd put the chicken breasts to bake on low.

"Smells good," DJ said as he entered the house. He seemed pleased that I'd still be seeing the therapist weekly, and he was happy that I'd called his parents.

"They'll take their jobs very seriously. Dad may even agree to text you." He laughed.

He offered to take another walk with me after supper. He hadn't had time to go to the gym after school. "You don't have to rush home every day. You can do whatever you normally do."

"This is what I normally do, for now, and I can go tomorrow. I just had duty this afternoon. No big deal. Next week, will you go on the fieldtrip with me and my class?"

"Really? A fieldtrip?"

"Yes, a fieldtrip. It will be fun." I considered for a moment and then agreed.

The next afternoon, Molly called and invited me to go to a movie with her, but I had to politely decline. "Oh, I'm sorry. I wasn't thinking. Darren said you might want to get out some."

"It's very thoughtful, Molly, but I'm not allowed the screen time, yet. Maybe we could go out for lunch or something this weekend," I suggested.

"That would be great. I'm free Saturday."

"It's a date, then. Thank you for calling."

DJ offered to drive me to meet Molly. He was determined to find me another pair of sunglasses before I went to meet her. We went into two different drug stores before we found a decent pair. They were dark as pitch but more fashionable than his dad's.

"That's better," he said.

"I was getting used to the other ones," I said.

"Yes, well, that doesn't mean they look good just because you're getting used to them. Besides, I'm taking you with me next week and teenagers are cruel beasts and might not be willing to be seen with you in public."

Molly was waiting in her car when we arrived at the restaurant. She was smiling her cute smile, waving. She radiated perky. DJ squeezed my hand before I got out of the car. "I'll be back in a bit. I'll wait here for you. No need to rush, I have several errands to run and then we'll go by the grocery store before mass."

Molly was a sweet girl. She was the epitome of a kindergarten teacher. She giggled and drew me in with her smile. Her eyes were wide with wonder and she seemed to be delighted by the simplest things.

She told me about herself and her hobbies. It was only her second year teaching. She loved the kids and the school. Her words were sincere. She asked about my interests and when I would be able to return to school.

"The neurologist won't release me. He's already made it clear that I'm not returning for the rest of the year." Molly looked genuinely disappointed.

Before the end of our meal, she asked about Darren. I wasn't surprised that the conversation turned to him. He was really the only thing we had in common. Her eyes did that fluttering thing when she spoke of him. I couldn't help but smile. I didn't think so, but I wondered briefly if I did the same thing when I said his name to my therapist.

We walked to the front of the restaurant. Darren was parked just outside. I could see him reading on his tablet. I thanked Molly and she gave me a quick, friendly hug. She followed me to DJ's car, and he got out to say hello. We chatted briefly before he walked around and opened the door for me. Molly watched his every move, assessing with her big eyes.

"I'll see you Monday, Darren," Molly said before she stepped back toward her car.

"Thanks, Molly. Have a good rest of the weekend," DJ said smiling.

We picked up a few items at the grocery store and brought them back to the townhouse. "How was lunch?" he asked.

"Good. I had a nice time with Molly. She's a sweet girl."

"But?" he asked, hearing my tone.

"No buts, really. I think she genuinely likes me. She doesn't seem like someone who has any malicious intentions, but I think she'd like to be friends with me to get to you."

"Really?"

"Yeah, really." He looked at me, studying my expression.

"And you don't like that," he smiled, momentarily amused.

"No, I don't like that," I said impatiently.

He laughed. "Good. Let's keep it that way." I made a face and stuck out my tongue.

After the grocery store, we were running a little late for mass. The church was full when we arrived and the order of worship had already begun. Standing near the back of the sanctuary, I felt a little awkward. Something felt off. DJ wasn't singing like he had at his parents' church. He patiently and dutifully allowed me this experience, but I suddenly realized that it was familiar, but not connecting me to any tangible memories. I felt good there, but I didn't necessarily feel whole. I went through the motions and did all the appropriate things, but I was continually drawn back to Christmas Eve and the genuine connection I had to a family and how I was drawn into worship by the music. As soon as the service concluded, I was ready to go.

"Are you okay?" DJ asked when we got into his car.

I shrugged. "I don't know. Something felt different today. Do you ever want to go to church for yourself?"

"Sure, I've gone on occasion." There was hesitation in his voice.

"I can feel an explanation is needed." He intentionally diverted his eyes as he pulled out of the parking lot. "Out with it," I demanded.

"Isn't it obvious?" he asked teasingly.

"No, it's not."

"Well, if I had intentions to marry you, then I also had intentions to convert."

"You'd be willing to do that?" I asked. "Does that align with your beliefs?"

He chuckled and shook his head like I should understand. "Beth, I can still have my own beliefs, but I couldn't have our children considered bastards in the eyes of the church."

"What are you talking about? Could they do that?"

"If I didn't convert and the church decided not to bless our union, then yes. Our marriage would not be sanctified and our children would be illegitimate."

"That's stupid. I figured they'd accept all children, since we aren't supposed to prevent them."

"Well, you aren't supposed to try and make them, either, outside the Sacrament of Holy Matrimony. The Roman Catholic Church has very rigid ideals about what marriage is and isn't."

"Good point," I conceded. "Well, next week, we'll visit a church you like.
Let's find one that has good music and will welcome our illegitimate children,"
I laughed. He eyed me suspiciously.

CHAPTER 21

"It's not a good idea. I don't know anything about your kids."

"Well, I'm asking you to chaperone a fieldtrip. You've seen *Rain Man*, right?"

I nodded. "I think so."

"Well, think about Dustin Hoffman's character on steroids. My kids are off the charts in IQ, but off the other end in their ability to cope and adapt to everyday situations. They have a variety of tendencies and obsessions. Some are diagnosed, but regardless, we do our best to work the strengths and overcome the obstacles. Today is already challenging enough for these guys. Breaking their routine is like removing their limbs; it's crippling. You're kinda like them. You're not quite at home in your body, either. These kids are super-intelligent yet aren't comfortable in a variety of environments. Socially, they're fundamentally different from anyone else."

"What's today's fieldtrip?" I asked.

"The mall."

"Why the mall?"

"They're teenagers and teenagers go to the mall. They will each be given twenty bucks. They have a list of what to purchase. They will work in pairs, but they each have to engage with an employee, make a selection of color among the limited options, and be satisfied with the change given."

When we arrived at school, Darren introduced me to Gary. He was a lanky, teenaged boy with dark brown hair and incredibly blue eyes. Darren explained that he was diagnosed with autism when he was five. He was later reassigned with Asperger's when he was seven. He was high-functioning and intelligent but so socially inept that his classmates called him Sheldon.

Gary wasn't the least bit phased by the information Darren shared with me. It was fact and he was fine with that. "Yeah, my parents really hit the jackpot. They get me, whatever you want to call it, and my brother, Rick, with Down's Syndrome. Do you know the statistical probability of getting both ends of the bell curve?"

"No," I answered. I had no idea how to calculate that.

"Well, it's one in an incredible crap shoot. I could figure out complicated algorithms when I was seven, but I still couldn't tie my shoes. Do you know how much mocking can be made over old-man, Velcro shoes? They have to bring in a college professor three times a week for my math. It's in my IEP, yet it's not written anywhere for anyone not to bully me for Velcro."

"Sit with Gary," Darren instructed. "He gets anxious when we cross the railroad tracks. We have seven to cross to the mall."

"Not if you take the interstate. There are no tracks anywhere near the I-10," a petite brunette interjected. I later learned her name was Roxanne.

"Do you know that Velcro wasn't invented by NASA?" Gary began, picking up with his last train of thought. "It's just a nasty rumor. It was invented in the forties by a man from Switzerland. Their profits are in the millions. Whoever made a profit on shoe laces?" he asked rhetorically.

"Gary, how old are you?"

"I'm fifteen."

"You don't talk like a fifteen-year-old."

"You don't look like a forty-nine-year-old, either."

I stopped and looked at him. "You think I'm forty-nine?"

"Of course, but you've preserved yourself well. You could be in commercials." He examined my face and hands and neck. "My mother would be fascinated."

"How old do I *look*?"

"I'd say close to thirty, but Darren is twenty-eight, so I'm thinking you might be the same age. Window or aisle?"

"Aisle," I said.

"Good, I really wanted the window."

We sat in the first bench, right behind the driver's seat. "Why are you afraid of the railroad tracks?" I asked.

Gary didn't answer. Darren eyed us. He was amused by our interaction. "He thinks when I open the door, the train will somehow fly off the tracks and into the bus."

Gary shook his head. "It's not *exactly* like *that*, Darren. You make it sound completely irrational. There's logical reasoning behind my neurosis."

Darren followed everyone onto the small bus and sat down in the driver's seat. "You drive a school bus?" I asked.

"Yes, I drive a school bus. Being a special ed teacher sometimes requires I drive my students, so when I was doing my first internship, I got paid fifty cents more an hour if I could drive a school bus. So, I learned to drive a school bus."

"How much did it cost you to get your license?" Gary asked.

"I don't know, probably a couple of hundred bucks, total."

"So, it took you four hundred hours to recoup your investment. Did you even work that many hours in a summer?" Gary interjected.

"No, really, you have a post grad degree in special education and nearly enough hours to claim a doctorate, and you drive a school bus?" I asked, unable to conceal the condescension.

"Yep! Talk about job security."

"Are you sure this is the right bus?" Gary asked.

"Yes, Gary, it's the right bus."

"It says number twenty-seven, but it smells different from last time. Did they use a different cleaner to disinfect the buses at the bus barn?" Gary removed his tablet from his backpack and texted a note to himself.

"I've already submitted his application for employment to the school board. He needs a position in quality control or inspections," Darren said as he buckled himself into the driver's seat. He checked the mirrors and then started the bus.

"You live with Darren, right?" Gary asked.

"Yes, we're roommates, but I'm not his girlfriend."

"Oh, I know. He's not sexually active."

I hesitated. "I don't think this is a conversation I need to have with a student, ever." I was very uncomfortable.

"No, Miss Rust, I mean to say that you're his roommate, but not his girlfriend."

"That's correct."

"I was just making an observation that he doesn't have a girlfriend."

"How do you know that?" I was genuinely curious.

"Well, he doesn't have the look of a man who has a girlfriend, and he doesn't smell like a man who has a girlfriend."

"What do they *smell* like?"

"Well, not only do they have traces of a woman's perfume and deodorant, and sometimes the traces of other feminine hygiene products, but also there's an elevated level of pheromones released. I think it's related to their testosterone levels. Sexually active males actually produce more testosterone than non-sexually active males."

I caught Darren's eye in the large, rearview mirror. He smiled, knowing I was getting an ear full of Gary's knowledge. "I haven't yet proven it or found studies to support my theories, but I know it's directly related to pheromone output. Am I boring you?" he asked.

"No, not at all. I honestly didn't want to come today. I've had a rough few weeks, but I'm surprisingly having a good time, so far." I smiled at him reassuringly.

The bus entered the mall parking lot. Darren locked the bus and threw his backpack over his shoulder. The students checked their watches, programmed the app that linked all their phones, and then proceeded into the mall together. It was like watching a SWAT team plan their maneuvers.

"Now, we have the fun of the agenda. Roxanne prefers hers laminated. Any deviation or delay will cause her to hyperventilate. We usually synchronize our watches before we go anywhere together. Nick refuses to engage with odd numbers, so he's forced to carry an odd amount of change after his purchase. Penny will have to choose a color that is not in her current color palette. She's into yellows right now and she has to pick between blue and green. It may take her the entire time to decide."

"What about Tommy?" I asked. I'd heard his name the most.

"Oh, he's going to need to stay with me and Roxanne."

"Why?" I asked.

"So that I don't offend the sales person. It isn't their fault they aren't knowledgeable about every product they sell. I also must practice not criticizing their hair color or their sense of fashion," Tommy said, quoting verbatim what he'd been instructed. He managed to capture Darren's tone and inflection almost perfectly.

"How do you do this?" I asked.

"They're pretty great kids. Sometimes, I imagine I'm traveling with a small village of superstitious, dark-agers." Darren laughed. "That, and they keep me connected to what's most important."

I walked with Gary as each group went in their assigned direction. Gary walked directly toward the candy store. "Why are we going in here?"

"I always go here first. They have candy corn year-round."

"Is candy corn on your list?"

"No, but I will get some with my own money, and if you don't tell, I'll share with you. Do we have a deal?"

I smiled and nodded. I didn't see the harm in a bag of candy corn shared with a boy who went to the candy store first. He was a man after my own heart. He examined each bag carefully and then chose the one with an appropriate number of candies.

"I'd like this divided evenly by three, please," he said to the girl behind the counter.

"Who's the third bag for?" I asked.

"Penny. It will make her happy to hold a yellow bag with yellow candies."

"That's thoughtful of you."

"No, it's really not. I just know if I don't do something, she'll obsess all the way home. I'll offer her a trade."

"I'd still consider that thoughtful."

"Perhaps, but I'm only thinking about myself."

"So, what's *your* challenge?"

"I don't have one." I looked at him skeptically. "This is my third year with Darren. I've already passed his tests. He doesn't think artificial colors are good for kids. I agree with the research, but I still require candy corns if I go to the mall." He paid for the candy bags and then handed me the red bag. "You like red, don't you." It wasn't spoken like a question.

"How do you know that?" I asked.

"Because you have red trim on your shirt, there's red on the tips of your shoe laces, and you're wearing red lipstick. I don't actually like that color on you, but I'm not supposed to say that. Instead, I think I should suggest politely that we go to a cosmetics counter and pick a new color."

"How about not?" I replied. "Is it cool for guys to pick ladies' lip color?"

"No, but that doesn't mean that I couldn't learn. There's always room for improvement."

"So, why did you come today if you've already passed the tests?" I asked trying to change the subject from my offensive lips.

"Because you needed a partner. Besides, I think Darren will be relieved to know you had a good day. He's been very concerned about you."

"How do you know that?" I asked opening my bag and sampling the contents.

"Because he frowns sometimes when he's just standing there with his own thoughts."

"That doesn't mean he's worried about *me*."

"No, but it's the same look when he got the call you were in the crash. Mrs. Ramsey had to cover our class for the afternoon. She's awful and talks to us like we're a bunch of retards. I think her IQ is two-thirds what it should be to work with students. There should be a minimum IQ and personality quotient required to be an educator. My fourth-grade teacher was the only qualified teacher I've

had other than Darren. She recognized true genius. Unfortunately, she doesn't

recognize it, now." His eyes were telling.

"Was *I* your fourth-grade teacher?

"Yes, well, you look like her, but you aren't *her*. Hey! Look! You want to

play video games?" He nearly ran to the arcade and hastily put his money into

the coin changer. He handed me a pair of blue nitrile gloves. "You don't want to

touch anything in here with your bare hands." I closed my bag of candy and

slipped it into my purse. "I performed an experiment for my fifth-grade science

fair with the number of germs detected on one video game and the particular

strains of bacteria and viruses on that one game. I then paid tokens to random

test subjects so that I could swab their fingertips and fingernails. It was

astounding the correlation of germs and player's hands. There was also a high

correlation of nacho cheese which is unable to grow bacteria, itself. My results

were inconclusive as to why bacteria couldn't grow on nacho cheese sauce, but

that was a tangent of my findings and deviated too far from my hypothesis. Was

that too much information?"

"Possibly, yes. What game do you want to play?"

"Pacman!"

"I love that game!"

"I know. Most girls do. It's the pink ghost."

"Really?"

"Yes, really."

He placed tokens in the machine and we began playing. We played for an hour before we'd lost all of our tokens. Then, his watch beeped.

"What's that for?" I asked.

"It says we have twenty minutes to make it back to the food court to eat."

"Do you eat food court food?"

"Yes, I like Chick-fil-A and Subway and even the noodles at that wok place, but I don't like many of Darren's *approved* options. Besides, I think he has a closet Christian thing. I think I'll choose the pretzel place on the way. Do you like pretzels?"

"Yes, but it's not a meal."

"You're right. Do you want a pretzel, anyway?"

"What do you mean by the closet Christian thing?"

"He shops at Hobby Lobby for all of our decorations and art supplies, and he eats Chick-fil-A at least three times a week. You don't think there's some correlation?"

"Sure, I guess," I said as I removed the gloves and discarded them. He then produced scented hand sanitizer and squirted an ample amount into my hands. "Thank you, Gary."

He ordered the pretzels but was specific that the knots were balanced on each side. "I know it doesn't matter to you, but it's important to me. The pretzel makers should be more mindful of symmetry."

When we finally made it back to the food court, everyone was together and on-time. "How was your morning?" Darren asked.

"It was good. I didn't know I was assigned a task."

Darren winked and gave Gary a quick, approving nod, acknowledging his efforts. He then guided his charges toward their respective menu options. Once we were served, I sat between Roxanne and Penny. They didn't say much, but didn't seem offended by my presence, either. Penny was tall and athletic looking. She had pretty coloring.

"Do you swim?" I asked Penny.

"Everyday." She nodded.

"Competitively?"

"Sometimes."

"On a team?" I asked, truly curious.

"Yes, but not today." The subject was instantly closed.

"Roxanne, how are we doing on time?"

She checked her watch and laminated agenda. "We have ten minutes before we must arrive at the bathrooms to relieve ourselves before we depart."

"Do you play any sports, Roxanne?"

"No, ma'am. I don't like to lose, but I bowl sometimes with my brother and his friends, and I play golf with my dad. I don't play against anyone, and I haven't kept score since I was seven. That way, it's called *fun*. The numbers distract me from the game."

Later that evening, I asked more about the students with whom I'd spent the better part of the day. "They all read on-level or above, but I have to bring in a math professor from the university a few times a week. They love movies, but

I'm only allowed to show them for teaching purposes. It took us a month to make it through *The Breakfast Club*. They kept wanting to watch certain parts over and over again.

"Writing is challenging because their minds move about ten times ahead of their patience to write in a conventional way. Sensory issues with pens and pencils can also be an impediment, so they type or write mostly through voice recognition software. They could probably build a bomb faster than you could make a sandwich, and thankfully, their social issues limit their ability to amass an army to take over the world. If they were the least bit charismatic, we'd all be in grave danger." I laughed a little thinking that he was making a joke. "No, I'm serious. It's both horrifying and fascinating to think what they might be capable of. My goal is to help equip them in whatever way I'm able, so they might make their way in the world a little easier."

CHAPTER 22

Later that week, I rode to my next therapy appointment. My driver this time was distracted and not as friendly as the last one. He seemed impatient. I wondered what had him all stressed.

I proudly reported that I'd done all of my homework. She smiled and nodded approvingly. "Excellent. This week, I'd like you to extend your circle a bit more. Find at least one new person to call or reach out to. Can you easily think of one more person?"

I thought for a second and then considered Sadie. "Yes, I will."

"Very good. How is the journaling going?"

"I haven't made any real connections, but I haven't dreamt of the crash in a week. I haven't had any episodes, either, so I've just journaled about current things and past episodes."

She nodded and made a little note in my chart. "Have you considered my suggestion regarding regression therapy?"

I nodded. "I'm willing to try just about anything."

"Good. Let's get started, then. We aren't going to do anything scary or delve into anything uncomfortable. This isn't some crazy, ritualistic mumbo jumbo. I'm going to lead you into a relaxed state and attempt to guide your memories to the surface. This may take several sessions to work through the layers of your psyche. I want you to relax and take a few deep breaths."

I did as she instructed. I closed my eyes and allowed my mind to follow her directions. She gently guided me through several exercises. I wasn't frightened, but I also knew that she was nowhere close to my memories. I couldn't feel any connection at all to the dreams. She was knocking on a door to an empty room as far as I could tell; there was no answer. She didn't seem frustrated by that fact and neither was I.

"I'll see you next week, then," she said as I departed.

That night, I dreamed about the Volvo, again. I was driving it this time and singing out loud to the music on the radio. The scratch on the dashboard caught my eye. I shook my head remembering how it had gotten there.

We didn't need another one of something, but *he* just had to have it. It didn't fit. It was too long and *he* knew it. His resolve and stubbornness won out, and we'd forced it into the car, laughing. As soon as we shut the hatch, he knew he'd scratched the dash. I wasn't mad, though. I was thoroughly amused.

It was the first dream I could recall about the vehicle that wasn't the crash. It was a good dream and I didn't wake startled or frightened or gasping for breath. DJ was already gone when I awoke. I went through my usual daily routine and talked with Tom and Mary at different times during the day. I walked and fixed dinner and journaled.

The next morning, I found Sadie's post-it note amid all of the discharge paperwork from the hospital. Of all the people I could talk to, she could probably be the one that wouldn't think I was a crazy person, or she could tell that I was completely mad.

"Hello, Sadie? This is Beth."

"Oh, honey, it's so good to hear your voice."

"It's good to hear yours, too. How are you?" I asked

"I'm fine, nothing the good Lord can't get me through. How about yourself?"

I hesitated. I really didn't know how to answer that question. Where should I begin? "I'm okay. I was wondering if maybe you have some time to talk? I'm making efforts to expand my friend circle. My therapist has given me homework to speak to other humans besides my roommate. I don't know very many people right now, so I hope you don't mind being included."

She laughed her deep laugh and I could practically see her broad smile through the phone. "I'm off all day today and tomorrow. What does your day look like?"

"I'm pretty much free anytime. Except for therapy appointments and church, I don't get out much. I can't work for the rest of the year and I can't drive, so," I said leadingly, "I can meet you somewhere, too."

"Where do you live?" I gave her my address and she laughed. "Oh, my goodness, we're practically neighbors! How about I come get you for lunch. Marcus will be home after his shift. We can eat together if that's good for you."

"That sounds nice. I'm free the rest of the day."

"Well what a coincidence, so am I. Let me get a few things together and I'll come pick you up. I should be there by noon."

I was relieved to hear her voice; I was relieved to hear that she was pleased to hear from me. I felt a great sense of anticipation at being welcomed into her home again. She pulled up in a seventies, gold Cadillac. I couldn't help but shake my head and smile.

I slid onto the broad leather seat. I felt like a little kid in this huge vehicle. My hands instinctively stroked along the seams in the seats and I could smell the faint traces of pipe tobacco.

"Don't you go hating on my car," she said reading my expression. "Her name is also Sadie and she's prideful. She belonged to my husband. It's my town car, now. I allow my eldest son to keep her running and show her off at area car meets, but I enjoy taking her on a spin as often as I'm able. It's not practical to drive her to and from work. She gets bored just sitting there in the hospital parking lot. She prefers to be appreciated."

I laughed. "I wouldn't dare hate. She's beautiful. Was she new when you bought her?"

"No, but she was only a few years old. My husband saved for over a year to buy her from a friend of his who was being sent overseas. He was still in the military, but was just getting out. He was ready to settle down. He thought it was the best car to raise a family. Little did he know, we probably conceived more than one of them right in that backseat. Sadie's a fertility goddess not to mention being the best-riding sedan made." She laughed her big laugh and drove us back to her house.

I walked into Sadie's home; it was comfortable and easy there. I realized the contrast of something that our townhouse lacked. It didn't have a sense of comfort and welcome. Mary and Tom's house had that same feeling, even Allison and Lance's had some of that same feeling, but Sadie's house reeked of it. Perhaps it was their faith or having kids there; I wasn't sure.

"How long have you lived here?" I asked.

"Oh, gosh, well, nearly forty years, now. My late husband and I bought it the first year we were married and raised five kids together. Now, it's just me and Marcus. He's waiting for his girl to finish her deployment. I expect they'll find a place of their own after that."

"He has a girlfriend?"

"I do," I heard him say as he entered the backdoor. "But she'll be my fiancé as soon as she gets herself back from Afghanistan, and I get a ring on her finger." He walked over and kissed his mama's cheek and then bent down and kissed mine, too. "It's good to see you, Beth. The smell of my mama's cooking lure you back over here?"

"Indeed."

"She's expanding her friend circle. You want to join?" Sadie asked Marcus.

"Sure, but it's not like I have to go to meetings or anything, huh? I'm going to change."

"No, I don't think so. She didn't mention it. You do have to be friendly, though. You think you can handle that?" she hollered toward the back of the house. They both laughed.

Sadie went to the stove and turned it on; the crackle of the fire in the gas burner sounded familiar to me. She gently stirred the pot and took a taste. She didn't replace the lid on the pot and showed me to her small dining room table. She served me a glass of iced tea and sat down next to me.

"So, what's on your mind these days?"

I shrugged. "Not much. It's pretty boring, but I'm surprisingly content."

She smiled. "The Lord gives you what you need, when you need it."

"So, who all is in your friendship circle?" Marcus asked as he reentered the dining area, wearing a pair of jeans and a flannel shirt.

"Darren, of course, his mom, Mary, and his dad, Tom, my co-teacher, Molly, and you and your mom."

"Seems exclusive enough. You may include me. What is the purpose of this little group?"

"My therapist has tasked me with speaking daily with another human being that is not Darren. I suspect it's not healthy to fixate on only one other person in the world. I did pretty well last week, but she told me I needed to expand it by one more this week. I chose your mom. I wonder if I'll get bonus points for including you, too."

Sadie stood and walked back to the stove. "It's ready; let's eat."

Marcus stood and bowed his head. I stood and did likewise. Sadie blessed the food and thanked God for my joining them. She prayed for my memory and for peace in this journey. We served our plates. It was rice and gravy with peas and carrots on the side. She offered me some bread and butter and refilled my glass. I was so full after we ate, that I could hardly bend in the middle.

The conversation was good and we laughed and carried on and joked. It was fun to observe their generational interaction. I liked the idea of family and connectedness that ran deeper than what I currently had. I wanted real, genuine interaction and the trust that came from committed love.

"Marcus," I began, "Would you be willing to drive me past the crash site?" He hesitated and eyed Sadie. "You're the only one who knows."

He looked to his mama for confirmation. She shrugged. "Can't hurt. She needs to know and see."

Marcus nodded. "Sure. I'd be glad to. Darren hasn't driven you by?" I shook my head. "It's not close. You okay with a little drive?" I nodded.

"How do you eat like this in the middle of the day?" I asked after my second helping. "I'm ready for a nap."

"This isn't always the middle of our day. Sometimes it's the beginning and sometimes it's the end, depending on what shifts we're currently working," Marcus explained.

I yawned big. I couldn't help myself. "Do you mind taking me home. If not, I may crash right here."

Sadie patted my hand and gave a nod to Marcus. "Do you mind if I take you?" he asked.

"Not at all." I stood and placed my dishes in the sink and began rinsing them. Sadie shooed me off and gave me a big hug. "I'll call you tomorrow and check in," she said. I thanked her and walked toward the Cadillac.

"I'm not allowed to drive Sadie," Marcus said as he approached another car parked on the street.

"Why not? Did you lose a bet or something?"

He laughed. "No. When I was seventeen, I took her out without permission. She didn't take too kindly to that and broke down on me. As you can imagine, it didn't go over well. My daddy was beyond enraged. He was a big man. I thought he was going to kill me for sure. My lifetime consequence is that I may never drive her again. She can sense me."

"You're pretty superstitious."

"It has nothing to do with superstition. I know where I'm not welcomed."

Just as Marcus was pulling into our complex, I had a thought. "Marcus, when can you take me back to the scene of the crash? I know you showed me the pictures, but I'd like to have a clearer understanding of what happened, and you're the only one who can tell me."

"I don't go in until late tomorrow. I can take you before lunch."

CHAPTER 23

I was asleep when DJ got home from school. He found me sacked out on the sofa, but I soon rallied. I was almost giddy all evening. A day out with new friends was just what I needed, not to mention Sadie's cooking.

DJ noticed a marked difference in my demeanor. We laughed together while we ate grilled cheese sandwiches. I ate a little, but I was still full of rice and gravy. I played the keyboard and texted with Tom. He cracked me up. Some of his responses made no sense. Autocorrect was not his friend. I recorded myself playing and sent him and Mary an audio clip. They seemed pleased with our regular interaction.

I sat next to DJ on the sofa. I took his hand and cuddled in next to him while he read. "DJ, may I interrupt you for a moment?" He muttered his ascent. "I'm going out with Marcus tomorrow morning."

He looked up from his tablet. "Did he ask you out?" His jaw tightened slightly and his eyes were unnecessarily focused. He let go of my hand.

"No, he's doing me a favor. I want him to take me to the crash site. I want to see, and he's pretty much the only person who can tell me."

"Are you sure that's a good idea?" I nodded. I was sure. "I don't like it, Beth. What if it causes another seizure? What if it makes you have another nightmare?"

I shrugged. "I'm willing to take that risk."

"I don't think it's a good idea," he said firmly. "I won't allow it."

"I'm not asking your permission. I just thought you should know what I was planning on doing."

He looked angry, almost like I'd betrayed him, somehow. "Who are you going to ask to sleep with you afterwards, me or Marcus?"

I sat up and pushed myself away from him. My stomach hurt like his words had punched me right in the gut. I stood and clutched my stomach and held my hand over my mouth. I was afraid I was going to be sick. He could read the pain in my eyes. He knew he'd crossed a line. "That was hateful. Why are you being mean?" I asked. I was so frustrated and unable to stop the tears that flowed down my cheeks. Why did I have to cry? I wanted to prove a point.

He set his jaw and lowered his eyes. "I didn't mean it that way."

"Well, what way did you mean it?" I asked angrily.

"I meant that if he takes you and gets you all stirred up, who's going to be the one there to pick up the pieces? Who's going to be the one who sits with you all night at the hospital?" His voice rose along with his frustration.

"I've only asked you to sleep with me because you said I could. If it's such a bother, I won't do it again," I said defensively.

His jaw clinched, and I fisted my hands trying to regain some control. I couldn't read any trace of his thoughts on his face. I couldn't tell if he was angry with me or himself. He wouldn't look me in the eye.

"There are questions I need to answer. Please accept that." He wasn't accepting anything. He just sat there, masked and unmoving. "I'm going to bed. Goodnight," I said in a huff. "And for your information, Marcus has a girlfriend, a serious one. It's nothing like that between us. I've only spoken to the man three times."

He looked up and glared at me. "Four," he corrected. "You've spoken to him four times."

I glared back at him but it was useless. I hated the distance between us. I knew I needed to reconcile this before I went upstairs. I took a deep breath and began again. I wouldn't go to bed like this. It wouldn't do me any good; I wouldn't be able to sleep if we weren't right.

"DJ," I began with a softer tone, "I would appreciate your support on this. If you'd like, I can make it a time when you're both available. Maybe he'll have some time over the weekend. I'm sorry, too, that I mistook your comment. I know the old Beth probably didn't need three or four conversations with a man before she, well, had sex with him," I blurted. "I'm not that person, but it hurts that maybe you doubt me." My voice caught on the last few syllables.

He didn't move or speak. He just sat there looking at me. I wiped the last of my tears from my eyes. "Goodnight," I said, again, and walked up the stairs with a measured pace. I went through my evening routine like a robot and fell onto my quilt, quietly sobbing. My wonderful day completely dissolved into tears.

It was probably midnight when I finally heard DJ come upstairs. I heard him hesitate in front of my door. He knocked lightly. "Beth, are you sleeping?" he whispered into the mostly dark room.

"No." I sniffed.

"Are you still crying?" I could hear his remorse.

"Yes, some, but not as much."

"I'm sorry. I know you need to do hard things to get better. I'm frustrated that I can't fix everything for you, and I'm jealous that you're spending time with another man."

"You're jealous?" I rolled over to look at him.

"I hate to admit it, but yes. I reason that I'm being protective and looking out for you, but I can't justify my reactions; they're primal and deeply rooted. It's definitely jealousy."

I sat up. "I'm sorry, too. I shouldn't have just sprung it on you like that. I was so excited when he agreed. I feel like I can finally get a mental picture of what happened."

I think I saw his shadow nod. "Goodnight, Beth."

"DJ," I began.

"No," he said flatly.

"But I think you need me as much as I need you." He sighed. He had to feel the pull from across the room. "I want to hold you and reassure you, somehow. Please," I begged. Did I have the power to draw him to me? "Please," I said again. "You know neither of us is going to get any sleep if you don't."

I'm pretty sure he rolled his eyes before he gave in. I got up and blew my nose and brushed my teeth again. When I returned, he was already in the bed. I cuddled in next to him and he kissed my head. I adjusted my breaths with his, and within a minute, we were both sound asleep.

The next morning, I felt him leave the bed when his alarm sounded from the other room. Once I heard the water run in his shower, I found my bathrobe and went downstairs. I made him a cup of coffee and an egg sandwich to go. Food was my meager attempt at a peace offering. He thanked me and kissed my forehead. "I hope something good comes of today."

"Me, too. Have a good day, *Dear*."

"You, too, *Darling*," he said and smiled his genuine, DJ smile.

***

When Marcus picked me up in the squad car, he was in full uniform. We drove through town and then for another twenty minutes along the interstate. He then got off at an exit and backtracked along the opposite side, heading back home. He pulled over and stopped the car. I sat there just looking over into the wooded area a few yards from the road.

"All three vehicles were traveling southbound. When I arrived, the 18-wheeler was jackknifed in the center of the road right here. The cab was tilted over. The other vehicle plowed into those trees; your vehicle ended up there." He pointed through the windshield to a place next to the trees.

"May I get out and see? May I get closer?"

"The grass is pretty high but sure." Marcus waited for a break in the traffic before he got out of the car and walked around to open the door for me. The noise of the cars passing was loud and intimidating, but they slowed slightly as they approached the patrol car on the side of the road.

IMPACT

I stepped out onto the shoulder. The gravel crunched under my boots and the wind gusted with each passing vehicle. Marcus walked down the slope with me. He held my arm twice to help me balance.

"Here. This is where your car was. It was facing this way." He used his large hands and body to recreate the scene. "When I arrived, you were unconscious. I tried to get your attention. Your airbag was partially covering your face and you were bleeding, but I could assess through the windshield that you were still breathing." He looked at me cautiously making sure that what he was telling me wasn't too upsetting.

My expression was carefully neutral, so he continued. "It was then that I approached the second vehicle and called for backup and a second ambulance was dispatched. When I reached the white Volvo, I knew the occupants were most likely gone. You can just sense death sometimes." Marcus shuddered slightly before he took off with the story, not being as guarded with his words. "The tree was practically in the middle of the vehicle; it could have been planted there. The tow truck driver had to break out his chainsaw before he could remove the vehicle. They worked a long time to get that couple out. Their bodies were a mangled mess. The best we can figure is that the 18-wheeler collided with the Volvo and sent it careening over the slick road and into those trees.

"You were most likely trying to swerve out of the way and plowed into the Volvo, forcing it further into the trees." He was using his hands again. I followed him as he led me to the second vehicle's location. "The driver was nearly split in two by the steering column. The airbags didn't have a chance to save them. They were forced into these trees at an incredible speed. You can still see the damage. You know, I enjoyed physics in high school, but this is when you realize how deadly those formulas can be. The strangest thing, though, when they extracted the couple from the vehicle, the driver, the woman, was clutching to the passenger's chest so tightly they had to cut his clothing to set him free from her. She was literally hanging onto him for dear life."

I felt a wave of nausea and my hands were clammy. I could feel my right hand form a fist reflexively. It wasn't an actual memory. It was more like reconnecting with a dream when you first awaken. The traces of the dream were just faint threads of connection and made no real sense when I spoke them aloud.

Some things Marcus explained made perfect sense. Others, not so much. I could sense the other person in the vehicle. I was reaching for him, but my hands were empty. My heartbeat increased and I could feel my breaths growing shallow. Everything he said was so close to my nightmares.

Marcus continued and then retraced his steps, returning to my vehicle's location, and then described how he'd climbed onto the 18-wheeler to assess the driver's condition as he'd done on the day of the crash.

"That poor fellow was in bad shape. He had to be airlifted. He was conscious and complaining of chest pains." Marcus' words were far away, now. "The firetruck and ambulances arrived within minutes. They were able to get you out pretty quickly."

I closed my eyes and could hear them in the distance. I could hear the sound of breaking glass and the men's voices shouting orders. I was there and I could hear everything going on around me.

"Beth, Beth," I heard Marcus' voice. His large hands were on my shoulders. He was shaking me gently. I forced myself to take a deep breath and return to the present. "Are you alright?" he asked, concerned.

"Yes," I finally answered. "I can hear it. I can hear the shouting men and the sirens." I opened my eyes and smiled. I was breathing heavily, now, and my heart was racing, but I was so happy to recall something. "Thank you," I panted, catching my breath. Marcus wasn't sure if he should return my smile. I could read concern all over his face. His eyes were wide, examining me for shock. "I'm good," I assured him. He wasn't convinced, but he nodded and gave me a little smile anyway.

"Come on, let's go. I think you've had enough."

CHAPTER 24

I watched the crash site as we passed it on the way back into town. "Are you hungry? May I buy you lunch," I asked.

"Sure. What are you in the mood for?"

"Do you know any good burger joints?"

"I think I know a couple," he chuckled.

We were parked in the patrol car, eating outside of an old drive-in. A huge burger lay in the wrapper on my lap. I had used about ten napkins already and had barely made a dent in it. The onion rings were amazing! Marcus insisted that I order the chocolate shake. He was a genius.

"To be so little, you sure do pack it away," he commented.

"Is that a good thing?" I asked.

"Most women don't eat in front of men. They pick at food and complain about their waistlines."

"What's your girlfriend like?"

He smiled broadly and shook his head. "She's about my height. She's taller than me when she wears heels. I like it when she wears heels." He smiled at the image in his mind. "She's a lot like you, though, fair skin, brown eyes."

"Your girlfriend's white?" I asked, wiping the side of my mouth.

"Yes. Does that surprise you?"

"A little. Where'd you meet her?"

"We were stationed together. I didn't reenlist after my daddy passed. She and I kept in touch, and one thing led to another. I see her as often as I'm able. Her unit was deployed six months ago. She'll be home in less than a year. I miss her like crazy. I pray to God she says yes."

"Does she eat in front of you?"

He laughed. "Yes! She's a good cook, too. Part of the reason I fell in love with her. That, and she can take me to the mat every time we spar. She's a blackbelt."

"Impressive. You're a pretty big guy. What does she do in the military?"

"She's a systems analyst. She also writes programs on the side."

His phone rang, interrupting our conversation. He checked the number and answered it. "Yes, I can come by. Now? Okay, but I have to be on duty by four." He disconnected and turned to me. "Do you need to be home right away? I need to go by my brother's shop. He's got a truck he wants me to look at. It's on the way back to your house."

"I don't mind, if you don't mind me tagging along. Is he a car dealer?"

"Sometimes. He's a mechanic and resells vehicles he's repaired. He has a separate lot that he allows folks to park their cars. He makes a little on the side by allowing sellers to park their cars there."

"I'll hopefully be able to drive, soon. Maybe I can look around."

Marcus was in the market for a new truck, well, a new to him truck, and his brother was helping him look. "I have a strong suspicion that Sadie Cadillac corrupted my last truck. It was running fine when I moved home, and then little by little it began to break down. She's got it in for me."

"I think you need to learn the definition of superstitious."

Marcus and his oldest brother, Tony, went to inspect a vehicle on the other end of the lot, a gray truck. I wandered around among the other cars and ended up behind the shop. There, parked between an old truck and a cute little sportscar, was a black sedan. I was drawn to it instantly. I traced my hand along the hatchback and followed it to the driver's side door. I looked around to see if I could find someone to unlock it for me, but I was alone. I tried the handle and it opened easily. I slid onto the leather seat and placed my hand on the steering wheel. *This was nice.* I liked the way the leather felt under my hands and the smooth contours of the gear-shift and the contrasting, woodgrain trim. *The woodgrain trim…*

My breath caught. I'd only seen this view in my dreams. I closed my eyes and allowed myself to relax into the comfortable seat. I eased my head back onto the headrest and felt the way the seat pressed against my back and ribs. I held onto the steering wheel and imagined driving. I could see the wipers going back and forth in steady increments combatting the constant splattering of rain across the windshield.

It may be a different color, but I knew every inch of this interior. I smiled to myself. It was a happy place. There had been laughter here and love and connection. How many miles had we driven? Would we need to stop again before we got home? The tank was nearly full. Oldies played on the radio. We were singing along.

I adjusted the wipers, decreasing the speed. The sun peaked through the band of clouds and I smiled at the most amazing rainbow. "Look, honey," I said aloud and pointed into the sky. It looked like we were going to drive right into the band of colors. A momentary distraction. Just then, a wave of fear washed over me. I clutched the steering wheel, but I couldn't avoid the inevitable. I couldn't anticipate the sporadic movements of the 18-wheeler. It happened too fast. I couldn't stop. There was nowhere to go.

The forceful impact sent us careening out of control. Metal grated upon contact. Sparks flew and the force jerked us around against our seatbelts. I couldn't retain control of the vehicle. My hands clutched the steering wheel even tighter, but it was no use. We were going into the trees and I knew it would end there.

The pain and pressure returned. The familiar sense of drowning and the inability to breathe. I had to get to him. I had to know he was okay. There was no response. The emotional pain of his absence was greater than the physical pain in my torso. I sobbed because the wave of sadness was greater than the wave of fear.

Amid that sadness, I heard or maybe sensed another impact, even more forceful than the first. The face of another victim flashed across my limited line of vision as her vehicle swerved out of control and nearly flew into mine. Her eyes were full of fear and then resignation. This was the end; we could see death in each other's eyes. Even in the odd colors of the rainbow's reflection, I could see her face clearly; her face was *mine*. I didn't bother to brace myself. Resignation. Impact. Light. Cold. Darkness.

I was rigid and unmovable. I was screaming, hysterically. I couldn't release the steering wheel, and my right hand was fisted into a tight grip against the passenger seat.

"Beth, Beth," Marcus' voice was far away again. "Damn it, girl, talk to me! Tony, help me." Large hands unwrapped my fingers from around the steering wheel while others scooped me gently from the seat. "Call Mama."

Marcus cradled me close to his chest as he carried me into the shop. I sobbed into his shoulder. He lay me gently on an old sofa and Tony placed a damp cloth over my forehead. "Yeah, it's Marcus. No, she's not responding. She's just staring out and crying. We could hear her screaming from across the lot. Okay, we'll meet you there. No, I don't have his number. Yeah, I'll check her phone."

He patted me down and pulled my phone from my back pocket. He held me close and rocked me gently, soothingly, as he scrolled through my contacts. He texted a message, one-handed, while I clung to him. I couldn't regain control of my body. My chest constricted making my breathing and heartbeats sporadic. My eyes were opened, but I couldn't see anything. I was in total darkness. It was horrifying.

Marcus made to lift me from the sofa. I went rigid, refusing to go. "Come on, Beth, I'm taking you to the hospital. Mama's going to meet us there." I went rigid again and lurched forward, vomiting; my entire lunch wasted across the floor. More hands wiped my face and the cool cloth returned.

Moments later, I was in the backseat of the patrol car. Tony was riding next to me, holding me securely, wiping my face. I felt clammy and pale, like all the blood had drained out of me. Marcus turned on the sirens as we pulled out onto the road. They were surprisingly loud in my ears. Sirens were a good sign that help was on its way. Sirens meant I'd soon be out of pain, reliving the impact in waves. The darkness wasn't painful. I settled into it like a cloak of protection.

I was coming around as we entered the hospital's emergency entrance. I turned to look at Tony. He had his mama's eyes. I blinked and made a weak effort at a smile. "She's coming around," he said. I could see more clearly now and make eye contact.

I rested my head on Marcus's shoulder as he lifted me from the backseat and carried me through the sliding doors of the ER toward the reception desk.

"Lt. Miller," I heard a pleasant voice say, "your mother called. Follow me. Dr. Saunders is on his way." He followed the nurse through a separation in the curtains. Marcus laid me gently on the narrow bed and the nurse raised the side rails before she began her preliminary examination.

Sadie arrived moments later. "What happened?" Sadie asked, looking at both of us. I looked to Marcus. I couldn't answer with the thermometer in my mouth.

"We went to the crash site. She was fine, I swear. Then, we ate lunch and went by the shop. She was looking around at the cars. When we found her, she was screaming and clutching the steering wheel. It took us both to pry her off. She's got a fierce grip."

"Honey, can you recall what happened?" I nodded. I felt like my eyes were wide and permanently opened. Everything was clear and bright. The nurse removed the thermometer and moved to my other side. Sadie moved in and took my hand and looked searchingly into my eyes. She was performing her own examination. "You're okay, now, aren't you." She didn't say it like a question.

I nodded again. She could tell I wasn't completely crazy. "What did you tell Darren?" I asked Marcus.

"I texted him; he's on his way. I didn't say anything, except I that was taking you to General." He handed me my phone. He was disappointed. I could tell he was upset with himself for agreeing to help me.

As soon as the doctor arrived, Marcus excused himself. "I have to be on duty in an hour. I'll check in with you, later." He kissed his mama on the cheek and then patted my shoulder.

"Thank you, Marcus. Please thank Tony for me, too." He nodded once and left the room.

"Beth, how are you feeling?" Dr. Saunders asked.

"I'm okay. My head doesn't even hurt."

"I'm going to need to do another EEG and we might want to bump up our timeline for another CT scan."

"It wasn't a seizure," I said flatly.

He looked at me skeptically. "How can you be sure?"

"It was different. I swear. It's not the same."

"Can you describe what happened?" Dr. Saunders asked.

I told him about driving to the crash site. I explained how for the first time I had a memory, a genuine memory, not a dream. "Please believe me. It wasn't like the seizure." Then I explained how I sat in the car at the shop and my mind was flooded with the entire accident. "It all came back in a rush. I couldn't stop the memories any more than I could prevent the crash. I could hear everything, and although I couldn't respond, I knew everything that was happening to me. I didn't when I had the seizure. Do you see?"

"I'd still like to be thorough."

"I understand. Run the tests, but I don't think you're going to find anything," I said confidently.

Sadie grinned slyly as Dr. Saunders left to speak with the nurses. "You're aware, he only lets certain patients speak to him that way. You must be special."

"I sort of lost it at our last appointment. I think he's afraid I'll make another scene."

"Is there anything you're not telling us?"

I cocked my head to one side. "What do you mean?"

"There's something you're not saying about your memory."

I shrugged. It was all too crazy. "It was horrifying. I was reliving the entire incident, the pain, and seeing it all in slow-motion and in real time, simultaneously. I can't explain what I saw. It doesn't make any sense. I need to process it a bit more before I can put it into words."

"Well, when you're ready, I'll listen, you hear?"

The nurse wheeled me to the EEG machine and began hooking me up to the tiny electrodes. I lay there for an hour in total darkness. I was hungry and bored and rather impatient to be released. I thought about the image of my frightened and resigned face, my spikey hair with the bleached tips, my red car thrust through the rainbow.

The rainbow...

Sadie and Darren were together when I was returned to the ER. Darren was wearing his gym clothes. Marcus' text must have interrupted his workout. He stood and walked toward me as the nurse helped me onto the narrow bed. He couldn't conceal his disappointment, either.

"I'm sorry, but it's not what you think."

He glared at me and shook his head. "It apparently doesn't matter what *I think*," he whispered, barely containing his rage.

I lowered my gaze, ashamed for having disappointed him. Nothing I could say would convince him at that moment, so I thought it best to keep silent. He would be careful not to make a scene in front of Sadie. I could feel her watching our exchange. She stood and patted my hand.

"I'll leave you both to it. Darren, would you like a cup of coffee?" she asked.

I looked up to see his hardened features. He shook his head, but didn't divert his eyes from mine. "No, thank you."

"DJ, it's not another seizure. I didn't do anything bad, I promise."

"Really? Nothing bad? You're in the ER because it wasn't *bad?*" His words stung like they tasted bitter.

"Please, let me explain," I pleaded and made to take his hand. He casually moved his hands away and stuck them in the pockets of his hoodie. His eyes were still hard. "I'm sorry for making you worry, but I'm not sorry for having the first actual memory come to the surface. I'd do it all again, if it meant knowing more."

"What the hell, Beth? Are you serious?" he asked, disbelieving.

"Yes."

CHAPTER 25

Sadie and Dr. Saunders returned together. "I don't like saying it, but you were right. It wasn't a seizure. I think you and your therapist may have to discuss some post-traumatic stress symptoms in your next session. I'll be contacting her."

"Thank you, Dr. Saunders. I feel fine, now. May I go home?"

He looked at Darren. "Anything you'd like to know?" He had to be sensing the tension between us.

"Do you work with many PTSD patients?"

Dr. Saunders nodded. "More than I care to. Head trauma doesn't typically occur in calm and serene settings. There are usually extreme circumstances. They tend to influence the recovery."

"Does PTSD cause the person to be unusually stubborn and stupid?" DJ looked directly at me.

"No, not the stubborn part." He eyed me, then, too, and raised his eyebrow, challenging me to disagree with his assessment. "You're free to go, Beth. I think your therapist is more qualified to help you deal with this side of your recovery. After what I've seen with the EEG, I'm satisfied to see you again in a couple of months. I'll have my nurse call you to make the appointment."

"Thank you," I said, genuinely.

Sadie came over and looked at me again. "You scared my boys half-to-death. I thought I was the only one able to put the fear of God in them, but I was mistaken."

"I'm sorry, Sadie. I'm so embarrassed. I threw up at the shop. I just wanted to know."

She placed her large hand lovingly across my cheek. "Curiosity has killed many a fair cat. Be careful." I nodded.

She turned to Darren, then, and looked him straight in the eyes. "Don't hold this against her. She didn't know. Gentleness," she said, and this time, he nodded obediently. He wouldn't dare mess with her, either.

"I'll call and check on you tomorrow." She leaned over and hugged me.

The ride home was quiet. The rest of the evening was quiet. I made us each a sandwich and waited for DJ to come down after his shower. We were much nicer to each other after we ate.

"Do you want to talk about what happened?" he asked.

"Yes, I would." I told him about being at the crash site and understanding what Marcus had found when he arrived. I could remember bits and then I could hear the sirens and men giving commands, but not like when I'd dreamt it. The accuracy was different, somehow.

"You didn't lose it there?" DJ asked.

"No, I didn't. We went and had lunch and then we went by Tony's shop. I was just wandering around the lot looking at cars while they went to look at a truck. One caught my eye and I sat down inside of it. I haven't been behind the wheel of a car since the accident. It was then that the memories flooded in. I couldn't stop them. I was overcome with the feelings and the memories and the emotions." I could feel the wave of sadness touch the edges of my eyes and tears welled in them against my attempts to avoid crying. "DJ, I felt and saw everything. Some things were off, like I could see both sides of the accident. It was horrific, but there was the most amazing rainbow." My voice cracked and I had to wipe away the tears streaming down my cheeks.

His expression softened and he moved closer to me. "Were you in a great deal of pain?" I nodded. He sighed. He didn't like knowing that. "Come here," he whispered and allowed me to lean into him.

"I'm truly sorry. I just want to wake up and know, you know?" He wrapped his arms around me, and I held onto him, filling my lungs with our closeness. "DJ, how can I convince you that this was actually a good day?"

He shook his head and chuckled low in his chest. I smiled a little. I knew we'd be okay and that he had forgiven me for disappointing him earlier.

***

"I don't need you to drive me to the therapist. I can Uber. Remember, I'm supposed to talk to people other than you," I said in a singsong voice.

"I know, but I can take you today. My kids are in an assembly all morning about the dangers of drug abuse, and then they'll have the fun of Cajun dancing with a local band after lunch. They can manage alone for a few hours."

"Who's in charge?" I asked.

"No one. They can be mainstreamed for assemblies and school functions. They know I expect them to participate fully or they'll be required to do supplemental resourcing."

"Punish work?" I clarified. He laughed.

***

I dutifully entered the therapist's office. She smiled and eyed Darren in the waiting room. He smiled his DJ smile and gave a little wave. She asked how I was feeling. She asked me to explain in detail what happened the day before. She was pleased that I had journaled some before I went to sleep.

"Dr. Saunders mentioned PTSD. Is that what you think I'm experiencing?"

"I think you definitely have reason to be. The memory you describe is from different perspectives. Have you noticed how you describe it?"

I nodded. "It doesn't make sense. I can see different parts from different angles. I see the beginning from the white Volvo and the end from the red Honda. I don't know how that's possible." I could hear the frustration in my voice.

"How have you done on your other assignments?" she asked changing the subject.

"I like how you do that."

"What?"

"Change the subject when it gets frustrating for me."

"You're very intuitive, Beth, and extremely observant."

I smiled, satisfied. I'd been right about her tactics. "I've done well. I added not one, but two, to my circle of friends, Sadie and her son, Marcus. Sadie was my nurse in the hospital and Marcus happened to be the first officer on the scene. Convenient, wouldn't you say?"

"Indeed." She scribbled something in my chart.

"So, how do you treat PTSD?" I asked.

"Delicately. Patiently and with an understanding that you may not be fully aware of what may trigger an episode. Keeping physically, mentally, emotionally, and spiritually healthy, along with a conscious awareness of your environment, are the best defenses for your mind. I can only help with two of those areas. The physical and spiritual are your responsibility. The awareness will come in time."

She led me through a brief relaxation exercise. Like before, it didn't bring anything to the surface. The knocking she did at my mind's door, was light and not the least bit agitating. I made my next appointment and she said to continue as I'd been doing. Contact with others was vital to my well-being.

DJ dropped me off back at the townhouse, confident that I could manage myself for the afternoon. Sadie called me after lunch. Tom and Mary texted me, too. They didn't know anything about the incident, so Mary called me right away and wanted to know more about what happened. She was the only person that responded appropriately in my opinion. She actually sounded happy and matched my enthusiasm about remembering something significant, even if it had made me go a little crazy.

"Beth, it sounds like you've made a breakthrough. I can't wait to tell Tom. This is absolutely wonderful! Please tell the officer that we appreciate his willingness to help you." Her warmth and her smile radiated through my phone.

That afternoon, I started a pot roast. Before he'd agree to let me pick one out on our last grocery run, I had to convince DJ that I could cook it. I was right. Apparently, my old self paid close attention to food preparation, I just never implemented any of that knowledge. The house was smelling rather amazing. The potatoes and carrots were almost tender.

As I was closing the oven, DJ called. "Hey, do you have plans for dinner?"

"Yes, it's nearly done, why?"

"Is there enough for three?"

I hesitated. "Sure, it's pot roast. We'll have leftovers for days. Who's coming with you?"

"Molly," he said, like she was standing right there with him.

"Great," I said, trying to evoke a positive response. Would he be able to read my expression over the phone?

"Alright, I'm nearly finished, here, and then I'm going to the gym. Molly and I should be there by 4:30 at the latest."

"Is she working out with you?" I asked.

"Yes, she just joined our gym last month." *Convenient*, I thought.

***

Molly arrived a few minutes before DJ. She was all smiles when she hugged me. "How are you?" she asked.

"I'm good. Thanks."

"Darren will be here in a few minutes. He said he wanted to go by the store on his way home. It smells amazing. What are we having?"

"Pot roast. How was your day? How are the kids?"

"It was good. This year is much better than last year. I finally joined the gym. You were right. It's a nice place and super convenient. I wish I had done it sooner. You were right about that personal trainer, too. He's adorable and so helpful. Darren introduced me and he showed me around. He said he could give me a proper workout with the machines when I go back. Maybe you'd like to go with me, sometime."

I smiled. She was enticingly sweet. "Thank you, Molly. I might start doing that." I walked over to the stove and turned everything off. It would keep warm in the oven until we were ready to eat. I took out a block of cheese from the refrigerator and a box of crackers and placed them on a plate on the counter. Molly and I nibbled a bit while we waited.

Darren arrived and came through the door with a loaf of French bread and a bouquet of fresh flowers cradled in his arm. "Mmmm, smells good. I could get used to this." He placed his keys on the entryway table as he passed.

The flowers were beautiful and I smiled. I felt a little foolish. Surely, he wasn't bringing me flowers. He was just trying to brighten up our home; they would make a pleasant addition to the kitchen table, I reasoned.

"Here, these are for you," he said as he presented me with the flowers.

"Thank you. They're lovely. What's the occasion?" I stammered a little, completely taken by surprise. I lifted the bouquet to my nose, taking in their light fragrance.

"Sadie said, *gentleness.*" I nodded, understanding. *Thank you, Sadie*, I thought to myself. "I thought you might like them, and they promised to make you smile if I brought them home," he said as he kissed my cheek. I caught his eyes. They weren't mocking or joking at all. "And they didn't lie." He smirked knowingly. Was he offering me a reprieve?

My smile didn't waiver, but my stomach did that tightening thing, and I know my eyes did that ridiculous fluttering thing, too. I wondered if that's what it felt like to swoon. Had Molly not been standing there, I may have attacked him. I cleared my throat. "Do you want to get cleaned up before dinner?"

"Yes, I'll go upstairs and change." He turned and took the stairs two-at-a-time.

"That's so thoughtful. He's got to be the most thoughtful man," Molly commented.

"He's pretty great," I said absentmindedly. I felt a little vulnerable, standing there, holding the flowers. I supposed I should put them in water or something. I looked in the cabinet above the fridge and found a vase. I trimmed the edges of the stems with the kitchen scissors and arranged them. Molly helped and chatted easily around me.

We snacked on a couple more crackers and then set the table. DJ came down the stairs, looking pretty adorable in jeans and a button-down with his hair still damp from the shower. I took dinner from the oven and served our plates.

DJ poured us each a glass of wine and Molly placed them on the table. I sat down last. "This is going to be good," he said as he inspected the contents of his plate. He hesitated before he picked up his fork. He was considering something. "Let's return thanks," he said.

I nodded instinctively but didn't know why. We never prayed. He took my hand and then Molly's. I reached across the small table and took Molly's hand. She smiled like it was familiar to her, too. Was DJ doing this for Molly's benefit or his own? I'd never heard him pray aloud before. He cleared his throat and gave thanks. It was a simple prayer, but sincere. I liked it; I liked all of it.

Dinner was delicious. Without tooting my own horn, I was a pretty good cook. We laughed together and Molly was funny and relaxed with us. I watched their interactions with new eyes. Molly's sweetness poured out easily. Her smile and eagerness for Darren's attention wasn't much different from the way she spoke to me. It was just her way.

DJ got up from the table and turned on the oven. "How about some dessert?" He opened the drawer inside the fridge and pulled out a tube of cookie dough. Molly and I both clapped like little kids. Maybe, deep down, we had more in common than I first imagined.

DJ cut a few slices, rolled them out into little balls, and placed them on a cookie sheet. He then cut a huge chunk and thirded it. He handed me and Molly each a wedge of the cookie dough and I took a sip of wine. "This wine pairing goes well with pot roast and cookie dough. How did you know?"

"It's already in the Bonus category," DJ smiled as he placed the rest of the tube in a zip baggie.

Molly helped me clear the table and DJ loaded the dishwasher while the cookies baked. "You ladies up for a movie tonight? It's one of my last nights off before classes begin."

"No thanks. I need to leave in an hour. I have duty in the morning and I want to be sure to be on time. I hate morning duty. I much prefer afternoons."

We visited some more over dessert, just casual conversation. Molly spoke a little about her family and how she'd stayed local after she finished her education degree. Her parents wanted her to come home. They didn't think a young, single woman had any business living in town alone. She argued that she didn't technically live alone because she had two roommates and they shared a house near the university. They just didn't understand her need to live independently.

"They think I should be married already and starting a family. I'm not ready for that. I keep toying with the idea of taking some extra classes to make them think I'm not really finished with school. I'd like to get library certified, but I think for now, I'll just keep teaching and enjoying the kids. Mrs. Moore has been really supportive since you've been out. She thinks I can handle it; it's very encouraging."

Molly excused herself before eight-thirty. She thanked us for dinner and expressed hope that she'd like to do it again. "Hey," she began before she left. "I was wondering, if y'all don't have plans Saturday, would you like to attend a concert with me?"

"What kind of concert?" I asked.

"Well, it's actually a collaboration of choirs and some local ensembles."

"Anyone we know playing?" DJ asked.

"Well, no one you probably know," Molly began and then hesitated. She tucked her hair back behind her ear and looked down. Her ear was the slightest shade of pink darker. "There's this guy from church. His name is Dan; he sings and plays violin. He was just hired on as an assistant music director at my church. He's helping with the young-adult ministry, too. Anyway, I want to go to the concert, but I don't want to appear too eager. So, I thought if you guys came along, it would look better, and it's something to get you out of the house, Beth, that doesn't involve screens."

I smiled and nodded. "I would absolutely enjoy a concert and to get a look at your *friend*." Molly returned my smile and this time the blush covered her neck and cheeks.

"What time?" DJ asked.

"It starts at four, but I don't know when his group performs."

"It will conflict with mass," he said looking at me.

"We aren't going to mass, remember? We have to consider our illegitimate children."

"What?" Molly asked. We'd completely confused her.

"Never mind. Don't worry about it," DJ said shaking his head. "Where is it and what time would you like us to meet you there?"

Molly smiled all over. "Thank you. I know the music will be good, but you're doing me a huge favor."

CHAPTER 26

DJ and I stood together at the door and waved as Molly drove off. "That was fun," I said. "Thank you for inviting her. I wasn't sure how enjoyable it would be for me if she were gushing over you all evening, but it's just her personality. I'm glad I said, yes."

"Me too. I don't think we have to worry about her making you jealous anymore, thanks to Dan." We both laughed.

I followed him to the sofa and sat down beside him. "Thank you for the flowers. That was very unexpected." My stomach gave a little flutter and I couldn't hide the smile. DJ looked at me, thoughtful, reflective, and a little bit calculating.

"I was hoping they would elicit such a response."

"Are all girls that predictable?" I asked, rolling my eyes.

"No, but I thought it might be a reasonable place to start."

"Start? Start what?" I eyed him cautiously.

"I'd like to add a new dimension to our friendship." He took my hand and turned to face me.

"What?" I asked, truly confused.

"Do you remember when I said that you should wait until you knew yourself better before you kissed me, again?" I nodded, but he could read the disappointment on my face. "Well, I've been thinking a lot about Christmas Eve and since we've been home, and your little episode this week." I wasn't sure where this conversation was headed, but I liked the way he was holding my hand and stroking my knuckles with his thumb. After a few minutes, he asked, "What do you think about courtship?"

"It's a very old-fashioned word, why?" I asked, completely distracted by his thumb. He then massaged down each finger, lingering on my fingertips. I closed my eyes, enjoying the tingles that ran up my arm. "That feels really nice," I commented.

"Good," he said as he gently squeezed the skin between each of my fingers. My lips parted a little and my face went slack. I was so incredibly relaxed after only a few moments of him rubbing my hand. I could feel myself sinking into the sofa.

"So, what do you think?" he asked, as he rubbed the thickness around my thumb. I was having a hard time paying attention to what he said.

"It's great." I'm pretty sure I would have agreed to just about anything he suggested at that very moment.

He stopped rubbing my hand, but didn't let it go. I opened my eyes to see why he'd stopped. He was so close to me. It took me a couple of seconds to blink and focus. He'd removed his glasses and was looking intently into my eyes. I didn't understand why he was so close to me, but I liked it, and I wasn't going to dare do anything to make him move away from me.

The intensity of his eyes held me in place. I remained perfectly still, pinned against the sofa cushion. My heartbeat was steady, but I could feel my breath catch slightly on the inhale. The familiar fluttering in my stomach was now a tight band of solid aching and longing.

"Do you still want to kiss me?" he whispered. I could almost feel his lips forming the words when he broke the silence. I nodded slowly, afraid that any sudden movement might break the spell I was currently under. There was a change in his expression and I could see the smile and anticipation rise to my eyes. He placed his palm on the side of my face. He tilted his head slightly to the side and our lips met somewhere in the shortened distance.

Thank you, Lord! I exclaimed internally, feeling the relief of finally being able kiss him. My only external exclamation was an exhale and maybe a sigh. My heart leapt inside my chest and I placed my hands around his neck, bringing him closer to me; he came willingly.

He allowed his hands to move down past my shoulders to the small of my back. He pulled me closer and I rested my legs over his thighs. I was practically sitting in his lap. We stayed in that position for a long time, kissing slowly. It was the best feeling in the world!

Like Christmas Eve, our kissing felt natural. It was sweet and settling. Neither one of us expressed desperation or demand. Our lips fit together perfectly, and I didn't want to stop kissing him, but I needed to catch my breath. DJ sensed the change and moved his lips to my cheek and the side of my head. He kissed me gently and slowly over my earlobe and down my neck and back across my cheek to my lips. Conversation moves slowly when it's constantly interrupted by kissing.

"Why did you decide today? What changed?" I asked breathlessly.

"Nothing really. I was just praying hard for a sign."

"What was the sign?"

"There wasn't one. Mom told me I wasn't properly encouraged and needed to be more supportive of your desires. Dad said I needed to stop being a dolt and get over it. Then, Gary; it was something he said in class today that gave me the courage I needed."

"What did my buddy, Gary, say?" I smiled imagining what could've come out of that young man's mouth.

DJ smiled, too, and kissed me again, gently and briefly. I honestly wanted it to last longer, but he answered, instead. "Well the first thing he did was he agreed to do something I've been trying to get him to do for two years. The second thing was that he told me he was ready to attempt a new level in calculus with his professor. He's been frustrated lately and really distracted. I haven't been able to put my finger on what's been getting to him, but then I was able to figure it out. It is directly related to his third thing."

He kissed me again, making me wait for the significant point of impact on our current positions. "And the third thing?" I asked when he released my lips again.

"The third thing he said to me today was just before lunch. He came to my desk and asked if he could have a word. 'Darren, life is too short, and I know I have to overcome my fears.' He was so freaking sure of himself that I didn't doubt him for a second. He could've found a way to fly to the moon at that very moment and I would've believed it was possible. Then I watched as he sat next to Penny and asked if she would like to go see a movie with him on Saturday. It was so incredibly sweet and painfully awkward at the same time." He laughed and shook his head. "I figured if Gary was willing to overcome his fears today then surely, I could make an effort as well."

"The flowers were planned?" I asked.

"Yes. Pretty much since lunch. Penny smiled so broadly when Gary sat next to her and started talking to her. I couldn't help but think how badly I wanted you to smile like that at me." More kissing. "When he stood from the table, he'd grown about a head taller, and gave me a little nod like he'd just presented the king with the dragon's head. I wanted that same confidence."

I smiled beneath his lips. "I'll need to send Gary a thank you note. And Molly?" I asked, curious.

He sat back and looked me in the eye. "Molly was *not* planned. We were talking at school and I was trying to figure out how to make tonight a good night. I thought maybe dinner with her would be relaxed and casual. We've always had fun when she's around. That hasn't changed. I also thought that her seeing the two of us together would make it easier somehow for the three of us to be friends. I really like her, and I think she's a sweet girl. Maybe we can help her out on Saturday. I'm also thankful it wasn't awkward or made you jealous." His smile lingered in the corner of his mouth. "Maybe she was just serendipitous." He kissed me again, longer this time, and with a little more insistence than before.

There was nothing calm about my heart now. His kisses were dancing along a fine line. I needed to breathe and maybe drink a glass of cold water or maybe keep kissing him. I wasn't sure the right decision. I finally released his mouth and took in a lungful of air. That helped, but his hand on my leg and his lips on my neck did nothing to align my thoughts.

"Courtship?" I gasped, aloud. It was the only word I could remember.

He chuckled and he stopped kissing my neck. "Yes. May I court you?"

"Does it include kissing?"

"Absolutely." He kissed my neck again.

"Does it include anything else?"

"A commitment to know each other intimately and assurance that we both desire to be married." He returned his attention to the tender skin under my earlobe.

"*Intimately*. I like that word." He was absolutely driving me crazy.

"Nope, not like you're thinking. Not until we're married."

"Are you proposing?" I asked.

"Not yet."

I furled my brow as the idea that this was as far as he'd go until I married him sank into my brain. We'd gone from flowers and a kiss on the cheek to marriage in a matter of an evening. I sighed. I was being greedy. I needed to be satisfied with this. This was good and I assured his mother I wouldn't muddy the waters.

"Am I allowed to sleep with you?"

"Sometimes, if you can behave yourself." He laughed and I pushed his chest away from me.

"You've thought this through," I said, wanting to see his expression.

"You have no idea." The mask of his emotion was gone. He looked as vulnerable as I felt. He smiled his best DJ smile and I kissed him with a loud smack and hugged him close. I was happy and he knew it, and he knew he was a huge reason for that happiness.

CHAPTER 27

I think I floated through the next couple of days. I don't remember touching the ground. DJ went to work. I contented myself at the townhouse. I journaled. I spoke happily to four other people, and even Marcus texted me twice. He was pulling extra shifts working security to make more money for his new truck. While everyone else worked, I listened to music and played the keyboard. In the evenings, after dinner, DJ and I talked and held hands and we kissed; we kissed more than I played the keyboard, and I played my keyboard a lot.

I slept amazingly well. No nightmares. No memories. Nothing that was the least bit upsetting. I woke up early each morning, eager to see DJ before he left for work. I happily anticipated his arrival each afternoon. He kissed me in the kitchen, but I nearly burned dinner, so he had to stop. He kissed me in the dining room but not in a passionate way. He let me wrap my arms around his shoulders from behind in the mornings if he made it to the kitchen first. He kissed me most passionately on the sofa, but he never kissed me upstairs or anywhere within four feet of the staircase. It was like an invisible forcefield. In fact, he never touched me at all beyond the stairs, not even my hands.

Saturday arrived. Darren went to the gym early. He returned and we made breakfast together. He smiled all the time, too. I felt strong and invincible and extremely confident. This was the connection I'd been longing for. This was the foundation for everything good I could imagine. I wanted to get this right because we could build a life together and be a family.

Molly texted to verify that we were still planning on meeting her. I asked what she was wearing. She called me in a panic. "What do you mean by that? I'm wearing a skirt and boots and a scarf. Should I change?"

"No, Molly, I wasn't sure what I should wear. I was just asking so I wouldn't be too casual."

"Oh, okay. I thought you didn't like what I'd chosen."

I laughed. "I can't see you. How could I know what you've chosen?"

She laughed nervously. "My roommates aren't home and I've changed clothes three times already. I'm so nervous. Maybe this is a huge mistake."

"Molly, calm down. It's not really a date, is it? You're just going to a concert to hear a friend's performance. Take a deep breath. Do you want us to pick you up?" I asked.

"Could you? I don't want to be a bother." DJ would agree; it would be no trouble.

Molly looked adorably nervous. She must really like this guy. DJ took my hand across the center console and squeezed it gently, giving me a cue to say something to encourage her. "Molly, you look really pretty. Can you tell us a little bit about Dan?"

"He's tall and has a beard. He's from Texas and has the cutest accent. He's only lived here a couple of years. I think he's probably closer to your age than mine, but he was so sweet when he asked me if I'd like to come see him perform. We talk some at church, but there are always people around. I really don't know if anyone else we know will be there. I'm not sure who all he invited." She took in her bottom lip in a pout. She was doubting herself.

"Do you have some lip gloss?" I asked.

"Yes, why?"

"I think you should put some on; brighten your lips a little." She smiled and dug in her purse. The distraction helped settle her.

We purchased our tickets and went into the small auditorium. We chose seats close to the stage. I tried to engage Molly in conversation, but she had a hard time focusing. She kept looking around. She read the list of performers. Apparently, Dan would play one song with an ensemble and sing with the choir for two numbers.

Finally, the concert began. Coincidentally, the men happened to be on risers close to our end of the stage. Molly nudged me and pointed to a tall man with a beard on the highest riser. The music began and I was instantly drawn into it. It was soothing and stimulating and an enjoyable way to spend the afternoon. DJ held my hand much of the time. I could feel the energy in the room and the affection flow between us. Molly was completely focused on Dan and watched every move he made.

At intermission, I followed Molly to the bathroom. When we returned to our seats, Dan was standing there, talking with DJ. "There they are," DJ said, giving a nod over Dan's shoulder. Molly slowed her pace as we approached.

Dan turned and smiled. "Hi," he said.

"Hi," Molly replied.

"I'm really glad you came." She smiled. "I wanted to catch you before the end. I need to get back. I was just telling Darren to ask you if you could hang around for a few minutes afterward." Molly nodded. "Okay, I have to get back. We're up soon." Dan walked quickly back to the stage.

We managed to get Molly settled again. Poor thing. "What do you think?" she asked.

"He seems nice," DJ said.

The rest of the concert was good with a finale of all the singers singing acapella. We stood near our seats, waiting on Dan to return. People were milling around among the sounds of polite chatter and instrument cases closing. Molly continued to look for him. He was hard to miss. He had to be at least six-three.

"Thanks for waiting," I heard his voice from behind us. We all turned. He held a violin case in his left hand and extended his hand out toward DJ and shook his hand. He then turned to me. "Hello, I'm Dan."

"Hi, I'm Beth," I said shaking his hand. "The concert was lovely. I enjoyed the music."

"Thank you. It's good to meet you." With all the social convention out of the way, he turned his attention toward Molly. "I'm glad you came. You look really pretty."

Her eyes fluttered a little, but she soon recovered herself. "Did anyone else from church come?" she asked.

He shrugged. "I don't know. You're the only one I invited."

The poor girl blushed all over. I cut my eyes to DJ. He was having a hard time concealing his amusement. "Hey, are you hungry? I was about to suggest we go eat. Do y'all have any plans?" I asked.

"No, nothing. I was about to ask the same thing," Dan said. "Do you mind if I get out of this tux? I'd really like to get comfortable."

We agreed to meet at a restaurant near the auditorium. It was a glorified sandwich shop, but the food was good and the conversation was even better. We laughed and enjoyed the casual interaction among us. DJ and Dan got along well. Their lighthearted conversation made it easy for Molly and me to be included.

"Molly, can I give you a ride home?" Dan asked.

"That would be nice, thank you," she said.

I went to the ladies' room with Molly again. She was so excited that she grabbed me and hugged me. "Oh my gosh! I can't believe this is happening. Since the guys split the check, do you think this counts as a date?"

"I have no idea, but the fact that you were the only one he invited, might mean he's interested in asking you out." I had no knowledge of dating, but I knew it would be best for her to be her own sweet self and just be honest with him. "Relax. Be yourself. You're precious, and I think he might like you, too."

We each hugged Molly in the parking lot and she thanked us for coming along with her. She turned and gave a little wave as Dan ushered her toward his truck. It was a full-size Ford that looked to be nearly three feet from the ground; he had to give her a boost into the cab.

DJ opened the door for me and smiled. "What?" I asked.

"That was possibly the most entertaining thing I've witnessed in a while. I'm glad we said yes."

"Me too, but you know what?" He shook his head. "I haven't kissed you for several hours. I may have forgotten how."

"Mmmm, I think I can review that with you."

CHAPTER 28

On the ride home, I remembered something DJ had mentioned the night before. "I was wondering what you've wanted Gary to do for two years?

"Attend a math competition in Texas."

"Why?"

"He's that good. Want to come, too? It would mean a couple of nights away."

"Where will Gary stay?"

"In the dorms with the students."

"Us, too?"

"No, we'll stay in a hotel, nearby."

"Will he be the only one going?"

"No, Penny and Nick, too, but they've been before."

"So, what time are we going to church tomorrow?" I asked.

"You were serious?" he replied.

"Yes, I was. I think we need to find common ground in that regard. I feel selfish enough as it is when it comes to our relationship, like it's been mostly one-sided since the crash. I want to level the playing field a little, be equals in that decision."

DJ looked solemn, reflecting on what I'd said. "That's a big deal, you know, leaving your church."

"I don't feel like it's *my* church, and I doubt it will ever be *our* church." DJ took my hand and kissed it.

"I talked with Dan while you were in the bathroom. He and Molly like where they attend. How about we give it a try? If Dan is playing, we know the music will be good."

The next morning, we arrived at their church. It wasn't a huge building, but it was comfortable and welcoming. We found seats, but didn't see Molly or Dan. The musicians entered the stage to lead the time of worship. Dan was there, singing along and smiling. At the end of the first song, he saw us and gave us a wink and a little nod.

The sermon was most fitting. The pastor was in the middle of a new year's series. He preached on new beginnings and being born again. That held my attention. He taught and read from scripture. I couldn't remember if I even owned a Bible. DJ opened an app in his phone and followed along. I leaned in and read over his shoulder. When he realized what I was doing, he leaned back and put his arm behind me on the chair and brought his screen across for me to read along.

The way the pastor spoke, resonated in my mind. I felt like I was experiencing a new beginning. I couldn't help thinking that this was an opportunity to begin anew with DJ and my life's decisions. I was so filled with hope by the service's end. After the last song, Molly came over and gave me a big hug.

"I'm so excited to see you, here."

"How did it go last night?" I asked.

She smiled. "Great! We're having lunch today."

"That's great!"

Just then, Dan came over and shook DJ's hand. "Welcome. It's good to see you, again."

"Thanks," we said together.

He looked at Molly and raised his eyebrows. She gave a brief nod. They were already able to communicate wordlessly. "Hey, you want to join us for lunch?" Dan asked.

"Sure, if you don't mind us crashing," DJ replied.

"We'd love it," Molly said.

We followed them to an out-of-the-way BBQ place. We were seated and served quickly. The conversation was again lively and enjoyable. We were laughing at something Dan was telling us about his hometown and some of his uncles when a stranger approached our table.

"Hey, Beth," he said. I looked up in anticipation after hearing my name, but I didn't recognize him. "You're looking good. It's been a while." The way he said it made me feel uncomfortable.

"I'm sorry. I don't know you."

"Wow! That's a low blow to my ego. It's me, Jake. I thought we had some good times," he said leering in a creepy way. I took his meaning. Everyone at the table took his meaning. I felt DJ stiffen at my side.

"She's had a head injury. She doesn't remember you." DJ said flatly.

"That's a good one," this guy, Jake, said laughing. "I'm sure she's told you a number of things. She's good like that."

I was mortified and looked down. *This wasn't happening; this wasn't happening!* At this point, Dan and DJ stood at the same time. "Would you please excuse yourself," DJ said politely through clenched teeth.

"I believe the lady has grown bored with you," Dan added. His smile was friendly, but his presence was anything but.

Jake eyed both of my protectors and paused like he might say something else and instantly thought better of it. "See you around, Beth," he finally added flippantly as he walked away from the table.

Molly took my hand. "Are you okay?" she asked.

I shook my head and whispered, "I'd like to go home, now." I looked at DJ pleadingly. The look of disgust on his face made my stomach hurt. He nodded and helped me to my feet and placed his hand on my back. He pulled out his wallet and put a couple of bills on the table.

"Thanks," he said to Dan. "We'll see you guys later."

Molly hugged me and I whispered an apology before DJ escorted me from the restaurant and directly to the car. He unlocked the door and opened it for me. I sat down in the seat, but DJ wouldn't look at me. He slammed the door behind me, unable to control his anger.

The silence before he got into the car was deafening. I felt nauseated and disgusting and ashamed but without the actual memories to connect to my physical reaction. DJ hesitated before he opened his door. He was obviously trying to calm himself before he faced me alone. His hand lingered on the handle for several seconds before he opened it. He got into the car and shut the door. He started the engine and gripped both hands onto the steering wheel and took another deep breath. I sat quietly. I had no idea what to say. Obviously, he didn't either. He put the car in gear and pulled slowly out of the parking lot. Each movement he made was deliberate and precise.

"I'm sorry," I whispered again. It was too hard to speak and not throw up. DJ took my hand and held it but didn't say anything. It felt wrong allowing him to comfort me. I'd hurt him again and I loathed myself. Tears welled in my eyes and I moved my hand from his. I didn't feel worthy to accept his comfort.

"Beth, that wasn't your fault. That jerk isn't worth it."

"How many jerks like that are there out there?" I asked rhetorically. "How many losers have I fucked?" I asked, unable to control my tone of voice.

He shook his head, disappointment layering every breath he took. I closed my eyes and tried not to cry, but it was useless. The tears fell and fell and fell. My eyes were too blurred to focus on the ride home. I walked toward the townhouse, not allowing DJ to touch me. I could feel myself retreating into a very dark place. As soon as DJ opened the door, I bolted upstairs and slammed the door to my bedroom. I wrapped myself securely in my quilt and wept. I cried until I fell asleep. It was the only escape I had.

A couple of hours later, I heard a light knock on my door. "Beth, may I come in?" I opened my eyes and for half a second couldn't remember why my eyes felt puffy or why my pillowcase was damp. "You've been up here for a while; may I come in? I'd really like to talk."

Come in was what I said, but I really wanted to bolt the door and stay alone in my misery.

DJ stood across the room at the doorway. "Are you okay?" he asked.

I scoffed. "No, I'm not okay."

He nodded. "I know that, but I don't know what else to say. Do you need anything? I made you some tea."

"Tea's not going to fix this."

"It's what I've got right now. Would you like to come downstairs?" I shook my head. "Please, we need to talk." I knew I needed to face him sooner or later. I rose from the bed but kept the quilt around me. He moved from the doorway to give me space to pass him. He didn't touch me, keeping his careful upstairs distance.

Once we were downstairs, I saw the steaming mug on the counter. I adjusted the quilt over my arms and took the mug in both hands, savoring the warmth and the calming aroma.

"Sit down. Make yourself comfortable. I don't plan to leave until we get some things straight." I stood there, looking at him. I didn't want to sit and there was no way I could get comfortable, but I was being petty. I had to be mature enough to face this issue head-on.

I could see, now, why my former self had distanced herself. I understood why she'd asked him to move out. She hadn't deserved him and neither did I. It didn't matter if I couldn't remember, truth was truth, and the truth had blindsided me. I wasn't prepared or equipped to deal with any of it.

Once I was settled, he sat facing me. "Beth, I'd like to begin." I nodded, but I felt the familiar wave of nausea pass over me. I took in a calming breath through my nose in hopes of settling my stomach. He didn't look upset anymore, but I couldn't read his expression. His mask had returned. I'd enjoyed its absence the past few days. "I'm not angry with you. I'm sorry that it ruined our perfectly good day, but I'm over it and I'd like for you to do the same."

"How can you do that, just pretend like it's not a big deal?"

"I choose for it not to be."

"Well, it is. I've apparently been with numerous others and still you desire me like you can't see any of that."

"I don't; they've always been nameless and faceless."

"That's stupid. Jake was neither."

"Probably, but I love you, and I've always been able to see past that."

"That makes you an even bigger idiot."

He took offense to that. "No, that makes you the most important thing in my life and you know it." He raised his eyebrow in challenge. It was the first time he'd declared his love for me directly. "How did you feel after church this morning?" My face couldn't conceal the truth. I'd felt good, really good, and that joy leaked out over my entire body. "There, see. We couldn't have heard anything better: new beginnings, new life, fresh starts, do-overs. This is our second chance. This is our fresh start. I'm still in awe of that fact, the simple fact, that you woke up, and for the first time you are willingly returning my affection. You even initiate contact with me. Do you know how long I've wanted that?"

I imagined it, but I didn't answer that question. "How can it not bother you? I'm sickened every time I've been confronted with it."

"Understandably, but that shouldn't define you. That's not who you are, anymore."

"How can you be so sure?"

He shrugged. "I just know."

I accepted his words. They were truth, too, and I knew it. "I'm embarrassed and I don't like hurting you."

"You didn't hurt me. I was angry, sure, but not at you. Hell, I wasn't even that embarrassed. All I could think about was getting you out of there."

"I feel awful for Molly, too. What must Dan be thinking about Molly's slutty friend." I lowered my gaze to the untouched tea in my hands.

DJ took the cup gently from my grip. He placed it on the table behind me. He took my hand and forced me to look into his eyes. "You are not a slut, and I'd appreciate it if you'd stop referring to the woman I love, in any such terms. You're beautiful and you're mine. Beth, please don't think less of yourself." I tried to lower my gaze again, but he held my face firmly. "No, you will look at me and hear this clearly: I love you. Do you understand that?" I nodded obediently, held in his gaze. "Do you believe me?" I nodded again and smiled a little. "Are you going to let this ruin the rest of our evening?" I shook my head.

"Good. May I kiss you?"

I smiled big and took his face in my hands. "Thank you. I love you, too." The words came out and he looked at me in astonishment. Once my words settled over him, he pressed in and kissed me gently for a very long time.

CHAPTER 29

Monday morning came too early. I trudged downstairs in my bathrobe and put on the kettle for tea. I made coffee for DJ, too. I scrambled some eggs and made toast. DJ smiled when he saw me at the stove.

"Good morning." He kissed me on the cheek. He didn't want me distracted when I cooked for him.

"Do you want it to go?" I asked as he poured his coffee.

"No, I have time. Remember, I have class tonight. I won't be home until ten."

I tried to mask my disappointment by turning back toward the stove. I'd have fourteen hours alone to figure out how to fill. Playing the keyboard was fine, but I needed to find a new hobby or something to occupy my mind and my time.

At nine that morning, I received a text reminder. Apparently, I had an appointment with a Dr. Carol DeRosen the next day. I didn't know her and she wasn't listed in my contacts, so I Googled her. She was an ob-gyn. *Great*, I thought. Of course, I remembered when DJ told the doctor in Chicago that I was due for another birth control injection in January. I decided I'd go through with the appointment. I had some questions, well concerns, really.

DJ came home just before ten that evening. He was surprised to see me up. "How was class?"

"Good. How was your day?"

"Good." I rose from the sofa and hugged him. "I wanted to see you before I went to bed."

"I'm glad you're up. I need to talk something over with you."

I looked up into his eyes. "What?"

"First things first," he said before he kissed me. "Secondly, my professors want me to submit my dissertation proposal this semester. They'd like it before spring break."

"That's great!" I said responding to the wide smile on his face. "I'm really proud of you."

"Thanks."

"But?" I could tell there was something more.

"But that means I'm going to have to commit plenty of time to it." His brow furled. "That's time I won't be spending with you."

I understood and nodded. "I'll figure it out. I was thinking earlier how I needed a new hobby. Please don't let me distract you. It's too important to delay."

My response pleased him. He hugged me closer and I asked if he'd like something to eat before he went to bed. He ate a bowl of cereal and we visited briefly before he kissed me goodnight.

I decided before I fell asleep that I'd do whatever I could to help out. I'd make him breakfast in the mornings and be encouraging and figure out constructive ways to spend my days.

***

I arrived at the gynecologist's office about thirty minutes early for my appointment. I thumbed through a magazine. Several women passed in and out of the waiting room while I waited to be called. I watched as women in varying degrees of pregnancy, from baby bumps to full, round bellies, signed-in. They were each attractive and beautiful in their own ways, and I felt a physical longing, an emptiness, a craving from my heart and my womb. I imagined what that must feel like, a little person growing inside me. I imagined what it would be like to make love with DJ often enough, but now I had the added glimpse of what it would be like to be married to him, starting a family together. *Dr. and Mrs. Darren Fitzgerald.* Would this become my new obsession? Not only did I want DJ, I wanted his babies, bad!

I was called to the back and weighed and shown into an examining room. The nurse asked me several questions.

"Any changes to your medical history?"

"I'd say," I said and gave the nurse a brief description and let her update my information. She then gave me a sheet and a hospital gown to change into. Apparently, this was my yearly check-up as well.

"The nurse practitioner will be in to see you. Dr. DeRosen was called out on a delivery."

The nurse practitioner came in, reading my chart. "Hello, Beth. Good morning." She looked at me. "You don't recognize me?" I shook my head. "I'm Sharon," she said smiling. "Is this all true?" she asked gesturing to the chart in her hand.

"Yes."

"Wow!"

"I know."

"How did you know to come in today?"

"Text reminder. I had to Google the doctor's name."

Sharon laughed a little and nodded. "Interesting. Any issues other than the memory?"

"No."

"Well, as you can see, today is your yearly check-up and quarterly Depo injection," Sharon said.

"Before we do this, may I please ask you a few questions?" Sharon nodded. "I have no knowledge of my medical history. I know I had an abortion when I was nineteen. Have I ever been treated for any STDs?"

Sharon flipped through my chart and shook her head. "No, are you having any symptoms?"

"No, I just want to make sure I don't spread anything." Sharon nodded, understanding.

"Are you nervous about the examination?" I shook my head. "Alright, let's have a look, shall we?" The nurse helped me lean back onto the short bed and Sharon began the examination. I forced myself to relax and focus on the ceiling above me. In a few moments, the nurse covered me and helped me back into a sitting position.

Sharon removed her gloves and asked, "Do you have any other questions?"

"Do I have anything in my chart that may indicate reasons why I'm on birth control other than to prevent pregnancy?" Sharon shook her head. "Have I had any abnormal lab results?"

"No, nothing. From our perspective, you're in good health. I've been seeing you for the past three years for your injections. Dr. DeRosen usually does your yearly examination. I don't see any concerns before that, either. You've had no other pregnancies listed and no history of anything out of the ordinary."

I sat considering for a few moments. "I don't think I want to continue with the injections; I'd like to get to know my body better in its natural state."

Sharon nodded. "You've been on the injections for nearly five years. It may take six months to a year for your body to return to its *natural* state. It takes a while for the hormones to completely leave your system and for your cycles to become normal again. You'll have to use other forms of contraception to prevent STDs or pregnancy."

I nodded. I understood. "I'm not sexually active and I'm confident it's not going to happen for a while."

"Very well, then. You're done here. We'll see you in a year unless you need anything else. I hope things improve with your memory."

"Thank you, Sharon."

I dressed and waited outside for my ride.

***

DJ texted me and asked me if I had plans for dinner. I replied that I was defrosting chicken. He replied with a thumbs-up. I spent the afternoon texting with Tom while the meat marinated. I played on the keyboard, trying to figure out some new songs. They were complicated, but I pressed on. It would take me a little while to master them.

I talked a little while with Sadie during my walk. She was on a break between shifts. She asked what I was doing Sunday afternoon. She was off and thought she'd invite us over for dinner. "Marcus won't be home until close to four. We'll plan on eating around five."

I chopped vegetables for a salad and then pulled out an old cookbook from the back of the pantry. It had apparently been Gram's. I recognized her handwriting. She'd made little notes in the margins of several of the recipes. As I perused the desserts and cakes section, I saw my name a couple of times. *Beth's favorite* was written next to the recipes for a chocolate cake and the chocolate frosting. I wondered how many times she'd made that cake for me.

I sat down and began reading the recipes. Each one contained an explanation of some kind, where the recipe originated, when the recipe was served most often, and sometimes a little anecdote about the person who had submitted the recipe. It was both entertaining and enlightening. I really didn't seem to have the attention span since the crash to read or listen to a novel. Perhaps, I'd take up cookbook reading, instead.

DJ came in and I happily welcomed him with a kiss. I felt a little like June Cleaver, welcoming Ward home from the office. Maybe I should don a set of pearls. He ran upstairs to shower; he'd already been to the gym.

"Sadie invited us to dinner Sunday evening. Do you think we can go?"

"We should probably discuss my schedule this semester. I have class Mondays and Thursdays. I'd like to study and write on Tuesdays and Wednesdays and leave Friday nights and Saturdays for you. We can plan on church either Saturday afternoons or Sunday mornings and then I need to hit the books again Sunday evening to prepare for Monday."

"That's only two nights out a week. I think I can manage."

"I can't study and write here."

"Why not?"

"Because it's hard for me to concentrate."

"Concentrate? You read here all the time."

He looked a little sheepish. "Well, now we kiss here all the time, too, and honestly, there are times when I'd rather kiss you than read."

That made me smile. "So, it's not a good idea to go to the library with you, either."

He shook his head, smiling. "Please don't."

I sighed. Five nights seemed daunting in comparison to the two or three that I was imagining. "Will you start tonight?" I asked. He nodded. My eyes pricked a little at the thought that he'd be leaving again so soon. I'd been looking forward to his being home all day. I didn't cry, but he could read my disappointment. He reached across the table and took my hand. "It's okay," I said. "I'll get used to it. Can we still have breakfast in the mornings and supper together on the nights you don't have class?"

He considered a few seconds and nodded. "Yes, that would be good for both of us. What did you do today?"

"Read a cookbook, took a walk, texted with your dad, talked with Sadie for a few minutes, and I went to the gynecologist."

That part he wasn't expecting. "Everything okay?"

"Yeah, it's fine. I got a reminder yesterday. I'm all good."

"Where did they give you the shot this time?"

"I didn't get it."

He slowly cocked his head to one side, considering. "Why not?"

"I don't need it. If I'm not having sex, then I don't need birth control, right?" I shrugged like it wasn't a big deal. He smiled approvingly. "Besides, I don't want to be on any medication unless it's absolutely necessary. I'm ready to be rid of my other meds as soon as I'm able, too. They make me feel tired sometimes. I really want to know how this body feels without anything else. I've had something to numb or relax my brain since the crash."

I rose from the table, knowing he didn't need to put off his plans for the evening. DJ loaded the dishwasher while I put the leftovers away. He didn't say or ask me anything else. I had no idea what he was thinking about as we worked in silence.

"What time will you be home?" I asked.

"Ten." I nodded and tried in vain to keep my eyes from pricking and my stomach from aching a little. "I'm sorry," he said.

I took a deep breath and hugged him goodbye. "I'm going to be fine. I just need to get a plan, that's all."

He kissed my head and held me closer. "Thank you. It's not forever, just a couple months." He then kissed me goodbye and released me completely. He grabbed his backpack from the bottom of the stairs and the keys from the entryway table. I gave him a little wave and then bolted the door behind him.

CHAPTER 30

I had to get a plan. I had to figure out what to do with myself. I texted Molly and asked what day or days would be convenient to go to the gym with her. I texted Sadie and told her to please just plan on having me on Sunday; my plus one would be studying. I called Mary after her shift and asked if she had any ideas about how I might spend my time.

"Go online and see what they offer at the library. Our branch here has classes all the time. Also, see what you might be able to do at your gym. You mentioned yoga once."

Molly sounded excited that I reached out to her. She was so willing to hang out with me. We decided to go to the gym on the same days that Darren had class so that I wouldn't miss dinner with him. She also thought it was a great suggestion to check out the library. "Oh, and Wednesday evenings, we have activities at church if you want to come along. We usually have a study and discussion."

By the second week, I was getting into a routine. I did go to the library. The first class I attended was an adult coloring class. The next week, I attended a book talk about women in business. Most of the attendees were retirees. They were a lively group and seemed to be searching for ways to spend their days as well. In the upcoming weeks they would begin a few extended sessions in sign language and crochet. I figured I should give them a try; they were both useful things to know how to do.

So, my plan worked pretty well. Working out was good with Molly. I slept well on those days. Sadie's was a place of refuge with comfort food and great companionship. She knew I was feeling lonely and did everything in her power to make me feel welcomed and at home. Marcus was there sometimes, too. We were an odd threesome.

I went out a couple of times with Molly and Dan, but I felt like a third wheel. They didn't need chaperoning and I honestly didn't like feeling babysat. I enjoyed my time with DJ, but it didn't feel like enough.

After the first week, I significantly lowered my Friday night expectations. DJ was asleep on the sofa before 8:30. The week had caught up with him. He was so peaceful lying there. I sat for a good hour and a half just watching him sleep, gently stroking his hair. It was the most physical contact we'd had all week.

Saturdays were better. He apologized for falling asleep on me, but it happened every Friday night, so I came to expect it. Without the distractions of kissing, the dreams returned. They weren't as intense as they were in the beginning, but I still woke panting.

My therapist tried to catch glimpses of them with me, but it only came during my nights alone without any other stimulation or distractions. Some mornings, I woke exhausted from not sleeping soundly. I didn't want to complain to DJ, but I missed him terribly and longed for him to hold me when I woke in the night, alone and afraid.

Several nights, I could hear someone calling to me. It was a man's voice, faint and far away. "Victor?" I whispered. He laughed. "Victor, stop it. Stop teasing." He laughed again. I could hear the smile in his voice when he called to me. His intrusions into my dreams weren't frightening. In a way, they were settling.

DJ's nights were longer and longer by the second month. My dreams of this man continued. I rarely saw his face, but it became a comfort to hear his voice and to know he would be there again each night. I much preferred to dream about this man than the crash. The colors in my dreams had changed, too. They were altered somehow, like I was seeing everything through a prism refracting light.

I'd fallen asleep on the sofa again waiting up for DJ. When I stirred, I knew it had to be well after midnight. "Hey," I whispered sleepily and reached out to hug him.

"Hey, yourself," he said, but he wasn't smiling. He knelt back and rested on his heels.

"Is everything alright?" I asked, realizing he didn't seem happy to see me.

"Who is Victor?" he asked, concerned.

"What?" I asked. I didn't know what he was talking about.

"Victor. You were saying his name when I came in."

"I don't know what you're talking about." He didn't believe me.

"Beth, I distinctly heard you say his name."

Then it came to me. "Victor's the man calling me in my dreams. I can't see his face, though. He's always laughing and being playful. I wish he'd quit teasing me."

"What are you talking about? You dream about this man often?"

"Sometimes. It's better than reliving the crash."

"Are you having nightmares, again?"

"Sometimes."

"Why didn't you tell me? Why didn't you come to me?"

"I didn't want to bother you."

He sighed in exasperation. "I've left you too much, haven't I?"

I shrugged. "I miss you."

"I miss you, too. You're dreaming about another man and having nightmares. That can't be a good sign." He tried to smile, but it didn't make it to his eyes. He was exhausted, too.

"Would you like to join me?" I asked scooting over on the sofa.

He shook his head and his heavy eyes looked like they might stay closed if he let them fall. "Let's go to bed."

I was hoping he meant together, but I wasn't sure. He turned out the lamp near the sofa as soon as I made it to the staircase and followed a couple of steps behind me, keeping his careful upstairs distance. "Goodnight," I said as I entered my bedroom. He didn't say anything as he entered his room and shut the door. I brushed my teeth again and got in the bed. I punched the pillow under my head and fell back asleep almost instantly."

It only felt like a couple of hours had passed, but the early morning light was already threatening at the side of the curtains. DJ's alarm would be going off soon. I rolled over to find him in the bed next to me. I didn't know he was lying there, but God, it felt good, probably the reason I'd slept so soundly. I cuddled into him and forced my arms around him. I breathed slowly into his chest and settled again into a state of total relaxation.

When his alarm sounded from the other room, DJ stirred and wrapped his arms around me securely. He kissed the top of my head. "Good morning," he whispered into my hair.

"I didn't know you were here."

"Yeah, you were pretty out of it, last night."

"What time was it when you came in?"

"After midnight."

"Why were you so late?"

"Got carried away. I wanted to finish a section. It took me longer than I thought."

"Hmmm," I murmured into his chest and then eased away from him. He needed to get up. He held me tightly, though, and wouldn't let me go.

"Stay, please," he said. The alarm beeped in the other room, but he ignored it.

"Don't you need to get up?"

"Yes, but I'd rather hold you right now." I smiled. I'd rather hold him right then, too.

A few moments later, he begrudgingly released me and took a shower before he came downstairs. I had breakfast waiting for him and a to-go cup of coffee. I'd also packed him a snack and a sandwich. I didn't know why, but I felt like he wasn't eating well when I couldn't see him in the evenings. He kissed me goodbye and I smiled for the first time in a couple of days.

I went to the library to continue my crochet class. I was able to chain stitch consistently and managed to make a chain that was taller than me. The instructor was an incredibly patient woman. She said I was ready to learn to single crochet. The sign language class was easier. I apparently knew some already; I just needed to be reminded. I knew the alphabet and a number of signs for normal things like colors and foods and making simple requests like *When will dinner be ready* and *May I use the bathroom*. It was easy to use my hands in both classes. They were accustomed to nimble work.

I passed through the lobby of the library and saw a new sign. They were hosting a reception honoring a donation to the library. In the corner of the sign was a photo of a smiling couple. I recognized them instantly. What were they doing there? I read the poster more closely. *Please join us to honor the generous gift to our library given in memoriam by Katherine and Victor Hebert.* Under their photograph were their names in bold print.

"Victor," I whispered touching his face on the photograph. I knew his face. I knew that smile. I knew his laughter and his propensity toward mischief. Staring into his clear, blue eyes, I put my fingertips on his lips and my other fingertips touched my own. They were cold and I couldn't stop the tear that fell down my cheek.

"Beth, honey, are you okay?" my kind instructor asked. She touched my shoulder and I turned to her, not wanting to remove my eyes from Victor's. I hurriedly wiped the tear from my cheek.

"I think I knew them," I said numbly.

"Oh, I'm sorry. They passed away a few months ago. They were patrons of the library, very generous. They had no family, so I suspect their fortune will bless many organizations."

"They were wealthy?"

"Exceedingly, but you wouldn't know it from the way they lived. They weren't excessive. They traveled often and donated heaps of money to St. Jude's after they lost their son to leukemia. She was a beautiful woman, inside and out."

"You knew her?"

She shook her head. "Not personally."

I returned my gaze to the photo. The woman was a blond with vibrant blue eyes. She was smiling the kind of smile that said she was accustomed to having her photo taken. She looked confident and kind. She stood a couple of inches taller than her husband, but he didn't seem to mind.

My instructor patted my arm and bid me farewell. "See you next week." I smiled and nodded, but didn't move from in front of the poster. I needed to go, too; I had a therapy appointment that afternoon and DJ and I were leaving town for the math competition the next day. I needed to pack.

This particular Uber driver wasn't talkative at all, so during the drive to my therapy appointment, I took the opportunity to search this couple on my phone. Why hadn't I done it before? I was initially curious about the couple in the Volvo, but I was too preoccupied with other things to follow through. There were pages and pages listed with their names. They must have attended numerous fundraisers and social events. Wow! They were extremely popular.

Katherine was pictured over and over again with different organization leaders. Victor was also pictured, but he wasn't nearly as photogenic. The camera loved Katherine and from the look on Victor's face in more candid shots, he loved her more. I knew that as fact, but I didn't have any physical connections to this couple; they were only in a foggy memory.

When I arrived at the therapist's office, I was feeling frustrated like I couldn't get through a wall of memory to the important stuff. I was just banging my figurative head against it. The feelings were intense and limiting at the same time.

She sensed my agitation as soon as I entered the office. "What's new?" she asked.

"I think I knew the other couple in the crash. I keep dreaming about them. I know her from my dreams of the crash, but recently I've been dreaming differently. I know them, well him, Victor. I saw a picture of him today and I know him; I know him well."

"Interesting. Would you like to try and tap into that right now? It may be closer than you think." I nodded and tried to relax and follow her guiding through my brain. We hit the same wall repeatedly that I'd faced in the car on the way over. I felt too addled to relax fully. "What are you thinking about right now?" she asked.

"Why do I remember this man, but I can't remember Darren?" The frustration boiled over.

"Perhaps you've compartmentalized your past and are just now unlocking those memories. Perhaps the pain and trauma of the accident has forced you to protect the most important parts of your relationships."

At the end of our session, I still felt uneasy and anxious. There was a nagging at the back of my mind like a little hammer tapping and tapping. *Great*, I thought. I was surely going to have a headache if I didn't let it go or get some answers.

DJ had class and I promised Molly I'd work out with her after school. I went home and finished the laundry and packed my suitcase so I'd be ready to leave the following afternoon. Molly and I had a good workout in the evening yoga class and then we picked up Chinese. We brought it back to the townhouse and ate together.

"How's Dan?" I asked.

Molly smiled and said that he was fine, but that he was going out of town for a few days to see his family over spring break. "He invited me to go with him."

"Are you going?"

"No."

"Why not?"

"My parents haven't met him, yet."

"Why not?"

"It hasn't been convenient and I'm not sure I'm ready for that."

"Ready for what?" I asked.

"Ready for them to expect more just because I brought a boy home to meet them."

"In case you didn't know already, he's *not* a boy."

She rolled her eyes wide and giggled. "I *know* that very well, but you know what I mean." I honestly couldn't say that I knew what she was talking about.

"Wouldn't it please them to know you were dating a music minister?"

She laughed out loud. "No, absolutely not!"

"Why not?"

"He's technically a part-time employee at our church. They'll see him as a part-time musician. They don't think *musician* is a stable profession and they wouldn't appreciate his day job, either."

"What's his day job?" I asked, truly curious.

"He's a hauler and diesel mechanic. His company services area farming equipment and machinery."

"That sounds like steady work. He must make a good living to drive that truck."

"Oh, it's not the money. He makes a good living, but it's uneducated, blue-collar work. To be from a small town, my parents are insufferable snobs. They sent me to college and expect me to marry a college-educated man. It wouldn't be right for me to be better educated than my husband."

"That's terribly confusing," I said.

"You have no idea." She rolled her eyes again.

"So, why can't you go visit his family and meet them, anyway?" She shrugged like she didn't have anything to defend that argument. "Aren't you curious?"

She nodded. "You sound just like Dan. He's been egging me on for a week, trying to get me to agree to go."

"I don't see how it can hurt anything. He likes you a lot. That's evident. I hope it works out."

"How are you and DJ?" she asked.

"I think we're good, but I haven't seen much of him. He's working so hard. I hope he gets done with this proposal soon. I miss him like crazy."

"You have the next couple of days together. You'll have fun."

"I hope so."

***

DJ stayed late again, after class, to meet with a few classmates and speak with one of his professors. He texted me, so I decided to take a hot bath and go to bed. Molly's afternoon and evening distractions helped me postpone the headache that had threatened earlier. I took my headache medicine and tried to go to sleep. I was tired and relaxed after the bath, but I had a hard time giving in to the rest.

My thoughts returned to the poster and hints of dreams flooded forward and crashed into the same wall. When I woke, I was screaming bloody murder. I was gasping and sobbing and convulsing. I had no control over my body. DJ held me tightly against his chest.

"Beth, it's okay. You're safe. I'm here. Please, Beth, wake up." He was pleading for me to respond to him. I was grasping for something to hold onto. I was clinging to him for dear life.

I finally found my voice. "Save him!" I screamed.

"Who?" DJ asked, almost matching my intensity.

"It's too late! He's dead!" I screamed.

"Who? Who's dead?" DJ asked, concerned.

"Victor! Victor's dead!"

"Who is Victor?" He sounded frustrated.

"My husband! He's dead!"

"Beth, you aren't making any sense." He shook my shoulders trying to get to me to wake up completely. I blinked. It was DJ; the remnant of the dream retreated quickly behind the wall and then it was gone, leaving a faint trail of color behind.

"DJ," I panted.

"Yes."

IMPACT

"DJ," I repeated and found his lips in the dark. I ran my hands through his hair and pulled him closer to me. He wasn't prepared for my assault. I kissed him and pulled at his shirt but couldn't get close enough to him to satisfy my need to be reassured. He was alive and I was alive, and current ran between us like a fire. I pulled him down on top of me and wrapped my entire body around his, all the while kissing him deeply.

Then, I felt the shift, the change; he'd gathered his wits and had regained control. He was bigger and stronger than me and easily pulled himself from my grasp. He wasn't giving in so easily.

"Beth," he sighed. "Please, no." He begged me to stop. He was begging me. Maybe this was harder for him than I thought. I eased my grip on his shirt, untangled my legs from around his hips, and allowed him to sit up.

"Are you awake, now?" he asked breathlessly.

"Yes," I panted in reply. Emotionally, I was spent from the dream. Physically, I had a hard time controlling my desire.

"I could hear you screaming before I walked through the door. I couldn't get to you fast enough." He stroked my face with his hand and rested it against my back.

"I'm okay, now." My breaths were slowly returning to normal.

"What the hell is happening to you?"

"I don't know," I said honestly. "I'm remembering things that make no connection to my life. I don't understand." I leaned into his chest, allowing his

271

presence to settle me completely. "DJ, will you sleep with me for what remains of the night?"

He hesitated for a long time before he answered me. He rubbed the scruff of his beard and exhaled in resignation. "Yeah, give me a few minutes."

CHAPTER 31

DJ had to leave early to pick up the van for the trip to Texas. I was going as an official chaperone. I took an Uber to the school and met them just after lunch. DJ's substitute had already arrived. She was a mousy woman, but Tommy promised to be on his best behavior.

"Don't make her cry," Darren warned him before we left.

The five of us piled into the van. "You have until the state line to do whatever you need to do on your phones, then it's my time. Got it?" Penny rolled her eyes dramatically. Gary and Nick seemed fine.

It was like riding with mutes until the state line. I closed my eyes and dozed a bit in the quiet of the van. DJ pulled into a gas station and we all got out to relieve ourselves. We all bought snacks and bottles of water.

When they buckled back into the van seats, they were smiling and almost eager for what was next. DJ asked me to pull out a box of cards from his backpack. "Just read them aloud. They'll keep score. The loser has to sing car karaoke with me."

"Am I playing, too?" I asked, cautiously. What the heck had I signed up for?

"Of course. That wouldn't be fair to exclude you," he said jokingly.

The questions were incredibly difficult. The topics covered movies, history, science, and art. They each seemed to have their own niche in the game. I did alright with history and art, but I absolutely knew nothing scientific. They could answer most of the questions and even spell the answers. *Show-offs!*

"This isn't fair!" I protested.

"Fair?" Gary asked. "It's a game. Nothing is ever fair in a game."

"There is always a probability of success, but fairness is never a part of the equation," Nick interjected.

"I need to go to the bathroom," Penny said.

Nick rolled his eyes. "Why can't a girl go more than an hour before she has to pee?"

"Because I have a uterus and I'm currently menstruating and the additional fluid I'm retaining adds pressure to my bladder."

"Sorry," Nick said meekly.

"No need to be sorry. It was the correct answer to your question."

"Serves you right," Gary said. "You know better than to make generalizations."

Darren raised his eyebrows toward Nick who was looking at him in the rear-view mirror. It was so hard not to laugh, but I knew it would be terribly inappropriate if I were to burst out laughing.

I got out of the van with Penny and walked into the gas station. I had to pee, too, but thankfully no one commented on my uterus or asked if I were menstruating. I wasn't.

"Is Penny short for anything?" I asked as we washed our hands.

"Penrose," she said smiling. She was a beautiful girl with deep blue eyes and caramel blond hair, her skin tanned and toned from swimming. I could see her on the cover of *Sports Illustrated*.

"That's a pretty name."

"Thank you. It's where I was conceived."

"Where's Penrose?"

"England. My parents were studying abroad. Is Beth short for anything?"

"No, just Beth." She nodded acknowledging that. "Did you enjoy your movie with Gary?"

"Which one?"

"I didn't realize there was more than one."

"Uh huh, we've been to three. I like going to the movies with him. I like doing a lot of things with him."

"That's good. What kind of things?" I was trying to make casual conversation.

"Kissing." She smiled. I wasn't prepared for that reply. I had no idea how to talk with teenagers, and I'm sure my questions were loaded.

Once we were back in the van, we began playing a version of *Name that Tune*. Points were awarded for title of song and name of the artist or band, and a bonus point if you knew either the year of release and whether or not it was a cover. DJ started a playlist from his phone before he pulled out of the parking lot. The playlist contained random songs from numerous decades. I was surprisingly good at this game. How many hours had he spent compiling this playlist? It was fantastic. We all sang along with the songs we knew the best.

Although, I'd gained a considerable amount of points in the music category, I couldn't win. I would be stuck singing car karaoke with DJ. He knew I didn't like losing. He smiled. "Pick your poison," he chuckled. I looked at the teenagers in the backseat. They were absolutely no help at all. They were lively and had enjoyed the game. They were also happily relieved that they weren't forced to sing a duet with their teacher.

I didn't care what song we sang. I was having fun and would be a good sport about losing. "Go ahead, pick whatever you want to sing."

He chose Elton John and Kiki Dee's version of *Don't Go Breaking My heart*. We hammed it up for our audience and before the end, they were singing along, too. They were good sports, and it was a great way to end our afternoon of traveling.

DJ chose a restaurant close to the university for dinner. It was still early enough that it wasn't crowded. We sat at a large circular table in the corner of the dining room. "We have a little over an hour before we have to check in. You guys okay?" he asked. They all nodded. "Any questions?"

When they didn't speak up, I asked, "How exactly do you compete in math?"

Nick explained, "We have to take a test in the morning. They'll be graded and we'll be ranked according to our scores. Then in the afternoon, we'll have individual and group problem solving. We'll finish up around eight tomorrow night. There will be a geek mixer until midnight and then on Sunday morning, we'll have an awards ceremony. Penny and I both ranked last year in testing and individual problem solving. Now with Gary, we can compete as a group, ourselves. Last year we were placed with a guy from Dallas. He was okay, but Gary will be better to work with. We already know what he can do."

"Do you study or prepare for this?" I asked.

"I read through questions from past competitions. I don't know if you can truly study for something like this. The questions are new each year. They seem pretty straightforward, but then again, not everyone reads questions the way we do. I think we'll do alright," Gary said.

Gary and I were the only ones at the table. Everyone else had gone to the bathroom before our food was served. "Things are different, now." Gary said. He was staring at me.

"What do you mean?" I asked.

"You and Darren. They're different from when we were at the mall. He smells like you all the time." I blushed and couldn't contain the smile that threatened to spread across my entire face.

"Is that a good thing?" I laughed a little.

He shrugged. "It's definitely not bad and he's happy. Are you getting married?"

"I don't know."

"Do you want to?"

"Why do you ask me such pointed questions?"

"Are they pointed?" he asked curiously.

"A little, yes. I'm not accustomed to being questioned like this. It's a little uncomfortable."

"Oh, I'm sorry. I just thought it was the next logical step in your relationship. You both seem different from our fieldtrip, like you're together and happy. I don't know how these things work. I'm curious and you're easy to talk to."

"Thank you, Gary. I am happy and yes, I'd like to marry Darren. I don't know when or how that will happen, but I do love him."

Gary nodded accepting my answer. "I know that. He loves you, too."

"I think you're alright, Gary. I enjoy our little chats."

"Me, too."

"Are you excited about the competition?" I asked.

"Not particularly. I just didn't want Penny to be alone for the weekend with Nick, again. He can be a real jerk sometimes. He isn't very thoughtful and last year made Penny feel really stupid when they didn't win. It wasn't her fault." He shook his head. "Besides, I'd like nothing better than to outrank him on our test scores. He thinks he knows everything."

"Penny is a pretty girl."

He nodded again. "She has a pleasant exterior, but that's just the container she came in. Her mind is even prettier," he said and his eyes changed as he watched her return to the table. *Lord, have mercy!* This boy had it worse than me.

CHAPTER 32

The hotel where DJ had made reservations was across the street from the university where our three charges were staying. The lobby was packed with teachers and parents. DJ recognized several other teachers he'd met in years past. He introduced me and after some brief discussion about their top students, we excused ourselves.

DJ was beat after a long week of late nights and the drive. He went directly to the shower and got ready for bed. I put on my PJs and thumbed through the hotel magazines. "What time will we head over in the morning?" I asked.

"We can't be there until after lunch. We aren't allowed to be anywhere near the students until after they've completed their testing. It's very strict. We'll be able to observe their individual and group competitions, but only from a distance. It's not like watching anything interesting. It's quiet, but I enjoy watching my team compete. I'm curious as to how they figure things out together and are forced to communicate their ideas."

DJ rubbed his eyes and yawned. "You're exhausted." He nodded. "How much longer until you can just focus on class?" I asked.

"A couple of more weeks. I turned in a rough draft to my professor. He's checking for errors and areas that may need more explanation." He stretched his neck down and flexed his shoulders.

"Here," I said gesturing for him to come closer and sit in the desk chair. "May I?" I asked.

"May you what?"

"Rub your shoulders."

"Sure." He looked hesitant like I didn't know what I was offering. He sat down and looked over his shoulder at me.

I placed my hands on the top of his shoulders and could feel the tension and the knots as soon as I began rubbing them. He closed his eyes and exhaled. Gradually, he relaxed under my touch; I could feel the tension leaving him. He leaned forward onto the desk and I rubbed the middle of his back between his shoulder blades. He groaned slightly as I massaged down his spine. I then focused on his neck and the base of his skull. Goosebumps ran down his arms. I smiled, pleased with myself. *Bonus*, I thought.

The massage lasted less than thirty minutes, but my hands were growing tired and I was losing strength. I could feel myself relaxing, too. "Thank you," he mumbled when my hands stopped. His voice was muffled with his head down on the desk.

"So, can we sleep in tomorrow?" I asked. "Not worry with an alarm?"

"That sounds great," he said stretching as he rose from the chair. He yawned again, bigger this time. "What bed do you want?" he asked.

"I'll take this one." I gestured to the one closest to the window. I went to the bathroom and brushed my teeth and washed my face. When I came out, DJ was already asleep in the bed I'd called.

Now that we were a kissing couple and technically *courting*, I wasn't sure about sleeping together and kissing in hotel rooms. He should have made me a list of rules. I lay down beside him and made myself comfortable. He put his arm around me and nuzzled me closer to him. I was relieved that I wasn't breaking any rules.

We slept past seven the next morning. We dressed and went downstairs for breakfast. The lobby was bustling with parents and teachers. Some were chatting, others were reading the newspaper or watching the lobby televisions, catching up on sports scores and current events.

"You brought a new contender," a loud, male voice said from two tables over.

I looked up to see who had spoken. DJ smiled at the stranger. "Yep."

"How old is he?"

"Fifteen."

"How many more years you got with him?" the stranger asked like they were discussing thoroughbreds.

"Two."

"That'll be a good run," he said and returned to his breakfast.

"What would you like to do this morning?" DJ asked, returning his attention to me.

"I have no idea what my options are."

"There's a park, not too far from here, and a museum, and we can grab lunch before we return. There will be a brief break before the individual competition begins, so we can see the students. With it being Gary's first time, I'd like to be there before they go in."

"He's a special one, isn't he?" I asked, already knowing the answer.

DJ smiled and nodded. "Yep, sometimes you get a student who really gets to you differently from the rest. He's been that kid for a long time."

"Why did you get him before high school?"

"I probably should have had him from the time he came to our school, but that was before Mrs. Moore became our headmistress; she has a very different philosophy. She gets it better than most administrators," he said appreciatively. "Also, his parents hadn't quite accepted his differences. They were hopeful he'd grow out of it and be *normal*. They were also dealing with their younger son with Down's Syndrome much of that time. I'm sure Gary was put on the back burner for a couple of years. He was mainstreamed for all of his elementary years. Once he hit middle school, though, it all came to a head. I was called in on several occasions to mediate and help him negotiate his terms. He was ready for a change. His parents wanted to keep him in the middle school for social reasons, but the middle school teachers didn't want him anymore. I expect the middle school students didn't want him anymore, either. They didn't know how to accommodate his needs. I didn't really, still don't, but he and I get along and could figure things out better. I'm a bit more altruistic when it comes to dealing with challenging students. I believe that true education is greatly self-guided and organic in nature. Sure, we give them plenty of guidelines and timelines, and we educators have managed to suck all the life and fun out of gaining knowledge. Standardized testing and norms and objectives and scopes and sequences do nothing to improve an already gifted mind. So, yeah, he's a special one, indeed."

I loved hearing DJ talk about his greatest passion. It was engaging and drew me in entirely. After breakfast, we went back to the room. I wasn't particularly interested in going to a museum or a park, but I would do whatever to be with him. It was Saturday and we didn't have to run errands. We could just *be* together.

He was texting on his phone when I came out of the bathroom. He looked concerned. "Is everything okay?" I asked.

"Yes. Just checking in with parents. Reassuring Penny's mom that she's not getting pregnant on this trip and that she's not secretly sneaking off with Gary or Nick. I also have to comfort Gary's mom that he's fine and wasn't abducted by aliens."

"Really?" I asked.

"Not the aliens part, but she has a terrible fear he's going to be abducted."

"It sounds like you have to manage their parents as well."

"You have no idea. They have been conditioned to be responsible for everything for their children. Their instincts are in overdrive, and I have to work just as hard to gain their trust as I do the students."

"You're pretty amazing," I said and I know my eyes did that gushing girl thing. He smiled broadly. I think he liked that response. "It's probably why you're so patient with me and all my crazy."

"Yes, you are a pretty special one, too," he said downplaying his feelings for me.

He stood and walked toward me. He put his phone down on the TV stand and took my hands. He looked down at them and sighed. "I'm sorry we've not had very much time together these past couple of months. I miss you, and I worry that you're not okay. I also hate that I'm not there to help you through the rough spots."

"Other than the dreams, I'm doing okay. I know this week was unusually rough for both of us. I'm doing what I can." I shrugged. "It's definitely testing my patience on both fronts."

He leaned over slightly and kissed me. He held me close and kissed me gently. I was relieved to know kissing was allowed in hotel rooms. I smiled and it distracted him.

"What?" he asked as he took in my expression.

"I'm glad to know we can kiss here."

"What do you mean?"

"Well, we only kiss downstairs at home. Night-before-last when I kissed you in my bed, you didn't allow it. You don't touch me at all upstairs. You take my hand in public and you even kiss me sometimes when we're out, but it's not overly mushy and wouldn't make anyone uncomfortable. You're very careful with me."

He nodded once. "Yes, I am. With good reason, wouldn't you say?" He stepped back from me. I hadn't meant for my words to cause him to move away.

I sat down on the bed and watched him as he crossed his arms and leaned against the wall. He looked determined and bothered. "And to be clear, you didn't just kiss me in your bed, you attacked me."

"Indeed," I sighed.

He pursed his lips and furled his brow like he didn't want to ask the next question that was pressing. It pained him and I knew exactly what he was about to ask. My stomach sank when he spoke the words. "Who is Victor and why do you keep dreaming about him?"

I swallowed hard and my mouth went dry. I didn't know exactly how to answer that question. I'd been screaming his name in my dreams for two nights this week. I'd seen his face. I knew his smile. His laughter was present all along. I couldn't accept that he was dead and there was no saving him. I felt sad and my heart ached at the loss. I'm sure the emotion washed over my entire face. I couldn't conceal the pain. "He's the man in the Volvo."

"Do you remember seeing him?"

"Only in glimpses, but I know him. He's the one in the car with me from my nightmares. He's the one I want to save and I can't. He laughs and calls after me. I can't explain it."

"Did you know that couple?" he asked trying to make a connection.

"Not that I know of, but it's like I'm in the Volvo every time I dream of the crash, and I only wake up briefly in the Honda. It's very confusing. I saw their picture at the library on Thursday. They made some big donation and were being honored. I wasn't expecting to see them; I was caught off guard. Later, I searched them on the internet. I feel an attachment to them that I can't reason away. I'm sorry if hearing his name upset you. I can only imagine what you must have been thinking."

He furled his brow and nodded once, but he didn't uncross his arms or remove the mask from his face. Thankfully he didn't look mad, just bothered, cautious. He eyed me for a few moments longer and then sighed, "Let's get out of here, get some fresh air."

He drove us to the museum, but they didn't open for another half hour so we walked around the gardens and grounds, taking in all the beauty. Even in the late, southern winter, there were buds and blooms and lush evergreens. Birds chirped and squirrels chattered and scurried around us.

DJ took my hand as we walked. It was nice and felt right. He stopped at the end of one of the pathways and turned toward me. He looked deeply into my eyes. "I didn't think the worst of you for screaming another man's name. I want to make that perfectly clear. I honestly just wanted to know he wasn't hurting you or you weren't in any danger, even in your nightmares."

I felt relieved. He brushed my bangs back from my face. My hair was growing out and my bangs were nearly past my eyebrows, nicely covering the scar. He held my face and kissed me. The concern and conflict from earlier were gone. He'd accepted my explanation and didn't want to press me. Good thing, because I didn't know what else I could have said to explain any of it.

We arrived at the competition after our morning out. Everyone had gathered outside the auditorium. Nick motioned for us to come over to their side of the room when he saw us come in.

"How was it?" Darren asked.

"Piece of cake," Nick said confidently.

"A lot like last year," Penny said.

"Gary?" Darren asked.

"Fine. It was very similar to the posted questions. Like I said before, straightforward. I'm satisfied," Gary said. Penny smiled smugly, looking at Gary. If I didn't know better, she was hoping he'd beaten the socks off Nick.

"Do you need anything before you go in?" Darren asked. They each shook their heads.

"I have to go to the bathroom," Penny interjected. Nick rolled his eyes. I walked along with Penny. She was chatty and didn't mind me tagging along with her. She stared at me in the bathroom, watching me in the mirror as we washed our hands.

"What?" I asked, feeling a little self-conscious. Surely, she'd be polite enough to tell me if I had anything in my nose or teeth.

"Gary's right. You do smell like Darren. Do I smell like Gary?"

"I have no idea." I laughed a little, but she was completely serious. "I haven't noticed. Would you like me to compare?"

"I don't think we do, yet. Perhaps in time if we ever live together. I'm just curious. I don't know very much about dating and relationships. I read articles online, but they aren't very informative. Girl magazines are stupid. They give such insipid advice, like a girl can't be logical about her feelings."

"What does Gary say?" I asked.

"He says that we have to maintain mutual respect and communicate our thoughts and feelings without making it a personal attack or placing blame when we have conflicts."

I smirked. "I think he's been talking with Darren."

She nodded. "He gives good advice most of the time."

***

The afternoon competition went smoothly from what I could tell. I finally just put in my headphones and listened to music. DJ was intrigued and sat on the edge of his chair like it was riveting. I didn't understand any of what I observed. The individual problem solving was set up on different tables and they had to go to each station and read laminated instructions or study an illustration or a diagram. On one table was a three-dimensional model of whatever they were trying to figure out. It was all beyond me.

There was one table that the students returned to for further examination. Gary was one of the few students who hadn't needed to return to it. DJ smiled, seeing the gears working in that young man's mind.

We ate dinner together in the dining hall on campus. It wasn't too bad for cafeteria food, and they joked that they were happy Tommy wasn't with them.

"He'd have had a field day with this crew," Nick laughed.

The evening session consisted of the team competition. Nick took the role of leader. "Since this is your first time, Gary, I don't expect to win, but take mental notes for next year. I want this before I graduate. My application to MIT won't be complete without it."

"How much better will it be if we take it two years in a row?" Gary asked, confidently.

"It might get me into their summer program or even Harvard's or Princeton's," Nick said, smugly. "Do you think you're capable of making that happen?"

"Why do you doubt me?" Gary asked. "We're supposed to be a team. You obviously can't win it by yourself."

Nick looked at Penny. She looked as determined as Gary. "You're right. I can't. I'll do my best to remember that." He was arrogant even in his attempt to submit and be a team player.

"You guys are going to do great. Remember to rely on each other's strengths and communicate your thoughts before jumping in and making your own calls. You may not be seeing everything clearly." He looked at Nick pointedly. "Remember to verbalize your thoughts, Gary, and communicate with one another, otherwise you're going to get sloppy and waste time. Penny, do not look away from your table, even when you're finished. Stay together and only make eye-contact with your teammates." She nodded, obediently. It was a great pep talk. I felt rallied, too.

This session was much more interesting to watch. Each group had their own table. The instructions were less than a half-page of typed information. That seemed daunting to me. Nick looked knowingly at Gary. He was almost grinning. They passed the paper across the table to Penny. She read through the instructions carefully and then blinked her eyes disbelievingly. She tossed her hair back over her shoulder, looking more like a vixen than a genius girl at a math competition. She was going in for an attack. She winked at Gary and he smiled his goofy, *I love this girl's mind* smile and they began.

They shook their heads a couple of times and seemed to disagree with something they'd done in previous steps. It wasn't easy for them. It was challenging, but they enjoyed every second of it. Thirty minutes into the task, Penny pulled a hair elastic from her wrist and put her hair back in a ponytail. She was serious and focused and began sketching something on the graph paper. It appeared that neither Gary nor Nick disputed each other. Perhaps that was the greatest challenge for them.

The ninety-minute session was coming to a close. The minutes were ticking away. The ferocity of the earlier problem solving had passed for many of the tables. It was just a matter of working through the problems and checking their computations. Gary passed his work onto Penny and she checked over it, although she'd watched his every step and pointed out things as he went along, all the while sketching and measuring along the graph. Nick was writing frantically.

"He's writing out their explanation," DJ whispered close into my ear. "They have to both prove it mathematically and give reason for their approach to the problem. The explanation is key. Nick doesn't show it often, but he has the ability to convince just about anyone with his words. He'll charm the judges. Thank goodness he doesn't have to present it in person."

"You really enjoy this, don't you?" I whispered.

He smiled. "You have no idea," he mouthed silently and refocused on the competition.

We only had a few minutes to see them before they were whisked off to the geek mixer. They were smiling, though, and felt accomplished. "Have fun. Don't think about it anymore. No obsessing," DJ warned. "Eat plenty of crap and fill your heads with mindless teenager things. I want you to stay up late and sleep the entire way home tomorrow. Understand?" They nodded, smiling. "Oh, and Nick, stay away from those Midland boys. They're trouble. Just go and find some nice girl and dance with her. You can't get into too much trouble that way."

He eyed Darren and raised his eyebrow. "Is that a challenge?" he asked.

Darren shook his head. "As long as she's not from Midland." Nick laughed with him and the three of them left with all the other students toward their party.

"I'm sure there's a story behind that comment."

"Yes, there is, and the gentleman who spoke with us at breakfast is their coach. He's antagonistic and his boys do just about anything to get Nick disqualified. If Gary does as well as I think he will, they'll be after him next year, too. Eliminate the competition. That's who beat Nick and Penny last year.

I'm hoping they knock them down a notch or two with their technical merit."

CHAPTER 33

Once we were back at the hotel, DJ asked if he could watch some basketball. I didn't mind. He'd not had any time recently to do anything fun. I dozed on and off when the game went into overtime. I was so tired, but I wasn't sure why. I didn't feel like I'd overexerted myself today. I supposed it was just our day together and being so comfortable. We'd not had this much closeness in weeks.

DJ kissed the top of my head and eased away from me out of the bed. "Where are you going?" I asked, sleepily.

"I forgot something in the van. I'll be right back."

I don't remember him coming back into the room. I don't remember much about the rest of the night. My dreams were easy waves of color and light, and the peace of lying close to DJ returned my previous joy.

We got up early, ate breakfast, and made our way to the morning awards ceremony. The Midland coach was the first to greet us. He was wearing cowboy boots and a large hat. He was surely dressed for Texas.

"Good morning. Fine day for a win, wouldn't you say?"

"Indeed," DJ replied in a friendly, noncompetitive way. I admired the way he kept his emotions in check. I wanted to say something antagonistic and probably a bit sarcastic, so it was a good thing this man hadn't spoken to me directly. I smiled politely.

"Ed Greerson," the man said, putting out his hand toward me.

"Beth Rust," I said and shook his hand. He eyed me a bit warily and raised his eyebrow when he realized we had different last names. He tipped his cowboy hat toward me.

"Nice meeting you," he said to me and then turned his attention back to DJ. "You've got a nice little filly, here. Hope your team's ranking doesn't embarrass your attempt to impress her."

"Oh, I'm not concerned about that," he said confidently. "Our team has already won her over, now it's just a matter of seeing the results of their efforts." DJ dipped his chin, dismissing him with a simple gesture.

We found our seats in the final assembly. The students were seated down front, near the stage. All three of them ranked in the top ten. Penny was one of two girls on the stage. Gary and Nick both received top rankings for their test results. They were among the top five students. A Midland boy, a senior, placed first. Ed looked over at DJ smugly and nodded once.

Gary placed third in the individual competition. Nick was obviously bothered that he got fourth overall. Gary had beaten him by only one or two points. Then the team competition was announced. Nick, Penny, and Gary were called to the stage. Nick was beaming! They were awarded a huge trophy for their efforts. He high-fived Gary and even hugged Penny in his excitement. Coach Greerson wouldn't make eye contact with either one of us. He sat there in disbelief.

"Congratulations!" we said together as soon as we could make our way down to the student section. The three of them were pleased with their efforts.

Once we were in the van, they chatted excitedly as we headed back onto the interstate towards home.

Not twenty minutes into the trip, our charges' excitement waned. They'd eaten and the accumulation of the past three days had caught up with them. They yawned and their eyelids looked heavy. Penny leaned into Gary's shoulder and he put his arm around her. They looked peaceful as they drifted off to sleep. Nick cradled the trophy affectionately on the back seat and managed to sleep with it in his arms. He was so proud!

I reached over and took DJ's hand. He smiled. "This has been a fun weekend. I'm glad I tagged along."

"Me, too."

"Are you going back to the library tonight?"

"I don't know."

"It's fine if you need to; I understand. Sadie invited me to dinner, so I won't be alone."

"Okay, tell her I'll drop you off before six, if she can bring you home."

I was a little tired on the drive, but I forced myself to stay awake and help keep DJ alert. "What do you plan to do once you complete your doctorate?" I asked.

"Like how I plan to celebrate or career options?"

"Both, but I was actually thinking career more specifically."

"I want to continue to teach, that's for sure, but I'd like to become an adjunct professor and teach some undergraduate classes. I think I have experience to pass along to other teachers. What do you want to do, Beth? What goals do you have, currently?"

I wasn't expecting that question. "Personally, or professionally?" I had begun to construct a fantasy existence, daydreaming about our life as husband and wife, with children and friends and family, traveling to see Tom and Mary and introducing Michael to his cousins, but I was unsure about my ability to teach and manage a classroom. I shrugged, "I don't know."

"I don't believe you," he said in a low voice. I looked behind me toward the backseats. Everyone's ears were plugged with headphones and their eyes were closed. "They can't hear us," DJ said confidently. I looked at the side of his head. He caught my eye and then turned back to face the road. "Go ahead, I'm listening."

"As far as working; I have no idea. I get a sense that I'd like to be able to return to my students, but I have nothing to base that on. The rest is silly and I'm not sure I'm in the right frame of mind to follow through. I have a lot of time to daydream, so it may not be very realistic." I hesitated before continuing. The silence wasn't awkward; it was just silent and DJ was being patient to let me go at my own pace. "I'd like to be your wife and start a family," I finally whispered.

He froze. He didn't look away from the road. I wasn't sure he'd heard me. My stomach sank thinking I'd have to repeat it louder. Then, he finally exhaled. "Are you serious?" He cut his eyes at me. I nodded with a nervous smile. I swallowed, again, relieved the saliva had returned to my mouth. "I'd like that, too," he said solemnly, and I could hear emotion in his low voice. My smile broadened and I learned over and kissed his hand.

"Do you think I'm ready?" I asked. "It's been nearly four months since the crash and I'm not really better, you know?"

"I don't know why we couldn't move in that direction. Do you have a timeline?" he asked.

I shrugged. "I think it's long overdue, but I'm not exceedingly patient."

He chuckled. "Are you talking about getting married or starting a family?"

"Can't they happen simultaneously?" I asked.

"Absolutely, but do you imagine a particular wedding day or venue?"

"I'd like your family to be there and I guess our few friends, if that's possible, but I don't want a big, fancy affair. I think I'd like to hold a bouquet and wear a simple dress, something feminine, and my boots. I want to promise all the right things and make it official."

"You've given this some thought."

"Yeah, like I said, I have a lot of time to daydream. What have you always envisioned?"

He chuckled, again. "To stand before God and promise to love you, to exchange vows and rings, and then take you away for a few days and claim you forever."

"What am I wearing?"

"A huge, puffy, white dress with a headpiece that makes you look six-feet tall," he said seriously.

"That's BS!" I exclaimed.

He laughed. "Beth, honestly, I've only recently begun to think of the reality. It doesn't matter what we wear. I see you. I see your eyes and your smile, and it's a sunny day."

"So, we're being wed at a nudist colony?"

He rolled his eyes and shook his head. "No. There are clothes because I get to undress you before I make love for the first time."

Something in the way he said *first time* made me hesitate. Surely, he'd had sex before. Surely, his first time wouldn't be with me. My opinion of his self-discipline and masochistic nature peaked. I let go of his hand.

"You're serious." I said.

"Dead serious." He looked over at me.

"You've never? Really? How is that possible?"

"I hadn't before I met you, and you know what our relationship has been since."

"DJ, that's a lot to put on me. You know my past."

"Now you know mine," he said flatly.

We neither said anything for a long time. I didn't know what to do with that information. No wonder he wanted to wait. His logic made more sense now. I stared out the window. Penny sat up and announced her desire to stop. Everyone was moving slowly from the van. They'd spent all of their mental energy on the competition and it seemed to ooze over and tap into their physical energy. They all stretched as they got out of the van and DJ pumped gas.

IMPACT

I didn't make eye contact with anyone as I got back into the van. "You okay?" DJ asked. I nodded solemnly. The kids were all awake, now, so he played music and we didn't really talk the rest of the way home.

After we dropped off the kids and he'd given appropriate responses to their parents, DJ drove us home. I went into the townhouse and DJ carried my suitcase upstairs. He then went across the hall to his room.

I wasn't upset with him. It just felt awkward. I'm not sure why I assumed anything else, but I had. He said he'd dated but never was in love with anyone, but I also knew from my journals that love had very little to do with sex.

299

CHAPTER 34

DJ drove me to Sadie's for six. "We're not done talking about this," he said before I left the car.

"I know. I just need some time to process. I never imagined someone our age would still be a virgin. I was surprised, that's all. I shouldn't be, but I am. Did I know before?"

He nodded. "I kept very little from you." He leaned in and we kissed. "I'll be home by ten."

Sadie's house wafted love all the way to the curb. She'd pan-fried porkchops that she served with coleslaw and green beans. I loved Sadie's cooking. Her daughter-in-law had brought over a pound cake. She put on a pot of decaf and we sat on her front porch swing eating dessert. Sadie could tell something was on my mind.

"Beth, you seem unusually preoccupied this evening. You tired after your weekend?"

"No, not really. We had a good time with the kids. They're amazing!"

"Things okay between you and your roommate?" Sadie asked in the way she referred to DJ.

"Things are more serious. We're talking about getting married and what that looks like. He lets me imagine a future that's filled with love and family. I want it so badly."

"What's wrong with that? The two of you have been through a great deal from what you've told me, and I believe we all deserve a slice of happiness. What else is eating at you?" Her sixth sense and motherly instincts rarely rested.

"I keep dreaming about the couple in the Volvo, the husband, especially. I don't know why I survived when the other two people in the crash didn't! Why am I still here? I saw the pictures! There's no logical reason I left that crash virtually unscathed!"

"Honey, there's a lot in this world we can't explain. I don't know the reason, but I have faith enough to know that it's not always for our understanding. Give your all and love for as long as you can."

"Why do I keep seeing the other couple in my dreams?" I asked.

"I think that's a better question for your therapist. What does she say?"

"She has no idea, either."

Marcus came in from his extra shift, working security at the theater. He changed clothes and fixed himself a plate. He came outside and sat with us. It was a pleasant evening. "My girl's coming home early. Her unit got word last week. She'll be home before the end of the summer." He smiled broadly.

"That's great! I can't wait to meet her."

"That makes two of us," Sadie said.

"You've not met her?" I asked, surprised.

"Not officially. We've spoken over the phone a couple of times. I've seen pictures and she's a pretty girl. She makes my baby smile, so I think I already like her." She cut her eyes at Marcus playfully and winked.

301

Sadie drove me home in Sadie Cadillac. Marcus was tired and had an early shift the next morning. I had a couple of hours before DJ returned from the library. I sat at the keyboard and tried to play, but I was distracted. There was something nagging at the back of my mind. I went to my computer and Googled Victor and Katherine again.

This time, the couples' Facebook pages came up. I was able to gain access into their lives from a different vantage point. Their personal pages weren't filled with as much of the social and philanthropic. There were older photos of the couple with a little boy. He was a beautiful child. He had his mother's beauty, but his father's coloring and vibrant eyes.

A haunting feeling washed over me. The feverish, unresponsive child I'd seen when I'd wakened Michael that morning before Christmas. I felt sickened. I knew that boy just like I knew his father. Had I taught him? Had he been in my class? That wasn't possible. The timing and our ages were all wrong. How did I know this child? I showered and got ready for bed. It was all too weird and bizarre to even obsess over, but I knew there were too many factors to disregard a connection.

It was just before ten when I heard DJ come in the front door. I was sitting on the edge of my bed rubbing lotion over my feet and hands when he popped his head into my room. He was smiling, broadly. "Looks like you're ready for bed. May we talk?"

"Sure, come in."

His smile turned sheepish. "I'd like to kiss you, so I'd prefer we go back downstairs."

"You can kiss me here. I give you permission. I'm not going to attack you... again; I promise." I rolled my eyes and raised my hands in surrender. "Besides, I just put lotion on my feet and I was about to get into bed."

He took the two steps from the door and sat down next to me. I eased over and crossed my legs under the covers. I sat up straighter against the pillows. DJ leaned in and kissed me gently on the lips. There was even less passion than when he kissed me in the kitchen. He sat back and looked at me. He leaned in and tried again.

"Wasn't what you expected?" I guessed.

"No."

"Sorry. Move. I'll go downstairs with you," I said, resigned.

He stood and I followed him to the kitchen. He turned toward me and took me into his arms at the base of the stairs. He completely enveloped me in his embrace. He kissed the top of my head and I moved my arms around his waist. I lifted my face from his chest and he bent his face to mine. *That's better*, I thought as he kissed me and the little tingles and twinges in my midsection fired off. His breath tasted of fresh peppermint. The minor inconvenience of getting out of bed was worth this feeling.

I eased my arms up and around his shoulders, drawing him even closer to me. Whatever passion had eluded the kisses he'd attempted in my bedroom flooded through him, now, and I allowed it all to wash over me like a warm wave. Our kissing was the perfect diversion. It never failed to keep me grounded and secure in the moment.

He walked me gently to the sofa without breaking contact. He eased me down and I pulled him down next to me. In seconds, I straddled my legs over him. I removed his glasses and ran my hands through his hair and over his shoulders. His hands groped my back and held my hips and waist securely against him.

My eyes were closed, but I knew every inch of his body without sight. I knew every inch of my body at that very moment also. I knew exactly where he was touching me and where I was touching him and where our bodies were nearly fused together.

"DJ," I gasped when he began kissing down my neck. "You don't actually think this is a safer kissing place than my bedroom, do you?" I panted. I leaned my head back and took a deep breath. He shook his head and the stubble of his beard tickled my neck. That only aroused my senses more, and I forced his mouth back to mine.

My hands went to his neck and my fingers nimbly unbuttoned his shirt while I kissed him. I was disappointed when my hands reached into his shirt and instead of finding his bare chest, he was wearing a t-shirt underneath. I frowned and sat back looking at him.

"Sorry," he said. He could read my expression clearly. "It's a t-shirt not a bullet proof vest."

"Hmmm. You wore it intentionally, didn't you?" I sounded petulant.

"I do most every day, but not for the reason you're thinking." I removed myself from his lap and stood. "Where are you going?" he asked.

"I need a drink of water." I turned toward the kitchen and fixed myself a glass from the sink. I guzzled it and then refilled the glass. I walked back toward the sofa and offered it to DJ. He took a sip and then returned it to me.

"Why did you stop kissing me?" he asked.

"Because I know it's not going anywhere and because you said you wanted to talk and because of what you said this afternoon."

"I figured."

"So, let's talk."

"I spoke with my professor this evening. He thinks my proposal is ready for submission."

"That's awesome!" I smiled and jumped back into his arms, pride and relief and excitement for all of his efforts. "I'm so proud of you."

"I still have some minor work to do to polish it up, but I'm relieved it's done."

"Me, too." I kissed him and held him close.

"I'd appreciate if you'd read it through for me. Find any obvious grammar errors."

"Sure. Have you told your parents?"

"Not yet, I wanted you to be the first to know."

"They're going to be so excited! Wow! What's next?"

"I'll submit it to the committee for review. I'll be selected as a doctoral candidate and then hopefully complete the process in the next couple of years. I should be eligible to sit for the exams next semester."

We were both smiling and delighted by this news. No wonder our kissing had accelerated so quickly. He was happy. I was happy. He kissed me again and held me close. "What else is on your mind?" I asked.

"I was hoping we could talk about your reaction to this afternoon's bombshell."

"I'm sorry I reacted so negatively. That was incredibly immature and judgmental on my part. I have no right to think of you differently because we've made different choices. I was taken by surprise and my response was ridiculous. I feel even more ridiculous because I don't even remember having sex with anyone, so I don't know why I responded like that at all."

He laughed. "I hadn't thought about it that way. You don't remember anyone else, do you?"

"No. I know what I've read about myself and I know what you've told me. I'm well-aware my body knows what to do especially when you kiss me like you did ten minutes ago." A blush rose to my ears. "But other than that, I don't have anything to compare it to."

He smiled and drew me closer. "Good. That's something we'll discover together, then."

"Speaking of that, do we really have to wait until we're married?" I sounded petulant, again.

"I'd like to."

"But why? Why is that so important to you?" He sighed, resisting my pleading tone. "Wouldn't you agree that physical love is important between two people who love one another?"

He took in a deep breath and let it out slowly. "I agree with that, wholeheartedly, in the protection of marriage, absolutely."

"Is it because of God?" I asked.

"That's a loaded question. I'd like to try and articulate my thoughts and feelings in a way that you can accept and hopefully understand." He sat back and diverted his eyes, remembering. "When I was fifteen, I ran with some guys whose sole purpose was to have sex. They spoke non-stop about it. They were in constant pursuit of this Holy Grail. I didn't understand; we were only fifteen and I'd been taught differently. Two of my five friends had sex with the first girls who said yes. The other three were a little choosier, but still, it didn't take them long to find girls who were agreeable. I thought it was a stupid quest and they razzed me plenty for my decision to abstain." He cut his eyes and shook his head sharply. The memory wasn't a pleasant one. "Fortunately, my dad was transferred and we moved.

"By the time we were seniors, one guy had already gotten two girls pregnant; a second had been on more than his share of antibiotics and seemed prone to crabs. The final straw, though, for me, happened at the end of our senior year. Two of the other guys, twins, and I were drinking late. We'd kept in touch after my dad got transferred, and I'd gone back to visit them before graduation. They both encouraged me to wait.

"We were at their dad's fishing camp, sitting around the firepit. We'd had plenty to drink. 'It's not worth it, man. I mean, yeah, it feels good in the moment, but it's not like it's the greatest thing in the world when you look beyond it. I wish someone had told me that and shaken some sense into me. I met this girl last summer and she's the most amazing thing in the world. We've dated all year. I don't know; it's like she's different from anyone I've ever met and I want her to be the first and only, but she won't ever be. Kinda sucks, you know?'

"I did know, and when I met you six months later, that's exactly how I felt. It still is." He looked tenderly into my eyes and stroked my cheek with his thumb.

"But," I began as a rebuttal.

"No, buts." He placed his thumb over my lips. "All through college, I heard the same tales. As a grown man, I hear even more lamenting over past relationships: regrets, comparisons, and unplanned pregnancies. Do you have any idea the number of men paying child support for one-night-stands?" I shook my head. "I don't want any of that."

"But we aren't a one-night-stand, and I think God would understand."

"Yes, I'm sure God would understand and forgive us if we asked. Marriage was instituted for our protection, though. There are rules for a reason. It's not to limit our impulses or punish us. Marriage elevates sex from a carnal act into a blessing. I'd rather wait for the blessing."

"I've never thought about it like that."

"Not many people do. Besides, we're adults making adult choices and I think we can wait a few more months."

My stomach tightened and excitement pounded in my chest. "Months?" I clarified. He nodded and I waited expectantly for his reply.

"I'm thinking this summer will be exceptionally sunny."

I could hardly contain my excitement. "Really? Are you proposing?"

"Not yet. I just want you to clear your calendar." Joy, pure joy, radiated through me like combustion. I couldn't get close enough to him to satisfy my need to express it adequately.

"Darren James Fitzgerald, I love you."

"I love you, too, Beth."

CHAPTER 35

For the next two weeks, I floated on thin air. I went to my appointments; I attended my library classes. I learned to make a dishcloth and began a hat. Everything I saw was beautiful and amazing; everyone I spoke to probably thought I was high. No one was naturally this happy.

I followed up with Dr. Saunders the week before spring break. DJ couldn't come because he had an advisor's meeting to submit his paper. His meeting ran late, but he said he'd try to meet me there. Waiting in the neurologist's office was like waiting in perpetual hell. Waiting in perpetual hell alone was even worse. I read through every magazine. I went to the bathroom. I'd even eaten the crushed-up granola bar from the bottom of my purse. I finally put in headphones and rested my head against the wall behind my chair. I was bored out of my mind.

I opened my eyes with a start. DJ was standing in front of me smiling. "Did they accept it?" I asked hopeful. He nodded and kissed me. "I'm so glad you're here. I'm about to lose my mind."

He chuckled. "Again?"

I laughed. "Okay, I need to stop saying that."

"Yes, you do. Here, I brought you something. Close your eyes."

I held out my hands eagerly and opened my eyes wide with excitement when he placed a huge Styrofoam cup into my hands. "Thank you!"

"You're welcome."

"How did you know?"

He shrugged. "It wasn't hard to guess. You've been here for a couple of hours, and your patience has probably turned into starvation. Am I right?" I nodded and took a huge sip of the chocolate shake. I sat happily until the nurse called me back into the examination room.

"It isn't polite not to share." Dr. Saunders said when he noticed my shake cup. "Where's mine?"

"It isn't polite to make me wait for two hours to see you, either. It's my reward for patience." I smiled and blinked my eyes innocently.

"Some things can't be avoided." He raised his eyebrows and greeted DJ like he pitied him a little for having to wait with me.

DJ shrugged. "I just got here; you haven't kept me waiting."

"Anything to report?" Dr. Saunders asked.

"Nothing. No episodes. Some dreams, but lessened in severity. I'm still seeing my therapist weekly," I said.

"Headaches?" he asked as he shined the little light into my eyes.

"Only one a couple of weeks ago." Dr. Saunders nodded in approval at that.

"Energy level?"

"Good. I'm not as sleepy all the time. I think not having to take the headache medication helps. When do you think I can begin weaning from the seizure medication?"

"I don't see that happening right away. I'd like you to be episode free for six months before we begin altering the dosage. I'd also like to schedule another CT scan before making any decisions."

"I have a couple of questions." I said.

"Go ahead," he said, documenting something on his tablet.

I cut my eyes at DJ and decided to ask the lesser of the two evils. He and I hadn't discussed either one of these topics. "I was wondering, with our headmistress's approval, if I might be able to go and observe in my old classroom. I could go for short periods of time and just be present. I think there's a little part of me that misses it." I could see DJ's smile out of the corner of my eye. That pleased him.

Dr. Saunders crossed his arms and considered my request. He didn't say anything for several seconds. "Short periods like a half-hour?"

"Yes, please."

"Okay. I can allow that. If you manage that well, then you may increase that time gradually."

"Thank you." I smiled.

"What else is on your mind? Let's hear it." Dr. Saunders placed his hands in his lab coat pockets and took a more casual stance.

"Darren and I plan to be married this summer. We'd like to start a family. I guess I'm asking if there are any reasons why that shouldn't happen, neurologically or with the current medication."

DJ was watching me closely. The look on his face wasn't shock, but he was definitely not prepared for what'd I'd just asked. Dr. Saunders nodded solemnly and then smiled.

"Congratulations." He looked at DJ and considered him as well. He could read the surprise on DJ's face. "These are valid concerns, but you don't have anything to worry about. Your medication is safe for pregnancy. If you happen to get pregnant while you're on it, we won't make any changes until the baby is born. If you're anticipating pregnancy, then I recommend you begin taking a multi-vitamin and high levels of folic acid every day. I'll write you that script along with the scan orders before you go."

"Thank you," I said. Dr. Saunders shook his head slightly like he was arguing with himself. "What?" I asked.

"You two weren't engaged before the accident, were you?" He looked at my hand. No ring.

We both shook our heads. "No, that's a recent development," DJ said, but his eyes flickered with a bit of mischief. "We aren't technically engaged, yet."

"I see." Dr. Saunders furled his brow and then grinned slyly. "How many shakes does it take for you to wait patiently for that?"

I laughed. "You have no idea," I said dramatically.

"I'll see you in six weeks. Behave yourself. Don't be stupid. I can't do anything for the stubbornness." He laughed and left the exam room.

I moved down from the examination table and gathered my belongings. DJ stopped me. "Wait." I looked up questioningly. He kissed me. "I wasn't expecting any of that."

"I know. Sorry. I don't like wondering all the time and making guesses. You said we were being adults. I want to be sure, too, but for other reasons and he seemed like the right person to ask." He nodded and seemed to be considering something. Doubt flashed across his face or maybe it was a question, but he quickly shook it off. "I think we have reason to celebrate, tonight. Want to see what Dan and Molly are doing? Maybe they'd like to celebrate, too."

"Sure," he said.

They were already on their way to dinner, so we asked if we could join them. As of Monday, Molly was still on the fence about going to Texas with Dan. He was leaving Friday afternoon, so she only had a day to decide. "Were you planning on going home for Easter?" I asked her after we worked out Monday afternoon.

"No," she said.

"So, your parents won't even miss you if you go to Texas."

"Nope."

"You still aren't sure?"

"No," she said in a sigh. She looked petrified.

"What's the big deal?"

"What if they don't like me? What if they don't think I'm good enough for their son?"

"What if they adore you and think you're perfect?"

"That's even greater pressure." She paled.

"What are you talking about?" I asked.

"Then I won't have a choice but to introduce him to my family. Can't we just date and keep it simple?"

"Sure, but is that what you truly feel for him? Simple? Easy? Casual?"

She shook her head. "No. I don't feel any of those things."

"Alright, then, put on your big girl panties and go and meet his family!"

"I'll talk with him again. His sister friended me on Facebook. She seems really sweet."

"I'm sure they're harmless. Go! You'll be regretting it, if you don't. I was so nervous when we went to Chicago, but I'm very glad I did."

***

Dan and Molly were already seated in the booth when we arrived. Dan had his elbow propped onto the table, facing Molly. The way he was leaning over, his broad shoulders completely blocked her from view. She looked so small next to him. Her features were petite and feminine, but he could have scooped her up in one hand if he wanted. Her big brown eyes looked over and widened as we approached. He was holding her hand and smiling.

Dan stood and greeted us and I eased into the booth across from Molly. She was beaming. "Did you decide to go?" I guessed.

"Yes." She nodded enthusiastically and then cut her eyes at Dan. "He threatened to kidnap me if I didn't agree to go willingly."

"I didn't say that. You make me sound so sinister." She giggled. "I simply told her that I'd like to take her to lunch before I left town and to please pack a bag with a couple of changes of clothes; it would be a very long lunch date. She completely mistook my meaning." He put his arm around her and hugged her close. He was happy that she'd finally agreed to go. They were an adorable couple.

After dinner, we went home; we were both tired. We tried to stay up a little while to be together, but I was falling asleep next to him on the sofa. "I need to go to bed," I said, yawning.

"Me, too. I'm beat." He stood and stretched and offered me a hand.

He kissed me goodnight before we went upstairs. "I'll see you in the morning," I said. "I love you."

"Goodnight. I love you, too."

I hadn't dreamt of the crash or Victor in weeks. I hadn't even woken upset. I'd slept well and held out hope that in my current joy, everything had passed somehow. So, I was more than pissed when I woke sobbing and nauseated and overcome with grief. I was definitely mourning a loss. I couldn't lift my head from the pillow. A part of me was dying and I couldn't breathe. I felt like my heart had been removed in the night. I tried to be still and hoped the feeling would pass. I dozed on and off. I couldn't tell how time was passing.

"Good morning." I heard DJ say in a comforting voice. "You've been asleep a long time. It's nearly ten. You okay?"

"I don't know. I don't feel well."

He came into my room and looked at me more carefully. "Are you hungry?" I shook my head. I had no appetite. "Do you feel like you have a fever?" He put his hand on my forehead. His eyes were concerned. "You're warm." I was warm but didn't have the energy to care. Lethargic, I definitely felt lethargic. I blinked and my eyes stayed closed. "Want me to take you to the doctor?"

I shook my head. "No doctors. I just want to sleep, okay?"

"Okay. I'll check on you again. I was going to the gym. Do you want me to stay?"

I shook my head. "No, go. I'll be okay." He kissed the side of my head and patted my shoulder. He adjusted the quilt over me and I heard the door shut and bolt downstairs.

I felt someone's hand on my head, stoking my hair. "DJ?" I asked.

"No, baby, it's me. It's Victor." I opened my eyes and he was there, lying next to me in the bed. He was so real. I could see every detail in his face, his loving smile. He held my gaze, purposefully with those clear, blue eyes. "I've missed you," he said. "It's been too long since I've held you." He placed his hand on my cheek. I shook my head slightly. "We're caught between worlds. You can't hang on like this. I'm not here, anymore. You need to let me go, baby." I shook my head again. I didn't know what he was talking about.

"Katherine, baby, remember when we had to do it before? It's hard, but you can do it. Let me go; choose a different life."

"Why do you keep teasing me?" I asked, with a chuckle in my voice.

He laughed. "You can't resist it, can you?" His smile was lovingly playful.

"Victor, why?"

"I don't know, baby, but I need to go. Can you do that for me? Can you?" His eyes were pleading.

"I don't know. I don't understand what you want me to do."

I blinked sleepily and he disappeared, but his touch remained. Soon, I returned to a deep sleep, but it was anything but restful. I felt like I was thrashing against strong, mental restraints. I couldn't wake myself. I couldn't avoid the inevitable waves of memories. They started out slowly and clearly and then the waves turned turbulent, bordering on violent. The perspective of the crash was all wrong and the inconsistency bothered me.

The rainbow. The crash. The vehicles. The colors. My face, Beth's face, flying toward me, resolved and accepting of her fate. The bright light. This time, though, I could feel the jolt and the sudden force upon impact. The bright light. The cold darkness. The excruciating pain and choking were temporarily abated and then the sirens and the men shouting and then silence.

"Beth, honey, wake up. It's me, Sadie. I need you to look at me. Open your eyes." I shook my head. She shook me harder, rousing me from deep sleep. "Beth." Her voice was insistent and commanding. I couldn't fight her imposing tone. I opened my eyes and blinked against the light.

"What?" I asked impatiently. My voice was husky and thick.

"Beth, I need to take your temperature. Open your mouth."

I did as I was told and she placed the cool thermometer under my tongue.
She took my wrist and her hands felt cool against my skin. She removed the
thermometer from my mouth. "102 degrees."

"Hmmm," I groaned and tried to roll away from her. "Go away," I moaned.
"Leave me alone."

She chuckled. "Beth, honey, do you hurt anywhere? Do you have a sore
throat?"

"No, I'm hot and everything just aches me all over," I complained.

"It's probably the flu. She needs some Tylenol and plenty of liquids. What
do you have?"

"I think we have some canned soup in the pantry, but other than that,
nothing."

"Hand me my bag and get me some water. I'll stay with her until you get
back. You might want to stock up. You've been exposed, now, too."

"Great! What a way to spend spring break." I heard DJ grumble as he left
the room.

"Don't forget the bendy straws. It makes it easier to drink." Sadie sat back
down on the edge of the bed and helped me sit up enough to swallow the
capsules she'd placed into my hand. I was so weak I could hardly hold my head
up. She then eased me back into the covers and tucked me in. Even under the
quilt, I was shivering.

"This sucks," I said.

"Yep, every time," she agreed.

I heard her open a drawer and then she put socks on my feet. She went to my closet and found a hoodie, too. She sat me up and helped me into it. "That should keep you warmer." She tucked me in again.

"Did DJ call you?"

"Yep, sure did. He was worried when you didn't get up and he said you don't even own a thermometer. That boy sure does love you." I smiled a little, but didn't open my eyes or reply.

The Tylenol kicked in before DJ returned. I was a little more coherent and much more alert than before. I still couldn't lift my head from the pillow, but at least I wasn't hallucinating.

Sadie made herself comfortable and sat next to me on the bed until DJ returned. "How long has your husband been dead?" I asked.

"A little over five years. You already know that."

I nodded. "How long did it take you to grieve his death?"

"Longer than it took me to fall in love with him for sure. I don't know if I'm completely over it; I loved that man fiercely."

"What did you do to let him go?"

"This is a strange line of questioning, Beth. What is going on in your mind?"

"Victor. The man from the crash. I have to let him go. He just said so." Tears flowed from my eyes. "It's so hard."

IMPACT

Sadie rose from the bed and dampened a washcloth. She wiped my face tenderly. "I don't know who's talking to you, but he's right. If he's gone, you have to release him. You can't cling to the past and you can't keep what doesn't belong to you."

Tears flowed from my eyes. Involuntary sobs wrenched my chest. There was a hollow void where my heart should have been. Sadie held me close and let me cry. She couldn't have known why. She surely couldn't read my thoughts. None of that mattered; she just let me cry. Tears and tears and more tears. She held me close and rocked me back and forth. She muttered and soothed me with her deep, resonating hum. Maybe my fever hadn't gone down as much as I'd thought.

CHAPTER 36

DJ returned at some point. Sadie had released me after I drifted into another wave of sleep. She made me drink some water and I could hear the two of them talking in hushed tones over me. The daylight was bright at the edge of my curtains; I guessed it was still afternoon.

"Beth, I'm going now. I'll check on you again this evening. I'm going home to make you some soup." I think I nodded, but I wasn't sure.

"Sadie," I whispered, "I need to pee."

"Come on, honey, I'll get you to the bathroom." With each fevered step, my head ached. Chills ran down my entire body when I sat on the cold toilet seat. She patiently waited for me to finish and then made me wash my hands and face. She also made me drink another few sips of water before she allowed me to lie back down. She was so bossy.

DJ was left to command over me. He woke me a few times to give me more water and Tylenol. He wasn't as bossy as Sadie, but he was just as insistent. It was night when I heard Sadie return. She brought me up a mug with a bendy straw. I had to sip some broth. It tasted good, but I couldn't drink very much. I liked the crushed ice in the ginger ale better, but I wasn't sure how much of that I could stomach, either.

I spent all day Friday in the bed and again all-day Saturday. There were large gaps in time, but I could hear DJ and Sadie talking sometimes. I heard Victor talking more, but he wasn't making any sense, either. Sunday, I opened my eyes and my head didn't hurt when I blinked. It didn't hurt when I walked to the bathroom. I wasn't shivering constantly. I considered for a few moments that I might live.

I looked at myself in the mirror. I was paler than usual and my hair was standing up in every direction. "Beth." I heard DJ say.

"I'm okay. I need to brush my teeth." I had the worst taste in my mouth.

"Okay." He sounded exhausted. I went back into my bedroom and found him lying in my bed. "I heard you get up."

"What time is it?"

"A little past two a.m."

"I think I'm going to live." I said.

"Good, because I may need you take care of me, now." I felt his forehead. Sure enough, he was running a fever.

"Do you want to go back to your bed?" I asked.

"No, I'm good here, if that's okay with you. I don't think I can make it back."

"That's fine. Do you want anything? Do you need anything?" He shook his head and kept his eyes closed. "Text Mom and Dad and Sadie later. They'll wonder why I don't reply." He shuddered. I put the quilt over him and held him close to keep him warm. I was still exhausted, so it was easy to fall back asleep for the rest of the night.

Later Monday morning, I texted Sadie, Tom and Mary. They were sad to hear that DJ had fallen ill, but they were relieved that at least we were taking turns. Sadie said she'd come by after her shift and bring more provisions. She was a godsend. She refused to let me do anything, except let her in the door. She heated the broth on the stove and brought it up to me. DJ sipped some, but crashed again as soon as he downed some Tylenol and a few sips of water.

Sadie didn't judge us for being in the same bed. She said it was actually more convenient given our current state. She demanded that I rest and set an alarm to help me remember to administer regular doses to keep our relative fevers down.

"I'll check in with you again in the morning. If either of you gets considerably worse, call me." She looked at me for a long moment. "You having any more crazy dreams?" she asked.

I shook my head hesitantly, unsure of how to answer that. "Was I hallucinating with the fever?" I asked.

She shrugged. "I don't know the answer to that, but you were convinced. You still are, aren't you?" I nodded. "You need to rest and regain your strength. You'll figure it out when you feel better."

"Sadie, thank you. I don't know how we'd have managed without you." Tears welled in my eyes.

"Honey, you're going to be fine." And I knew her words meant more than recovering from the flu.

She tucked me into the bed, again, felt DJ's forehead, and then turned out the light. She left the hall light on, and I heard her leave. I was back asleep in seconds. My fever was virtually nonexistent, but as I drifted off to sleep, I could see Victor, again, lying between me and DJ. I could hear his voice.

"Katherine, you are so beautiful." He stroked my cheek again. "Do you know how much I love you?" I nodded. I sensed his love. I couldn't doubt the intensity of his eyes. "I'll understand if you don't want to join me, but whatever you choose, do what you got to do, baby, but I need you to let me go."

Tuesday morning, I was able to heat some broth for DJ and made sure he took his medicine. I walked him to the bathroom and helped him stay warm. He let me hold and cuddle him when the fever spiked and he was shivering uncontrollably. Other than cooking for him, it was the first time I could remember taking care of him; our relationship felt more balanced. It was the first time that he needed me more than I needed him. I liked that feeling.

By Tuesday afternoon, I felt well enough to take a bath. I texted Sadie to tell her my intentions. She asked if I needed her to come over. I didn't. I could manage a bath on my own. I must have been feeling better because for the first time in days, I could smell the sickness in the house. I felt the overwhelming need to disinfect every surface. It felt good to scrub the germs from my body.

I changed my pillowcase and threw my toothbrush away. I was not going to reinfect myself if I could help it. If DJ roused in the next day or two, I would be sure to change the linens and bleach everything.

Lying in the bed, next to DJ, I realized that the bed was extremely crowded. The memory of Victor was there, too. The strangest thoughts came to mind. He'd called me Katherine. If he were my husband, then I must be his wife. If I were his wife, then I wasn't Beth; I was Katherine, but how did I get into Beth's body? I was so confused. It didn't make sense.

I found my journal and began reading through my notes and memories from my dreams. Each and every one ultimately returned to the rainbow and the crash, waking screaming and clinging to the person in the passenger's seat next to me. This was completely insane. The fever must have made me delusional. None of what I was thinking was possible, but that didn't change the fact that I needed to grieve Victor's death. I needed to acknowledge the last few moments with him. I needed to put our past to rest, but where did that leave me in the present? I wanted the nightmares to end. I didn't want to continue waking in the night screaming another man's name.

I don't believe in reincarnation, I told myself several times through the course of the afternoon. *Is it like I'm possessing someone else's body?* "No, I'm not possessed!" I said aloud and DJ stirred but didn't wake.

I was absolutely obsessing over this new revelation, but if I spoke it aloud, they'd commit me. Maybe I wasn't over the flu, after all. I lay there staring at DJ, completely conflicted between what my heart and body felt for him and what my dreams told me about Victor. There were few words to describe the confusion and turmoil.

Sadie checked on me via text. She said she'd been called into the hospital because so many nurses were out with the flu. She wouldn't be able to stop by again. I was more than a little relieved. She'd notice my furled brow and read my expression. She would know something wasn't quite right with me. She'd pry and not let it go until she got an answer that satisfied her. I wasn't ready for that sort of interrogation.

Less than twenty-four hours later, DJ's strength rallied. His fever broke in the wee hours of the morning. He'd sweated so much that I had to put him in his own bed and change the sheets on mine. I found him a change of clothes and made sure he had plenty to drink. He'd need to rehydrate. I managed to eat a few saltines and drank more broth. I still felt hungry, so I scrambled myself some eggs and made toast. It tasted delicious. With my bed clean with new linens, I decided I'd disinfect all the surfaces of my bedroom and bathroom. On top of everything else, I was probably turning into a germaphobe.

DJ called me from his room. He was trying to get out of the bed, but was too weak to make it to the bathroom by himself. "I think I'm hungry," he said once I'd gotten him back into bed.

"Want some toast?" I asked.

He nodded and grabbed my hand before I left the side of the bed. "I'm so glad we're better, but I had very different plans for this week. None of them involved the flu or lying in bed." He blinked lazily.

I laid my cheek on the top of his head and stroked his back. I was disappointed, too, that DJ's break was spent sick. We hadn't made any plans, but I had been looking forward to ten days without classes or appointments or time apart.

"I'll bring up some broth and toast in a few minutes. Try and drink some more water before I get back." He squeezed my hand and I felt conflict again. I was looking at the man I loved, but I was haunted by Victor's words. What could this all mean?

Thursday morning, I woke and heard DJ's shower running. That surely was good news. We were considerably weakened, but on the road to recovery. I went downstairs and made us some eggs and toast.

He took his time coming down the stairs. I wondered if I looked as pale as he did. We ate breakfast and it was the first time in days that I'd laughed or even smiled. It felt good. We had three more days of break before DJ would have to return to school. That should be enough time to regain our strength.

"So, what did you have in mind for spring break had we not been attacked by the flu?" I asked.

"I thought we could drive into New Orleans for a couple of days and walk around and see the sights. I thought we could listen to some bands in the French Quarter and maybe find a nice restaurant for brunch." He smiled but his eyes flickered with a hint of mischief. I'd missed his eyes all week.

"That sounds wonderful. Have we done that before?"

"Yes, but not romantically. Once, you were incredibly intoxicated and I basically babysat you all weekend. Another time, we went with friends for Mardi Gras. That was a lot of fun."

"So, what places would you consider romantic?" I asked leadingly.

"Just about any place with you." He looked so damn handsome. His brown eyes were piercing and he furled his brow considering.

"What?" I asked.

"I know our home isn't all that romantic, but I'm thankful I share it with you. I also thought our break would be the perfect time to give you this." I looked at him expectant. He stood and put his hand in his pocket and got down on one knee. I think my heart skipped a beat or two and then it took off with a jolt. He was holding out the most beautiful ring I'd ever seen. I blinked and swallowed. "Beth, will you marry me?"

I smiled and my hands flew reflexively to my mouth. They only slightly muffled the squeal. I think I nodded but I know for sure that I flung my arms around his neck and kissed him. He smiled and laughed. "Is that a yes?"

"Yes! Thank you. Yes!" I exclaimed breathlessly.

My hand was shaking as he put the ring on my finger. "This was my grandmother's ring. She and my grandfather were married for over fifty years. I think that's a good sign. How does it fit?"

"Perfectly," I said, admiring the sparkly diamond. "Do your parents know?" I asked.

"They sent me the ring, but they had no idea when I'd ask you. I think they've been waiting all week for us to recover. I'm proud they kept their composure so well."

"Let's call them. We need to tell them we're getting better, too."

Tom and Mary were excited. Mary put us on speakerphone so they could both hear at the same time. We sent photos of the two of us together and the ring on my hand. Mary sounded like she was wiping away tears as she spoke.

Even Tom's voice was deeper and full of emotion. "We're happy for you two," he said. "You'll be family officially, now."

When Sadie called to check on us, I couldn't wait to share the news. "Oh, honey, that's great!" she exclaimed. "Poor thing's been waiting all week."

"You knew?" I asked.

"It wasn't hard to tell something was up. He was so disappointed when I came over that first time. You know I had to ask." She laughed her big laugh and I thanked her again for taking such good care of us.

CHAPTER 37

We spent the next day lounging around the house. We sat outside and attempted to soak up some sunshine. I felt the need for a few extra doses of vitamin D and whatever else the sunshine could provide to kill lingering germs from my body. DJ thought it was ridiculous when I rolled up my lounge pants and attempted to let the sun reach my knees.

"Just put on some shorts and a t-shirt. You aren't cold, anymore, are you?"

"No, but I don't want to change, either; I'm comfortable." He just shook his head. "DJ, thank you."

"What for?" he rolled his head toward me, but his eyelids were only partially opened. The sunlight was shining brightly over us.

"For being so incredibly patient with me and for loving me."

"It's not that hard." His smile broadened against the sunshine.

I laughed. "I think we have different ideas about what hard means."

"When do you plan to ask Mrs. Moore about coming back?" he asked.

"I wanted to talk with Molly first and get her opinion. I don't want to upset the kids or confuse them. Since I don't remember my students or even how to manage a classroom, I was also going to suggest that I begin observing in a different classroom where the kids don't know me. That way, I wouldn't be as much of a distraction." He nodded, approvingly.

He took my hand and fiddled with my fingers. He gently moved the ring with his thumb. "You're welcome to hang out in my classroom, too."

"That wouldn't be a distraction?" I asked coyly.

"For me or for the kids?" He paused. "What about wedding plans? Do you know where?"

I shook my head. "I don't really care about all that. I guess a part of me wouldn't care if it happened right here."

"I think we can figure out a place a little more memorable than here." He chuckled.

The rest of the afternoon and evening we spent resting. I fell asleep watching more basketball. We forced ourselves to go to bed before ten, but restful sleep eluded me. Hints of dreams and conversations, knowing I needed to purge myself of whatever was happening, made it difficult to rest for more than a few moments at a time. My mind wouldn't stop racing. It was like a family of flying squirrels was were jumping from thought to thought through my mind. Not only were they active, but they were incredibly noisy.

At seven o'clock, I heard DJ's alarm. I heard him get up and go into his bathroom. I begrudgingly did the same. I needed to clear the cobwebs from my head. After a long, hot shower, I went downstairs for breakfast.

"How did you sleep?" he asked when I joined him at the table with a mug of tea. He must still be feeling weak, too. He didn't get up and great me with a kiss.

"Not great. My days and nights are off. I think we need to get out of this house today and do some shopping. I'm sure we're out of everything."

"Yeah, that sounds good," he said distractedly, but then turned his gaze directly to mine. "Was there another reason why you couldn't sleep?" I swallowed and my eyes widened.

"What do you mean?" Could he read my expression that easily?

"Beth, I can tell you're wrestling with something. Please tell me." He took my hand from across the table. I looked down at the hand he was holding. My engagement ring glimmered in the light. "I heard you talking in your sleep. I heard you wondering out loud if you were making a mistake. Will you talk to me, please?" He must have thought I was questioning our engagement. That couldn't have been further from the truth. I looked up briefly, but I couldn't look into his eyes. He frowned. I took a deep breath, but it got stuck somewhere in my throat. I forced it down with a swallow.

I contended with whether it was the right time or if there was ever a right time to tell DJ, but I couldn't disregard his concern. Tears burned behind my eyes but didn't fall. My shoulders stiffened and I shuddered from the anxiety that rose in my chest and arrested my lungs. My silence would hurt him, but it was a long time before I could answer him. Victor's words and touch lingered and shame washed over me; somewhere, deep inside of me, there was love for Victor, too.

"It's not about our engagement. I have no doubts about that." My smile was genuine and reassuring. DJ returned my smile, but his eyes were full of concern. I took another deep breath; thankfully, this one made it all the way to my lungs.

I had no idea where to begin, but I needed for him to know. I stared at our hands to ground me.

"It's going to sound crazy. I... I don't know how to explain it." I could feel his eyes on my face. He was willing me to make eye-contact with him. I lifted my eyes and looked into his. God, they were beautiful. I felt so afraid, but I knew if I didn't get it off my chest, it would continue to put a wedge between us. "DJ, I want you to know that I love you, and no matter what, that won't change." His eyes searched my face for why I might need to say that. He scowled. "There's no logical reason why I survived. I should have died upon impact, but I didn't."

"It was a miracle," DJ whispered.

"Perhaps. There's no denying something supernatural happened on the day of the crash. Something beyond explanation."

He cocked his head trying to read my expression. "Supernatural?"

I nodded. "It sounds crazy enough in my head. There's no telling what it will sound like when I say it out loud." I sighed. "As you already know, there's a rainbow. The dreams return me to it often. It's the farthest I can go back. I drive into the rainbow and the colors absorb me and the cars. From the beginning, my perspective has been all wrong." He nodded, cautiously following my explanation. "I think I know why."

"Go ahead," he said leadingly. The tension between us thickened. He was holding my hand more securely like I might evaporate. I needed to be grounded, so I didn't resist or complain.

"Victor and Katherine Hebert were in the Volvo. Katherine was driving. I see everything from her vantage point. I saw my face, through the windshield. I saw my spikey hair and resigned expression in the memories that flooded with Marcus that day. I think when the vehicles collided, some part of Katherine collided into Beth as well." God! I sounded completely mad, but I couldn't stop. I had to explain. "The colors in the rainbow were almost tangible. There was a force even stronger than the impact. I'm only beginning to make the connection and understand. When our cars struck, some part of my soul went into her body in the rainbow."

"Some part of *my* soul?" he clarified, "*your* soul?" I nodded. "Not *Beth*?" I shook my head. "So, you're saying you aren't Beth?" The grasp on my hand was now cautious. His face, too, and tone were hesitant like he was mentally entering a minefield.

"I know Victor. Sure, I dream of him, but I *know* him. He spoke to me in the fever, and I know I need to release him and move on. As you know, he's the one I'm clinging to in the Volvo. He's the one…" Tears began falling down my face. "He's the one I was bound to, but it's just a small piece of who I am." DJ's expression was unreadable. I wasn't sure he believed me, so I continued, "A piece of my soul belonged to another," I said dispassionately. "I know I was married to Victor for a long time. I had a child and a husband and that longing hasn't gone away. I think I even had a dog. Do you think I'm making all of this up?"

Darren shook his head, hesitantly. "Not at all. I can't explain or understand it, but I don't doubt you. I can tell when you're lying. You haven't exhibited any of your tells."

"What are they?" I asked.

"Nope, then you might be able to conceal them. You always think I believe everything you say. Initially, I do. I want to believe you're honest, but we both knew the truth would come out sooner or later."

"This is the truth as well as I can explain it. I'm sorry."

He shook his head, not fully comprehending anything I'd said, or perhaps he was considering his next words carefully. "Now you claim you aren't completely Beth; you aren't her."

"I am Beth, but I can't remember my past. The amnesia part is real. Physically and emotionally, I know who I am. The music, the foods, you, especially you. There are too many consistencies to deny. The only way that I can explain it is that there's a part of Katherine, too." I tapped my chest for emphasis. At that point, he released my hand. He slowly wiped his mouth with the palm of his hand and rested it on his chin in a scholarly consideration.

"Does Katherine talk to you like Victor?"

"No."

"Is there anyone else in there?" he asked cautiously.

Great! He was definitely considering who to call to have me committed. "I don't think so. It's pretty simple and new in here, except the Victor and Katherine thing."

He nodded once, slowly, considering that, and then chuckled once, sardonically. "Interesting," he said flatly. He stood and walked away from the table, pacing. After a few moments of awkward silence, he exclaimed, "Damn it! I knew this was too good to be true!" He ran his hands through his hair exasperated. His hardened eyes glared at me. "I knew it wasn't you as soon as you opened your eyes. Although I've loved you since college, you didn't recognize me. You were gone." He turned and paced again. He muttered indiscernible phrases to himself as he paced. I was the crazy one, but DJ was losing it. "She never returned my affections, so I resigned myself to be her friend," he said like his thoughts were far off.

"You still are, but why are you speaking of me in third person like I'm not here?"

He blew out a huge breath, unable to contain his emotions any longer. "This is so damn confusing! From the start, I felt like I was cheating on her, but it was you and it was her, and it's not her! God! I don't know what to do!" He groaned in frustration.

I stood to face him. "I thought you should know. I want you to be happy with whatever and whomever I am. I want you and I love you. I want to do whatever I need to do to make this work. I need to figure out how to release Victor so I can be completely yours. I can't be someone I'm not, but I want you to love *me*, this Beth."

He grabbed my shoulders forcefully. "Don't you think I know that? Don't you think I want that, too?" He held onto me tightly, controlling his urge to shake me. "God! I want the Beth I used to know, but she would have never looked at me the way you do, with attraction and longing. She would have never taken my hand or eased into me the way you do. She would have never kissed me! She would have never agreed to marry me! She made me crazy sometimes, but she never provoked me to madness! That's all you! If I choose to believe you, I'm losing my fucking mind!" He released me and walked across the room. He hadn't harmed me physically, but I felt like he'd thrown me, dismissing me completely. He flicked his glasses onto the table in frustration and rubbed the bridge of his nose.

I took a step toward him, but he bristled. "I'll leave you to your thoughts, then," I whispered. He looked away and I retreated upstairs.

Once in my room, I collapsed onto the quilt. I regretted telling him. I regretted the pain I caused him. Every fiber of my being ached for him, ached for his comfort, ached to comfort him. The tears I'd managed to keep at bay burst forth in a torrent. I couldn't breathe between the fits of tears, gut-wrenching sobs, and convulsions.

Not two minutes later, I heard the door slam. It startled me and I froze when I heard DJ's car start. "This is BS!" I screamed at the top of my lungs. "Way to go, Beth! You really know how to fuck things up better than any other living human! Why must you continually torture him? Why do you have to be so selfish? He deserves more!" *Great!* Now I was talking to myself like I wasn't Beth, either.

I rose from the bed and wiped my face, determined not to let this defeat me. I'd been honest and it cost me, but it didn't make any of it less true. An hour later, I was pacing the floors. I'd cleaned every surface, folded laundry, and started the dishwasher. My tears and wallowing had been short-lived. I began vacuuming the downstairs when my phone rang. It was Sadie.

"Hello," I said.

"How are you two lovebirds?" she asked in her way.

"Oh, Sadie," I began and burst into tears, again. They were only managed while I busied myself. Between sobs, I continued. "We've had a fight. I don't know what to do."

"Is he there, now?"

"No, he left, and I don't want to be here, either."

"Want me to come and get you?"

"Yes, please."

I dressed and went outside to wait. Not ten minutes later, Sadie Cadillac pulled into my parking space. I got into the car and Sadie's arm pulled me over into a hug. "You're going to be fine, child. Cry if you need to, but I'd prefer you wait till we get to the house to let it all out. Sadie Cadillac's leather can't take the saltwater."

I wiped my eyes and nodded, holding it together until we got into her house. She planted me on the sofa before she went into the kitchen. When she returned, she handed me a box of tissues and a glass of iced tea.

"Drink up and we'll begin when you're ready." I took a sip of the tea and then used the first of many tissues to blow my nose. Sadie sat patiently beside me, but I didn't know where to begin. I continued to drink and cry and wipe my eyes and nose. When my glass was empty, Sadie took me into her hug and patted me comfortingly. "I'm sure it had to be bad if he left. That boy doesn't leave," she speculated. "Did you decide you didn't want to marry him?" I shook my head. "Did you tell him what really happened in that crash?" I gasped and pushed away and looked into her large, dark eyes. How could she have guessed? I nodded cautiously. "And he didn't take too kindly to it?" she asked leadingly. I shook my head. "Would you venture to explain it to me?" she asked.

"I think you'll have me committed," I laughed nervously.

"How about you let me be the judge of that?" she asked sternly. I told her most everything I'd told DJ. She watched me carefully as I spoke, but she reserved any judgement until the very end. "That's a lot for a mind to comprehend," she said when I'd concluded my explanation. "I may need some time to mull that over."

"I'm crazy, aren't I?" I asked. "You know the right people to take me. They'll treat me well. They won't beat me, right?"

Sadie laughed so big, I jumped. "Oh, child, no one's taking you anywhere. I told you before that I didn't see a lick of crazy in your eyes and that still stands. You believe it, so to you it's truth. Now you either convince others or not. Does Darren know where you are?" I shook my head. "Text him," she demanded.

"I didn't bring my phone," I confessed.

Sadie shook her head and sighed as she fished her phone from the bottom of her purse. "Looks like he's already home," she said as she texted a brief reply. She muttered something under her breath.

"Does he sound angry?" I asked.

Sadie chuckled low, "No, child, he only ever sounds worried, like he's got no control in the world when it comes to you." Tears leaked again and I curled up into the sofa cushions cradling the box of tissues. "You want to stay here a while?" she asked.

I nodded but didn't look at her. "Please."

"Do you want to be alone? I need to start Marcus' supper. He'll be home soon."

"May I just stay here?" I asked, feeling small and spent.

"Sure thing." She patted my hand as she rose and walked toward the kitchen. There was something easy about this house. I drifted off to sleep to the familiar kitchen sounds.

I woke to Marcus and Sadie eating at the small dining table. They were speaking in hushed tones but stopped as soon as they realized I was awake.

"Hungry?" Sadie asked.

"Yes, please, but I can get it myself." I didn't want to interrupt her meal; she was already wearing her uniform. I fixed my plate and sat down across from them. "You work tonight?" I asked, but the answer was obvious.

"Yes. You're welcome to stay here if you need, but I have a feeling roommate won't take kindly to you sleeping in another man's house."

"Thank you. Can one of you give me a ride?"

Sadie looked at Marcus and he nodded. "No trouble," he said. I wondered briefly if she'd told him. He wasn't looking at me too crooked, so I guessed she hadn't told him everything.

Sadie hugged us both before she drove to the hospital. I ate a second helping after Marcus convinced me. He scooped the serving onto my plate like he was doling out chow in a mess hall.

"You need to keep up your strength to sustain a good battle. You don't want to peter out halfway through. Your opponent will smell victory in your weakness. Stay strong, well fed, and hydrated." He refilled my glass with water. "Tell me when you're ready to go home."

I nodded and ate everything on my plate. When I was finished, I stood and rinsed my dish in the sink. As I placed it into the dishwasher, I stopped midway at the strangest thought. "Marcus, does Tony still have that Volvo?" I asked.

"I think so. You interested?"

"Not exactly. Can you tell me again about the crash?" He was shaking his head cautiously. "Was there a rainbow?" He looked surprised at the mention of that.

"You remember that?" His dark eyes widened with curiosity.

I nodded. "You made no mention of that at the scene, but it was really unusual?" I guessed.

His brow furled. "Strangest thing I've ever encountered, an unnatural occurrence to be sure."

I smiled, satisfied that I hadn't made it up. He'd seen it too. "Will you take me there again?" He eyed me warily and shook his head, refusing me. "Please," I begged. "I need to know more. I think it will help me. I think I need to sit in the Volvo again."

He shook his head, completely defying me. He was bigger and stronger and more solid than any man I'd ever met. "Darren will be pissed," he said.

"Darren wants me to get better. Darren wants to protect me, but I need to know."

He considered for a second and then refused me. "No, I won't do it. The last time I took you anywhere, I had to carry you to the hospital."

I put my hands on my hips and looked straight into his eyes. I wanted this, and I was determined. "Marcus, you are the only one who can answer my questions. You were the only one there."

His jaw tightened and I could see he was struggling. He sized me up and shook his head again. "You think I'm going to let a little hundred and twenty-pound white girl tell me what to do?" he challenged.

I raised my eyebrow returning his challenge and smiled to soften my request. "No, but I'm hoping that you'll be my friend and consider it. I know there's a risk that it will take me to a different place, but each time I've had an episode, I'm able to recall more of that day. I know it's scary for you and Darren to witness, but it's where I have to go to remember."

"Does he know what you're planning?" he asked.

I shook my head. "I just now had the idea."

"I won't do it unless you tell him, and he and my mama are both there. I won't do this alone with you. I've seen some scary shit deployed and on the job; but you, girl, take the cake. I don't want to touch you and your crazy with a ten-foot pole. I know my limitations."

I thought Marcus was overreacting, but I agreed to his conditions. "Okay, but your mama says I'm not crazy."

He laughed big like Sadie. "Well, she's not afraid of anything and may be a better judge, but I know what I can handle. You ready to go?"

"Yes. Thank you."

We rode in virtual silence to the townhouse. "You need me to walk you in?" he asked when he put his car in park. "Mama said he left after you two had a disagreement." He looked at the ring on my hand. "Does it have anything to do with that recent development?"

"Not directly."

"Are congratulations in order?" he asked.

I blinked back the wave of sadness. I refused to cry. "I hope so, but I'll keep you posted. My feelings haven't changed."

He looked over me entirely, assessing my size and ability to handle myself. "I'd feel better if I walked you in."

"He's not going to hurt me, Marcus."

"I know. I didn't mean to imply that. As your *friend*, I'm not going to allow you to walk in alone and just leave you." He walked me to the door and followed me inside.

"Beth?" DJ's voice rose hopefully from the kitchen. I detected a note of relief in his tone. He didn't sound angry, but my stomach tightened just the same. He walked toward me. His eyes were expectant, but then he hesitated briefly when he saw Marcus come in behind me. He looked into my eyes, but I saw no emotion beyond the color. He would stay masked until we were alone. DJ pressed on without missing a beat. "Marcus, thank you for bringing her home. I told Sadie I'd come and get her."

"No problem," Marcus said as he put his hand out to shake DJ's. He assessed DJ and the townhouse in one brief glance. Apparently, everything met with his approval. Before he left, Marcus faced me and put his large hands on my shoulders. He held my gaze. "You call me if you need anything." His eyes were sincere.

"Thank you." I smiled to assure him.

"I'll see about what you requested. I'll let you know soon." He kissed my cheek and turned back to DJ. "I'll come back, too, if you need me. Don't hesitate to call."

CHAPTER 38

DJ opened the door for Marcus and thanked him again. DJ shut the door behind him and stood there for several seconds facing it. He took a breath to settle himself and then turned to finally face me.

"Beth, I'm sorry I left. I won't ever do that again." His words were a promise. "I hate it when I can't get to you, and I did the very same thing." His emotions were still masked, but they weren't easily contained. He seemed frustrated with himself. "What did you tell Sadie?" he asked.

"I told her everything," I confessed.

"Of course, you did," he said flatly. "What did she say?"

"She said she needed some time to mull it over, but that I wasn't crazy."

"Good, that makes one of us," he said sarcastically. "And Marcus?" I shook my head. "What did you ask him to do?" I told DJ what I'd like to do. I explained about how I thought sitting in the Volvo at the crash site would help me. He looked at me with familiar hesitation, but he didn't look angry. "I don't know if I can witness that," he said after I explained.

"I understand. I'll let you make that decision if and when it happens. Where did you go?" I asked.

He rolled his eyes. "I just drove for about an hour and then went to the store. It doesn't sound logical, but it helped me think to do something normal, routine."

I nodded. "Yeah, I cleaned for nearly an hour."

"I noticed," he said with an amused glance around the room. "If this is how we fight, we'll always be tidy and well-stocked." He laughed once, but it did little to relieve the tension. Although, I'd cleaned the downstairs thoroughly, the air carried the remains of distance. Awkwardness lingered.

"I don't want to fight. I've upset you, and I regret…"

"No," he interrupted, "never, ever regret honesty. I needed to know what was going on between your ears. I can't do anything about it, but I'm glad you told me. It somehow makes sense of a few things." He took my hand, then, and led me to the sofa. I was thankful he could still touch me. It was only a few steps and he released my hand, again. I sat on the edge, unsure of what to expect.

"Beth, you were one of the most tormented souls. You were rarely settled. I've wrestled all afternoon with everything you told me this morning, and as frustrating as it may be, I still desire to be with you! I love you with everything I am." His eyes were sincere, almost pleading. "I can't believe I'm actually saying this out loud," he said with a disbelieving tone. He sighed again, resigned to acceptance. "Whatever part of you was replaced, freed you from the past that haunted you. I want to believe that you're no longer tormented, that you've found peace."

He believed me. I smiled, relieved and filled with joy. I cautiously reached for his hand. He didn't move or avoid my touch as he'd done before. He didn't even look away.

"May I hold you?" I asked tentatively.

His eyes were suddenly pained. "Oh, Beth, how can you ask me that?"

"Because I don't know the answer, and I don't want to be rejected," I laughed nervously. "Do you still want to marry me?"

"At this very moment, yes. We both have some things to figure out, but that offer still stands." I smiled broader at that, but tears welled in my eyes. He was still out of reach and hadn't answered my first question. "Why did Marcus feel the need to walk you in?"

"He's a friend. He's got a protective instinct. He wanted to make sure I'd be okay."

"I felt like I was being sized-up by your big brother. I think you made a mark on him when he helped pull you from the car." He blinked and shook his head. He didn't like speaking of the accident. "I sensed his protectiveness the first time he came to the hospital."

"Does that bother you?"

"No, I'm glad to have back-up."

I moved forward and put out my arms for a hug. It wasn't easy for him, but he gave in and allowed me to wrap my arms around him. He even allowed me to draw myself close to his chest, breathing deeply for the first time all afternoon. He didn't quite reciprocate the closeness I desired. I lifted my face to kiss him. He was looking off.

"DJ?"

He looked down and caught my eye. He lowered his chin and gave me a brief peck on the lips. I tried not to look disappointed, but I couldn't hide it.

"I'm sorry. I promise to do better," he said.

"I understand." I gave him a little squeeze around his midsection before I released him. "What would you like to do tonight? Basketball? Are you hungry?" I asked.

"Not particularly. You?"

"I ate at Sadie's"

"You wouldn't have thought to bring me a plate?"

"Sorry, no." He turned on the TV to find the game he was looking for. "I'm going upstairs to take a bath," I said.

When I went back downstairs, DJ had fallen asleep watching the game. He was lying on his back snoring lightly. I smiled to myself. I couldn't help it. I silently hoped that the morning would be better between us.

***

Saturday morning, I woke to the familiar smells of breakfast. Mouthwatering bacon wafted up to my bed. I ran downstairs smiling, but I stopped short when I saw Sadie sitting with DJ at the table. I froze.

"Is this an ambush?" I asked cautiously.

"Your roommate invited me to breakfast. He thought I'd be hungry after my shift. He makes a pretty good cup of coffee, too, so I have no complaints." She chuckled her low laugh.

"We aren't ambushing you, Beth," DJ said sincerely. "I hoped Sadie could put my concerns to rest. Are you hungry?"

"Obviously, the bacon," I said.

He rose and pulled out a chair for me. He then fixed me a plate of toast and bacon and poured me a mug of coffee. "It's decaf," he said.

"Thank you." I smiled meekly. "So what conclusions have you two come to?" I asked taking a sip of the coffee.

"That we care very much about your well-being, and we are willing to see you through this," Sadie said, eyeing DJ with a hint of warning.

DJ took my hand. "Beth, I'm not going to pretend that anything you said yesterday pleased me, except the fact that you are willing to do whatever is needed to deal with it." He rubbed his thumb over my knuckles. "When will you see your therapist again?" he asked.

"Not for another week. She's on vacation."

"Are you sure you want to go through with this without her?" Sadie asked.

"Honestly, I trust you three more than I do her. She's good at what she does, but I think I'm better off figuring it out on my own. Does Tony still have the Volvo?" Sadie nodded. "May I pay him to tow it out there?" She nodded again.

She was eyeing me carefully. "What if this doesn't go like you think?" she asked.

I looked at DJ and then back to Sadie. "Then I promise to tell my therapist everything and agree to whatever treatment or specialists she recommends." She nodded solemnly. "I really do want to get better," I said convincingly.

"We'll all be available tomorrow afternoon. Marcus will pick you up on his way home. I'll meet you there after church."

"What about Darren?" I asked Sadie. We both turned our attention to him.

"I told you I wasn't sure I could witness that. I'm going to reserve my decision until tomorrow. I want this to help you, so I'm willing to let Marcus and Sadie take the lead."

My stomach tightened as his words sunk in, but I didn't hide the disappointment. "I hope you change your mind," I said and smiled again meekly.

"I need to be on my way," Sadie said as she rose from the table. "Thank you, Darren, for breakfast."

"Thank you," he said as he stood to see her out.

"Thank you, Sadie. I'll see you tomorrow." I rose and hugged her goodbye. I sat back down and finished my breakfast.

DJ walked Sadie out to her car. When he returned, I stood to rinse my plate and put it in the dishwasher. I wasn't sure what the next twenty-four to thirty-six hours would be like between us, so I focused unnecessarily on cleaning the kitchen. I went perfectly still and closed my eyes when I felt DJ's arms wrap around me from behind. He breathed in slowly at the back of my head and kissed down my neck.

"Beth, I'd like to enjoy my last full day of spring break with you. Can we just enjoy being together?" I exhaled slowly, relishing his touch. "Go out to eat? There are bands playing downtown tonight, too."

I smiled and nodded and turned slowly to face him. "I'd love to spend the day with you. No more crazy talk, I promise." He leaned in and kissed me, gently at first like he was testing his own resolve, but I didn't want gentle or resigned. I was excited that my plan was coming together, and I was greedy for an entire day alone with him. I would do my best not to cause any conflict or make waves between us. His response to my kiss sealed the deal, and since I wasn't cooking, he wasn't cautious either. I leaned back into the counter and gently pulled DJ into me. My fingers moved through the hair at the nape of his neck and he sighed. The way his hands moved down my arms to my hips, I knew he missed this, too. He moved his lips and I sighed as he kissed below my ear.

"Get dressed and let's get out of here," he whispered. Was that a pant I detected in his breathing? I smiled thankful that he still desired me. I gently embraced him again and pressed my palms to his chest. He took a step back and allowed me to go upstairs. I could feel his eyes on my back.

We began our day with a brief walk through the farmer's market. We bought some fruit and a couple of bottles of water. DJ stopped and produced a hammock from his backpack. I helped him hang it on the hammock posts and we made ourselves comfortable. The day wasn't yet too hot and we enjoyed the gentle breeze as we rocked back and forth. We watched a variety of dogs play catch with their humans. They were eager and anticipated each ball or frisbee thrown.

"Favorite dog?" DJ asked.

"Labs. Lab mixes. Mutts."

"That's not very specific."

"I think it depends on the dog."

"I agree. Nothing less than forty pounds, full-grown. Favorite cat?" he asked.

"Outdoor."

He laughed. "Agreed."

"Did you have pets growing up?" I asked.

"Sure, dogs. Always dogs. I thought when Dad retired, he'd get a dog, but ends up Michael is allergic, so pet-free it is."

"Hmmm," I pondered. "So, whose room will we share once we're married?" I asked.

"I'd like you to share mine. I have a much larger closet and your mattress is lumpy."

I pushed him away playfully. "It is not!" I protested.

"Mine is a far-superior mattress."

"I wouldn't know."

"No, you wouldn't."

"May we keep the quilt?" I asked.

"Absolutely! Had I known it was in your closet all along, I'd have claimed it years ago. I love sleeping under that quilt."

"When did Gram give it to me?" I thought maybe I'd had it in college since I'd mentioned it in my journal.

DJ turned to face me. His eyes looked a little sad. I could sense something more connected me to that collection of fabric I was so attached to.

"She never had the opportunity to give it to you herself. We found it among her many treasures. It was in an unmarked box in her cedar closet. When we opened it, we found a note in Gram's handwriting: *Beth and DJ's wedding quilt.* You were so pissed at her presumption, but it was the last bit of her love and comfort that I could find when everything went downhill. I know you felt it too, so you allowed me to continuously wrap it around you. It's still a comfort to you, isn't it?"

Tears began to leak down my cheeks as I gazed into his pained expression. "How on earth did you stick around so long?"

"I made a promise to Gram; I made a promise to myself. I've never regretted either one."

"You're very persistent."

"Maybe." He shrugged.

"So, the quilt was intended for us all along," I said. No wonder I continually marveled at its ability to comfort and keep me safe.

"Yes, it was." He smiled and moved the bangs that had fallen into my eyes. "Your hair's getting longer," he said.

I laughed and wiped the tears from my face. "I should probably think of an actual style now that it's getting longer." I tucked a few strands of hair behind my ears.

"You're going to let it grow out some more?" he asked hopeful.

"Yes, I planned to. My natural color is nice and I think it's a healthier texture now without all the chemicals. I'll get it shaped soon so I can let it grow more uniformly. I'm thinking I'd like to get it to my shoulders at least." He

smiled. That pleased him. "What is it with guys and hair?" I asked rhetorically.

He kissed me instead of answering.

"Uh hum," a deep voice cleared his throat loudly. I opened my eyes to see

Dan standing there. "Sorry to interrupt you two, but it didn't look like you were

coming up for air any time soon." We laughed and I sat up a bit more in the

hammock.

"Hello, Dan," I said and saw that a huge chocolate lab was obediently

sitting next to his human, tail wagging and tongue lagging. "Who is this?" I

asked. "May I pet him?"

"This is Rex, T-Rex, and he'd love it."

I eased out of the hammock and let him sniff my hand before I patted his

head. "He's beautiful. I didn't know you had a dog," I said as I played with his

ears and stroked down his back.

"Thanks. I brought him back after Easter. He was getting fat at my sister's.

She's too indulgent. She's great with kids, but not with hunting dogs." He

laughed.

"How was your trip?" DJ asked stepping out of the hammock.

"It was great, but I'll let Molly give you her side of it. Thanks, Beth, for

encouraging her. You're a good friend. She just needed a little push." I nodded

as Rex licked my face.

"Is she here?" I asked, giggling as Rex pressed his big head into me, nearly

knocking me over. He looked full-grown, but he was still playful like a puppy.

"Rex, heal!" Dan commanded. Rex sat and calmed himself, but his tail thumped on the concrete in a steady beat. "She'll be here soon. She had some errands to run this morning. Getting ready for school, again. How was your break?" he asked.

"Flu," DJ replied.

"Awe, man, that sucks."

"Yep. It's our first day out. Hope to enjoy it." He looked at me.

Just then Dan's phone buzzed. "She's here." He looked up trying to see her from a distance. Rex was distracted by Dan's change and looked up eagerly. He barked. "Yep, she's coming, boy. He's grown quite attached," he said, amused, but I suspected he wasn't just talking about the dog.

Molly came into view. Rex stood anticipating her. She saw the three of us together, waved, and quickened her pace.

"Beth, DJ!" She hugged me. "It's good to see you! I'm so glad you're better."

"Us, too," DJ said.

Molly greeted Dan with a light peck and then turned her attention to the dog who was not waiting patiently at all. "Good boy. Good Rex." She reached into her pocket and presented Rex with a treat. "Sit," she said sweetly. He obeyed. "Lie down," she said. He obeyed in anticipation of the treat. His huge tail whipped around frantically.

"You're going to make him fat," Dan complained.

"It's his dogfood you left at the house; it's not really a treat," she argued sweetly.

He grunted a little disbelievingly. "When it comes from you, he thinks it's a treat."

Molly and I were both petting the dog when she grasped my hand. "What's this?" she asked surprised. I beamed. "When did this happen?" she asked in a way that sounded like she was left out of something important.

"Two days ago!" I exclaimed with unconcealed joy.

Molly hugged me, again. "Congratulations! Oh, my! How exciting! When?"

"This summer?" I shrugged.

"Where?" she asked looking at DJ. He shrugged this time, but I was relieved when he returned her smile.

Dan moved the leash and reached out to shake DJ's hand. "Congratulations, man, that's great!"

Rex was impatient to begin his exercise. Dan released him from his leash and threw a tennis ball. Rex ran and retrieved for the next twenty minutes, running through a series of commands. It was impressive.

Molly and I sat in the hammock and made small talk with the guys between throws and commands. The topic of lunch came up. We agreed to meet at a place with a patio so Rex wouldn't have to stay in the back of Dan's truck.

"Want to work out again, Monday?" Molly asked. "Back to our routines?"

"Yes. How was Texas?" I asked.

"Good." She smiled up at Dan. "I liked everyone I met. He has a huge family. His mom had everyone over on Easter. They had a big Easter egg hunt on their property for all the cousins. Then, they do an adult hunt for gift cards and cash prizes. It's crazy competitive. The big teen cousins are in charge. They hid them in the hardest places. I loved every minute of it. Then on Monday, as we were driving home, I called my folks and asked if we could stop by for supper. It was only about an hour out of the way."

"How did that go?" I asked, surprised. I looked at Dan for his response.

"They weren't exactly prepared to meet the likes of me," he said, "but by the time we'd finished dinner, I think I'd won them over." He chuckled.

"Yes, you did," Molly conceded. "Thankfully, their only complaint was our age difference. He's only seven years older than me. Geez! I can't seem to please them." She sighed. "The things I thought they'd question, they accepted, but they still had to find something. He and my dad got along, and I don't think he'd question anyone who stands a head taller and put his arm around his daughter so confidently." She blushed slightly; her ears turned the slightest shade darker.

"Don't get the wrong impression. They're nice folks. They want what's best for their daughter. They were just surprised it came in a different package than they imagined." Dan smiled down at Molly and she blushed all over, this time, blinking her eyes wide. She bit her lip innocently, but it was anything but innocent. Dan cocked his head to one side and shook it. "My parents were easier, but my whole family was there, so they all welcomed her with open arms. My grandma and great aunts are probably plotting and planning our entire future."

"They were precious and funny," she giggled. "They can plot all they want."

CHAPTER 39

After lunch, Dan and Molly took Rex back to Dan's. DJ and I went to the townhouse to rest and change before we returned to hear the bands downtown. Dan and Molly weren't sure they'd come meet us; Dan had to be at church early.

Once we were inside the townhouse, I fixed myself some juice and went upstairs. I lay down on the quilt and adjusted my pillow. I examined the stitches again with my fingertips. Each and every stitch, hand-sewn delicately, and lovingly pieced together. Gram knew that DJ was right for me. She knew long before I did. "Thanks, Gram," I whispered before I drifted off to sleep.

I dreamt of the quilt, being completely safe and secure in it. Comfort, warmth, embraced in love. The quilt images drifted into images of DJ, but the feelings were all the same. He took my hand and kissed my cheek. He reached over and held my cheek in the palm of his hand. He eased his hand from my shoulder and down to the small of my back. I wasn't sure if I were dreaming at that very moment, but then the sweet aroma of fresh-baked cookies bombarded my senses and I knew I wasn't dreaming anymore.

"Cookies?" I asked.

DJ kissed my forehead. "Yes."

"That's a nice way to be awakened, very gentle." He let me ease into his side. "Cookies and bacon are great, but this is an even better way to be awakened." I smiled and looked up into his dark eyes.

"I love you, Beth."

"I love you, too," I said sleepily. "Should we bring this quilt on our honeymoon?" I asked.

"Heck, yeah!" He laughed. "Want a cookie?"

"Heck, yeah!" I said, mimicking his tone. "Did you sleep?" I asked.

"Not much. I just watched some TV and caught up on games I've missed. Do you still want to go out tonight?"

"Absolutely."

DJ pulled out mugs from the freezer and poured us each some milk. The cookies were still warm. "You were smiling when I went in to wake you. Is it safe to ask what you were dreaming about?"

"This time, yes. I dreamt about how the quilt makes me feel and how much love went into every stitch. Just before you woke me, I was dreaming about how you make me feel the exact same way."

He smiled at that. "I'd say that was a good dream."

"Me, too. I think that's why I was smiling."

"What do you want to do for supper?" he asked as he cleared the plate and mugs from the table.

"Will there be food downtown?"

"Yeah, there should be food trucks. Want to get something there?"

"Sure, that sounds good."

Food truck food is delicious. Outdoor concerts are even better. We danced and sang and enjoyed one another for the remainder of the evening. Dan and

Molly never showed, but DJ and I danced for nearly two hours. By ten o'clock,

I was beat, happy but tired. The evening was humid and I was extremely sweaty

when I got into the car. I directed all the vents on my side toward me and turned

up the AC.

"It's forecasted rain tomorrow." DJ said as we made our way through

downtown traffic.

"Is that a warning or are you just making conversation?"

"It was on my mind. I'm just sharing the information. I didn't intend to put

you on the defensive."

"You didn't. I've had a wonderful day and I'm really glad we've had a

couple of good days. Church tomorrow?"

He nodded. "Dan's leading tomorrow; I look forward to it."

I smiled over at him. Our hair was matted down from the humidity. I

brushed my bangs back with my fingers and cooled my forehead.

"I hardly see your scar anymore; I'd almost forgotten about it."

"I see it every time I get out of the shower. It's looking better. I'm

definitely not shocked by it anymore."

Once we were home, I kissed DJ goodnight at the bottom of the stairs and

thanked him for a lovely evening. It was probably too formal and forced, but I

meant it sincerely. We were an engaged couple who had gone on a date. I

thought it should be acknowledged. We just happened to be an engaged couple

who went to their respective rooms to shower and sleep in separate beds.

Sunday morning arrived too early. My stomach tightened with nerves and my lips looked unusually pale. I took several deep breaths to get me through my normal, morning routine. I thought about my expectations for the day. Expectations sounded too concrete; I had hopes. One, I wanted to do whatever I needed to do to release Victor. Two, I hoped this exercise would allow me to move past this incident towards the life I desired with DJ. Three, I prayed for a deeper clarity than before, some healing, and to close the proverbial door on this piece of my life.

I looked down at the ring on my finger. I liked how it glistened in the sunlight. I wore my boots and jeans to church knowing I would be walking around in tall grass with Marcus. DJ still hadn't said yet what he'd decided. I smelled coffee and knew he was already downstairs.

"Good morning," I said and walked toward him, anticipating his smile. I smiled, but his expression wasn't a pleasant one. He looked pained. "What's wrong?" I asked not really wanting to know the answer. He blinked and swallowed hard. He looked like he was going to speak and then looked away. "DJ, please look at me. Tell me what you're thinking." He blinked again and I thought he might cry. He let me put my arms around him and he put his head down as he hugged me. "You don't have to do this today. I'm okay to go alone."

He shook his head. "It's not that." His voice was husky. "Alli called me early this morning. Mom collapsed at work last night." His grip around my shoulders tightened and he took a deep breath before he continued. My breath caught and the worry for Mary was instantaneous.

"Is she okay?" My voice was barely above a whisper.

"She's stable. They're running a bunch of tests. Dad texted me back a little while ago. He's been with her all night. They aren't sure, yet, what's going on."

As his words sunk in, tears began to fall. "What do we need to do?" I asked, not knowing anything else to say.

"Wait patiently and pray."

I nodded into his chest. "DJ, I'm sorry you aren't closer. I feel like we're a million miles away." I released him to grab a tissue to wipe my nose.

"Yeah, I know what you mean."

"Do you still feel like going to church?"

"I do," he said.

"Is this decaf?" I asked as I gestured to the coffee pot.

"No, sorry. I've been up for a while."

"Why didn't you wake me?" I asked as I started the kettle for tea.

"I thought about it, but you were sleeping well. Today is going to be challenging for you, so I didn't want to limit your sleep on top of everything else. It's not like the news wasn't going to wait another few hours."

"Do you want me to postpone today's plans? I can call everyone right now."

"I considered that, but there's no reason to change your plans. You believe you need to do this, and if there's the slightest chance it will help you, then I'm not going to ask you to delay it."

"Thank you, but if anything changes, you'll let me know immediately?" I asked.

"Absolutely."

***

We finished breakfast and attended worship as we'd planned. We were both preoccupied with various thoughts. I had a hard time focusing on the message and an even harder time sitting still. Molly sat with us and could tell things weren't normal.

"Are you two okay?" she asked.

"My mom's in the hospital. They're running tests. She collapsed at work last night."

"I'm so sorry, Darren. I hope she's alright."

"Me, too," he said.

"Beth, are you okay? I know you've gotten close to Darren's parents."

"It's not only that. I'm concerned about Mary, of course, but I'm going back to the crash site this afternoon to see if I can remember anything else."

She nodded. "That's going to be hard, isn't it?"

"I'm afraid so." DJ took my hand and I looked down at our clasped hands. Was this the right thing to do? Was this the right timing? I had so many feelings and disconnected thoughts. I had no idea what was going to come of any of it.

"I'm sorry we can't hang around today," DJ said, saving me from the awkward silence. "I'll see you in the morning, at school." Molly hugged me and wished us both good luck.

Once we were in the car, I put my hand on DJ's arm. "Wait, DJ. I want to ask you something." He looked up curious. The intensity of his brown eyes sometimes made me hesitate. "Would you rather me as I am right now, desiring to spend the rest of my life with you, with no memory of you but only memories of another man, or would you rather me like I was before the accident?"

He moved his hand from the gear shift and looked directly into my eyes. "That's a shit-loaded question, and I don't like either option in its entirety."

"If you choose me how I am right now, I wouldn't have to go through with this little experiment."

"True, but you'd never be satisfied, either. You'd always wonder, and I don't want you dreaming of another man if I can help it."

"Have you decided if you're coming with me?" The thought of being alone made my stomach ache. The thought of having to endure the onslaught of emotions that were sure to come made my heart ache.

"I don't want to, but it will keep me distracted until we know more about Mom." He sighed. "I'm waiting for easier."

"I'm sorry. I won't ever ask you to do this again, regardless the outcome."

"Text Marcus. Tell him we'll meet him at the crash site. Are you hungry?" he asked.

"No, I think I'm too nervous to eat."

"Want a shake or smoothie?" he asked.

"That might be good. I guess I need to have something on my stomach, but I'm afraid I'm going to throw up, again."

"Okay, we'll wait."

It began raining just as we pulled out of the church parking lot. A steady stream came down all the way as we drove to the crash site. Tony was parked in his tow truck and Marcus was in the patrol car. Sadie had ridden with Tony.

When they saw us drive up, they began getting out of their cars. DJ got out with an umbrella and walked around to my side of the car. I put on my raincoat and walked to meet everyone.

"Thank you, all. I couldn't make this happen without you."

"Do you mind? I'm going to stay in the truck," Tony said.

"No, I understand. Please." I could imagine how uncomfortable this would be for a practical stranger. "I appreciate your bringing the Volvo for me." He stepped back and returned to the comfort of his dry cab.

"You ready?" Sadie asked. I nodded.

"I know this is going to be hard to watch if I lose it again, but let it play out. Unless I lose consciousness or have some kind of seizure, please don't make me stop. I need to see this to the end." My eyes were pleading as I looked into each of their eyes. Sadie was smiling, encouragingly. Marcus looked pale, if that was possible for such a dark-skinned man.

DJ's expression was a mixture of concern and regret. "We'll be right here," he said.

I took a deep breath. "Okay, Marcus, it's your turn. Will you walk through the events again? Then, I'd like to sit in the Volvo, and if needed, explain to me exactly how you found the couple."

He sighed and looked me over carefully. "I don't like any of this."

"I know, none of us do, but hard things have to happen sometimes."

He pursed his lips and then looked at me. He wanted to make sure he was doing the right thing. His dark eyes were steady, but his brow furled and his jaw stiffened. "Alright, let's go."

"Start with the rainbow," I said.

"Very well."

He began his story much like he'd done the first time, but this time, he began describing the weather and the break in the clouds and sun and the rainbow. I closed my eyes and allowed his words to draw me back to a different time. Marcus included a few more details than he did before. He also included sounds and smells and specifics that he found meaningful.

I was aware of his voice and the rain falling and everything he described. Images swirled around in my mind, but they were more tangible than my dreams; they were memories, actual memories. He took my hand and led me down toward the Volvo. I barely opened my eyes, not wanting to lose the connection he'd helped me create.

Once in the seat, I again closed my eyes. I fastened the seatbelt and felt every surface within my reach: the curve of the steering wheel, the gear shift, and the way the contours of the leather seat pressed gently into my lower back.

Marcus' voice was far off, now. He was still talking and describing things around me, but my focus was no longer on his words. The rain fell across the windshield in small waves. I could hear the wipers beating in my mind. The steady rhythm was similar to the cadence of Marcus' voice.

"Describe how you found the victims," I whispered when there was a break in his retelling, but his words weren't necessary. I didn't know exactly what he said, but the wave of emotion flooded over me, and I no longer needed his explanation.

I was thrown back into the seat as the force of the impact with the truck sent us reeling. My body convulsed like I had been hit and my head thrust back into the headrest. My hands were rigid on the steering wheel, and the familiar pain from the impact wrenched my body. The pain, the searing pain and pressure in my chest returned, the choking and gasping from blood and tears.

"Victor," I called out, in a gasp. "Victor," I panted. "Victor, are you okay? Please tell me you're okay." I choked on every word. My hand reflexively reached for him in the seat next to me. I opened my eyes and he was there. I smiled and sobbed in relief. "Victor, Victor, please, please tell me we're going to be okay."

"Hey, baby," his familiar voice replied. "You're going to be fine. You're going to be just fine." He smiled, reassuringly, and then blinked lazily.

My right hand clutched at his shirt. I had to hold onto him. He was the most important thing. I could feel my grasp tighten around the buttons on his shirt. If

I could have, I would have reached directly through his ribs and grabbed his heart.

"Baby, it's time. Let me go, and you can come, too."

I shook my head and the sobbing continued. "No!" I cried aloud. "No!"

"I know it's hard, but you can do it. Take a deep breath and just let me go."

The agony of the pain and pressure on my chest finally took its toll. I was choking and convulsing and gasping for breath. I heard the screeching of tires and metal. I was paralyzed by the fear of the oncoming vehicle. I was suddenly seeing the vibrant colors of the rainbow. I turned back to Victor. His deep blue eyes were pleading. I heard the other vehicle approaching, time slowed, taking in every detail.

"Now, baby," Victor whispered. "I love you, and we won't ever be separated again."

"I love you, too," I whispered and gradually released my grasp on his shirt. I felt him slip away, taking a piece of me with him. I was altered, but I was freed. I heard the oncoming vehicle again and turned to face it. Blurred by tears, I could hardly make out the red projectile coming straight for me. I blinked to correct my vision and saw my face, my resigned-to-death face.

"Beth," I heard a faint voice in the back of my mind. "Beth, where are you hiding?" I knew this voice. I knew that familiarly loving voice.

With what remained of my strength, I called out, "Gram? Gram, is that you?"

"Yes, sweetie, it sure is. It's time to move past all of this. Find DJ; he's going to take you home."

"I love you, Gram," I whispered.

"I love you, too, sweetheart. Hang on."

Just then the two cars collided. I was thrust through the blinding light into complete darkness. It was cold, but the pain once again disappeared. I knew it would be over soon. I knew I would awaken on the other side of this nightmare. I would awaken not knowing myself and not recognizing my own life, but I would awaken.

The jarring, the impact, the rain. The loud, commanding voices, Marcus' voice between the shouts, between the waves of unconsciousness. "Lady, can you hear me? I'm here to help you. You're going to be okay. Stay with me, now. Ma'am, I need to see you, open your eyes. That's it, one more time and you'll be out. You're going to be just fine."

The final wave of unconsciousness took me under and I tried desperately to find my breath. It was shallow at first, but gradually, I could feel myself coming out of the depth of the darkness, out of the depths of the unknown.

The rain fell around me, peacefully and steady. The sound of the drops was reverberating off the umbrellas and the windshield, and muffled through the top of the car. I gently released my hand from the steering wheel and touched the scar over my eye. My other hand came to rest on my face and together my shaking hands gently felt the contours of my eyes and cheeks and mouth.

My eyes were closed, but I could sense that I wasn't alone. I took several deep breaths to control the shaking. It wasn't just my hands. My entire body was vibrating uncontrollably and my heart was racing. *Breathe,* I told myself. *Breathe.*

My hands traced down my neck to my chest, feeling the beats of my heart violently through my clothes, commanding them to return to a normal rhythm. In a few moments, I lowered my hands to finally rest on my stomach. I pressed my abdomen to make the breaths stay and to prevent me from throwing up.

Finally, the violent shaking subsided and I was able to regain some control of my body. I turned my head toward the open door and opened my eyes. The first thing I saw was DJ's face. He was kneeling next to the car, watching me. His hands were poised like he was ready to pull me from the car. I looked into his eyes and I remembered every detail of him, his eyes, his smile. I remembered waking up to his kind face, but not just this time, each time. I remembered his younger face as well as the one I'd awakened to after the crash. Tears flooded my eyes. "DJ," I said weakly and smiled to the best of my ability. "DJ, I remember you."

I reached out to touch his face and he leaned in and kissed the palm of my hand. Our combined relief was palpable, and I wanted nothing more than to touch him and be with him. I tried to move to get out of the car, but I was too exhausted. "Hold me," I said. He reached in, unbuckled my seatbelt, and scooped me up into his embrace. I cried again, tears of relief this time, relief that this nightmare was over.

I could feel Sadie's hands on me. She took my face in her large hands and forced me to look into her eyes. "You're just fine, aren't you, honey?" I nodded weakly and leaned my head back into DJ's shoulder. "Come on, we'll get you home and in bed. You need rest," she commanded.

DJ and Marcus managed to carry me up the hill and place me in the back of DJ's car. DJ kissed my forehead and shut the door behind me. Sadie sat with me, holding me closely to her side. For the first time after an episode, I didn't feel nauseated. I looked at Marcus through the window and smiled. "Thank you," I whispered and he read my lips and gave a nod like a salute. DJ shook his hand and thanked him. He then started the car and drove me home.

I was able to walk myself into the townhouse and all the way upstairs to my room. Sadie helped me remove my wet clothes and into my pajamas and a hoodie. DJ joined us and handed me a cup of tea.

"Thank you. Thank you, both." I wiped away a couple of tears with the back of my hand. They were tears of joy and relief.

"I'll leave the two of you, now. Marcus will be waiting downstairs for me in a few minutes. He stayed to help Tony with the truck." She eyed me carefully and gave me a thorough once-over. "You did it, didn't you? You let him go." I nodded. "I'll call you tomorrow and check on you. You rest and drink plenty of water. Your brain needs the hydration." She hugged me and then turned her attention to DJ.

"Roommate, you call me if you need me." He nodded just as obediently.

"Thank you, Sadie, for everything," he said. She hugged him and said she could see herself out.

I sipped the hot tea carefully. DJ sat next to me on the bed. His dark eyes glistened with anticipation. "You remembered me? What did you remember?"

"I remember waking in the hospital. Not just this time, but every time I saw your face, your kind face and your eyes." I reached up and touched his cheek. "I heard Gram's voice, too, and she called me sweetheart."

He laughed. "Yes, that's what she called you. Beth, I'm so relieved you remember me."

"My body's never been able to deny you. This body has loved you since the beginning. DJ, I *loved* you. I can feel it."

His eyes filled with tears. "But you weren't *in love* with me until recently."

"I don't think that's completely true, either. I felt love, trust, honor, and respect from the beginning – sexual love, too. I can't explain the emotions and security I feel when my ears hear the sound of your voice or our hands touch. Please be assured that you were loved."

He stroked the side of my cheek with his thumb. "What else do you remember?" he asked cautiously.

"Very little and I'm okay with that. It's mostly feelings and stronger emotions than I felt before, like somehow, they've been released. This is a fresh start for us. This is our second chance. I think I'm in a better place, now, healthier, you know?"

He smiled, accepting my resolve and took the mug from my hands. "And Victor?" he asked hesitantly, raising his eyebrow.

I sighed. "He's gone. I hope their souls can be at rest, now."

He leaned in and kissed me. I wrapped my arms around his neck and pulled him closer to me. I wanted to feel his heartbeat. I wanted our bodies to be too close to separate. Just then his phone buzzed in his pocket. He sat back and answered it.

"Dad?" he asked when he answered.

"No, son, it's Mom," Mary said. We were sitting close enough that I could hear her voice, too.

"How are you?" he asked.

"I'm going to be okay. My blood sugar is all out of sorts and they think I'm dealing with some blood pressure issues. We'll get it managed." Her voice was reassuring. DJ sighed, releasing the worry he'd been carrying all day for his mom. He continued to stare at me while they talked. His expression gradually returned to its normal countenance. He smiled and pulled me closer into his side.

They talked for a little while longer. He didn't want to keep her from resting. The doctors planned to keep her another day and then she'd be home. She promised to call again when they were settled. He spoke with his dad briefly; then, he put his phone away and turned his attention back to me.

"Are you hungry?" he asked.

"Yeah, I am."

"Good, let's go downstairs and eat. I'm suddenly starving."

CHAPTER 40

So much can change in a year's time. I stood waiting in the hall for Molly to bring the kids back from recess. Mrs. Moore was gracious enough to allow me back in the fall. Molly was an excellent lead teacher. I was content to be her assistant. She managed things well and we made a great team. In time, I could see myself capable of managing a classroom again on my own, but for now, this is where I belonged. Things came naturally, and I loved every minute of it.

She and Dan were engaged at Christmas. They'd be getting married over the summer. They had decided to marry in Texas with all of his family. DJ and I hoped to attend, but it would depend on the timing. Her parents had finally accepted Dan. He said that when he went to ask her father's permission to marry Molly, he wasn't convinced he'd won them over at all.

"He kept me waiting for an hour before he'd see me," Dan complained. "Swore he'd had an emergency at work, but I think he was hesitating. It's got to be hard to agree to allow a man to take your daughter's hand. I pray we have sons."

I looked down the hall, anticipating the children, but DJ approached me instead, smiling. My eyes did that silly fluttering thing. A part of me hoped that never stopped. He looked to make sure no one was watching along the empty hallway before he kissed me. "How's your day going?"

"Good," I said.

"You feeling okay?"

"Yes." I beamed as my hands automatically went to the fullness of my round belly. "He's active today."

DJ smiled, proudly and put his hands over mine. "Hey, little guy, stay up; we'll read tonight," DJ promised, addressing our unborn child. "I'll see you after class. I love you." He kissed me again, quickly, and I watched him walk back down the hall to his classroom. His kids would be returning from lunch soon.

I thought fondly back to our wedding day. After the events of last spring, we didn't want to wait. We called Mary and Tom and asked if they minded terribly if we went ahead and got married immediately. Tom laughed at our impetuousness but Mary sounded a little disappointed. She wanted to be there. Mary wasn't allowed to travel until they regulated her blood pressure medication.

"We'll stream it live so you all can see," DJ assured them.

Dan joined us in holy matrimony on a Friday afternoon, just after school, in the quiet of a nearly empty church. The day was sunny and the afternoon sun streamed in the windows along the western side. I held a bouquet of daisies and wildflowers. Molly agreed to be my attendant and Gary was most assuredly our best man. Nick had driven his classmates to the church in his mom's mini-van.

Sadie cried quietly, dabbing her eyes when she picked me up to go to the church. "Lord, child, this is a great day, indeed." She fussed over me and my dress and my hair again before she left me at the back of the church. She hugged me and couldn't stop smiling as she made her way down to the front to find a seat.

Gary and Penny were so happy for us. They waited with me at the back of the church until DJ arrived. "Will you change your name?" Penny asked.

"I planned to, why?"

"I don't know. I just wondered if that sort of convention is still required."

"I think she should," Gary interjected. "It simplifies things when the couple shares a name. It's too confusing with hyphens and maiden names. I mean, if you didn't like his last name, then maybe he could take yours instead, or you could make up one together. Either way, a couple should share."

Moments before the ceremony, I once again found myself alone with Gary. Penny had gone to help Nick and Roxanne with the tripod. Roxanne wanted to take pictures for her photography elective and Nick was our official videographer. He'd be streaming the entire thing from DJ's phone.

Gary turned to me. "Beth, I'm glad you and Darren are getting married. I've known him for a long time, well a relatively long time considering my age, and I know this is going to be good for both of you. You've changed since the fieldtrip and even more since the math competition. It's nice to see you more like the Miss Rust I remember."

"Thanks, Gary."

"Who's walking you down the aisle?" he asked.

"No one. I figured since we didn't have music, we'd all just meet up at the front of the church."

379

"That's not very traditional. It's probably bad luck if you don't play music and get escorted. Wait here. I'll be right back."

He and Tommy found Pachelbel's *Canon in D* on Spotify, and Tommy said he'd play it when we were ready to begin. Just then Marcus walked into the back of the church. "Is DJ with you?" I asked.

"Yep," he said, smiling down at me. "It's unlucky for him to see you, so he's already in the sanctuary. Nothing like a police escort to get you to the church on time." He laughed.

"Yes, that's exactly what we need, an escort," Gary said when he returned. "I take it you and Beth are friends?" he asked, inspecting Marcus.

"Yes. Why?" Marcus stiffened at Gary's way of asking questions.

"She needs an escort. Would you be willing to give the bride away?"

Marcus's chest puffed out proudly. "If you have no objection, I'd be honored to give you away," he said smiling.

"Thank you, Marcus. I have no objections." I smiled, but my eyes pricked a little. I was suddenly moved to tears. "I can't think of anyone more qualified for the job."

Tommy started the music. Nick streamed every detail to DJ's family. They'd all gathered at Allison's house because Michael convinced them their Wi-Fi was superior. Marcus took my hand in the crook of his elbow protectively and proudly walked me down the aisle.

DJ had been right. What we wore and the venue didn't matter. We looked into one another's eyes and promised to love and honor and cherish for the remainder of our days. We exchanged rings and promised all the right things before God, surrounded and witnessed by our small circle of family and friends.

After our brief, but official ceremony, we all went to Sadie's for supper. Her sons' families had prepared more food than we could possibly eat, even with five teenagers in tow. After a pleasant evening with our friends, DJ lifted me over the threshold and carried me into our home where we spent the entire long weekend together, having food delivered when Sadie's leftovers ran out.

Once we were inside, we couldn't keep our hands to ourselves. Now that I was his wife, he kissed me without any hesitation or reservations. He kissed me as we traversed the stairs. DJ could kiss me upstairs; there was nothing guarding his reserve. Once in his bedroom, he undressed me like he was unwrapping the most precious gift he'd ever received.

For the next three nights, we came to know one another *intimately*. I liked that word. We made love before we slept. We kissed and made love again before the sun was full in the sky. We slept together under Gram's wedding quilt and dreamed and planned our life ahead.

EPILOGUE: DJ

The definition of insanity is doing the same thing over and over, expecting a different result. For the better part of the past thirteen years, I was definitely insane.

"Beth, please wake up." How many times had those words come out of my mouth? This girl, this woman, was the center of my universe, and I was helplessly attached to her. From the first time I laid eyes on her, I was in love.

I was eighteen and she had the prettiest smile. I loved how she ran into class every morning with a messy bun of light brown hair. Her face would be flush and her eyes sparkled with relief that she'd made it to class. But her smile; yep, it was definitely her smile.

I knew she was a mess, that she had issues. I knew it before she even spoke to me directly. So, am I insane sitting with her again, waiting, hoping, praying she'll wake up and see me and love me, and forget that she asked me to move out two days ago? I can't do that. I made a promise. Maybe I should come clean and tell her the whole story.

I remember the first time I rode with Beth to Gram's house. She wanted to prove to her grandmother that she'd made a friend at school. "It's nice to meet you. You can call me Gram, too, DJ."

Gram was elderly. Come to find out, she was actually Beth's great-grandmother who had raised Beth's mom after Beth's grandmother, died. Gram may have been elderly, but she was spry, lively and full of energy. I loved her instantly. Being a military kid, I'd never lived close to my grandparents. We'd visit summers and holidays, but by the time I was thirteen, they'd all passed away.

Over the next year-and-a-half, I spent many weekends at Gram's house with and without Beth. I helped her ready her garden seasonally. I helped her clean gutters. She paid me in cash and home-cooked meals. One Halloween I even helped her make trick-or-treat bags for her neighborhood.

"You're a good friend to Beth. Thank you," Gram said once after we'd planted enough tomatoes and summer squash to feed a small village.

"She's a good friend, too." I said, defending her. "I came here not knowing another living soul. She makes life here pretty great."

"I'm glad to hear that. She's not had an easy life. I've done what I could, but I wish I'd been there from the beginning."

"I know; she told me about her parents."

About six months before her death, Gram called me. "DJ, I need you to come by the house."

"Sure, what do you need done?"

"Nothing. I just need to discuss some things with you."

"Yes, ma'am. Do you want me to bring Beth?"

"No, just you. Bring your appetite." That was easy enough. I was a nineteen-year-old college student. I was hungry all the time.

As soon as she served my plate, I could tell the conversation would turn serious. "DJ, I know this is a lot of information, but Beth doesn't have any other family, and I know she'll listen to you when the time comes."

"What time?" I asked as I devoured a huge bowl of banana pudding.

"I've made some changes to my will. Everything will go to Beth. My health isn't what it once was. There are things my doctor tells me, and I'm not sure how much more time I have, so I'm being proactive."

"Does Beth know?"

"Absolutely, but she's not accepting that anyone else will ever leave her. She thinks I'll live forever and that isn't so. I need you to promise me that you'll look out for her. I can see the way you look at her. She's not just your best friend, is she?"

Gram's light eyes looked deeply into mine. I couldn't deny the feelings I had for Beth. She'd managed to carve out a huge place in my heart without even trying. "Gram, I love her." I'd never confessed those words out loud, not even to myself. "I've never felt this way towards anyone, ever. I'll do anything for her."

"You're a blessing to us both, DJ."

"I wish Beth felt the same way. She definitely keeps me in the friendzone."

"The friendzone?" Gram asked for clarification.

"Friendzone means I'm her best friend but not her boyfriend. I'm allowed to hug her and hold her and spend most every moment of the day with her, but I'm not allowed to kiss her or even take her on a date."

Gram laughed. "But you two talk all the time about your future and all the things you want to do. Most of those experiences, you talk like you'll be together."

"I hope we are. I can't imagine a future without her."

"Be patient, son. You're the first young man she's ever trusted. She'll come around; you'll see." Gram patted my hand.

"I'm not very, patient that is."

Gram laughed. "My first husband was the love of my young life. We spent ten years together before he died of cancer. We never had children. My second husband was a good man and gradually, patiently courted me. He wooed me over time and made me realize that our friendship was even strong enough to endure marriage. We were married for thirty-five years.

"We had Beth's grandmother, but Suzanne died and left us Beth's mother, Jennifer. That girl was wild! She got pregnant before she was sixteen. Beth's daddy was so young. He didn't know which way was up most of the time. Then the drugs started, and it all went to hell from there. Jennifer ran away when she found out she was pregnant. It worried me to death. She thought I wouldn't understand. Broke my heart. I received a few photos, but it wasn't until child services called me that I knew I'd have someone special to raise. Beth was such a sweet child. She never went against my wishes. She never, ever rebelled. She also never made a friend until you. She didn't fit in here." Gram's words were always with me.

***

When I received the call at school, yesterday, I was half out of my wits with worry. Frantically, I made it there just as they were settling her in the ICU. When they finally let me in to see her, she was heavily sedated, bruised, pale, and weak. I held her hand and stroked along her knuckles. Her eyelashes fluttered slightly.

"You can talk to her," the nurse instructed. "She'll begin coming around as we wean her from the sedation. It may take a couple of days."

"Beth, please wake up," I began. When the nurse left me alone, I was able to speak freely, "I promised Gram I'd be here for you. I love you and I don't want to move out. I'm insane for even thinking it will be different, but I want you and I need you so much. I'll be satisfied if you'll just wake up. The townhouse is so quiet. I miss you. I'll leave if that's truly what you want, but you know it isn't. God, I want to climb in this bed and hold you and tell you it's going to be okay.

"Remember that time at the lake and you wished on that shooting star? You said you wanted me to be your best friend and be with you forever. Little did you know that I wished for the very same thing on the very same star." We have to keep promises – the wish on a star and my promise to Gram. I promised you I'd always be here for you, even after everything: the abortion and suicide attempts. I made a promise and I'm a man of my word.

I stroked her knuckles and kissed her head. I whispered her name, calling to her, praying she'd return, begging God to give me another chance. Maybe I'm not as insane as I thought. God answered my prayer. I did the very same thing I've always done, but this time, I'm thankful for a *very* different result.

ABOUT THE AUTHOR

Kelda shares her south Louisiana home with her husband, their four children and

four wacky dogs. With a passion for education and young people,

both young in age and young at heart,

she has homeschooled her four children through graduation

and has tutored students for over a decade.

In addition, Kelda holds a BA in elementary education and an MA in

counseling. Her fictional writing began in 2016 while facilitating a novel writing

class with her students. This is her first published work of fiction.

She self-published two non-fiction works: *Call Their Hearts Home* and

TWPH-Insights into Living with Teens.

When she's not writing, she's watching movies, listening to audiobooks,

knitting, quilting, or crocheting, all the while, playing great music in the

background like a soundtrack. Writing is a compulsion that occurs amid the

chaos of life and dogs and constant interruptions.

She believes life is full of opportunities to love.

Be embraced.